IRIDESCE

DAY WITHOUT DAWN
BOOK ONE

A NOVEL

CORDIA PEARSON

MORGYN
STAR
PRESS

This story is dedicated to all who love.

"It is not in the stars to hold our destiny but in ourselves."—— **William Shakespeare**

The Lady or The Tiger?

The choice is yours.

I wrote Iridesce without a prologue, then debated whether readers would like to explore Thea's history or uncover it while reading.

With that in mind, I have included Thea's origin story at the end of this book. (A fun sort of dichotomy, putting the start at the end.) I'd love to know if you read it first or after. Please let me know by sending an email to: cordia@cordiapearson.com or: https://bit.ly/49Cdfyn

Also, again not wanting to get between you and the story, there's a glossary as well. For the ebook, please use the table of contents. For the print version, it's before Thea's origin story.

FORETOLD

A CENTURY AGO,
FORGED UPON AN
ANVIL OF BITTER
ENMITY, A CHILD IS
BORN.

ON ONE SIDE OF THE
EMBATTLED BORDER,
THE SIRE, HER MOTHER
ON THE OTHER.

FORSAKEN, REVILED,
AND CAST OUT
THRICE, SHE WILL RISE,
A PHOENIX OUT OF
THE FLAMES, GRANTED
THE FIERCENESS OF A
SERAPHIM.

ACT ONE

MY LIFE, SUCH AS IT IS

ONE

COME TO REIN

They say I am nothing, less than nothing, worse than nothing. They're wrong, just not today. Two members of my foster father's cavalry block the border between my two countries. Only moments before, the road was open.

As we thunder their way, the senior Venari, eyes wide with disbelief, jabs a forefinger our way.

"Godsdamn it, Thea, this is no racetrack!"

Bad enough we're racing along the border. Run these warriors down, and Lycan and I will never join their ranks.

I ask my stallion for a halt. Amir rocks back on his hindquarters, his back hooves skidding through the shale.

Lycan is not so lucky with Hanan. Rather than crash into the two men, he sends his three-year-old careening down the hill.

Swift as the stand-off began, it ends. Amir halts, a length away from the veterans' warhorses, then tosses his head as if to say, 'Told you I could!'

The eldest Venari recovers first. "You idiot! Pell will turn you over his knee!" He spares a moment's glance for Lycan, who in the grasslands below, now fights Hanan to a halt. "And you, bonehead, good luck with justifying racing Thea, here of all places."

He and his second share a disgusted look. The elder warrior reins down the hill, then out into the lush, knee-high sea of green. He doesn't glance back to see whether I'll follow.

One last glimpse for the red desert of my birth, and I send Amir down the steep grade.

As we reach the flat, Lycan reins in alongside us, his face tight with apprehension.

I give him a 'what-is-it-with-our-luck' glance, then heave a sigh. Having done this stupid thing, we must answer for it now.

Trailing behind like errant children will only affirm our guilt. Instead, I bring Amir alongside the veteran's warhorse. As last year's Champion of Champions, on this year's favorite, I could reach Pell's command tent first. Just one problem. Do so and the a'Shara would tan my ass. I have no desire to endure the litany of disasters certain to follow such an event.

All too soon, the Sada encampment appears along the horizon. While our warriors protect the Sada's section of the A'talan border, this city of felted tents lets us follow the grazing.

The Sada make their homes in rows of private tents farthest from the Daharshan threat. Between them and the border, tents belonging to Venari and Venari-to-be. Nearest the border, our destination: the a'Shara's command pavilion, with the healers and armorers north of it, and the horse pens to the south.

The veteran reins in at the picket line, facing the pavilion entry. He leaps to earth, then hands his warhorse's reins to a first-year Venari-to-be. "Water and grazing only. My rotation isn't over."

The youngster nods, her eyes huge at the sight of two fourth years hauled before the a'Shara.

The Venari hooks his thumb our way to follow him, then strides for the command tent. In deference to the summer heat, its felted sides rolled up and tied into place.

More first-year Venari-to-be step forward, eager to claim bragging rights at holding Amir. We dismount and follow the veteran, his sheathed sword angled across his back.

Halfway to our destination, he glances over his shoulder. "Wait here." Doubtless, he's delighted at leaving us baking under the midday sun, with the wind off the desert our only relief.

Two members of Pell's elite guard wave the veteran into the pavilion.

Soon after, a muted conversation reaches us, then my foster father's deep voice. "She did what?"

The snap of the tent's felted roof drowns out the answer. My mouth goes dust dry.

Garin, revered as first among Pell's personal guard, steps into the light, then crooks a finger our way.

Brave as a whipped dog, I slink past him, for which Garin shakes his head.

Pell's at his map table, gripping its edges as if they are the anchor keeping him seated.

The sight of me thins his lips in their close-clipped frame of beard and mustache. "Daughter, in the name of Heaven, why?"

As I fumble for an acceptable response, my already sweaty skin turns clammy.

Pell brings his fist down on the table with such force, pens, and papers topple onto the ornate carpets below. "Thea, answer me!"

I swallow my heart out of my throat. "We sought to determine if Lycan's colt should race this fall in Azalais."

Though striving for reasoned, my words come out timorous.

Pell arches his brows in a manner suggesting an utter lack of foresight on my part. "Where the enemy could use your empty skulls as targets? Surely another possibility suggested itself, perhaps one of the ways?"

The ways, none of which are elbow distance from the country of my birth.

His eyes narrow as he waits for me to evince intelligence.

Before Lycan tries taking the blame, I do. "A'Shara, the lapse in judgment was mine."

Battle braids swaying, the a'Shara shakes his head. "Is that not the heart of the matter? You, acting without thought?"

The warrior who hauled us here stifles his laughter.

Lycan steps forward. "A'Shara, the blame is mine. I asked Thea to race Amir against my colt."

"None of which excuses endangering your lives or that of your stallions."

The creak of saddle leather and trotting horses heralds the Lightning Ulan's approach. My father holds up his hand for silence, then rises to review his forces. One hundred Venari strong, these are the ranks of warriors Lycan and I long to join. Me, in a moon when I turn seventeen and Lycan come this winter.

Khat, the Lightning's battalion leader, and Hasia, her second, lead the column. Next up, come the unit's lancers, their pennants fluttering. Swordsmen and swordswomen follow, then my calling, the archers. All salute their commander, who inclines his head, acknowledging their service. Should Heaven smile upon us and we become Venari, Lycan and I may serve as each other's seconds. It's a tradition wherein two warriors guard each other's back. If so, it will be both a first and the most daring pairing of all time: a Daharshan foundling fighting at an A'talan's side.

Lycan threads his fingers through mine, offering comfort and fortitude. Such caring underlines why he's become a safe port in the storm of my life.

The wind swirls, erratic in this heat, replacing the parch of dust with the aroma of roasting meat and baking bread off the gathering grounds. Not that I'll be eating soon with a stomach in knots.

When the last rider passes, my father turns back to us. His gaze hardens. "Step apart."

I do as commanded, my expression pleading for his forbearance.

Pell's gaze pierces me. "You lay with this boy, yet neglect to tell me?"

Before I can find the words, Lycan does. "Sir, we have not."

"Daughter, am I to believe this?"

My nod sends a ripple down the braid riding over my spine. That my father assumes I'd withhold an expected truth between parent and child appalls me.

"Indeed." He returns to his chair, then laces his fingers over a stomach lean and muscled as any of his younger Venari. "Hear me, and hear me well. The pair of you are a recipe for disaster. Seek other companions, or forget becoming Venari."

In the stunned silence that follows, the wind strains the tent's lofty ceiling.

"So, what's it to be?"

Lycan and I share an agonized glance. My father's given us a choice between two wretched extremes.

The nearer my possible ascension, the greater my caution in the presence of this man who fostered me. I love my father, nay, worship him. Since a tiny child, I've known who he is in our world: A'tal's most respected general and, last word on whether any Sada Venari-to-be ascends. Only as Venari will I gain a citizen's rights. Thus, I must forsake the first A'talan to deem me worthy of sharing his life, love, and fate.

Shoulders back, I meet my father's shrewd gaze. "I would be Venari, a'Shara."

He smiles, having expected as much. "Should obedience and restraint replace folly, I will revisit seconding the pair of you. Mind you, provided either of you ascends."

I fight for breath. Never has my father threatened not to make me Venari.

Lycan's hands fist. "A'Shara, this is wrong."

Pell's expression becomes flint. "Tragic enough when I lose Venari to the enemy. It's idiotic, when Venari-to-be offer themselves as easy kills along the border. And for what? Nothing more than good race footing."

Hot as the day is, ice slithers through my veins. I caused this mess. Not my father. Not the young man I hoped would protect me in battle, as I would him.

Lycan steps between me and Pell. "A'Shara, I would do anything to protect your daughter. Anything."

My father's laughter mocks this claim. "None of which you exhibited, racing her on the border. You want to be her lover, do better. Till then, leave her alone."

My tears fall like silent rain onto the open-throat shirt and leather riding vest I wear. For centuries, A'talan warriors have visited death and destruction upon Daharsha. As a creation of that enmity, I am heir to its legacy. Children who can't sob, our silent tears a shield against A'talan invaders.

My father turns to the warrior who hauled us before him. "Take their stallions to the horse pens, then tell Sojur what's happened. This pair's riding boot leather till tomorrow."

He's unhorsing us, leaving us on foot. I wrench free of my shock. "A'Shara, I beg of you, let me care for Amir!"

"Suggesting Sojur hasn't the knowledge?"

Sojur, the Sada Master of Horse, the man who taught me everything I know about horses and riding. What will he think if I don't bring Amir in?

"No, it's just that . . ."

"Yes?"

"I would explain our reasons."

"Pity you didn't think of that earlier." He waves dismissal to the veteran.

Lycan turns his back to the a'Shara, then compounds the insult by framing my face between his broad hands. "In less than a moon, you come of age. Ascend, but take no second. Come winter, I too will be Venari. However unjust we can survive this."

He parts my bangs, then blesses my forehead with a kiss.

Real crashes into possible. I tilt my head, offering my lips.

"Lycan . . . leave . . . now." Pell's tone brooks no further disobedience.

Our first kiss before my father?

Perhaps not.

I step back, mourning all the chances we've let slip through our fingers. Had I been braver, had he been bolder, were we one, my father would not, could not, break us apart.

Lycan's sweet smile promises we will prevail. As my dreams turn to dust, the best I can muster is a faint upturn of my lips.

Aware of the pressure I'm under, he doesn't take my response wrong. Hand-to-heart, he offers me reverence, then faces Pell, and repeats the gesture.

Unmoved, Pell takes his time acknowledging the honor paid.

The scorching light reflects off Lycan's polished knee-high boots as he strides from the tent. The last glimpse of the golden-haired man whose life I dream of sharing is his sword-crossed back.

Once on my own with my infuriated father, I step into parade rest. Innate Daharshan impassivity disguises my all too active terror of the a'Shara's displeasure.

He fills two goblets with water, then hooks a chair out into the open. "Sit."

"I prefer standing."

His eyebrows hood. "I said sit."

With all the enthusiasm of a steer led to slaughter, I do as told. My sword belt over the chair back, I accept the water he offers.

On the back of my left hand, a birthmark shaped like a Luna moth spreads her wings. For this symbol of the A'talan Mother Goddess, my sire abandoned me less than a day old along the border. The greater irony? His inexplicable birthgift of a just-weaned Daharshan filly left at my side.

Pell stretches his long legs out before him, then crosses them at the ankle. "I never thought to see the day, you crying over a boy. Long as you've held yourself aloof from love, I expected a measure of common sense."

I meet his gaze, and pray the rush of blood does not show on my year-round tawny skin. Throughout, my heart aches for Lycan.

"Sixteen years you have been my delight, till this summer. Any fool can be reckless, but a dead Venari serves no one. Either toe the line or I will let Mora turn you into a healer."

While I respect the Sada Wise Woman's skill, her magic terrifies me. Rare is the day she doesn't nag me about setting aside fighting and following in her path.

On a map of the A'talan-Daharshan border, my father traces the path we took racing. "Have you reached the age your birth land calls to you?"

"No, never."

The enmity between my two nations is a festering wound born of differences in religion, values, and the prejudice I experience daily.

His gaze drops to the outer shafts of my boots. Images of Selene, my hunting hound, and my birthgift mare, Windsong, lay there. Since a tiny child, he's carved these images into all my boots and saddles. "Do they still fit?"

"Yes, a'Shara."

"Excellent. Sojur would despair if you were still growing."

All my frustration with myself breaks free. "Disappointed? After what I did today, he'll never speak to me again."

My father's smile grows. "Last year's Champion of Champions? The girl who bred Amir, then gave him to her teacher? Trust me, Sojur will speak to you at great and detailed length."

"And call me what? Reckless? Foolish? Impulsive?"

He shrugs his broad shoulders.

I envision a well-deserved harangue from my teacher and stifle a groan. Whatever made me think racing on the border would go unnoticed? I shouldn't have agreed.

All my life, I have lived in the shadow of two great men, and done my best to emulate them. Yet, as my father says, this summer has not gone well. Worse, my struggle to prove my worth has placed a barrier of formality between us. Only with my crèche brothers, other orphans, and foundlings like myself, do I speak of the love I bear for the man we all call Father. Losing closeness with him hurts worse than a wound.

As he refills our goblets, the dense muscling of his left arm shifts his tattooed sleeve of inked ravens. One for every enemy warrior he's returned to their nameless god. Pell a'Sada is called the Scourge of Daharsha for cause.

While returning the water pitcher to the table, he notes my fixation. "Atar showed me his latest design for your Venari sleeve. Lovely, a stylized knotwork of grasshens in flight."

Grasshens, my father's favorite. I hunt them for him every chance I get.

Smile wry, he leans back in his chair. "Yet for your crèche brother to ink your sleeve, you must ascend. Be my triumph. Be the first, the only Daharshan to become Venari and an A'talan citizen. Prove your blood doesn't tell."

Blood tells: what the tribe says about me day in and day out. Only when racing in Azalaïs am I worth anything in their estimation. Him, using this adage, has me swallowing the thickness congealing in my throat.

Seeing this, he pays tribute to my misery. "The tribe will have a heyday with this story, same as the morning I found you, but didn't kill you."

How well he knows the path of my thoughts.

"So, how long have you and Lycan ridden together?"

"For a moon."

"Aryren mentioned a skirmish, wherein you two went after each other like wild dogs."

I wish my water goblet were a river into which I could leap, then wash away my embarrassment. "I didn't start limping till out of sight, which is why Lycan befriended me."

"Thereby emulating his sire, may he be born again . . ."

I bow my head in homage. ". . . amidst those who love him."

For a moment, we sit in silent reflection of life's many harsh realities.

There's a touch of sympathy in his tone when he speaks again. "I remember what love was like at your age. That said, after four years of training to become a Venari, you can endure the separation. Do you love Lycan?"

The abrupt shift from my daily dose of prejudice brings an unexpected blurt. "I don't know."

He arches a half-smile. "I credit your honesty, same as I credit Lycan for seeing beyond the losses your countrymen have exacted from his family. It is a measure of the man he may become. That said, I reserve judgment on whether he is the right match for you. He is a risk-taker, and you rise to the challenge all too well."

I look askance at my father. Is he saying he finds Lycan worthy, just not worthy of me?

My baffled expression brings laughter. "It's been too long, daughter. Either you're riding for Sojur or training with Aryren. We must make time to hunt together."

I pull a high, fast breath. To spend a few hours with him . . .

"Far as this summer's crazed behavior goes . . .," he pauses as Selene bounds into the pavilion, silky white hair afloat.

As she leaps, I bolt to my feet. Her paws thud onto my shoulders. "Please, Selene, down!"

She licks my face as if we've been days apart, her long feathered tail threatening to sweep the last of the papers off the map table.

Pell sighs. "All the warhorses you've trained, yet your dog . . ."

No sooner than I get her down than she lunges for him. It's not as if he needs proof of my loving her more than training her.

He points to the carpets. "Selene, sit."

Laugh-panting, she obeys. Selene adores the man who put her, a black-eyed, black-nosed puppy into my arms the day I turned ten.

He pets her, but his gaze stays on me. "Your dog obeys me. Will I be able to say the same of you?"

"Such is my hope, a'Shara."

"Thea, do better than hope. Come to rein. Evidence impeccable adherence to Venari principles and prove my seeking to elevate you isn't misguided. Remember, if you don't, I won't. How long before your birth day?"

Gooseflesh prickles. "Nineteen days."

He nods. "Nineteen days to make peace with Sojur, then give Sada tongues something besides your wildness to wag about. Go, and do just that."

I lay a trembling hand over my heart, then bow my head. While collecting my training sword, the shaking continues.

Throughout, my father's expression approves of the gravity with which I take his warning.

Despite the urge to drop to my knees and vow obedience, I know words unsubstantiated by acts are hollow. Instead, I snap a salute, then exit the tent.

Selene bounds alongside me, her long nose bumping my hand for yet more petting, which I do, yet wish my heart was as light.

I began this day believing love and citizenship were within my grasp, yet end it unhorsed, a laughingstock, with nothing to show for my efforts. Were that not enough, the worst is yet to come: Sojur, the man who taught me everything I know about horses and riding.

TWO

CLEAR THE WAY

I ron-gray clouds loom as we canter out of camp. It's been a week and I've not gone anywhere as there'd been no making peace with Sojur.

The Sada Master of Horse subjected me to a well-attended, public dressing-down. Witnesses to this rare event took avaricious delight in Sojur's litany of last year's Champion of Champions' many flaws and failures. Then, once finished, he salted his ire with a studied indifference to my presence. I responded with the only thing he'd accept in reparation: my best work, starting colts and training remounts. Throughout, keeping my head down and mouth shut.

It paid off this afternoon. Sensing the coming rain, Sojur told me to stretch my Daharshan mare's legs. With Selene at our side, in a matter of breaths, I had Windsong saddled, bridled, and the three of us gone.

Upon nearing the northern edge of camp, a clump of children spots us on the way and shout, "Go, go, GO!"

If their parents discover their little ones cheered on the Daharshan, they won't sit for days.

As we pass, I raise my hand in recognition of their courage. Rather than cheer, they scream and point forward.

The way, which had been open only moments before, is now a jumble of color. A dozen abaya-clad girls stroll across the road, their long gowns a swirl of bright colors.

Fast as I ask Windsong to stop, I pray she's faster.

The frantic children point at me till the young women turn and look. All but one race for the verge: Habibi, the only child of the tribe's wealthiest shepherd, her father's pride and joy.

Habibi twists my way, wrapping her hems around her ankles. Mouth a startled 'O', she topples onto her generous backside.

An arm's length away, Windsong judders to a halt. If she's hurt, weasel-like, blame will sink its jagged teeth into my rump. I leap from the saddle.

"Habibi, are you all right?"

Her shock curdles into venom. "Nomadi bitch, you've broken my ankle!"

Nomadi, a degrading word for Daharshans. Common enough whispered behind my back, just not shrilled into my face.

Honoring the Venari precept of others before self, I crouch to assess her injury. A heartbeat later, I'm on my rump with the dusty imprint of her shoe on my riding vest.

I roll up into a crouch. "No one kicks that hard with a broken ankle."

Busy worrying at her gown's hem, she pays me no mind. "My best abaya, ruined!" This shrilled, as her friends flutter and coo over this so-called injury.

These near-women are here for one reason only: to flirt with warriors entering or leaving camp.

I reach under my bangs, wiping sweat off my brow. In the doing, I miss Selene licking Habibi's cheek.

Habibi screeches, then smacks my dog, who yelps and cowers away, her tail tucked to her lean belly.

I grab Habibi's wrists, but wish I had her by the throat. "You hit those who offer you comfort?"

Silver bracelets jingling, Habibi struggles to wrench free of my grip. "Just wait till my father learns what you've done."

Leander may dote on this spiteful bit of fluff, not that it keeps me from getting into her face. "Hear me. Believe me. No one hits my dog, and I mean no one!"

"Go to hell, nomadi. Better yet, go home!"

All I wanted was to ride out and hunt, not play petty games with this shrew. Much as I'd like to smack her, I can't. If she were Venari-to-be, I'd pound her into the earth, then call the job well done.

As I come to my feet, she tries slapping me.

I bat her hand away, then arms crossed, address her as if she were reasonable. "Habibi, what if warning horns sounded, and Venari responded at speed? Or returned with wounded while you and your friends were on the way? Venari could die from such folly."

She rubs her ankle, ignoring me.

As if underlining my point, the thunder of horses and riders approaches. Eyes shielded, I look north.

Dust billows as Venari-to-be revel in the exhilaration of riding hard. Lycan heads this pack. In this heat, he wears as little as possible: leggings and a half-open shirt, its sleeves tied high. Tall and compelling in mien, he's proven a natural leader. I miss him like I'd miss breathing.

He signals for a halt, then leaps off Hanan. "Thea, what happened?"

I hook a thumb toward the girls now batting their eyes at his companions. "I had Windsong at a canter when this batch crossed the way."

With a hawk's pitiless gaze, Habibi watches our forbidden exchange. Though longing for Lycan may have me breathless, I'm not heedless of the raptor about to sink her talons into me. This girl is certain to use my father's proscription against me.

Wine-red lips a-tremble, she gestures to her foot. "Thea ran me down on her horrid mare and broke my ankle."

"Is that so?" Lycan's tone lacks conviction. "How did you come to be where Thea and Windsong could 'run' you down?"

She tips her head toward her friends, who now cast sultry glances at the young men in Lycan's pack. "We didn't see her coming."

Lycan laughs. "Either you're blind, lying, or stupid. Which is it?"

She gasps as if slapped.

Expression dismissive, he points to the verge. "Habibi, get off the way, now."

Like summer flowers rioting in the grass, this girl's ambitions are nothing more than her day in the sun. She tucks tousled, honey-colored hair behind her ear, then holds out her hand.

"Help me?"

She's flirting, same as with any Venari who gives her the slightest encouragement. Some women are too timid to blaze their own path, instead choosing to bask in the reflected glory of a partner. Not so Habibi. She's just spoiled and lazy.

Her feigned fragility does nothing for Lycan, who hauls her to her feet like a sack of grain.

The moment she's upright, she lets her ankle buckle, and tumbles into his arms.

He heaves her off his chest. "Broken ankle, my arse. You'd be screaming if it were."

Habibi goes wide-eyed. "You won't help me?"

He swings back onto his colt. "Girl, that's what friends are for."

Habibi sucks air, and it's an impressive inhalation. I'd lay silver she held her breath as a child whenever she wanted something.

"I . . . can't . . . walk."

"So?"

Never having ridden, Habibi eyes Hanan with distrust. "You're Venari-to-be, others before self, yes?" She limps toward the red colt, expecting Lycan's offer to take her back to camp.

He winks at me, a mischievous glint in his brown eyes. I stifle laughter when he sweeps Habibi onto his lap. She hasn't a clue of what's about to happen. She proves as much by smirking at me. While I was the one off to hunt, she's bagged the prey. Just one problem. Lycan's gaze and longing smile are for me alone.

"Good hunting, Thea."

Habibi squirms, seeking to reclaim his attention.

Were Lycan to dally with this girl, her father would come undone. Leander thinks his daughter deserves better than a grunt Venari. Nor does Habibi understand the force of nature Lycan is. If he wanted, he'd have this drifty-minded creature on her back, skirts rucked around her waist. Not that I had skirts to toss. Not that Lycan needed telling I wasn't ready.

He reads my regret, and a sad, tender smile curves his lips.

In that moment, I answer my father's question. Were I the one in Lycan's arms, we'd be counting the hours till dark.

Frustrated with his distraction, Habibi winds her arm around his neck, as she seeks to claim what isn't hers.

Lycan shoots me a grin, then nicks his colt's ribs with his heels.

Hanan responds, one moment here, the next, several horse lengths away. Habibi shrieks while hurling herself against Lycan like he's a wall to scale. Ignoring her, he blows me a kiss that I catch and press to my heart.

Habibi's shrieks fade as they disappear toward camp.

The other boys grin while lifting her friends onto their horses, thus clearing the way.

It grates. These girls would be as out of place on our training fields as I'd be in one of their sewing circles. Most Sada mothers frown on their daughters flirting with Venari or Venari-to-be. They prefer men who will live long enough to name any child they might sire. Still, their mothers' disapproval doesn't dampen these hearth-bound girls' exhilaration for a Venari's life. Not that they understand why we hold our lives with such open hands, or appreciate the ideals that allow us to accept death as our constant companion.

I could have offered to take Habibi back to camp.

No sooner than this idea arises and I laugh at its absurdity. Habibi would accept help from a Daharshan on a day without dawn. And when she runs to her father, 'broken' ankle and all, it will be my worthless word against hers.

No one, not even Pell, can assuage this tribe's aversion for their ancient enemy. Only as a blooded Venari will the Sada stop questioning my honor.

I bury my face in Windsong's mane, then breathe in the sweetest scent under Heaven's sky: sun-warmed horse. "My heart, now what?"

She whickers as if comforting one of her foals.

It's of no help, what with the possible repercussions of this encounter, perched on my shoulders like carrion crows.

Can I convince my father I did no wrong?

Tucked deep inside my saddlebags, lies a tassel made of Windsong's silver-white tail hair. A gift brought to perfection by my artist brother's silverwork, destined to grace Pell's sword pommel. Give it to our father now and he would see it as appeasement.

I sigh for yet another plan gone awry, then swing into the saddle.

Though damned for my blood, I will prove them wrong.

It's the how I'll accomplish this that escapes me.

THREE

HORNS OF THE BULL

A blood-spatter of poppies dance amidst the storm-darkened grasses. Our horses, sheep, and cattle thrive upon this verdant glory in which game abounds. Selene quarters a patch of wind-whipped grass, her intensity such that I slow Windsong, then nock an arrow.

With heart-seizing abruptness, a covey of grasshens explodes into flight. The birds level off as I pull, release, and nock again. By the time the flock is out of range, the brilliant blue of my fletching marks four downed birds.

While Windsong grazes, I gut the hens and toss the choice bits to Selene, who snaps them out of the air. With the birds in my hunting pouch, I rein for the Horns of the Bull. There, atop one of the twin buttes, I can see the whole of my world.

As we near the border, Selene peels off, in pursuit of some ground dweller. She'll find us once the chase is over.

We reach the towering buttes, then ascend the narrow trail winding around the northernmost spire. Windsong climbs with a Daharshan's casual disregard for danger, her hooves sending rocks clattering off into space. Cresting the ridge at the top, she halts square, her inherent power awaiting my command.

At our back, the Silverstone Mountains form a nigh-on impassable boundary between my two countries. To the left lies the grasslands, their verdant green veined with streams of mountain snowmelt. To the right, undulates the red desert where we were both born.

Venari warriors of all five A'talan tribes guard this bloodily contested sliver of land, from the Silverstones south to the sea, each to their appointed section. All share a common cause: deny the enemy access to A'tal's bountiful water and lush grazing, which is why my birth sire's people raid all too often.

Overhead, lightning spears heavy-shouldered clouds. Despite anticipating thunder's crack, my muscles snatch at bone when it comes.

Dark nostrils flaring, Windsong drinks in the wind, her attention fixed on something in the distance.

I follow the path of her gaze, and at first, see nothing, then in the middle distance, spot a raiding party skulking out from behind a rust-red dune. A pack of Daharshan Kian, headed for the border, and there isn't a single Venari patrol in sight.

A space of three horse-lengths separates the twin peaks, between which lies a jagged maw of rock. Retracing our steps down the northern spire would mean time lost, perhaps A'talan lives lost. A few heart-in-throat moments, and we could race down the southern butte, closer to a possible Venari patrol.

I dry my damp palms, then ask Windsong for something I'd request of no other horse. Something that could mean our deaths. I close my calves on her sides, and she bursts into a gallop, straight for the chasm. As we near the edge, my heart keeps time with her hoofbeats. Focus unwavering and trust absolute, I pray for wings to carry us over the abyss.

Windsong picks her spot, then launches us into the void.

Those moments, short as they are, and long as they seem, we are of the wind. The freedom of being airborne, purest exhilaration. Not answering to anyone, or found wanting, a rapture that will follow me into my dreams tonight. This mare is truly my Windsong.

We're mid-jump, when Sojur's words of wisdom resound in my head: While jumping, every joint loose upon landing.

Windsong's front hooves descend, hit. Her hinds scrabble at the edge, then thank you, Mother of All, grip. Heartbeats later, we're streaking around the curve of the second butte.

Trusting Windsong yet again, I let her set the pace.

One hand around the saddle horn and weight in the outside stirrup, I lean in as she pelts down and around the butte.

We reach the first switchback, and her scrabbling hooves launch more rocks into space. The change of direction snaps through her body, into mine.

Should a single hoof slip . . .

I grimace, picturing how little would remain for our Fires of Rebirth.

I squint through strands of hair freed from my braid as we whip another tight turn. The coming rain sings in my nostrils as the thunder rumbles overhead, big and bossy.

The invaders are out in the open now.

We reach level ground. My mare gives me her all as she flies up the rise to the border. There, with any luck, we'll find a patrol.

While competent with the sword across my back, I am deadly with a bow. Reins hooked on the saddle horn, I guide

Windsong with my legs, then nock an arrow. Will this be the day I kill someone whose blood I may share, whose color of skin and eyes are mine?

A rider's shadow crests the ridge above us.

Bowstring to my ear, I take aim, then equally swift, slack my bow.

It is my father, on his warhorse, D'jhat. The big gray does not move out of our way.

Sweet Mother in Heaven, be with us now!

Much as it is to ask, again I close my legs on Windsong's flanks. Tail dragging, she gathers herself for another leap.

Heartbeats shy of plowing into D'jhat, she catapults us up and over his backside. The moment she touches down, I ask for and receive a head-tossing, albeit hoof-stomping, halt.

Pell's brute of a stallion snorts, his black nostrils flaring blood-red, and flanks curdled with lather. The maneuvers I could not see were at speed.

I offer my father uneasy reverence.

I've never seen Pell fresh off the battlefield, fresh off a kill. Till now, I've drawn a mental veil over what happens when he crosses the border. As if compounding my error in judgment, he glances west where a Venari patrol now storms out from behind the dune that had sheltered the Kian. My reckless choice to leap the Horns? Pointless.

Pell swings his blade, showering crimson over the granite dividing my two countries. Blood of my sire or a brother?

Tail wagging, Selene rejoins us, oblivious to the straits I'm in.

My father regards me from a wintry distance. "Let me guess. While hunting, you spotted Kian and, seeing no Venari, judged the south Horn swifter than the north." This non-question asked while reining D'jhat head-to-tail with Windsong and noting the game bags on my saddle skirts.

"Yes, a'Shara." I don't meet his gaze while casing my bow and quivering my arrow.

"Daughter, how do you evidence restraint by risking your life and Windsong's?"

This he asks while drawing a thumb and forefinger along his blade, stripping away yet more blood.

Saddle leather creaks. Horses huff as his ulan trots around us, their riders keen to witness how their commander will deal with his nomadi brat.

I hide my shame behind the half-moon of my bangs. Why is it these moments always seem to play out before witnesses?

His warriors' presence sharpens my father's tone. "Child, I have done everything in my power to assure your place in this tribe. For every person who claims a karakal can't change their spots, I've argued the opposite. Was I wrong, standing between you and your detractors? Is my faith in you somehow misplaced?"

I meet his gaze while screaming inside: I did the right thing! For the right reason! Not words to say to my father. "With no patrols in sight, I thought Windsong could make the jump."

His sigh comes out heartfelt. "The danger, to you, to your mare..." he breaks off, then looks into the distance. "Imagine me waiting for first light, then giving your bodies to the Fires of Rebirth, and for what? We came in on that dune's backside, then decimated those bastards. While I applaud your motivation, were your mare less talented, I would have lost both of you today." He removes the hald around his throat, and buffs away the last traces of blood on his sword.

My skin clenches as if flea-bitten. Had I been born male and without my birthmark, that blood could have been mine.

"Child, the morning I found you, I vowed to make you one of us and have succeeded, perhaps too well. Your willingness to risk your well-being for others, though noble, is profligate. A dead Venari serves no one."

D'jhat chooses this moment to be the ugly-minded brute he is. Crest arched, he whickers with a deep masculine sound, while seeking to cajole Windsong.

She responds with flattened ears and a fiery squeal. Lest he have any doubt how far out of season she is, she snaps her teeth shut a breath away from his ash-colored rump.

The a'Shara views the drama between our horses as a mere irritant. He greets his mount's flirtation with a one-two of muscled calves, effective as any spur.

D'jhat grunts and moves away. While doing so, he brushes Windsong, who humps up to kick.

This cannot happen, not to D'jhat, little as I like the horse. I spin her hindquarters out of range. As I do so, D'jhat glares at me through the forelock he never lets me comb. Doubtless, the next time I try, there'll be a mouthful of teeth coming my way. Duck the bite, he'll still raise a bruise worth admiring.

Pell reaches between our two horses, then closes his fist on my pride and joy, a mecate rope I made from Windsong and her daughters' tail hair. Comprehension strikes. He intends to pony me back into camp.

I straight-arm myself out of the saddle, then shove my shaking hands under my arms.

"You'll be an hour walking."

"Better on foot than treated like a child."

With a glance, he confirms the sword across my back. "As you wish, so long as you know, this punishment is for the risk you took, not for seeking to save A'talan lives."

He backs D'jhat, the taut mecate telling Windsong she's with them. Meanwhile, I'm screaming in my head: Risk? Ascend, and I'll face worse than this every time you send me out on patrol!

Yet another thought I dare not voice. No one has the power to push the sun across the sky, yet in my world, Pell does.

"A'Shara?"

He pauses mid-turn toward camp. "Yes?"

I point to my game bags. "Grasshens, for you and Sojur."

He nods acknowledgment of the gift even as D'jhat shifts into a canter. Windsong follows suit, distant as the mecate on her bridle allows.

Unhorsed, again, Pell's favorite method of displaying displeasure with his crèche or any Venari-to-be. And this time, I brought it on myself.

The rain which has threatened all afternoon falls soft at first, then harder, as if Creation means to punish me as well. It's not long before the downpour hides Windsong's dark chestnut form. Pell, who as a'Shara wears white, remains visible longer.

Selene hips over onto my boot. I sink to my haunches, then wrap my arm around her. She swipes my cheek with her tongue, content just to be with me. If only I could say the same of myself.

When the Sada see Pell leading a riderless Windsong into camp, they'll know he unhorsed his Daharshan again. As if my lack of discipline needed bandying about. The same people who damn me as nomadi will savor every moment of pillorying me.

'Tis true. Blood tells.'

They're wrong. This Daharshan will be Venari, and this is the last damned time I'm leaving myself open to public scorn and humiliation.

FOUR

SISTER MINE

As we near camp, the sour taint of damp wool and doused cook fires greets us. Ever the princess, Selene sneezes, and drops to earth, then scoots her nose through hummocks of wet grass.

I slide my boot under her wriggling rump. "Enough, already."

She leaps to her feet and gives a mighty shake, silver-white hide traveling swifter than the lean body beneath.

"In case some part of me wasn't wet?"

My peevish tone earns me a good-natured shoulder bump on my leg as she takes off for the tent we share with Atar and Sahain. My crèche brothers are sure to greet her with a sloppy tussle. Other than Habibi, everyone loves Selene.

As I walk between this row of tents, grass frogs serenade the gloaming, in love with the warm wet. I'm relieved all tent walls have been pegged to earth. Were the sun shining, this would be a walk of shame, a litany of catcalls and sniggers over being unhorsed again.

Even as I celebrate my luck, my crèche sister's voice slithers through the near dark.

"Thea, we would speak to you."

What was I thinking, coming this way? No, not thinking, kicking myself while reliving my encounter with our father. And as always, speak to me, never with me. Beyond that, 'we' who?

I shield my eyes against the light coming through her tent flap, yet see no one else. Groaning at my utter lack of forethought, I splash her way.

Lips pursed at my state, Charra waves me inside. Her karakal green eyes are a perfect counterpart to her predator's heart. Were her plan to cut me down to size with a few well-honed words, she would have left me in the rain. No such luck tonight.

I brace myself for tonight's serving of bile, the darker part of my nature amused at dripping on her carpets.

Hands-on-hips, she regards me, waist-length copper hair spilling over her sapphire abaya. Pell gave his daughter will and fire. Her mother, a Covenant Master, bequeathed beauty and cunning, only to tire of life in a tent, and returning to Land's End.

I meet my so-called sister's gaze, which irritates her enough, she steps into me. "Is it true? Did you run Leander's daughter down?"

Of course, Habibi's father made his ire known to Jae, the tribe's headwoman, who promptly told Charra, her second-in-command on the tribal council.

I respond with the intransigence of silence.

With a father like Pell, Charra may act as if her mother's desertion isn't noteworthy. I don't believe it. A'talan children belong to their mothers. I've seen Charra's expression while tossing one of her mother's letters into a fire, not that our mutual lack of mothers has made for peace between us.

From my right, a male voice speaks. "Thea, is this true?"

I turn to Sojur, thrilled it's not Leander, and make reverence, hand-to-heart. "No, Master, it's not."

He holds up his hand when I start his way. "Think of Charra's carpets."

He braces himself on the chair arms, then rises.

A special boot disguises his missing right foot. I can't say the same about his hands. Five fingers between them. Though still Pell's second, my teacher no longer rides with the ulans, not after Kian took him apart a joint at a time. Toward the end, believing the pain too great, they ceased guarding him. On a dark moon night, he crawled to the horse lines, found his beloved mare, then somehow made it home.

While coming my way, he arches a dark brow. "How were you implicated in this mess?"

"A group of children cheered us on as Windsong and I cantered from camp. I waved to them, then faced forward, and found the way blocked by a pack of girls. Windsong stopped in time, but Habibi stumbled, then fell." I say nothing of the slurs cast.

Blink and I would have missed Sojur's quirk of a smile. "As suspected." He looks to Charra.

"Leander has no cause and Pell will concur."

She considers this claim, her aspect bright as any battle-ready Venari. "Perhaps."

Her tone suggests otherwise. Charra protects her sire from petty irritations, but for a chance at me, she'd trample a bull.

I've seen men stand tongue-tied before her, men who knew mortal danger. Mesmerized by her beauty, they've sought her favor only to discover Charra's heart has room only for two: herself and her sire.

Not among those enchanted, Sojur narrows his eyes and calls her hesitation to question.

Me, I silently call her every pungent name I know, and they are many. She thinks of herself as precious. She believes me dirt beneath her feet.

My teacher's tone remains measured. "Charra, what reservations aren't you sharing?"

She stabs a hard-eyed look my way, mindful Sojur is the reason I'm silent. "Thea's penchant for truth aside, my father's pet nomadi has injured a member of the tribe. Such is not the Venari way."

Sojur recoils from the slur and the loathing in her tone.

I don't, having grown up with it. Everything Charra is, I am not. Everything I am, she will never be.

My teacher rests his hand on my shoulder as if reassuring a flighty horse. "Charra, take care, lest your father deem your stance indefensible. Habibi knew better than to cross a way with a rider on it."

Her grass-green eyes glitter at the prospect of humiliating me. "We'll see about that."

No matter how unacceptable he finds her attitude, he says no more.

I drape his oiled rain mantle over his shoulders, then open the flap for him.

Charra crossed the line, suggesting my behavior unworthy of a Venari-to-be. The moment my 'sister' and I are alone, I scoop my fingers downward, then pinch upward. It's a rude gesture meant for a man, yet in Charra's case, appropriate.

She lashes out, cracking me across the cheek. "You wretched brat, once I plead Leander's case before council, you will never ascend."

Much as she wishes it otherwise, that decision isn't hers. With a tart smile suggesting as much, I bolt out of the tent.

Tonight, Sojur wears a Sada Venari's emerald haaka and knee-high boots over tight riding pants. The formal dress uniform suggests he's joining the a'Shara for the evening meal.

I match my pace to his uneven gait, keeping my shoulder within range should his missing foot unbalance his stride.

The rain has yet to ease, but for now, the land holds. If this downpour continues, by morning, the paths between the tents will be mud.

Pell's command pavilion appears. The loose-weave wool, now rain-swollen, sheds the downpour. From within comes laughter and conversation. We duck beneath the entry awning and into its lantern light. There, I remove Sojur's mantle, then hang it to dry.

When I turn back to him, his eyes go wide. "She hit you?"

I nod. Sojur knows how matters stand between Pell's daughters. Her slapping me is minor compared to what I must tell him.

"Master, the a'Shara unhorsed me again."

Momentary silence greets this revelation before he pushes my bangs aside with the thumb and forefinger on his left hand. "What will you do when you ascend? Crop these?"

Nothing could be further from my mind. "I haven't decided yet."

"Either put this 'forelock' into battle braids or have Atar shorten it. You're turning into D'jhat. Unable to see your eyes, I never know whether I should be dodging teeth."

Rare as it is for him to take a light-hearted tone with me, I can't raise a smile.

"So, why were you unhorsed?"

"I went up the Horns to watch the storm come in."

As Pell's second, Sojur knows every ulan deployment. He knows what I saw.

"From which you spotted the raiding party?"

"Yes, then jumped the Horns to seek a patrol."

One silent heartbeat follows another. "Windsong jumped clean?"

"Barely."

He shakes his head, face clean-shaven, hair close-cropped. "This constant striving to prove your worth will be your undoing."

Before I can justify my actions, Lycan ducks under the entry. The sight of me, drenched, gives him pause. He recovers, makes reverence to Sojur, then sheds his rain mantle.

He's wearing his best, however unexceptional. There's no privilege in his family, not with four to feed and clothe. That's the reason I crafted an agreement with Hanan's breeder. Reveal how Lycan came to afford Hanan, and the stallion service that slashed the red colt's price comes due.

My teacher voices the same question I'm asking. "Lycan, what brings you here?"

"I am to serve as the a'Shara's cupbearer." Regret fills his soft tone, and well it should. My father has given a beloved task to another, thus underlining his displeasure with me.

With an apologetic smile, Lycan lowers his head in farewell, then slips into the pavilion.

His expression contemplative, Sojur stares out into the pouring rain. "The Rowan are here to discuss fall racing in Azalaïs. Go. Change. As Amir's rider, you will be my cupbearer tonight."

However unweighted, monumental import rides on these words. Everything I've done wrong, and still he's giving me the ride on Amir, the Sada's best chance at this year's Champion of Champions winning horse. The same horse with which I created this mess, racing him along the border.

My reverence is profound with gratitude. "Master, I will do my best."

He holds one of his ruined hands to my cheek. "I know you will. That said, the sooner you leave, the sooner you'll return."

He's given me a gift that, though earned, comes when most needed. And for that, I manage a smile, then hold the tent flap open for him.

Venari in Sada emerald and Rowan sapphire fill the pavilion. Among them, Lycan stands behind the a'Shara. It's yet another reminder nothing in my life is a given.

Pell smiles a welcome for Sojur, then spots me in the entry. The warmth leaves my father's gaze as he reins me in better than Sojur, the greatest horseman of all time, rides.

FIVE

ART, DAY IN, DAY OUT

I n the tent I share with my two brothers, Selene lifts her head off my pillow. She sees it's me, and thumps her tail, then returns to prone. Yet more joy for this day: wet covers when the time comes to sleep.

Atar straightens from behind one of the three standing looms along the tent's felted walls. "Where have you been?"

"Getting my face slapped by Charra."

His ocean-blue eyes go wide. "Again?"

I nod, then jam my boot heel into the jack, and yank hard. The second boot comes off, reluctant as the first, both ankles raw from the long slog. Tall boots are not meant for walking.

Atar puts a double wrap around the warp of the loom he's restringing, his tawny dreadlocks bound between lean shoulders. In deference to the damp and heat, he's down to leggings.

While I unbuckle the right side of my brecca, he frees the left. "Was Charra in a twist about Habibi?"

The leather half-chaps land with a splat on the carpets.

"You heard about that?"

He rubs his goateed chin. "I've had a slew of company today, all fishing for gossip."

I sigh while unlacing my riding vest. A year older, Atar is an adult in the eyes of the Sada. His creative skills earned him the means with which he erected this tent. His invitation to join him delighted both me and Sahain, both of us eager to leave behind our crèche's current pack of noisy youngsters.

I pause, my skin-tight leggings now in the laundry basket. Atar's left a drawing on my clothing chest. It's me on Amir, bowstring to my ear, aiming at something hidden from the viewer.

"Atar, are you sure about this?"

He holds the sketch up to the light and smiles. "It won't be easy dyeing these colors, but imagine the impact, the movement."

I don't understand half of what my brother says about his art or its meaning, but as for impact, there's plenty. His tapestries paid for the roof over our heads, and the carpets beneath our feet. Equally amazing, he spoils his two rowdy Venari-to-be siblings with an extravagance of tack and clothing.

I nudge him with my elbow. "Remember me, the model? What do I know of art?"

"You are art, sister, day in, and day out." He adds the sketch to the stack on his drawing table.

I kneel before my clothing chest and paw through shirts, leggings, socks, and mantles. If I had my way, I'd cut this lot in half. That's not happening, not with Atar ordering this aspect of my life.

Considering the weather, I go with loose leggings and a tunic, its yoke a garden of embroidered poppies. Atar's design, executed by the tribe's top seamstress.

Once free of shirt, cami, and small clothes, I crouch in a copper bath basin while Atar pours sun-warmed water over my head. Such is the way of our world, a physical openness at odds with Daharshan propriety. One more reason I bless the day my sire dumped me and Windsong along the border.

As I wash the day away, my brother's gaze records my every move. In time, these mental images will appear in his drawings.

He shakes out the tunic as I dress in clean underclothes. "So, do you serve Pell tonight?"

"No. Sojur." This said while tightening the drawstring around my hips.

Atar bumps a knuckle down my ribs. "While there, eat. This is getting ugly."

I grin as he fishes my braid out from under the tunic. Who needs a mother with a brother like Atar?

"Why aren't you serving Pell?"

"Because he saw me leap the Horns of the Bull."

Sahain lurches to a halt midway into the tent, his arms overflowing with saddle, bridle, bow, and quiver. "Tell me you didn't." He slings his gear over a stand, then comes our way.

"I can't, and need to leave."

Sahain understands me, but this is one of those moments when I amaze him. He sighs while blessing my forehead with a kiss. "Stay out of trouble, sister mine."

Up on tiptoes, I return his blessing. "The girl unhorsed twice in a week? And to think, the day's not yet done." It doesn't earn me the desired smile.

Feet in sabots, and oilskin mantle over my shoulders, I pause in the entryway.

At his drawing table, Atar reproduces the chasm between the Horns of the Bull, over which a horse and rider soar.

Sahain, perched on a chair edge, shakes his head at me.

I wince him a smile, raise the mantle hood over my hair, then splash into the dark.

Ground lanterns now illuminate the command pavilion's entry. As I duck beneath its awning, a drift of smoke gray brushes my cheek: Pell's war standard, made of Kitan's tail hair. Serving the a'Shara for the first time, Lycan wouldn't have known to bring it inside.

The dawn we gave my father's warhorse to the wind, I was inconsolable. As a babe, Kitan was my first ride on Pell's lap. Twelve years, the gallant stallion served my father. I miss him still. Unlike D'jhat, Kitan never took exception to the one Daharshan Pell wouldn't kill.

War standard over my forearm, I observe every courtesy, and ease through the crowds of Venari inside. Upon reaching the map table, I hang the standard from a ceiling crossbar, then finger-comb out the strands. Finish to discover my father watching me with a touch of warmth in his gaze.

With an ulan's worth of guests, dozens of Venari-to-be are here to serve the wine sent west by A'tal's finest vineyards. Such gifts are one of the many ways our grateful nation pays tribute to those who stand between this country and conquest.

At the wine service, I seek and find Sojur's favorite. Its grapes grew atop the stark cliffs of Tradeah, near Azalaïs, where the five tribes race each fall.

My first stop is Gayleen a'Rowan, Pell's highest-ranking guest, and his counterpart in the Rowan tribe. I proffer the ewer, my bangs a shield against this woman's piercing gaze.

Her soft affirmation requires a hunter's senses, which exemplifies the light hand with which Gayleen commands.

Albeit, hers is a hand that packs a killing blow should anyone prove foolish enough to provoke her.

I fill her goblet to midpoint and glance up, seeking permission to move on.

Rather than dismiss me, she splashes a few drops of wine into the libation bowl, then sips. "Extraordinary. Is this Sojur's favorite?"

"Yes, a'Shara."

"So, Pell's child, were you justified, trampling this feather-for-brains Habibi?"

Embarrassment ties my tongue into knots, for which Gayleen tips my chin into the light. "What's this? Blushing?" She softens her words with a smile.

"Those eyes, so blue they burn, and the last thing all too many Venari see."

She looks to Pell in the chair beside hers. "Should the day ever come this one no longer pleases you, I'd take her into my ulans in a heartbeat."

My father laughs. "Provided her horses were part of the deal?"

"No, as she stands now, unarmed and unhorsed. You've done a superb job, rearing our enemy's child."

As she waves me away, I offer her reverence. All my assumptions about this harsh woman now need revision.

My next stop is my weapons master, Aryren, a woman who pushes all Venari-to-be till sweat flies and muscles scream. I've endured her brutal training that now people dislike fighting me for reasons other than my nationality.

Aryren shakes her head no.

Empty goblet between his ravaged fingers, Sojur smiles a yes. Beside him, Pell demurs.

From behind Pell, Lycan watches me, winter wolf hungry. We're miserable this close, yet apart.

While refilling my ewer, Kemu a'Rowan comes this way. He's one of a kind, a Rowan Venari with six years in the field, who, come the New Year, will become a Covenant Master. My mistrust arises from his second calling: mindhealing. Be it blocking pain, or should the courts so order, entering a person's memories, thus determining innocence or guilt.

The first time I saw Kemu, he was at his Venari father's side, one among many here to watch Sojur start Windsong under saddle. Three years old and still I sensed something fey about the weedy boy of eight. Despite racing against him over the past four years, my wariness in his presence has yet to ease. I pray wine is all he's after and that, once he has it, he'll join his a'Shara, Gayleen.

He gestures to the ewer I've just refilled. "For Sojur?"

At my nod, he extends his goblet. "Did Pell give that boy the honor of his cupbearer to punish you for Habibi's injury?"

With my attention on pouring his wine, I don't respond. Kemu knows just what message my father sent. Nor does hearing what's being said behind my back do anything good about my attitude.

"I hear you found Lycan a nice colt. Will we run against them in the three-year-old stallion qualifier?"

Shoulders tight, I shrug. How is it that this man knows so much about me? He thinks our racing rivalry and my being Venari-to-be means we share something in common. Nothing could be further from the truth. I cannot tolerate magic, his, or anyone else's. Call it what you will: racial prejudice, superstition, no matter. When I am near Kemu, apprehension reigns.

He savors the vintage with an upturn of chiseled lips. "Now I know why Sojur favors this wine. It's extraordinary."

In the main, Covenant men go clean-shaven. Over the two-day ride from Land's End to the Sada, Kemu's beard and mustache have made a strong showing. With his sculpted features, it has an impact, not that I let on.

He arches a brow, dark as a raven's wing. "Lost in thought, Thea, or just not inclined to talk?"

Rather than answer, I fake interest in the parade of servers arriving with tonight's meal. Throughout, I pray this thorn in my side will take the hint and leave.

"Or could it be you're silent because Pell unhorsed you for leaping the Horns of the Bull?"

I respond with the flattest, least-readable Daharshan expression I own.

Kemu's a swordsman like Pell, with the depth of chest and breadth of muscling it takes to prevail. His making light of most things is why I've never said or done anything particularly obnoxious in his presence. Nor is now the time to do so.

Rather than take offense, Kemu smiles as if my silence hasn't told him just where to stick his intrusiveness. "Word is you're racing Amir this fall. Any other hot prospects?"

As always, Kemu takes the edge off my steel. "You honestly expect an answer?"

He closes what little space there was between us. With wine casks behind me, I've nowhere to go, which he knows, and for that reason, persists. Amidst the general babble, his words are for me alone. "It would be a pleasant change of pace. Try as I might, I can't seem to engage you."

"Engage me?" I advance till we almost touch. "Do you have any idea just how much your magic makes my skin crawl?" At my soft snarl, his gray eyes go wide.

"Surely, you asked Mora to block your courses."

It takes all my restraint not to slap him for his presumption. "I endured Mora's magic to become Venari."

All female Venari do. If captured and bred, this particular magic assures no half-A'talan children are born into slavery.

He cocks his head as if a change in perspective will alter what displeases him. "Are you sure it's my magic that you find disconcerting?"

Heart dinning on my ribs, I seek a response other than my fist. "A'Rowan, your conceit exceeds your audacity, miracle that it is."

"Let's put that aside and address your flawed logic. Namely, tenacity and alignment with the natural order make magic possible. Not some absurd deal with an imaginary devil."

He's calling my fear of magic irrational. I lift the ewer chest high, odd shield that it is. "My life would be complete if I never spoke to you again."

His sapphire Venari marks catch the light as he passes his hand over his forehead. "Why can't I find the right approach with you?"

I laugh. "A mindhealer who has to ask? I despise magic, just as I detest your assumption we share a common ground."

I've shocked him into silence. Before he recovers, a scuffle has us turning toward the disturbance.

It's Habibi's father, Leander. He heaves through the crowd, his rude passage sloshing wine onto carpets half a century old.

"Out of my way, damn you!"

If he's here for me, I need to be out in the open.

I eel into the nearest clearing. Regrettably, Kemu follows. Before I can tell him to mind his own business, Leander clears the last resentful Venari and swings.

His fist connects with the same force as a mule's kick and splits my lip. "You savage!"

As I scrabble to regain my footing, Kemu shoves between us. I grab his arm, hindering the blow he's about to deliver. "My fight, a'Rowan, mine!"

There's no time to see if he'll respect my wishes, not with both of us getting out of Pell's way.

The a'Shara heaves Leander off me. "You dare hit my daughter?"

Never let it be said Leander lacks grit. He proves as much, thudding his chest into Pell's. "Curb your whelp, a'Shara, or I will. My daughter's ankle is so swollen, she can barely walk."

Pell's arm muscles bulge while he closes his hands around Leander's bull of a throat. "Strike, if you dare."

Leander's face turns red as he pries at Pell's grip.

Lycan clears the crowd, then addresses Leander. "Tribesman, I and nineteen others saw Habibi and her friends on the way. They forced the a'Shara's daughter down from a gallop to a halt, but she came nowhere near Habibi. Your daughter tripped. Which is worse: a wrenched ankle or dead?"

Though not completely true, I appreciate the exaggeration.

I step into my father's line of sight, hands open in a request to speak.

Pell nods, then releases the florid-faced shepherd. "Tribesman, mind your manners."

I go to a knee before Leander, arms low and out to the side. "First Law of the Venari: brothers and sisters-in-arms before self. Second Law: any member of the tribe before self. Leander au'Sada, I had no part in your daughter's injury."

Despite my humble words and mien, I pray Leander gives me cause so I can pay him back.

Gayleen comes up behind the glowering shepherd, then claps him on the shoulder, undaunted he's a head taller. "Au'Sada, hit this girl again, and you hit a 'defenseless' child."

This barb has the crowd guffawing. Even the youngest Venari-to-be can defend themselves. Beyond that, my manners have compounded the ass Leander has made of himself, for which he mutters a curse leagues beyond fragrant.

"You wait, girl. Once the council sees my girl's wrists, they'll have you digging latrines for a moon!"

Pell's brows crease, making this an accusation I must address. "A'Shara, Habibi smacked Selene. I kept her from doing it twice."

Pell strokes his beard, the start of a smile turning up the corners of his lips.

Leander gets where this is going: Venari closing ranks against a member of the tribe, for a Venari-to-be, whatever the color of her skin. He departs, his fury rising with the crowd's laughter.

As I watch him depart, someone's hand slides under my braid, and the tingle of a mindhealer's magic steals across my skin. I jerk free and whirl on Kemu. "Did I not just explain my aversion of magic?"

His expression suggests he's as irritated with my intransigence as I am with his assumption.

"Thea, what will it take before you accept a mindhealer's help? Ascended, wounded, and screaming?"

My father's presence tempers my response. "If that day comes, I will acquiesce."

Kemu leans in, speaking for my hearing only. "When, Thea, not if. Injury is a given in a Venari's life. I just pray whoever the mindhealer is, they can get past that thick skull and attitude of yours."

He pivots, stalks to where his wine awaits, then disappears into the crowd.

Sojur hands me a dampened cloth. "Have a healer see to that lip."

I nod, then offer reverence to my teacher, my father, and Gayleen.

It's easy to imagine the coming discussion. It's never welcome when the tribe interferes with Venari matters.

My detractors are welcome to charge, and sentence me in my absence. If serving the Sada, they can't order me back into camp to dig latrines.

I've had enough, more than enough.

I am taking myself hunting.

SIX

DEATH'S COURIER

A ll we can ask of death is haste, and under a hazy copper sun, I am her courier.

A buck sakier lies on the ground. Each labored breath strains his dark nostrils. Buried deep between his ribs, my arrow trembles.

He arches his head back as death rattles in his throat. His spiraled horns pierce the grass. His eyes close, and ribs still. He is here no more.

Mindful of how little divides the quick and the dead, I lace my hands atop my bow. One moment, he'd been muzzle deep in the grass, the next fleeing, hindquarters stark with cut muscle.

A year ago, another sakier shot across my path. Arrow already nocked, I raised, drew, then released. The horns on last year's buck were as long as my forearm. These are even longer.

I sink to my knees, and trace the black crescent moons stippling his honey-colored hide. He hadn't heard me sitting on Batal, waiting for game. I bow my head and thank him for his sacrifice.

"Mother of All, may this creature return to Your loving embrace, then be born again."

Such is Creation's Law, one dying that another may live.

When I grasp the arrow shaft and pull, the triple-headed blades catch on bone. Thrust deeper and at an angle, frees them. The fletching vanes, dyed the azure of my eyes, need no attention. I pass the razor-sharp steel through matted grass, and remove most of the blood.

Weapons back on my saddle, I dally my riata around the buck's horns, then swing up on Batal. Selene trots alongside as we head for camp, beneath a favorite kanga tree. There, I toss the riata over its strongest branch, and back Batal. Once the sakier's hind hooves leave the ground, I dismount and tie off. While I set to work, Batal wanders off to graze.

Steel sings on stone as I hone my gutting knife. A blade of grass, laid across its edge, should sever by weight alone.

Last year's sakier? All that meat and not a single word of praise. Not for a fifteen-year-old who yelled at Sojur, insisting she knew more about horse training than he did. Of course, Pell noticed the chill between his second and daughter. Naturally, Sojur explained why, which was when they closed ranks on me. In hopes my absence would ease their stance, I took myself hunting.

It didn't work.

Every time I brought game back to camp, they ignored me. I gave up on that idea, and tackled the horse pen's filthiest jobs, work no one else wanted. Still, my emotional winter continued.

When my name again appeared on Sojur's work list, it was for the worst of the worst. The buckers, biters, and boneheads.

I worked those reprobates without complaint, all the while lamenting the education my sassing had cut short.

Three interminable weeks later, Sojur halted the colt he was training, then hooked a finger my way.

I took his place in the saddle, riding that colt as if we were one. Finished, heart pounding and hope plummeting as Sojur remained silent. Then, with no change of expression, he spoke the sweetest words ever. "He's your ride from here on."

In the temper-trying heatwave that followed, Pell whistled me, sweat-blind, off the filly I was on. He slammed a pair of boots into my arms, then stalked away.

One glance and I knew the leather was from my sakier. I flew after him, and knowing me, he turned in time to catch my leap into his arms.

They are the same boots I wear today.

I glance down at them and see a sundered strand of grass to either side of my blade's now razor-sharp edge. I've sharpened my knife without an iota of awareness, then tested it. All of which is unbearably stupid with blood in the air. People aren't the only predators on the grasslands.

Knifepoint buried in the burnished hide over the sakier's breastbone, I slit down the midline. The guts spill out in a rush.

Not for me, the liver, liquid with blood, which I toss to Selene.

She snaps it from the air, then sinks to the ground, and eats with delicate manners.

I too settle to my haunches, and welcome the wind washing over me. Better the smell of death than digging latrines, with the Sada guffawing at last year's Champion of Champions brought so low.

It will take days, jerking this much meat over a banked fire, during which the scent could attract a passing karakal. The big cats are the grasslands' supreme hunters, which is why hunting alone isn't smart. As Sahain is wont to say, 'Not good, Thea, not good at all.'

I study the horizon, then come to my feet, unsure of what I've just seen. The wind never moves grass one section at a time.

Selene sniffs the air, then growls, flews high above her teeth. I grab her collar, then straddle her shoulders. A karakal can take down a horse. If this is one, we're dead. Selene, for sure, if she goes after the cat. They are savage hunters, sinuous and swift.

I tell my sweet dog I'm sorry for getting us into this mess, sorry I don't have the sense of a rock mouse. Throughout, I pray Batal's instincts will kick in and that he'll flee. If so, at least one of us will survive.

My worst nightmare becomes reality. The grass shivers, then parts as a karakal steps into the clearing.

Selene goes wild: lunging, growling, teeth snapping.

The karakal answers her with a snarl, its ivory fangs wicked as blades. Amber eyes steady, the deadly animal regards me, its tail flicking. The mass of shoulder and breadth of head suggests this is a male.

Bloody gutting knife in one hand, I tighten my grip on Selene's collar. Regret that I can't tell my father and brothers how much I love them, even as I pray Heaven will take our souls.

The twang of a bowstring snaps my head to the right. No one's fast enough to follow an arrow's path, not when the man bending the bow is my father.

As the arrow parts the fur over the cat's tawny shoulder, D'jhat marches from the tall grasses.

Silent as his arrival, the karakal disappears.

Pell halts D'jhat, then surveys the area. If seriously wounded, the big cat may come at us from a different direction. Statue-still, we wait.

Selene seeks the cat's scent, yet her calm says he's gone.

Pell notes my rigid stance while easing the draw on his bow. "Considering who Selene protects, I should have selected a sturdier dog."

Though swift as a tracker, Selene is no karakal's equal.

I bend and hug her, then thank the Mother of All for my father. She licks my cheek, affirming her love, then, tail wagging, returns to her meal.

Saddle leather creaks as Pell dismounts, arrow still affixed to his bow. He gestures to the hanging sakier. "Weren't we hunting together?"

I swallow spit thick as leather. "After unhorsing me twice in a week?"

"Which you took with extraordinary grace."

I marvel as he rests his hand on my shoulder. "A single line on Sojur's worklist: 'Hunting on Batal, Thea.' Knowing how much you love this site, I thought to start here."

I need to know. "What did the council decide?"

"To do nothing."

My surprise collides with relief.

"I told Charra her vendetta was over, that I wouldn't tolerate a Venari-to-be humiliated by such a feeble accusation. Daughter, can you not trust the love I bear you, and wait for my defense, rather than fend for yourself?"

I wish I could sob as others do, and release the pain, rather than standing stiff and silent, tears welling.

He holds his hand to those tears. "Sa, sa, little one, if it hurts, let it go."

The same words he used when I was little and faking bravery. The principles of our faith reworded for a child's understanding, by which we may request grace if death looms.

Overwhelmed, I press into his touch.

"The day will soon arrive when you must cease bringing down the prize by yourself. What say you? Peg this sakier closed, then return home?"

He's telling me to cease going it alone, and to count on others. Difficult as that is, I nod. "Yes, a'Shara."

My use of his title deepens the lines at the corners of his eyes. "Surely, daughter, you think of me in terms other than my rank."

His sorrow with my reticence pierces, even as his smile invites me to end it.

I race to Batal, retrieve the small packet from my saddlebags, then return to where he stands, his expression puzzled.

I proffer the tassel. "A token of my devotion." I swallow the lump in my throat threatening yet more tears, and make room for the sweetest word ever, ". . . Father."

SEVEN

FIX THIS

I sway side-to-side, my hands around Sahain's wrists.

He smiles at my rare moment of silliness. "Who are you, and what have you done with my sister?"

My answering laughter has him scooping me up into his arms, and spinning us till I'm giddy.

"Are you ready to settle down yet?"

"No, not really." I tip my head back and take in the gathering grounds from upside down. It's fitting. Our father put his foot down with Charra, turning my universe on its head.

Sahain indulges my whimsy, turning slower, trailing my long hair over the grass. Atar sees me, but Sahain gets me, what drives me, what keeps me awake at night. To him alone, I entrust my hopes, fears, and many failures.

The glorious aroma of roasting sakier drifts off the gathering grounds—my sakier, the jewel of tonight's meal. Hunger has me back on my feet, and freeing strands of my hair around Sahain's forearm.

"Thea!"

At Mora's familiar bark, I crane over my brother's broad shoulder, seeking what she wants.

"Come care for this!"

A bare-chested Kemu a'Rowan sits in a nearby gathering tent. Dried blood spirals his upper arm. His sultry expression awaits appreciation of his build and lack of scars. Such are signs of a ferocious and effective Venari. Equally disconcerting and however much it irritates me, the man is undeniably handsome.

The diminutive healer purses lips in a face as wrinkled as a withered apple. "Now, Thea! I have a birthing mother to attend."

My mood sours. She knows better than to ask for my help with a Covener.

Eyes narrowed, she crooks a forefinger my way, making her request a demand. When in the black robes of the Mother's Own, our Wise Woman acts the part, high-handed and imperious.

Sahain gathers my hair into a knot at the nape of my neck. "You can't win, so don't try. Besides, I want to know how the Rowan got nicked. That's not like him." Arm behind my shoulders, he steers me into the tent.

Mora thrusts a wound basket into my arms, a Mother's Mark tattooed on the back of her left hand.

I hold the basket away from me as if snakes writhed inside. "Grandmother, I am no healer."

"Tell your horses that. He's hurt. Fix it."

Much as it grates, I got myself into this mess by asking her to teach me healing for my animals. Along the way, she taught me to read and write, then made me something of a pet.

"Why me, when this camp is riddled with healers?"

It's a question that may get my ears boxed.

"Yes or no, you little ingrate? Everything I've done for you, yet you'd refuse something so simple for me?" She arches her brows, silver as moonlight.

She has cause. Her magic blocked my fertility when my first moon blood came. Not only that, she's mended my wounds whenever I've had need.

Kemu's a breath from laughter, watching the old woman tie me into knots. Just one problem. However great my debt, my priorities lie elsewhere.

"No. Ask one of your healers to do it. The a'Shara awaits us."

"For what? Fetch him wine? Laugh at his jokes?"

If there's a more irreverent woman alive, I've yet to meet her. Just as disturbing, my brother's glower deems my behavior churlish.

I grit my teeth, wishing I were up against anyone else. Mora has contrived this. It shows in her eyes, bright as the stars coming to life in the black velvet sky above. Either I give in or she'll make my life not worth living.

I gust a sigh of defeat and Mora's ire fades like the fiction it is.

"You won't know if the wound needs stitches till it's cleaned."

If this scratch needs stitches, I'd be amazed. Even so, I nod.

She harrumphs, but having won, places a blessing kiss on my forehead. While she walks away, her staff stabs the earth as if making her point again.

The laughter Kemu restrained in her presence breaks free. I round on him. "What's so funny?"

"You."

The fact my brother's grinning from ear to ear is of no help whatsoever.

I narrow my eyes at the ladder belly and bulging pectorals on display. After being roped into this chore, his relishing my discomfort does nothing for my mood. I gesture to his beard.

"Looking to piss everyone off?"

"Quite the opposite with you here."

My eyes go wide at the inference.

He's trimmed his beard in the Daharshan style. Chin and upper lip coupled, with the rest clean-shaven. Doubtless, he understands this potent statement of masculinity is a blatant invitation to someone of my nationality.

I cock my head as if considering a purchase. "You may want to rethink the beard. If captured and enslaved, looking as you do, the seller would come away rich."

Rather than back his ass down, my goad produces a devastating, one-sided grin.

Exasperated, I shake my head. "A'Rowan, if you want this scratch cared for, best you restrain yourself."

"So, about this 'scratch' . . ."

"Exactly. You couldn't wipe off the blood yourself?"

"It's a tad deeper than that, Thea."

"Is that so?" I lean in and part the skin. Blood wells.

Sahain's breath hisses past his teeth. "Mother in Heaven, Thea, show some care."

Appalled, I step back. "Kemu, please forgive me. I didn't know the cut was that deep."

Despite my fluster, his Venari sleeve registers. A snarling karakal peers through swirling grasses, between which his summer-tanned skin shows. What shocks are the cat's eyes, azure blue, the same as my own.

"Why, in the name of Heaven . . .?"

A tolerant smile defines his cheekbones. "Why not the fiercest predator on the grasslands? They mate for life and protect their own."

"Their eyes are amber or green, not Daharshan blue!"

"True." He tips his chin toward his shoulder. "Can we get on with this? I prefer my blood in me rather than out."

Not only is the coincidence too great, it's also plain he won't explain anything. "How did you get hurt?"

"Clipped a grasshen while hunting. She went to earth in a thorn bush. Either I went after her or left her dying for days."

I lean in, studying the straight-edged cut. "Thorn bush, my arse. I'd say someone found you in the wrong bed and came after you with steel."

Sahain's brows reach for his hairline. "Thea, that's uncalled for, and you know it."

Kemu waves my brother's concerns aside. "She's entitled to her opinions, however wrong-headed."

I turn my back on them while cleansing my hands with Mora's favorite tincture. "Chase the wrong prey at your own risk, a'Rowan."

"Thea!"

I glance over my shoulder to Sahain. "What?"

"Are you not the same girl whose father saved from a karakal today?"

Aghast he'd reveal something so personal, I dart a venomous look his way. If that wasn't bad enough, I spot Charra coming this way, red hair a stunning contrast to an emerald abaya.

Smile radiant, she kisses Sahain's cheek, then threads her fingers through his.

When she looks my way, miracle of miracles, there's no scorn on her face. "A'Rowan, I'll tell Gayleen why you're detained.

Something to keep in mind, our sister, cornered, not a good thing."

He touches a finger to his forehead. "Duly noted."

She smiles at Sahain. "Our father awaits." This said with teasing warmth.

Brows sky high, I watch them walk away. Something Sahain says has Charra laughing, then resting her head on his shoulder.

"So, are they one?"

I round on Kemu. "Are you out of your mind?"

"I certainly hope not."

I gust a sigh that denies any such possibility. Though unrelated by blood, Sahain would never align with my greatest enemy.

Now, doubly annoyed, I clean my way into his wound with an acrid tincture that makes my eyes water. As a mindhealer, I know he's blocked his own pain. Yet, I part the skin with caution, hoping to avoid another repeat of the bleeding.

"Is it deep?"

"Very."

There's no avoiding intimacy while driving a curved needle into his skin and drawing up the first knot. A skill I learned, sprawled over a thrashing horse.

"Was there any more fallout about Habibi?"

I shake my head. If he wants gossip, he'll have to get it from someone else.

"So, who brought down today's sakier, you, or Pell?"

"I did." One more stitch and I'm gone.

"The bow's your weapon?"

As if he didn't know. "At my height, it better be."

I lean in, weighing whether I can get away with one more stitch or if it needs two. Feel his breath on my cheek, and straighten, expecting to find him looking down my shirt. I'm wrong. It's my eyes he's fixated on.

"That blue. As Gayleen says, the last thing many Venari see, certainly the last thing my father saw."

I speak the benediction for his father's memory. "Born again . . ."

Broad hand over heart, he finishes the prayer, ". . . among those who love him."

We lock gazes, our faces a breath apart.

For a moment, time stops.

It restarts as he sighs out a deep breath. "Tell me, Thea, did you think I was filling my eyes with your beauty? Young as I was before losing my father, he taught me to wait for a woman's invitation."

I toss my bangs out of my eyes, peeved he's read me so easily and well. Question whether he would wait, only to remind myself he's Venari. He'd never cross that line. Push it, maybe. Cross it, no.

Last stitch in and knotted, I return the soiled instruments to their basket. While bandaging his arm, ask myself what about this man irritates me so? One thing's for sure. I don't believe a word of his story about how he got hurt, nor do I welcome his attention.

While I wash my hands, he works his bandaged arm into his shirt, then pulls it over his head. While tucking its hems into his breeches, he smiles at me.

Peeved, I park my hands on my hips. "A'Rowan, your aim is off. Way off."

"I don't agree. My aim is true. It's the quarry that's proven elusive."

I get the allusion and implicit request. Grudgingly, admit the lengths he's gone might work, were my instincts not screaming—run, this man has magic.

"I wouldn't trust you any further than I could throw you."

"And why is that?"

I gesture to his wounded arm. "This time, tell the truth. Who cut you, her brother, or a lover?"

A slow grin lifts his left cheek higher than the right. "Neither. Her father." He closes his broad, tendon-defined hand around his sheathed sword, then drapes the belt over his chest, settling the blade across his back. All this, done with the quiet competence of habit, his eyes so dark gray they're best described as black.

I tell myself, leave now, before you do something spectacularly stupid, then shake my head and free the knot Sahain put in my hair.

As I meet his gaze, it settles like nightfall around my shoulders. "If you've angered her father, I'd suggest hunting a different quarry, more in your league and tribe."

The mass of my hair sweeps across his chest as I turn and stalk from the pavilion.

Rich male laughter follows me into the dark.

That I wouldn't mind so much if not for the shiver passing up my spine.

EIGHT

FALLING

First light daggers the horizon and dawn-crazed birds cascade song over the grasslands. Amidst such peace, I have the luxury of singularity, thanks to a discovery made years ago.

One summer night, a Covenant glassblower spun a replica of the Great Henge at Land's End, to thank the Sada for their hospitality. Enchanting as watching the red-hot glass take shape was, the true beauty came once the structure cooled. An oil lamp placed in the Well of Souls bathed the crystalline spires in dancing colors. I lingered while others sought their beds. Come the dawn, in a community of thousands, I had the gathering grounds to myself.

That same bliss is now mine.

Nana, our head cook, doesn't tolerate uncovered hair in the cooking area and for the first round of bread off her baking stone, I comply. I wind my braid around my head while heading for her station, then bind it in place with my hald.

Breaking her coals open, I feed them hotstone, then swing the water kettle over the growing heat.

Nana and her crew arrive soon after, their expressions tranquil while indolently adjusting kerchiefs over their hair. Habibi is among their number. With Pell at the helm, even she can't escape her share of the work.

Her calm, the entire group's calm, disappears upon seeing me. Showing up for meals, that's expected. Yet after Leander split my lip, these women thought my days of cadging bread from Nana were finished. Hands dangling between my knees, I keep a 'guess again' expression off my face.

Nana halts before me, and perches her hands over broad hips. "Thea, you aren't welcome here, not after running Habibi down."

They cook. I hunt. It's all we have in common and, far for me, it's enough. I lace my fingers, then stretch my arms overhead.

"Are you banning me, Nana?"

We both know how well that would go over with my father.

Exasperated, she points to the kettle. "Is that boiling yet?"

I bend to listen for bubbling.

Several things happen in swift succession. A knee slams into my back and drives me into the flames. My hands plunge into blood-red coals and I scream while rolling out of the fire, burnt hands clenched to my midsection. Tears of pain stream down my face.

Habibi steps across me, and spits her curse into my face. "Nomadi scum! Leave, and never come back!"

I rise, then ride my attacker back to the dirt and break the blisters on her face. "You snake!"

I draw back my fist.

She shields her face, wailing. "I tripped, same as on the way!"

Before my fist connects, Nana yanks me off of Habibi. "That is enough! Pell didn't raise you to be a savage!"

I jerk free of her grip, and fall to my knees as what little was in my belly spews. The pain's worse than anything I've ever known.

No one moves to help. Either I wait till Venari arrive to break their fast or ask again.

"Nana, I beg of you, send for the a'Shara." These words, forced through my clenched teeth. Reminding her just who lies at her feet: Pell's daughter, a Venari-to-be. Ignore this request, and there will be repercussions.

Incapable of no more, I groan and subside on my back. There's whispering, then the sound of someone running.

Every breath is a lesson in suffering. How did Sojur survive those weeks of unrelenting pain? Even as I ask these questions, I pray for someone to break a pot over my head and knock me out: anything besides this.

It seems an eternity before the ground beneath me trembles with the approach of galloping horses.

I come onto an elbow and squint through pain-slit eyes.

It's the a'Shara on D'jhat. Sojur's at his side with Pell's guard hard on their heels. I wobble to sitting, then sway as darkness threatens to overtake me.

Dismayed at Venari riding into the cooking area, the women cry out.

Tack creaks. My father's spurs clash as he runs to me.

I raise my bloody, burnt hands to him. The right, not so bad, middle, and ring fingers a dull red. The best that can be said about the left is no bone shows. If this scars, how will I ride? How will I draw a bow?

Pell goes to a knee and braces my shoulders. His expression vows nations will fall. "What happened?"

My words come out tear-thick. "Habibi kneed me in the back and drove me into Nana's cook fire."

Habibi, all the women, start shouting at once.

Pell holds up a hand for silence and waits till he gets it. "You so swear?"

My answer's pain-staggered. "I so swear."

While my father cannot command opinion, justice is another matter. He rises and finds Habibi in the crowd.

She meets his gaze with an arrogant head toss. "Nana will vouch for me. It was an accident. I tripped."

The aplomb with which she delivers this bald-faced lie amazes me.

The a'Shara looks at Nana, who hesitates, and well she should. "I didn't see what happened. Perhaps someone else did?"

Habibi grabs Nana's arm, her fingers denting the older woman's flesh. "I did nothing wrong!"

Head pounding, flesh screaming, I can barely string a coherent thought together. How am I to prove her lie?

Pell gestures to his Venari. "Take this girl to Mora and tell her I want Leander's daughter Inlooked. I will have the truth."

Inlooking, whereby Habibi's memories will affirm I spoke true.

She backs away in terror as the Venari reach for her. "You can't do this to me!"

Pell narrows his eyes. "The innocent have nothing to fear."

Hard warrior hands close on Habibi's wrists and march her away, stumbling and wailing.

Sojur's lips thin with disgust as she passes.

The women whisper as Pell unwinds my hald, so old and often washed, it's gauze. Every layer reveals burns till the last.

His gift for herding horses, cattle, or least-loved sheep, and for its giver, it is precious, yet now ruined.

Concern scores lines around his eyes. "Had you been slower or she swifter . . ." he breaks off, then shakes his head. "I count the days till you ascend, and no Sada dare raise their hand against you."

Were my hands not bloody, they'd be around his neck. He's letting me ascend. As Venari, I will be any A'talan's equal, possessed of a citizen's rights. Yet the moment which should have been my triumph has become a barbaric nightmare.

I look at my hands, perhaps forever ruined. If I can't bend a bow, true ascension won't be possible. "Father, how am I to undertake my ascension hunt?"

"After the sakier you brought down yesterday? No one will question whether you've fed your people."

All this, thanks to Habibi, the girl who 'tripped.'

Pell lifts me into Sojur's arms. "Take her to the healing tents while I sort this mess out." His gaze shifts to me. "Whatever Mora wants, you will comply, which includes letting a mindhealer block your pain. Yes?"

Teeth grit, I nod.

With a grim, approving smile, he swings up onto D'jhat and departs. As Sojur reins Amir in the opposite direction, I sag against my teacher's body. For once, I may get justice, but at a cost that could sunder all my dreams.

NINE

BROTHER MINE

M ora holds her hands out in warding, blocking Lycan's entry to the healing tent. "You love sick fool! She's hurt, not dying!"

He sidesteps, then strides for the table where I sit. "I'll kill that godsdamned Habibi!"

Kemu stabs a forefinger my way. "You, stay!"

He turns, catches the younger man, and heaves him backward. "She's in agony, and you hinder us? How dare you call yourself Venari-to-be? Beyond that, kill Habibi and Pell will drag you till dead. Ours is a land of law, not lawlessness."

Lycan bulls into Kemu. "I saw you corner her in the a'Shara's pavilion. No way will you worm into her life!"

Over Kemu's shoulder, he sends me an agonized look. "Prevail, my beloved."

A moment later and he's thudding his fist into Kemu's chest. "Another time, a'Rowan, count on it." One last snarl and he storms from the tent.

His expression disgusted, Kemu turns back to me. "Don't you have enough trouble in your life?"

Mora huffs amidst sweeping supplies into her wound basket. "She does indeed, which is why Pell separated them. They're a disaster looking for a place to happen."

Kemu braces my back. "I've got you. Ease on down."

Hands curled into paws, I do as asked, and gasp as movement yanks flesh on fire.

Kemu sits on a stool behind me, and places his hands on my temples. "Mora says your only experience of mindhealing did not go well. You have my word, this will."

Moments pass as I wait for pain to cease being the whole of my universe. It does not happen.

Thea, don't make me force this on you.

His speaking in my mind plunges me into the past. I'm four years old. Blood gushes from a cut knee as a Covenant mindhealer unable to block my pain curses me. Horrid as the experience was, it was short. Mora told the woman to leave and never return to the Sada, then cared for me with medicine, not magic.

Show me this mindhealer some other time.

Reality wavers. He can read my memories?

I can. Now cease resisting, so I can block your pain.

The word 'yes' becomes my everything. 'Yes', to his magic. 'Yes', to whatever it will take to end the hurting.

Moments later, sensation shivers across my skin, then dives inward. Finding nerves on fire, whatever this is, silences the agony.

I tip my head back to see him. "The pain is gone."

A smile curves his lips. "As it should be. Close your eyes. I'll be with you throughout."

Exhaustion turns closed eyes into dreamless sleep.

When I wake, morning's shadows belong to late afternoon. I'm on my side, bandaged hands crossed at the wrists.

In a chair beside my bed, Kemu smiles at my befuddled expression. "You've been waking for the better part of an hour."

The horror of my burnt hands roars back, followed by a wave of bittersweet joy—Pell telling me I'll ascend, whether I can serve.

Someone has washed my hair, and left it unbraided. Rather than riding clothes, I'm in an abaya, its wide sleeves connected at shoulders, mid-elbow, and wrists. I look to Kemu, seeking assurance he had no part in dressing me.

"Trust me, Mora ran me out once it came time to bathe you."

I rise on an elbow and rotate my left hand. It's swathed in bandages. On the right, my little finger and palm are wrapped.

"How long will these stay on?"

"The right, a few days. The left, obviously longer."

"Can I ride?"

He arches a brow. "Don't toy with me, girl. You can ride whenever you want."

He's calling me to account and with cause. In battle, all Venari ride, reins looped over the pommel while their legs guide their warhorse.

"Want help with sitting up?" This asked while filling a water goblet on a nearby table.

I answer by rump-walking my back to the headboard, then draining the goblet he holds to my lips.

"Hungry?"

Hunger—what got me into this mess. I nod.

While he tucks a napkin into the abaya's neckline, the backs of his fingers graze my collarbones. Intentional or graceless? No, the latter can't be true.

His dark eyes narrow. "Do you know all your thoughts are mine, and the link between us will continue till you're out of pain?"

Appalled, I shake my head.

"Be that as it may, best you accept, I'll be privy to your thoughts for some time."

He gestures to a food tray on the table. "What do you want first?"

"The white cheese and bread."

He slits a round of bread, then tucks a generous slice of cheese into its interior. While he does so, again, I puzzle over his beard trimmed in the Daharshan style.

He chuckles, moving his chair closer to the bed. "Most women like it."

I beg my mind to shut up.

"It's been years since I fed my little sister, so some patience please."

I sink my teeth into the bread, and ravenous as I am, cannot pace myself.

"What do you want next?"

With a mitten'd left hand, I gesture to the orange. Its heavenly scent fills the air as he peels it, then pops the first section into my mouth. My delight settles the fur I've ruffled.

"The a'Shara sent these. Plainly, he knows what you love." This said while he frees the second orange of its rind.

I take a stab at not being so prickly. "What's with the abaya?"

"Mora hoped the Sada would see you as one of them."

The looped sleeves leave most of my tawny arms exposed. "Not a chance. All they'd see is a Daharshan."

"Oh, they'll see you any moment now. Mora will bespeak me when it's time."

"For what?"

"Tribal Council."

I come off the backboard swift as a shot arrow. "I did nothing wrong!"

He wipes an orange fleck off my lip. "Not you. Habibi."

"Oh."

He bends and retrieves something off the carpets. The spicy perfume of desert roses melds with the orange oil as he straightens. "A friend of mine found these on the A'talan side of the border. May I?"

I nod, amazed, then watch out of the corner of my eye as he plaits the tiny buds into a braid alongside my ear, and binds the end with a silver ferrule.

That ferrule is mine and could have come only from Sahain or Atar. Did he cobble this ploy together after Mora sent him away during my bath? Lycan loves the dramatic gesture, but Kemu is a man made for mockery and disdain.

"If that's how you think of me, no wonder I rub you the wrong way."

Blood rushes to my cheeks.

Thankfully, his attention flashes inward, the same as when Mora bespeaks someone, then returns swiftly. "Mora says the Council awaits you."

The Council, with all its haggling and stance-taking. I can't last that long.

"I need to . . ."

He rises. "I'll be outside."

The moment he's gone, I race for the chamber pot. I relieve myself, hems clumped between my knees, then find a pair of sandals among those at the entry.

The gown's hems swirl around my ankles as I come Kemu's way. While I do so, he holds hand-to-chest.

"You dressed like this, heart-stopping."

In my astonishment, I misstep. The abaya hems tangle my ankles and topple me into his steadying grasp.

In my embarrassment, I can scarce meet the warmth in his gaze. Why didn't Mora pick another mindhealer? I've made no secret of my aversion to this man.

He steadies me as I shake out the irritating mass of fabric. "Thea?"

His soft tone breaks my fixation with the unfamiliar garment.

"What?" It comes out sharper than intended.

"Mora didn't ask. I offered."

"Whatever for?"

He winces. "How is it a woman can wound so deeply in such a few words?"

In his estimation, I'm a woman?

"You are, and your beauty devastates."

I open my mouth, but nothing comes out. He finds the face of A'tal's enemy beautiful?

He closes what space there was between us. "Beyond beautiful. How could it be otherwise with your soul shining through such stunning eyes?"

No sooner than he says this, then his laughter depreciates the whimsy. "Now that I've confessed my utter infatuation, we'd best be on our way."

He takes my forearm, matching his stride to mine. The abaya ceases to be an object of irritation, which is a good thing, with his confession consuming the better part of my attention. Has this thorn in my side sought me out for reasons other than racing? No sooner than this question arises and I flush, then dart an anxious glance his way.

He's heard my every thought. It shows in his set jaw and gaze intentionally straight ahead.

I wish a chasm would open beneath my traitorous feet and swallow me whole.

It's nowhere near soon enough till we reach the sprawling expanse of the tribe's largest gathering tent. There, the Sada make grudging way as they seek to determine just how hurt the a'Shara's desert-born daughter truly is. The roses braided into my hair and an abaya earn me dismissive sneers.

I can easily imagine their thoughts.

We reach the tribunal. Sojur sits to Pell's right. Jae, our headwoman and most influential non-Venari in the tribe, is at his left.

Bandaged hand to pounding heart, I make reverence. Better trial by combat than Tribal Council. I tell myself all will be well. Charra's not steering the ship today. The sound of sobbing makes me turn.

Mora, in the robes signifying her rank as a Voice of the Mother, leads a short procession. Behind her, one Venari shoves a stumbling, weeping Habibi forward. Another leads Leander, his hands behind his back.

The extremity shocks. Yes, Leander split my lip. And yes, his daughter tried killing me. Yet for all the cruelties I've endured, I've never sought retribution.

Habibi, forced to her knees, buries her face in her hands.

A blade at Leander's throat keeps him silent, yet doesn't hide the loathing in the look he sends my way.

Pell speaks with the same depth and resonance he uses for addressing his troops. "Leander's daughter, I adjudge you guilty of intentional harm to a Venari-to-be. By our law, your fate is in Thea's burnt hands."

An angry rumble greets the a'Shara's pronouncement.

Leander's coal-hot gaze promises—hurt his girl and he'll see me dead. The animosity on Habibi's face puts the tribe's denunciation into a clearer perspective. She regrets not driving me face-first into the flames. Had I died, she could have made a show of mourning a 'tragic accident.'

Mora joins me, then scissors through the bandages over my left hand. "When you see what she's done, you'll understand why I do this."

The bandages fall away. The crowd gasps.

Weeping burns and ointment overlay my birthmark, the only thing revered about me. Even as I envision the ruin of my future, Mora thrusts the grisly evidence of Habibi's crime into her face. "Own your evil, girl. This is your abysmal doing."

Habibi tries looking away, for which Mora backhands her. "Coward, your hubris repulses me."

The crowd sucks a collective in-breath. This is not one of Mora's grandmotherly rants. The Mother's Voice rings in Mora's tone.

"I will not presume upon Thea's decision, but if she doesn't call for a horse and drag you to a richly deserved death, if you ever need help, don't look to me or my healers."

Mora turns back to me. "This wretch's fate is in your hands."

Habibi's expression vows unbending hate. Kill this girl, and I break faith with every principle I hold dear. I've never had the stomach to watch captured Kian dragged to their deaths. As for the thought of binding a raita around Habibi's ankles, it sickens me.

I force resolve into my voice. "I seek no recompense."

The sound of an angry hornet nest sweeps through the crowd, everyone talking at once.

Sojur contains a smile, but Pell's forehead creases. "Thea, are you sure?"

I bow my head. "My people before myself."

Leander, once freed, takes his daughter into his arms, their expressions devoid of gratitude.

I've done no good whatsoever in leaving enemies at my back, people who've learned nothing from my charity. This is the reason my father neither gives quarter nor spares lives while leading his ulans.

The crowd files past our tableau of misery. For every grudging nod of approval, dozens are rife with contempt. I can't do anything right in their estimation. No Daharshan can exemplify Venari precepts.

As Leander leads his sobbing daughter away, I seek affirmation from my father and teacher that I've done the right thing.

Their gazes are on the tent entry. I turn.

Sahain strides toward us. A red-fletched arrow juts from the quiver behind his shoulder.

Tomorrow, he turns seventeen, and our father has sent my brother on his ascension hunt. A hunt I will never undertake, thanks to a girl who tripped.

Pell greets his son, now almost his height and breadth as other Venari enter bearing a buck sakier.

Sahain turns my way and smiles at the sight of desert roses in my hair. He threads his arm through mine, then turns us to face Pell, the pair of us side by side.

Our father rests his hands on our shoulders. "Thea, you ascend in a week's time. In light of today's events, I offer you a choice."

His hard-eyed gaze seeks Lycan, yet softens upon returning to me. "Mora told me how your would-be second behaved in the healing tents. Not only did he defy my orders, he risked your wellbeing and will never be your second. That said, once an adult, you may do as you please where your private life goes. On this, I stand firm."

This morning, all I could encompass was Lycan's caring. The pain kept me from grasping the consequences of his breaking Pell's injunction. For this single act of defiance, the life we hoped to share is forever gone. Our a'Shara does not change his mind.

Pell speaks again, reclaiming my attention. "As for your future, Sojur would welcome you as his understudy and his quatrain. Or you can second Sahain, and ride with the Lightning Ulan. The choice is yours."

Without Sojur, I would not be a Champion of Champions. But since I was a little child, I've dreamt of riding with my father's forces. Praying that my teacher remembers what it is to be this age, I meet his expectant gaze, then bandaged hand-to-heart, making regret-filled reverence.

He nods, his formal expression barely containing his disappointment.

My heart breaks as I look to my brother, a man who is the light to my dark, even as I am the dark to his light. "It would honor me to be Sahain's second."

The a'Shara beams. "Then, it is so decided."

I kiss Sahain's cheek and he, mine. From this day forward, our lives will be intertwined for long as we live, be it fighting at each other's sides or stepping up whenever the other has need.

In a day of unbearable wrongness, one thing has gone right.

TEN
CELEBRATE

Determined to feed myself, I do so doggedly, spoon in right hand, bowl between my knees. Selene is plastered against my leg, her doleful gaze fixed on my food. I ignore her as best I'm able.

The bed we're on is one of four arranged in a cross. In the square formed by their feet, chafer lanterns keep our supper warm.

This is it. A few more days and our band will be broken. Sahain in two nights, me soon after. As Venari, all our needs will be provided: tent, food, tack, weapons, and clothing. Sahain may welcome his privacy, but me, not so much.

Atar sits near the entry, his back to the late afternoon light coming through the flaps. I nudge him with my toe.

He frowns, engrossed in the inner world of his drawing. "What?"

"Are you looking forward to being rid of us?"

Were his bewilderment not born of sorrow, it might be comical. "No, not in the least."

Sahain chuckles. "Are you sure about that? Neither of us stumbling in, stinking of horses, and pissing off would-be lovers?"

Atar sighs and shakes his head.

I narrow my eyes at Sahain in a warning to ease off, then look back to Atar. "Truly?"

"Yes, truly."

"What if I stayed?"

His expression brightens. "Would you?"

"Who knows what the future may bring? Lycan and I might not work out, and unlike Sahain, I haven't designs on scads of partners."

A hard-thrown pillow whizzes past my shoulder. My brother's intentional miss has me grinning. Sahain's more than competent with a bow. Selene, however, doesn't appreciate the jostling. She rises and crosses to Sahain, then flops down beside him.

My smile's sweeter than honey. "See, even Selene loves you."

While stroking her ears, he rolls his eyes.

Atar passes me bread, glistening with butter. "Please stay, Thea. Whenever I go off the deep, please remind me there's more to love than a handsome face."

He has cause. With his growing fame, men have sought his company for purposes other than love.

"Glad to do so. I wager once Sahain tires of catting around, he'll spend most of his nights here."

Sahain snorts. "Don't count on it, and whatever gave you the impression I 'cat' around?"

Atar joins in my laughter. "Says the man who rarely sleeps in his own bed."

To which our brother has no retort.

It's hard to imagine Sahain's open expression cloaked by a man's beard. It's equally difficult as envisioning us as adults with adult responsibilities. Still, whatever the future brings, these two men, our father, and Sojur, are the whole of my family.

A shadow falls over us. As one, we look to the entry.

It's Kemu a'Rowan, basket of wine over one arm, and jug of ale in the other. With the heat, he's down to shirt, leggings, and boots.

"What's this? I thought to restock your party, not start it. Name of Heaven, you three should be celebrating! Sahain's ascending and Thea soon after."

He grins at Sahain. "And you, getting drunk post-ascension hunt is a time-honored tradition. Show up clear-headed at gathering tomorrow and your ulan will question your worth."

Sahain grabs the double armload of gear scattered over the fourth bed that we keep for guests. "Please, join us."

Kemu puts the wine and ale at the foot of the bed, then his sword and flute case between us. "Do you need me to . . .?"

He mimics sliding his fingers up the back of my neck.

"No, I'm fine." I gesture to the case. "You play?"

He nods, then casts about till spotting a tray of glasses amidst Atar's unwound spindles. Filling one with ale, he sets it by my knee.

"Anyone else?"

He read my enthusiasm through our link. It irritates me so much I remind myself that this is Sahain's night. My soon-to-be second, who calls my aversion to magic lame, and already has the first wine bottle open.

Kemu twirls his forefinger between us. "Sorry. I should have asked, rather than read your thoughts."

I shrug, still annoyed.

Filling a glass with ale, he raises it. "To Sahain a'Sada and his-soon-to-be second, Thea a'Sada."

Thea a'Sada: who knew the day would ever come? The toast fills me with pride and amazement. I trade spoon for ale, touch rims with the others, then join them in making Thanksgift in the libation bowl. The chilled ale suggests the jug spent the day in one of our many snowmelt-sourced streams. I slant a questioning glance Kemu's way.

He gives me a wry smile of affirmation, then draws a folded cloth from the flute case. "Pell asked me to bring you this. It's a replacement for what Habibi ruined. Shall I unfold it?"

I nod, my throat tight with emotion.

He reveals a hald of Sada emerald, its ends tasseled in gold and silver threads. They signify the four pillars of a Venari's strength: courage, integrity, duty, and honor.

Sahain rests his hand on my knee. "You earned this for reasons beyond not taking Habibi's life."

All I can manage is a wan smile.

Selene rolls onto her back and wriggles as Kemu rubs her belly. "When hunting, she must be easy to spot."

Thanks to the ale, I laugh. "Other than winter, yes."

She rolls over and rests her head on his knee. Her eyes close as he strokes her head.

Her sweetness and the reminder of Habibi's hateful nature has me holding up my left hand. "Just think, if Habibi hadn't smacked my dog, none of this would have happened."

Kemu tops off my glass. "Drink. It will ease the ire."

Sahain greets this statement with wine-fueled laughter. "Not in this lifetime, a'Rowan. My sister is a Champion of Champions grudge holder. Never forgets. Never forgives."

"That's inconsistent with a woman who refused redress."

"Hah! Do yourself a favor. Don't cross her."

I slant Sahain a piercing glance. "Took you long enough to figure it out. Besides, it was only a grass snake."

Atar fights not to spit wine out of his nose. "A grass snake? There had to be a dozen of them squirming around in his bedcovers. I didn't know a man could scream that high."

I give Sahain my 'you had it coming look.'

Much to his discomfort, Kemu doesn't stifle his grin. "What did you do to piss her off?"

Sahain rolls his eyes. "Tracked her while hunting, then once the sun set, snuck up on her camp and coughed like a karakal."

I shake my head. "Idiot."

"No argument there." He holds up his thumb and forefinger, a breath apart. "That's how close her arrow came."

Kemu furrows his brows. "Why do anything so foolish?"

I glare at my brother. "Why indeed?"

He shrugs. "Just stupid kid stuff. At least with me there, you didn't have any bad dreams."

Kemu gives him a puzzled look, for which I slash my fingers across my throat, signaling Sahain to shut up.

He ignores me. "She's had them all her life, and often wakes up screaming."

Kemu's expression suggests either I explain or he'll get the story out of my brothers.

"I have nightmares of shapeshifters or karakels, their eyes aglow while slinking across the border. They kill me, then drag my carcass back into the desert for their cubs."

As Atar and Kemu gape at me, Sahain makes a sound of disgust. "Whoever told you that shapeshifter crap should rot in the seven hells."

"And just who do you think that was, brother mine, if not the human incarnation of a karakal? Whenever that didn't work, Charra threatened to ask a Covenant mage to place a curse on me."

Sahain's expression turns stricken. Little wonder. He's always seeking to convince me our sister isn't that bad.

Tiring of the topic, I drink. There's much to ponder: Habibi. Earning a role among people who would just as soon, I didn't. Whether my hands will heal well, or if Lycan and I will become lovers.

Immersed in thought, I'm startled back into the now when a flute's sweet, clear notes rise amidst dusk's soft light.

How is any of this fair? Not only is Kemu a decca leader and a soon-to-be Master Mindhealer, he's a musician. No matter. The flute makes an already wonderful night even better as Atar adds his lyrical baritone.

I wedge my glass beside Kemu's, refilling both as my brothers mark time to the music. The ale flowing through my veins eases my normal restraint in the presence of a stranger. So much so, as the last tinge of daylight bleeds into night's dark, I snag my tabor across my leg, then mark the beat with my right fingers.

Atar moves the food off the chafer lanterns. With their light dancing across the tent ceiling, yet more enchantment arrives.

When Kemu takes a break, Sahain retells the tale of his ascension hunt. His extravagant gestures cast dramatic shadows over the looms and walls. Atar's incomplete tapestries seem to come to life in my happy haze of ale. However silly, I say whatever comes to mind.

Needing to empty their bladders, Atar and Sahain help each other to their feet. Having led the charge in drinking, Sahain drapes his meaty arm over Atar's shoulders, then looks to Kemu.

"A'Rowan?"

"Yes?"

Convinced of a truth he's found in the wine, my brother laughs. "Put your spurs to it. It'll take your kind of grit to beat Lycan to the punch."

Howling at this so-called witticism, they stagger into the night.

In their absence, the silence deafens. I grew up with these knotheads, yet am appalled, my face on fire.

Kemu struggles not to laugh while setting aside his flute. "Pay them no mind."

I give him an incredulous look. "They're both getting grass snakes in their beds."

"Fair enough."

He gestures for me to lean forward. "For now, the ale keeps your pain at bay, but give it an hour and you'll be hurting." With the spider touch of his magic, he renews the mindblock.

When he stands, I try doing the same. Something's wrong with the horizon. While trying to sort up from down, my bare feet tangle in the covers and I trip, no better than Habibi.

With a head filled with wool and left hand bandaged, I don't break my fall. Instead, smack straight into Kemu's mass of muscle. Somehow, I restrain myself from drawing a fingertip down the visible part of his chest.

He sets me upright, then waits to see if I'll stay that way. "Are you all right?"

I blink, balance coming and going, doubtless, looking like an owl roused at midday. "A good night's sleep and I'll be fine."

Especially once I'm able to do what my brothers are.

When a yawn splits my jaw, thankfully, I have enough awareness left to cover my mouth. "Kemu, thank you for tonight and your help."

He smiles amidst settling his sword belt across his chest, then flute strap over his shoulder. "Sweet dreams, Thea."

"Same to you."

He laughs, a dark, captivating sound. "They will be if you're in them." With a smile and a wave, he disappears into the night.

I stand there, swaying, admitting a denied truth. The man's intrigued by me. What shocks is this particular river runs both ways.

ELEVEN

THE BLESSING

I sit Windsong atop a butte overlooking the border. True Covenant steel rides across the back of the knee-length emerald haaka I wear. Both are privileges extended to Sahain's soon-to-be second.

While awaiting the last guests for tonight's ceremony, a flight of Lunas whispers across the border. Hundreds of them, their moon-pale wings an icon of peace against the darkening sky.

I raise my birth-marked hand in greeting, upon which a Luna alights, her wings opening and closing, displaying the Eyes of Heaven. Then, soft as her arrival, she rejoins her companions feasting on the nectar-laden flowers in the grasses below.

I lower my hand, only to discover she's left her shimmer over my bandaged birthmark. Tell this story to restive children at bedtime, and they'd hiss shame for such farfetched nonsense.

Odd. Had I not been born with this mark, I'd be some Daharshan male's wife and likely a mother. Not sitting this priceless mare, who's eager to join the Rowan Venari now approaching from the south.

I bid this moment of reverie farewell, then, with my breath, send the Luna's 'stardust' swirling out into the growing dark.

As we descend the grade, the resonant voices of tabors echo over the grasslands. Sahain's ascension will soon begin.

This afternoon, Atar threaded the narrow battle braids he plaited into my hair with silver beads. Bound in a knot at the nape of my neck, it looks as if I've cut my childhood braid as many ascended Venari do. In celebration of this momentous event, he drew my portrait in full battle dress: eyes a startling blue over high cheekbones, jet black hair, and hands around the sword hilt, minus the bandages.

In four days, when I ascend, that same sense of being the master of my own life will be my daily reality. Or so I tell myself.

My haaka's panels ripple over Windsong's flanks as we follow the Rowan into camp. Sahain's uncomplicated ways have earned him friends among our neighbors, many of who are here to share his joy. With these numbers, the ulans will rank in squares, with those on the outer rims remaining a'horse.

I spot Lycan among the Venari-to-be serving as tonight's grooms. Tawny hair braided and bound, his smile comes slow and appreciative.

"Sun's ease, Thea."

If news of this encounter reaches my father, I pray he accepts the semblance of friendship we now present. "Sun's ease, Lycan."

Windsong nudges him for the treat she knows he has.

He feeds her a knot of sweet bread, his handsome face framed between her pricked ears. "Ah, my beauty, your beguiling lady must attend upon her brother. Will you help me ease the sorrow of her absence?"

With death soon to be my constant companion, the imperative to seize life compels me. I come to earth and it takes all my will not to kiss this glorious young man. All of which he knows, and for which he brushes my arm with his while loosening the girth I cannot.

I sigh.

He grins. "I'll find you afterwards."

Despite my fluster, I nod and vow a bold foray into the mystery of womanhood as he leads Windsong away. Only when they've disappeared into the mass, do I head for the tribe's elders: Mora, Pell, Jae, and Sojur.

My father is in his glory with yet another of his crèche ascending. His ulan leaders stand ranked behind him, among them, the dauntless Khat, head of the ulan we will serve. Hasia, her life partner and second, stands at Khat's side.

Knee to ground, I make formal reverence.

Pell smiles while signaling me to rise.

As I step into parade rest at Mora's side, her lips tighten. All my life, she's insisted despite being Daharshan, my birthmark suggests I could be a peacemaker, an Ah'rēnē with magical powers. Yet one more reason I chose my father's path.

Beside her, the tribe's headwoman, Jae, offers me a troubled smile. Little wonder. Habibi's life was mine to take. Jae must find it odd that the most hated person in her tribe did not respond in kind.

The music softens to a thoughtful refrain. Silence descends upon the ranks.

Sahain halts at the opening to our inner circle and smiles at me. For once, in honor of him achieving our mutual goal, I've abjured comfort for occasion.

The music ends, replaced by the sigh of the wind and crackling gathering fires. Into this mix, our father speaks.

"Who comes?"

Sahain draws himself to attention. "A warrior."

"Mindful that upon entering service, only death or dishonor will sever your obligations?"

"Yes, a'Shara."

"Then, you are well come, my son."

My brother inclines his head to our leading lights as he takes his place amidst Venari with half a lifetime in service.

Jae's smile is as genuine as it is gracious. "Sahain, once you are Venari, any mother, or child, the aged or infirm, will look to you for their very lives. Speak from your heart. Will you fight and perhaps die for your people?"

"I will, my lady."

"Then I give you my blessing."

Sahain takes a knee before Mora, then meets the wise woman's gaze. Though never a simple task, under these circumstances, it's formidable.

She rests her aged, skilled hands on his shoulders. "Sahain, the life you have chosen is that of a pasque flower, blooming at first light, and withering come dark. Are you willing to live within such a finite slice of time?"

"If the Creators so wish, yes."

"Wish?" She spreads her fore and middle fingers like shears. "The Mother and Father of All will snip the thread of your life as They see fit. Do you accept this as a given?"

He meets her challenge with courage. "Yes, Damă." A word we reserve for formal occasions and women of high rank.

"Then, so be it." She places her hands on his bowed head. "You have my blessing. Live without reservation and when able, take life with mercy."

Sahain nods, then rises to face our father.

I know and abhor what's coming. My brother won't explain the reason he chose this ancient custom. Does he dream of joining his ancestors, marked as they were? When my time comes, it will be a tattoo, not this savagery.

I move behind him, my arms around his waist, and breathe in his favorite scent, a mix of pine, cedar, and fir. My presence won't help him endure. That courage will be his alone.

Pell speaks. "Sahain, you have been in my care since a babe. What I do now, I do with pride."

I tighten my hold, knowing all too well the pain he'll soon endure.

The brand hisses. Sahain goes rigid in my arms as the stench of burnt flesh billows.

He thrusts his fist into the sky, the Sada Venari marks now three blazing chevrons between his left thumb and forefinger. The thousands join him as he shouts the Venari battle cry.

"Atla, Atla, Atla!"

'For A'tal.' My brother's first chance to make this claim.

Pell dusts ground malachite over the brand, which Mora seals with numbsalve. If only it deserved its name.

His smile transcendent, Sahain takes me into his arms. Our kiss is fierce with pride before we step apart, so he may kneel for Mora's blessing.

She lifts her face to the star-shot sky. "Mother and Father of All, you who are both the night and day, witness the bond this man swears to his people."

Jae takes Mora's place. "Sahain, speak and be heard. Act and be honored. Ask and you shall receive, for as Venari, you are one with your people."

As Sahain rises, Pell hands him his unstrung bow. "Consign this symbol of your youth to the fires of memory."

My brother grasps the recurve's ends, and forces the layers of silkwood in a direction they've not known since leaving the tree. The bow gives way with a tortured crack.

We roar jubilation as he hurls the sundered pieces into the nearest gathering fire.

In Sojur's ruined hands lies the bow Sahain will carry as Venari, its layers thicker and draw specific to a man of his build.

Aryren offers him a sword of Covenant steel. "Sahain a'Sada, you are one of my brightest stars. Land's End's foremost smith forged this blade, which I designed for you." She proffers the hilt.

He draws the sword, then takes a moment to admire the eddying waves formed on its edge during hardening. Grip reversed, he drives the steel into the earth. "Upon this sword, I dedicate my life to the defense of my people and country."

Aryren offers him a cloth to buff away the dirt, then holds the scabbard for Sahain to home the blade. There may be other swords in his future, yet none will mean as much.

At Sojur's nod, I step back, then loose a piercing whistle.

Those nearby know why and make way. A horse galloping toward the gathering fires is sufficiently odd that Sahain turns.

Batal skids to a halt, then extends his foreleg in a bow. The gelding springs back to his feet and nudges my brother.

I hatched this plan two years ago, while studying my coming three-year-olds, and seeking the best horse for Sahain.

Eyes bright, he turns to me. "You're giving me Batal?"

"The way you ride? You need a horse who can stay under you."

He laughs, acknowledging my concerns have basis. Nor does he have the silver to buy a warhorse of Batal's quality.

"A'Sada?"

We turn.

Were the five tribes to gather, the thousands in full battle dress would blind: Sada emerald, Rowan sapphire, Falili crimson, Mitanni violet, and Khadir saffron.

Kemu clasps Sahain's forearm, his sapphire marks beside Sahain's emerald, then leans in and whispers.

My brother nods in eager affirmation.

The Rowan grips Sahain's muscular neck. Moments later, a smile welcome as sunrise graces my brother's face, both of us now beneficiaries of Kemu's magic.

A roar of approval greets the sight of our newest Venari as Sahain swings up onto Batal. He reins for the horse pens, clasping the forearms of those eager to hail him as their battle companion.

Kemu comes to stand at my side. "So, that will be you in a few days?"

I laugh. "Not even close. Only those who must will attend."

"And why do you think that is, Thea? Perhaps others find your willingness to kill those whose blood you may share unnatural."

My greatest fear, which no one knows, revealed.

He reads my shock, not that it slows his intrusion. "Will you enter the ranks unmindful? On the mainland, you've seen how our willingness to die for this country inspires as much fear as it does respect. A'talans view Venari as a breed apart. Raised by Pell and taught by Sojur, I expected some measure of self-awareness."

In that moment, the earth sunders as the horror of one of my arrows piercing a Daharshan heart reveals the deepest of my hells.

Arms crossed, Kemu regards me. "Why not give our history some credence? I better than most know you fear killing your own kind, and well you should."

All the years we've known each other, and all the conversational gambits he's brought to bear, yet his magic remains a barrier I won't cross.

I meet his gaze, not hiding behind my bangs as I so often do. "History, in that we've raced against each other? What of it?"

His face has a touch of the desert, or at least an intimation of it with how he's trimmed his beard. It gives him the same unreadable quality for which they abhor my people.

I make reverence when he doesn't answer my question. "A'Rowan, thank you for my brother and myself. Please excuse me. I must join the a'Shara and my second."

He snags my forearm, detaining me. "If you join the ulans, your hands will run red with your people's blood."

I shrug, as if unaffected by his words. "They say the first time is the hardest."

"True, yet killing will haunt you. It does me."

Despite the crowds surrounding us, we might as well be alone in our tangle of confrontation. If he's uneasy about killing, how will I manage?

I force an answer. "It is the price I must pay to become A'talan."

His darkness turns into disapproval. "No, it is not. Rather than endanger your immortal soul, you could serve as Sojur's quatrain."

"And just how would that prove I'm an A'talan's equal?"

No sooner are these words out than their import strikes home. My struggle for composure fails. "I can't deal with this, not tonight."

He doesn't loosen his grip. "Four days, Thea, in which your brother doesn't have a second, while you fight with your conscience. Don't do this. Not to him or you. Hesitate in the field, even for a moment, and you become the danger."

Why make me look inward, and turn my prayers for the Mother's blessing into ash and despair?

An answer doesn't come.

I jerk free, bolting into the crowd, running from myself as much as him.

TWELVE

SUMMONS

We've abandoned the gathering tents for the glory of the evening sky and its cool breezes. Legs out to one side, I sit on a ground cushion beside my father's chair. Across from us, Gayleen a'Rowan mimes drawing a bow, illustrating her tale.

"I tell the boy he'll be fine just as the karakal snarls, one of those 'I'll eat you' sounds they make. A heartbeat later, the cat's in the air. The boy pulls back so hard, he buries the rear of the arrow's blades in his stave hand. Blood spurts. Strong as this boy is, he faints, and I release."

She pauses for effect. "To this day, that hide is in my command pavilion as a reminder for my Venari-to-be: 'Heed your teachers!'"

She chimes wineglass rims with Pell, then sits across from us.

A boy, fighting to be a man, and Gayleen wouldn't cut him a knuckle joint of slack. True, Pell destroys illusions of adequacy, but through example, not mockery.

I look to where crowds of well-wishers surround Sahain. I know his friends need time to accept his Daharshan second, but resentment roils in my gut.

On the back of Pell's chair, Windsong's tassel stirs on the pommel of his sword. The reminder of harmony restored between us eases some of my upset. When he rests his hand on my shoulder, it disappears completely.

I cross my arms over his knee and prop my chin atop them.

Bands of gold and emerald embroidery grace his ivory haaka's hems. Painstaking work, done by the woman my father adores: Enya, owner of The Sun, the inn where the Sada house during racing in Azalaïs.

Atar sits across from us, drawing board on his knees. To be near him, young women dare proximity to the a'Shara. Flowers-in-their-hair beauties who laugh prettily, other than the one who glares at me. A year ago, I walked into our tent to find her in Atar's arms, him naked and helpless with laughter. After that, she gave up on amending Atar's preference for male partners, and I earned her eternal enmity. Still, the girls keep coming around. My brother's just too beautiful, too talented, and too successful to resist.

I offer his once-lover a mild smile.

With a haughty toss of her hair, she turns her back on me.

Atar, witnessing this exchange, smiles while holding up his current drawing.

It's a portrait of a father and child. Pell, contemplative, stroking my hair, as I look off into the distance. Atar's chronicle of our lives, destined for our father's folio.

As he seeks a new subject, I follow his gaze. Among the drummers, I spot Kemu a'Rowan, his hands flying and timing perfect.

Doum, tek-a-tek-tek-a-tek! Doum!

With catlike instinct, Kemu looks up. He smiles as if our earlier conversation hadn't ended in disaster, which is when Sahain joins us.

He leans over Pell's shoulder, and speaks softly, giving me the perfect excuse to look away from Kemu.

Whatever's said, Pell rewards with rich laughter. "Indeed, two for service."

Sahain grins at me. "Even if one sits sullen as a hound left behind while the hunt is on?"

I scowl, proving Sahain's point.

Pell's brows crease. "Thea, what's wrong?"

My brother answers before I can. "Not what so much as whom, my a'Shara."

My a'Shara. I'd envy Sahain's privilege if it wouldn't soon be mine.

"Ah." Pell leans back, then seeks Kemu among the drummers. My brother didn't need to specify. "Did something happen?"

I blow out an exasperated breath. "No, it's just that he is so . . ."

Sahain finishes my sentence. "Handsome?"

This earns my brother a venomous glare. "More like arrogant."

Pell laughs. "That's the Covenant in him. As A'tal's teachers, lawgivers, and leaders, what's to be humble about?"

Elbow-on-knee, Gayleen leans forward, addressing me. "I, for one, wish there were more like Kemu, who, by the way, says you have reservations about facing your own kind on the border."

I straighten, gut-shot.

Before I can protest, Gayleen's off again. "Surely you appreciate the exceptional nature of what your a'Shara has achieved in elevating the first and only Daharshan as a Venari. Girl, do what you do best. Bend a bow, ride a horse, and serve your father."

She's left one thing off her list of injunctions: strangle Kemu a'Rowan. How in the name of all that's sacred am I to explain my uncertainty to Pell? Were the roast sakier in my belly not already sour, the next person to join us would have made it so.

"Father." Charra brushes Pell's cheek with a kiss, then hip bumps Sahain. "Have you seen your new tent?"

He pulls her into his arms. "I have. Are you the one I should thank?"

"I am, my darling brother."

He sweeps her into a kiss that has me wondering if Kemu isn't right. If so, there's no sin in the pairing, not that I don't wish better for my brother. Much better.

"May I join you?"

At the sound of Kemu's voice, I swivel. A rock would come in handy about now.

He makes reverence to the a'Shara, then lifts a questioning brow at my grim expression. "All's still well?"

"I'm fine." I leave teeth marks on the words.

Gayleen laughs at my slitted eyes. "Show some gratitude, girl. The man who blocks your pain only seeks to make you richer."

I stifle a groan, then look back to Kemu. "Who do you seek to buy?"

"Phillea."

"Knowing her price and conditions of sale?"

At his nod, I rise, then bow to the a'Shara and Sojur. Show some manners, and my father may give me a pass on Gayleen's revelation. That said, this confidence-sharing covener will pay.

"Do you want to see her?"

He glances toward the rising moon. "Please."

I lead the way out of camp. As our greatest asset, we graze our mares farthest from the border, where a few outriders can assure their safety.

Stars consume the sky as we pass into the grasslands. Amidst the grandeur of our surroundings, I lose a sense of the earth beneath my feet, and the fume of my temper cools.

Upon reaching a likely hilltop, I search for Phillea in the valley below. "There, the one with a white mane and tail."

Kemu sights along my arm. "Ah, I see her."

His looming has my nerves jangling. I write it off to his exasperating Covenant entitlement. If he didn't trim his beard in the Daharshan style, the sparks wouldn't fly so high in each other's presence. Praying his attention is on Phillea, I put some space between us.

"How many of these mares are yours?"

"A third."

"That many? I didn't realize you were rich."

I laugh. "Hardly. What I earn, I give to my crèche."

"Whatever for?"

"Without Pell, I wouldn't be alive. What he did for me, I do for others."

"Nothing set aside for a dowry?"

I cough, amused. "What A'talan would want half-Daharshan children?"

He faces me, plainly hot to address the tree I've felled across the conversation. "You think of yourself as Daharshan?"

"Are you blind? Of course I do, nor will any A'talan handfast me. Hence, I have no need of a dowry."

Annoyed, he looks back to the mares. "You're wrong, Thea. Bone-deep wrong."

On that disturbing assertion, I welcome the silence that follows, not that he lets it stand for long.

"All these mares, out of Windsong and her daughters?"

These words, spoken with warmth and resonance, reach where I ride. Not only has this bastard made my relationship with Pell formidable, he's been in my head ever since Habibi. For all I know, he could be there now, reading his effect on me.

I resist the urge to walk away, aware such appalling manners would shame my upbringing, thus force a response.

"All these mares from twelve years of breeding. First Windsong, then her daughters, then her son, Amir, whom we've bred to a variety of mares. All chosen for bloodlines that would nick with Amir's sire."

"Impressive. Introduce me to Phillea?"

I whistle her call and she raises her head, but does not come. "We'll have to go to her. Her filly must be asleep."

"Is she rebred?"

I murmur, "Yes," while starting down the hill.

"To which sire?"

"Amir, same as this year's filly." Who lays sprawled in the grass, all fuzzy mane, long legs, and stunning conformation.

Kemu offers Phillea his hand, then makes much of her as she takes his scent. "She is every bit as beautiful as I remember."

I cluck to her, resenting his play for her affection, and smile as she turns from him to nuzzle my cheek. "Not effective, a'Rowan, praising a horse you hope to buy."

He laughs, a husky sound that could be the downfall of any female. "What gain in pretending she's other than what she is? Two hundred tallens, correct?"

He's using his all-too-effective charm to ease my hostility. No matter. I know how to turn the odds in my favor.

"Grain vouchers, not silver."

"Four thousand bushels?"

"Five."

Stewing silence greets this. "Do you think I'm a wealthy steadholder?"

Steadholders: those on the mainland who hold the land apart, not sharing as we do. The truth is far more amusing.

"If the price is too steep . . . ?"

He blows out an irritated breath. "Word is you're riding Amir in the Champion of Champions race. The moment that becomes common knowledge, Phillea's price will . . . ?"

"Double."

We're both using the hanging response to good effect.

"Exactly. I'll dine on air to pay your price, but better that than losing my chance. Phillea's bloodlines are a legacy I hope will keep my father's breeding program strong. Could we meet in the middle?"

He's playing me, again. Same as while fishing for information the night Leander split my lip. Same as while feeding me oranges, and then there's tonight's crown jewel, sharing my concerns about killing my kind. All of which ends now.

"As you say, once word gets out about Amir . . ."

He sighs. "Fine, five. Plainly, this isn't your first negotiation."

It takes a moment to realize we've struck a deal. For enough grain to feed all my horses till spring. So, he may buy one horse, a mare he views as the means to continue his father's breeding legacy. All of which opens an unexpected doorway when he clasps my forearm to seal the agreement.

More than that happens. Moon haloing the breadth of his shoulders, he steps into me, his voice more sensation than sound. "Thea . . . ?"

My breath catches. Will he? Will I let him?

Kemu's masculinity arises from more than his looks. There's a quiet power in his stillness and assumption of success. All of which I'm not inclined to debate when his hands come around my waist.

A warning horn shatters the night.

We freeze, our faces a breath apart. Three times the call comes.

I want to cry and curse those who made me, for so many reasons. This pattern is for more than a Kian sighting. It's for an attack.

Kemu cradles my face between his hands. "Creators willing, we'll all return whole." And then, he kisses me, a kiss sweeter than summer apricots, sweeter than fall pears.

I breathe him in, reveling in the intimacy and marveling as we set aside every precept to which we dedicate our lives, all for a kiss.

With a groan of regret, he releases me and races up the hill.

I stay put, staggered, a sail in a stiff wind. That kiss was a Venari leaving for battle, and bidding farewell as a lover would. And not just any kiss. My first kiss, a kiss of such tenderness, I yearn for another.

The eerie wails of the warning horns summon everyone I love to war. My father and Sahain on this, his first night as Venari, with no second to guard his back, for which I damn Habibi. How many times have our teachers warned us, once we cross the border, there's no surety we'll return whole or alive?

Praying for everyone's safe return, and determined to do what I can in the horse pens, I take off at a run. All the while I plead: Please, please, please, let everyone come home safe.

THIRTEEN

MY SECOND

Throbbing Daharshan war drums reverberate over the grasslands. In answer to this taunt, Sada, and Rowan Venari charge across the border, backlit against a western sky shimmering with stars. Body armor be damned, they've gone from celebrating to grabbing weapons and gone.

I calm nervous mounts while other Venari-to-be saddle and bridle.

Battle stallions scream, their blood up with all the rushing and yelling.

From where Sojur sits Amir, he curses the chaos, and demands those under his command bring order to the process.

A raid during an ascension? This night will go down in infamy.

Sahain and I grew up assisting the ulans into battle, the pair of us flying as if winged. While I saddled Pell's warhorse, my brother armed our father. Throughout, we prayed for his and the ulans' safe return. The older we got, the greater our frustration at not riding with them.

Tonight, Sahain is with Pell, who is the heart and soul of the Sada, and my brother's description of me, a hound left behind during the hunt, fits all too well. If not for the damage done to my hands, I would be seconding Sahain now. During dinner, Pell agreed with Gayleen, that were I whole, he would have elevated us together.

The last rider departs, and the cleanup begins.

When Pell's in the field, Sojur's in charge. While reining Amir toward the command pavilion, he doesn't acknowledge my reverence. I tell myself he's preoccupied, yet fear his detachment is born of the choice I made.

Back at the gathering grounds, I sit on Pell's chair, head bowed and bandaged hands between my knees. I pray Lycan doesn't show up. Speak to me now, and I'd blurt a shattering truth. Another man kissed me, and I welcomed it.

All that's left is prayer.

Time passes, slow as rock turning into sand. My back slumps. My eyes shut. Venari sleep when they can, where they can, be it a'horse or on the ground. I am no exception.

Someone, shouting my name, wakes me.

"Thea, come quick! Mora wants you!"

With these hands, I can't stitch wounds, which leaves only horror. Heart hammering, I race for the healing tents.

Mother in Heaven, not Sahain, not Pell!

I stumble as a third name adds itself to the list.

Please, not Kemu!

A healer sees me coming and points to the tent Mora is in. When I bolt through the opening, she's already in a healing shift.

"Oh, Thea, I am so sorry."

"Who's hurt?" This question, never easy, tonight unbearable.

Her gaze shifts to behind me, and I spin.

Five Venari bear Sahain on his shield, among them, our ulan leaders Khat and Hasia.

A scream shudders out of me as I run toward them, only to have someone's arm catch me across the collarbones.

It's Kemu, his other hand pressed to a bloody cloth on Sahain's belly. "Go easy."

I match pace with the bearers. "Sahain? Sahain!"

His eyelids flutter, then open. "Thea?"

I kiss his clammy forehead. "I'm here."

They lift him onto a surgery table, where with practiced speed, other healers join Mora in cutting him free of his clothing. His gorgeous haaka, now black with blood, gets tossed aside. His shirt follows, a brief flight of shocking crimson.

Kemu slings me a stool, which I position at my brother's shoulder, then reclaim his hand.

Wound packing smacks into waste basins.

I tell myself, don't look, yet fail.

Healers' hands fly, rejoining veins and muscles in his belly, which is awash with blood. I once thought my speed exemplary at this task. No more.

Kemu cradles the back of Sahain's head, blocking what must be staggering pain.

My voice cracks while asking what haunts me. "How did it happen?"

"He took an arrow, broke it off, and kept fighting."

I rest my head on my brother's shoulder, begging the Mother and Father of All to save him. Men with my color of skin and eyes have done this. Gutted someone I love. Whose back I would have protected, had I ascended with him. Hard upon this knowledge comes the urge to do what I should have after the Tribal Council: drag Habibi to a well-deserved death.

A healer lays her hand on my arm. "We need to roll him on his side so the wound will drain."

I move out of their way, and while waiting, realize Khat and Hasia have left. Perhaps checking on other wounded?

Once he's on his side, I pillow Sahain's neck with my arm, our faces side-by-side. The air we share reeks of blood and the cleansing herbs used to purify his wound.

Mora halts across from me, her face a portrait of sorrow. "I prayed neither of you would suffer the heartbreak of the life you've chosen. Sadly, that's not to be."

Her words almost break me. "Does Atar know?"

"He and Charra will be here soon. Let's hope Pell returns in time. Far better in his family's arms than alone, somewhere in the desert."

I beg Heaven to take pity on us, to let Sahain wake. Instead, time marches on, inexorable and pitiless. Every catch in his breath, when his skin heats or chills, brings a rush of dread.

When he groans despite Kemu's mindblock, all hope plummets.

The Rowan gets an arm under my brother's shoulders and stabilizes him as Sahain gropes for something we cannot see.

"Charra?"

I kiss his cheek. "She'll be here soon."

His hand finds my face, and he smiles. "Dearest sister, we would have been great together."

"Unbearably good, you just wait." Even as I say these words, I know them as lies. He's slipping inward, preparing to leave us. "Someone, get Mora!"

There's a flurry outside the tent as Pell and Atar arrive. They brace Charra between them.

As she races to him, Sahain calls Charra's name, his voice hoarse with desperation.

She frames his face between her hands, then kisses him, a kiss filled with anguish. Heedless of the blood, she lies down beside him, then guides his hand to her belly. "My love, bless your son."

My knees buckle.

He kisses her with a tenderness which bespeaks of sorrow. "Tell him my heart aches, never to see or hold him."

She returns his kiss with equal despair. "I will, my love."

He drinks in her features, his hand held to her face. "Promise me your war with Thea is over. She will teach our son what I cannot."

Charra's face constricts as she fights for the poise so inherent to her nature. "You have my word."

As they treasure this, their last moments together, I see Charra anew. I beg Heaven, no, not this way. Don't make us sisters at the cost of the man we both love.

Charra holds her pain in while she makes way for our father. To think, all my life I've hated this woman, who now exemplifies the Venari way: others before self.

The a'Shara does what none of us have dared: lifts his son into his arms as he would when we were young and hurt. As he does so, in my heart, I hear the grace words he's not saying.

If it hurts, let it go.

My brother hears those words. As he seeks the place between extremity and peace, he looks upward as if there's nothing between him and Heaven's sky. "Father, thank you for everything . . .," his voice falters.

I hold in my scream as my brother's body goes lax in his sobbing father's arms.

Mora rests her hand on Pell's shoulder. "Without pain, among those who love him, no one could ask for more."

While she speaks truth, death has won.

She closes Sahain's eyes, then intones the ancient words. "Sahain a'Sada, may you draw wisdom from the life just left and once renewed, we ask that the Mother and Father of All grant you rebirth among those who love you."

I force the response, "Born again," past a tear-constricted throat.

My brother's death is meaningless. Proving nothing. Solving nothing.

Kemu takes my hands, then turns them over. "What would Sahain say about you hurting yourself while mourning him?"

I've clenched my fists so hard, fresh blood stains the bandages.

My father looks to Kemu. "A'Rowan, please, take Thea to their tent, then stay with her."

His next words are for me. "As Sahain's second, you will be at my side when we give him to the wind."

I nod as the sight of my father holding his dead son drives home a new reality.

My brother is gone, and our world is less without him.

FOURTEEN

GIVEN TO THE WIND

W hat's left of the night passes in Kemu's arms, sobbing so hard I can scarce breathe. If only this were one of my nightmares.

Time staggers on.

When the tears cease, their void fills with an emptiness that will never heal. With grim inevitability, my view through the tent flaps shifts from a tapestry of moonlit clouds to dawn's silver-gray.

In the bed beside mine, Atar groans as he sits up and rubs his eyes. "Did you get any sleep?"

I shake my head.

The tears start again, for which Kemu rocks me in time to my silent sobbing. The reminder of Sahain doing the same is more than I can endure. When I bury my face in Kemu's chest, he rubs my back.

"Come sunrise, I'll be nearby if you need me."

Through our link, he reads my confusion. "Having found and brought Sahain home, I'll be part of his honor guard."

I bite my lip and nod. This day's hurt has only begun. When the sun comes raging over the horizon, we will give Sahain to the wind.

Sheets rustle as Atar rises. "Kemu, you need to get ready. I'll take her."

Kemu nods, then renews the mindblock. Only then does he make way for Atar. While stepping into his boots, then settling his sword across his back, his expression questions whether I can find a Venari's self-control amidst a sister's pain. "Remember, I'm only a thought away."

It's a needed reminder. I nod, and make reverence for all he's done.

Compassion in his dark eyes, he answers in kind, then strides into the coming dawn.

Atar sits behind me, then unplaits my battle braids. Silver beads ping to the bedcovers. It's easy to imagine them as fallen stars mourning our shattered dreams. If I'd been at my brother's side, we might not have known this sorrow.

Once he's freed my hair, he plaits it into a single braid, then binds it with rawhide. We exchange last night's finery for mourning black and wait in the tent entry.

Throughout camp, wood flutes sound the call to gather.

All too soon, people bearing flower tributes file past, then the two a'Shara and Sojur on their stallions.

Pell inclines his head as he passes, vindicating our sorrow and restraint. His unsheathed blade lies across his lap, a promise of consequences to come. Consequences which I must be part of.

Sahain's ulan comes next, among which a friend leads Batal, draped in black. We share a moment of mutual anguish when he hands me the gelding's reins.

Next up, Sahain's honor guard: Kemu, and three members of the Lightning Ulan, bearing my brother's body to immolation.

My heart shatters.

Sahain lies on his bier, hands crossed over his sword pommel. A pristine haaka hides his wounds.

Their expressions grief-frozen, Charra, Khat, and Hasia follow. As they pass, we fall in behind them.

My vision blurs, part tears, part exhaustion. This is the last service we will do for a man we love: witness his ascent to Heaven.

We trade the encampment for the grasslands. There, a forest of funeral pyres stands stark against the paling sky. My family is not alone in our grief.

Pell, Gayleen, and Sojur halt their stallions before a lofty tower of silkwood, sandalwood, and kanga. Blood-red poppies, ivory moonflowers, and purple irises lie amidst boughs of cedar at its base. At each quarter, the heartrending scent of dark spices and bitter resins wafts from clay censers.

His honor guard walks his bier over the pyre, then lowers it into place. They draw their swords, then stand at attention, one at each corner.

All around us, the same ritual repeats.

I take my place at my father's left, vowing my behavior will befit the occasion.

At his right, her green eyes haunted, Charra exerts rigid control over her emotions. Of us all, she has lost the most: brother, lover, and her child's sire.

For once, my inability to sob when crying serves me well. The younger members of our crèche stand ranked behind us, gazes fixed on their big brother. The one person who was always there for them, be it ending fights or joining in their games, is gone.

First light knives across the grasslands. Mora lifts her arms to the sky, her voice powerful despite age's harsh edge.

"Mother, Father of All, enfold our beloved sons and daughters into Your loving embrace. May they draw wisdom and strength from the lives just left, then be born again amidst those who love them."

The grasslands echo with the benediction, "Born again."

At each pyre, Venari shatter their censers against the wood. Within moments, flames rush up the biers and engulf the bodies. Ululation resounds.

I make myself watch as the man who stood between me and my many troubles ascends to Heaven. Wish I could wail and rend my clothing, as so many others do. Families who've lost children, brothers, and sisters or lovers. Not for them a Venari's rigid control in the face of death.

As the wind drives the flames toward the rising sun, Mora faces the a'Shara. "Their spirits soar free."

Pell and Gayleen acknowledge her pronouncement with stiff nods, examples to us all.

My brother is gone, one among what, thirty or forty? I don't have the heart to count.

Charra cries so hard it takes Atar to keep her upright: the woman without a heart. How many other things have I gotten wrong?

Seeing the eldest in their crèche break down, our little brothers give up their battle. Who will they turn to now? Who will take up Sahain's legacy, part of which stands at my side, his nostrils wide for the smell of burning flesh. Had Sahain lived, we would have taught the boys how to ride on Batal.

I rouse from my misery and head for them.

My father's brows crease, questioning my leaving my post before seeing where I'm headed and nodding approval.

I halt before the eldest in his boy pack, Gitan, all gawky limbs, and sharp cheekbones. At my signal, Batal bows.

"Gitan, I entrust Sahain's horse with you."

I hold out the reins. "Any who wish to learn how to ride or hunt, I will teach on Batal."

Gitan crumbles under the weight of what I am giving him, giving all of them. I say nothing of fighting. Gitan's only moons away from declaring his intent to become Venari, and was counting on Sahain's mentoring. Perhaps I will offer later, when the price our brother paid while serving his country isn't so fresh.

I rest my hand on his. "Sahain would have wanted this."

Gitan nods, then does something unexpected: buries his face against my shoulder.

I hold my hand to his shaggy hair, bless him with a kiss, then step back.

He looks to our father, who gestures permission. The boys turn for camp, each with a hand on the horse entrusted to their care.

Charra comes to stand at my side, her gaze, like mine, on our little brothers. "Tonight, we'll pay Sahain homage, then offer remembrance in my tent. Please, join us."

I nod as this wrenching moment makes us sisters in more than name.

Pell reins D'jhat out of the crowd, then gestures to me.

One look at his grim expression and I know this isn't my father. This is our a'Shara. I come to attention.

He approves my response with steely eyes. "All Venari-to-be within a year of ascendancy will guard the border today. Gayleen and I are leading our ulans into the desert. Have a healer remove what bandaging they deem wise, then report to Sojur. He will assign you. Daughter, know your purpose is to sound a warning, rather than seek vengeance. Am I clear?"

He's read my intent all too well. Stomach in knots, I make reverence. "Yes, a'Shara."

Satisfied with my response, he heads for Sojur.

Atar joins me. "Is he sending you into the field?"

"No, I and other unascended will protect the border while the ulans wreak havoc upon Daharsha."

This is not an image my artist brother welcomes, so much so, he wraps his arms around me. "Sister, I cannot endure losing you as well."

I manage a wan smile. "You won't. Not now, not ever. You have my word."

He draws back in his gaze more faith in my promise than I can muster. "Come home safe."

I nod, kiss his forehead, then join the stream of Venari headed for camp. While doing so, I answer the question Kemu asked last night.

Given the opportunity, I will do what any second would, however unnatural it makes me.

I will take an eye for an eye and kill those whose blood I may share.

FIFTEEN

CAGED BIRD

B edlam reigns in the horse pens. Stallions scream and strike at grazing companions. Mares sink teeth in arms over-tightening girths. Rough bridling has geldings pinning their ears. This blend of Rowan and Sada has yet to go well.

Amidst this disorder, Sojur sits Amir. Unlike last night, he seethes with a stone-slow temper. Questions he rates as stupid or inane, receive curt, one-word answers. When his nostrils flare, I wince. The Venari asking has landed on the Master of Horse's list of the lackluster.

I wait till the crowd clears, in hopes his temper will cool.

Instead, upon seeing a bow in my unbandaged right hand, and the three fingers exposed on the left, his irritation flares.

As the silence between us grows, I fight to contain my anxiety. Finally, blessedly, he speaks.

"Unlike your father, I loathe the idea of you in the field. When the enemy learns of a Daharshan in our ranks, word will spread. Find her and kill her. This is the reason I'm sending you north to the spring where Pell and I found you. There, you will have the least exposure to the enemy. Nor will I tolerate you obeying the spirit of my command rather than its letter. You are there to sound the alarm, if need be, not exact vengeance. Am I clear?"

He is telling me I'm on a short leash, yet will ride. When Pell's in the field, such decisions are Sojur's.

I incline my head. "Yes, Master."

He gestures to the bow in my hand. "Not your greatest skill. Once Pell recovers enough to hear reason, I will force this issue. I didn't spend sixteen years teaching you, only to have you bleed out in Daharsha."

I lock my knees, staggered by the implications. If Sojur gets his way, my service will be for the ulans, not in them. Yes, I'll be a Venari, but free as a caged bird. Never to avenge Sahain or prove my blood isn't flawed.

As Sojur reins Amir for the command pavilion, there's a grim smile on his lips.

Once in the tack tent, the tang of oiled leather doesn't suggest which of my horses would be best for today. As I seek to sort this out, Lycan ducks through the flaps, his wild mane dull gold in the soft light.

He offers me a pained smile of sympathy. "Thea, I don't have the words. Whose saddle do you want? I'll get it for you."

My head clears. I decide. "Dafor's."

He raises a brow. "Is that wise? He's not that steady."

"Nothing like a day of watching shifting sand to cure impatience."

We're the only ones in the tent, which destroys any semblance of restraint. He holds out his arms, and I fall into them.

He lets me cry, patient with my pain, as patient as he's been with my odd behavior these past days. Only when I'm able to catch my breath does he frame my face between his hands, then kiss me.

I tell myself, look again, love again, and answer his kiss, desperate for anything besides the ache in my heart. His arms tighten around me, and our bodies meet. His breathing turns ragged.

"Not being with you last night tore me apart."

I murmur agreement, yet know without Kemu, I might have collapsed during my brother's ascent.

"If we do well today, ask the a'Shara to reconsider elevating me as your second?"

Sojur is right. Without someone who cares at my side, Pell will return me to the horse pens.

I breathe my "yes" into yet another kiss, which Lycan answers with equal intensity, both of us willing to chance being seen. Yet, we both know our duty calls, and step apart, our gazes that of shy children, unsure yet hopeful.

"I'll take your saddle to Dafor's pen. Ride out with me tonight?"

Tonight, Sahain's vigil, then what? Doubt treads hard upon hope's heels. None of which Lycan sees while leaving with Dafor's saddle in his arms.

Do we stand a prayer of winning my father's blessing? Equally unclear, are his arms the ones I want holding me while I become a woman? Even as I ask these questions, I know them as distractions from a larger issue.

Why send the Luna's blessing only to snatch it away?

No answer comes. Heart heavy and head overflowing with doubt, I shoulder my weapons, then head for the horse pens.

Dafor, a three-year-old Windsong grandson, takes my mind off my worries with a vengeance. First in the catching, then in the grooming, and of course, while mounting. I let him swirl around me a few times, then snag the saddle horn, and use his momentum to swing up.

No sooner are my feet in the stirrups and we're off, if crow-hopping can be called a gait. The only good is Sojur isn't here to witness Dafor heaving me skyward.

Tiring of his nonsense, I put him to work. A dozen direction changes later, revolt loses its appeal. I ask for straight and get it.

It's only while not flying through the air I notice our audience.

Brows arched for the show, Kemu sits his bay stallion nearby. "Gamar was a knot-head as a youngster. Is your colt from Windsong's line?"

I can't read his expression, not with the angle he holds his head. "Yes, one of Amir's sons."

"Three years old?"

At my nod, he reins closer, his hair freshly cropped so as not to become a trophy on some Kian's saddle.

"Thanks to the healing bond between us, I know just what took place with Lycan. Furthermore, I second Sojur's plan. Pell will agree when the pain of losing Sahain eases."

Mortified and furious, I'm moments from telling him where he to stick his meddling when Dafor lunges for Gamar. I demand a halt, then back him fast.

Kemu keeps Gamar within striking distance even as I battle Dafor into a semblance of manners. The moment he's under control, Kemu brings Gamar head-to-tail with Dafor, which puts us knee-to-knee.

"You can control your colt, but not yourself? Haven't I made my intentions clear?"

There's heat to his words. This isn't the same Venari who kissed me, then rode off to war. This is Pell calling me to order.

A'Rowan, you are an asshole.

Thanks to the mindhealing bond, my slur reaches its intended target. He reins Gamar out of Dafor's reach, then swings to earth, and crosses to us in a few long strides. His fist on Dafor's bridle keeps him in place even as his arm around my waist hauls me half out of the saddle.

I'm giving thought to planting my boot in his midsection when he brings his forehead to mine, and mingles our breath.

You have no idea how you frustrate me. One moment I am a fire in your blood, the next a pale infatuation.

My outrage explodes. "What's with this elaborate charade? Long as we've known each other, you walk on eggshells. Make allusions, yet explain nothing. What do you want from me, and why?"

"Want from you? Surely that's apparent."

I laugh. "Apparent as a stallion pursuing a mare in heat, which I am not!"

He winces. "Forgive me. Your being Daharshan has proven a greater barrier than expected."

"Then, why bother?"

He considers his answer, his leather cuirass creaking with each breath he takes.

"The first time I saw you, I remembered you."

"Remembered me? Just how the hells does that work?"

"Have you no sense of our past? Of the lives we've lived and the love we've shared?"

I've loved this man in another life? Say it isn't so! Panic has me heaving backwards, straining to dislodge his grip.

It's all the invitation Dafor needs. He surges at Gamar, only to be met by Kemu's checking hand. All this done second nature, his gaze fixed on me.

"Don't throw us over, not on a whim. So long as the healing bond exists, I can't respect your privacy. What you feel, what you do, I'm exposed to it all."

My skin goes hot at the thought of him in my mind while I kissed Lycan.

"Ask yourself, why did Pell put his boot down about Lycan? Could it be his decision grew out of concern for your risk-taking and ultimate wellbeing?"

I glare at him, for which he shakes his head.

"For once in your life, go slow. Mourn your brother. Throw yourself into the arms of someone your father doesn't trust, and your loss will be greater."

My denial crumbles at memories of Pell's expression, telling me I'd never be Lycan's second.

How am I to trust a man with magic, a man who terrifies me, yet plainly wants to be with me? A man, who did everything he could to save my brother, then held and comforted me when I most had need?

An unexpected willingness arises as I count on him reading my many fears: avenging Sahain, being caged by Sojur, and the consequences of these lives we've supposedly shared.

His intensity eases. "I know your concerns, which we will discuss at another time. Promise me you'll stay safe today?"

The risk he's about to take hits home. Like Sahain, Kemu could die. As I grasp the wound losing Kemu would leave on my already embattled heart, the breath I snatch catches on my ribs.

"If I give you my word, will you give me yours?"

"You already have it."

For a moment, it feels like he's had his say and that's all he wanted.

"Thea . . .," he breaks off, then draws me lower and kisses me, a deep pool into which I willingly sink.

I'm half on, half off a horse who'd rather fight than obey, even as my emotions slam me from pillar to post. Could this fire in my blood be love?

He breaks off the kiss and breathes me in, then releases Dafor. By the time I have my colt under control, he's on Gamar.

I make reverence, praying no one saw what just happened.

He answers with such grace and sincerity, I wonder about these lives he says we've shared.

He frees his sword, then turns Gamar west.

The resolute authority of his blade arching across the sky, then coming to rest on his brecca, daunts me.

While Kemu hunts nomadi, I'll sit this fool colt, and watch empty sand.

It hits like a fist.

I've used the curse that's dogged all my days to describe those who gave me birth, and for which there is only one solution.

I ask Dafor for a canter, then head north.

SIXTEEN

ZARIA

T he day ground on, dull in its sameness.

At first, Dafor did his best to distract me. He'd shy when birds flitted through the scrubby grass. When a rabbit appeared, he damn near splayed all four legs. This earned him a kick in the guts, and me a glare. Hunger finally won out. Head down, he grazed the rocky ridge between my two countries.

In the morning, our shadow selves stretched into Daharsha. Come midday, they huddled under us, and as the afternoon wore on, crept into the grasslands.

A day of doing nothing and no sleep took its toll. The sway of Dafor moving from one patch of grass to another turned my eyelids into stone. Promising myself only for a moment, I let them close, only to wake, dry-mouthed, and heart thudding.

Dusk's shadows now conquer the day. I've slept for hours.

I'm congratulating myself at still being alive when light flares deep in the desert. Sunlight off stone? Eyes shielded against the drooping sun, I spot two Kian with sufficient arrogance to announce their presence with silver on their tack. They know of this spring, thus head straight for it.

I swear softly, fervently. I'm on a horse, willful as a weed. Run and an arrow will end my life. With Dafor's reins over the saddle horn, then bow and quiver eased to earth, I slide off and urge him down.

Dafor lands with a disgruntled huff.

I sprawl across his shoulder, aware that given a chance, he'd end the indignity. Arrow nocked, I peer through a stand of grass between us and the enemy.

The Kian approach with caution. Even as I pray they can't see us in this cleft of rock, overhead a hawk screams. I glance up. By the time I look back, they've arrived.

Gold embroidery encrusts the hems of their azure riding coats. A buck Oryx lies slack behind one rider. He keeps watch as his companion dismounts, then crouches at the spring.

All this noted in passing, the greater part of my attention fixed upon the Kian's golden stallion. I can scarce believe this animal's beauty. A silver-white forelock spills between his pricked ears. His body color is that of molten gold. Ink-black nostrils flaring, he scents the air, then lowers his head and drinks.

Only a Haj could own such a horse, and the bejeweled saber hanging from this man's lean waist attests to the martial prowess it took to seize his station in life.

Dark eyes alert, the stallion raises his head, water sparkling on his muzzle.

The Haj lowers his hald, and cups water to his lips. His precise black goatee, with its connected mustache, suggests an imperious nature. While his skin is darker than mine, our eyes are the same intimidating blue.

Dafor, sensing the other stallions, shifts beneath me. I stroke his neck and murmur soft nonsense into his ear.

The second rider remains a'horse, an arrow nocked. His startling eyes are all that show between his hald and head coverings. He nods when the Haj points north. Once they're gone, I can sound the warning.

All's well till the Haj remounts. The golden horse brushes the bay. Their intemperate screams shatter the quiet. Dafor surges back onto his chest and bellows a challenge. Before he can gain his feet, I swing into the saddle and strain my bow.

With a hunter's preternatural sense of danger, the second rider ducks. My arrow disappears into the desert.

I rein Dafor south, my heels hammering his ribs. He erupts in a series of joint-bruising bucks. Before I can get him under control, a riata sails over my head, then bites into my arms. One sharp jerk and I'm on the ground, screaming profanities. My boot heels score lines into the gravel as the Haj drags me toward the desert.

Mother in Heaven, help me now!

The second rider binds Dafor's mouth shut with my reins, then yanks his head around to the saddle horn and ties him there. Dafor goes vertical, eyes showing white all around. Even as all this happens, calf-helpless, I'm hauled toward the drop in the border. We reach it, and the golden horse pauses.

I lunge backward, loosening the rawhide around my arms. Am halfway out of the loop, when the Haj leaps to the ground, lodging his saber point in the notch between my collarbones.

Parchment-thin skin is all that stands between me and death. I look from the glittering steel to the man holding it, and beg him with my gaze to ram the blade home. Hands-to heart, I pray he'll not rape me before killing me.

At the sight of my blister-covered birthmark amidst the now dislodged bandages, the Haj's eyes go bird-of-prey-wide. "Zaria?"

I bid farewell to life. Better death than face broken by hard male fists. Better death than savaged into womanhood, never to know love.

Mother, Father of All, I beg of You, take my soul.

I surge onto my elbows, seeking steel's kiss, only to have the Haj slam his boot onto my breastbone. My head smacks into shale. My ribs howl as they're forced against my sheathed sword.

"Nam, Zaria, NAM! Mia khadeen!"

Nam is no in Daharshan, but khadeen is what, child?

I still prey beneath a hawk. No. Not possible, yet he denies me grace. The breadth of his cheekbones, the shape and color of his eyes: all mine. Every time someone hits me by 'accident,' these are the features inflaming their hatred.

He breaks the spell by sheathing his blade, then closing his hand around my left wrist.

This is my last and only chance. I twist, free my fist, and swing for his face.

He bats the blow away with a distressing lack of effort.

I rear back to drive my forehead into his.

Air bursts free from my lungs when he buries his knee in my midsection, then seizes my shoulders in a bone-rattling shake.

"Nam, Zaria, NAM!"

Breath coming hard as my own, his calluses bite in as he turns my wrist, and brings my ruined birthmark to the top.

"Mia khadeen. Mia Zaria."

My child? My Zaria?

He draws my hand to his chest, the hard muscling under his clothing evident. *"Va Patra."*

Even I know Patra means father in Daharshan. My every assumption crumbles.

He whistles for the rider with Dafor. *"Baseem!"*

I am torn between my colt fighting his bonds, and the Haj now settling to his haunches before me. I have no illusions. Make a move, any move, and he'll be on me. Still, I can't stop looking at his eyes: my own brilliant blue.

Dafor subsides, trapped as I am. The man who's tied my colt into literal knots drops his hald as he comes our way.

I gasp. Had I been born male, his features would be mine. The differences between us are of sex and age. His skin, more weathered. Eyebrows thicker, starting low and winging up over almond-shaped eyes. Despite frequent wrong-headedness, my lower lip seems rounder. Perhaps the chinstrap beard makes his lips look thinner.

He kneels beside me. "Sister."

I tremble with disbelief. His A'talan is good as my own.

Hesitant, the Haj smiles. "Your A'talan mother taught us her language."

I'm half A'talan?

The Haj speaks in rapid Daharshan, a water-over-rocks tumble I cannot follow.

Baseem nods. "I will translate. Our mother raised me speaking A'talan and Daharshan. This is our father, Khalil, Haj of the Lawaan. I am his heir, Baseem. Our mother, Sabita, was once a Venari of the Falili tribe. Of all our father's wives, she is his one true love, his first wife, his Haj'ene."

He leaves me to wrestle with this. "First wife? Our Venari mother tolerates this?"

"Such is our way. The strongest stallion sires the most offspring. Have no fear. Sabita rules our father's hareem with an iron fist."

"You're half A'talan, yet heir?"

He smiles, this time a charming, one-sided quirk. "I refused relegation to the ranks of our sire's lesser sons. My advantage was our mother, not that my ascendance came without spilt blood. As heir, I too have a hareem, and among my children, a daughter who looks much like you. What would my little ones make of an unveiled beauty who rides a stallion and carries a sword the same as their father?"

It's easily imagined: this hawk-eyed male strewing blood and bruises among his half-brothers, then coming out the victor.

In his face, I see mine. My resistance crumbles. "Our blood isn't pure?"

He nods in solemn acknowledgment.

"Do we have brothers and sisters?"

"One true sister, many half-siblings, countless nieces and nephews."

I shake my head, yet cannot leave this inconceivable thing alone. "You are his heir, yet I'm abandoned?"

He gestures to my Luna, now visible amidst the ointment and burns. "This symbol of the A'talan Goddess . . .," he slashes his fingers across his throat, ". . . is anathema in Daharsha. Our parent's choice was to kill or save a child of love. They speak of you often and hope you are well. Sabita prayed that here, you would live the spiritual life your birthmark portended."

My mother, name of Heaven, the woman who gave me birth, then gave me up.

"Sister, how did these burns come to be?"

How, indeed?

"Among the tribes, I am anathema. Rare is the day someone doesn't remind me I am of the wrong nationality, and for which, a girl heaved me into a cookfire."

Baseem's eyes go wide. "The Sada are so wicked?"

I sigh. "Some are."

"The black you wear, is that not the A'talan color of mourning?"

Yet more acid churns into my already embattled stomach. I pass my wrist over my pounding forehead. "Daharshans killed one of my crèche brothers. Were you and the Haj among that number?"

"And endanger you? No, never! We do not raid the Sada lands. Every year, we make this pilgrimage, hoping to gain a glimpse of you. Would such people visit harm upon your home?"

The sun stills in the sky as the import of this strikes. When able to speak, my words come out in a whisper.

"My whole life, I believed myself abandoned."

Baseem barks a short laugh. "With the treasure of Daharshan filly left at your side? No, you weren't abandoned. Your birthmark and our mother's adherence to the A'talan faith sent you here, not a lack of love. Nor did our father leave till you were found. You, better than most, know the hate between our two countries brings pain to both sides."

His gaze shifts to the sword behind my back. "The weapons you carry suggest you're Venari-to-be. If so, why does your a'Shara permit you riding alone?"

It's the same question I now ask.

The Haj speaks, and Baseem translates. "Our father asks, is the filly he left with you well?"

I look to the mortal enemy who claims to be my sire. "Describe her."

Khalil's brows rise. "No markings, a dark chestnut with white mane and tail."

Now I need to throw up. Every assumption I've ever made, negated.

"She is my life."

"Her name?"

"Windsong."

A warm smile creates hollows beneath his prominent cheekbones. He gestures to Dafor. "Hers?"

I nod, temples throbbing. "A grandson."

A rapid exchange in Daharshan follows, for which Baseem nods. "Our father says if you must ride the border, it should be on a trained horse."

The same thing Lycan said, and I ignored.

"He asks by what name you are known, and whether the Venari who found you foster you?"

"He did, then gave me the name Thea."

The Haj speaks. *"Zaria eh Khamsin?"*

Khamsin, the same thing Mora loves calling me: the West Wind known for the destruction left in its wake.

My brother laughs. *"Aiee, Patra."*

Baseem holds his hand to my face. "Knowing you live will bring our mother such joy." His bittersweet smile suggests there will be sorrow as well.

"We must go. The danger of lingering is too great. Before we do, our father has gifts for you. Tell the Sada you found them on the border."

Khalil reaches beneath my arms and lifts me onto my feet.

I search this man's brilliant eyes, and seek the lie of his love, yet fail. My mother: Sabita a'Falili. This man: my sire, Khalil, Haj of the Lawaan, who now cups my face even as Baseem translates his words.

"Beloved daughter, if only I'd raised you. To this day, my people believe I gave up a child of sacrilege to the desert jackals, and for which, they praise my piety. I mourn all the days and joy we might have shared. Be well, my daughter."

He blesses my forehead with a kiss. *"Kahda, duene, mia khadeen. Mia Zaria."*

Zaria, my Daharshan name is Zaria. They bat me between them, a mouse between cats,. With everything coming so fast, I can scarce gather it in.

The Haj draws a falconer's glove over his hand, then holds his wrist up to the sky. "Remember." He whistles a pattern of notes.

The same sharp scream I heard earlier answers.

A small falcon plummets, her wings knifing the sky. She seizes Khalil's glove with razor-sharp talons, then settles with a rattle of pinions.

Khalil presents the tiny hunter to my bowstring guard. "Her name is Azize. If you need me, release her without jesses. She will find me, and I will find you."

Azize cocks her head, regarding me with eyes dark and flat as night. When Khalil hoods her, she takes a swipe at him with her razor-sharp beak.

My father chuckles. "Wicked temper, yet loyal. Come, meet Khamsin." He whistles again, a different pattern than Azize's.

The golden stallion steps forward, neck arched and his mien regal.

Khalil strokes the stud's forelock, then breathes into his nostrils. "Son of the wind, you are my best, my swiftest. Protect this, my daughter, Zaria."

I reach out to this masterwork of horse breeding, yet yank my hand back when a mouthful of teeth slash my way.

"Ameen, Kham."

The stallion's eyes, only moments before filled with wicked purpose, soften.

I tear my gaze off the golden horse. "Ameen means what?"

"Peace. Try again, Zaria."

Like training a puppy, they repeat my Daharshan name, teaching me its sad, sweet sound. When I raise my hand to Khamsin's withers a second time, he leans into my touch.

Khalil approves. "You will do well together. The word 'Ameen' is not enough to win his acceptance." He points to the saddle swell. "Azize's perch."

With a dignified shake of her talons, she steps from my wrist onto the swell.

I stare into the stud's eyes and groan. However much I would love to ride this horse, accept this gift and I betray the man who raised me, forsaking every principle he taught me.

I turn to the father and brother I will never see again. My already broken heart shatters in places that will never heal. Before my resolve wavers, I race to Dafor, free him, then throw away my warning horn. Without it, I have no way to summon Venari to hunt down my father and brother.

I swing up and ask Dafor for a gallop.

They are welcome to put an arrow in my half-A'talan back.

They don't, and the pain of that is even greater.

SEVENTEEN

MY FATHERS

No arrow flew, or pursuit followed. Affirming every word spoken by my sire and brother. For whom I have betrayed the father I love, and every Venari principle I hold dear.

Even at a gallop, I'll be the last rider back to camp. This will give Khalil and Baseem time to disappear into the desert. I can't lie, not credibly. Doing so would break the covenant I keep with the Mother and Father of All. Somehow, I must craft an explanation for my 'lost' warning horn, yet don't dare slow Dafor, Pell, fearing for my well-being, would send Venari to find me.

Today, my colt has displayed more bottom than sense. Once able to channel his aggression, he'll be a force to contend with, a courageous battle stallion prized by his rider, whoever that proves to be. Yet now, young as he is, he tires, shifting from gallop to canter. I hear a back-beat and turn in the saddle.

The path we're on has led Khamsin straight to us. From her perch on the saddle swell, Azize leans into the wind. Khalil's bow and quiver are still on the saddle's skirts.

The golden horse pulls up even with us, then tosses his head. He doesn't know racing Khalil's errant daughter will reveal a secret which must remain so.

I slash my arm at him, in hopes he'll break off this race. "Go back!"

Instead, the Daharshan pulls ahead of us, first by a length, then another. In his veins flows the heritage of the fastest horses in the world, the same quality breeders seek when crossing to Windsong's bloodlines. As the gap between us grows, he proves the superiority of pure blood.

Despite knowing Dafor's near the end of his strength, I don't dare let him slow. We must reach camp. When Khamsin thunders into the gathering grounds, he'll kill any Venari who dares lay a hand on him.

We crest the last rise.

Back-lit against the gathering fires, Khamsin rears, and dances away from those Venari who grab for his reins.

My first stroke of luck is Matsum, his back to me. He's a frequent onlooker when I work Dafor, and has voiced an interest in buying him.

"Matsum, please take Dafor."

He does so without asking why.

Venari are shoulder-to-shoulder and rows deep. A Daharshan stallion, here, in full war gear? Could this be the mount of the Kian who killed the a'Shara's son? If so, where is his rider?

I beg permission to pass, yet am answered by irritated snarls and outright refusals.

As the crowd closes in on him, Kham screams his rage. He's done with games.

I find someone smaller and bull past, earning a smack to the back of my head.

Pell and Sojur stand between the crowd and Khamsin. As I clear the last row of resentful Venari, Sojur reaches for the golden horse.

Kham rears, his front hooves scything the air.

I dive between him and my teacher. "Ameen, Kham, AMEEN!"

The Daharshan horse surges and arches his neck over me, guarding Khalil's daughter.

The sight produces a collective gasp.

I fist Kham's mane, then, quaking in my boots, meet Pell's gaze.

My father's eyes burn. "Explain this horse. Explain why your bow and quiver are on a Daharshan saddle."

My bow's on the offside?

I sink to my knees, arms out in supplication.

My father gives me no time to order my thoughts. "What have you done, Thea?"

With gaze and tone, I beg his forbearance. "Met my sire at the spring where you found me."

Incredulity rules the a'Shara's expression. "Your blood-father?"

I nod. "And an older brother."

In the silence that follows, I count each hammering heartbeat. My continuing existence trembles upon what happens next.

"And?"

"I had a choice to run and die, that or hide till they were out of range. I dropped Dafor in a swale, yet couldn't keep him down when he heard their stallions. I swung into the saddle as he shot to his feet. I got an arrow off before the Haj roped, then yanked me off Dafor."

Not wanting to miss a word, the Venari crowd close as they dare.

"Then what?"

"The Haj did a flying dismount." I lift my chin, exposing the dried blood on my throat. "Before I could shove onto his sword, the Haj saw my birthmark."

"He was a Haj?" Pell is having as much difficulty with this as I did. "Where are they now?"

"Somewhere in Daharsha."

"You're sure?"

His eyes narrow at my nod. "How long ago did this happen?"

"Perhaps an hour."

That he questions the time means he'd send Venari after my family, had I told the truth.

"In short, they're long gone?"

"Yes."

Khamsin looms, throwing my body into shadow.

I back him off Pell, hoping to distract my father from what I've left out. That the time was not so great. That my sire and brother rode double, and Venari could reach them.

My father closes the space I've opened between us. "Thea."

There's nothing for it. I meet his gaze, praying he knows none of this alters the love I bear him.

His eyes narrow. "Unbelievable. You're lying."

The snag in my breath is all the proof he needs.

He shouts. "Send three deccas after those nomadi bastards!"

I drop to my knees before him. "A'Shara, I beg of you, let them go. They make this pilgrimage every year, in hopes of catching a glimpse of me. Surely such men are worthy of mercy."

Pell draws back his hand, as if to hit me. Yet another first.

With a loud snort, the shadow towering over me warns Pell off.

Numb at having broken faith with the father I adore, all that keeps me upright is my grip on Khamsin's leg.

Pell whispers to Sojur, who draws back. "You can't!"

"I can and I will."

Pell turns, seeking someone. "Lycan!"

As the a'Shara growls an order, my would-be second, the man I thought I couldn't live without, makes reverence. We share an anguished glance before he turns and races south to fulfill the command.

Sojur grips Pell's forearm. "My friend, don't do this. You will regret it the rest of your days."

Pell shakes off his second with a snarl. "As will she."

I'm as good as dead. Hands over heart, I wait for the wound that will make it so.

The crowd parts and gives the council passage.

With every breath I take, my terror grows at what my father's about to do.

When he speaks, rage inflames his voice. "The first time I call upon your service, you betray this country. Were you of age, yours would be the ultimate punishment."

Dark and controlled as his voice was before, while passing sentence, his range, and volume beats against my soul. "I cast you out. By law, no tribe may shelter you. If still on the grasslands in three days' time, you become outlaw, thus subject to the whip of justice. Any Venari who crosses your path will be honor-bound to end your life."

As my world constricts, silence falls over the gathering grounds.

My place in the crèche, gone. The honor of a Venari and the rights of a citizen, denied. And who casts me into this deepest pit of the seven hells, if not the father I adore?

My life is over. I just lack the grace to lie down and die.

Voices, some shouting, some screaming come this way, then Kemu, bellowing. "Move, damn you!" The sea of people parts.

I hold my arms out to Kemu, and beg him to heal a wound he cannot. Gayleen stalks at his side, both soiled by the blood they've spilled today.

I whisper Khamsin's word for peace as Kemu reaches for me. He renews the mindblock, then rifles through my memories. Me, lying across Dafor. Khamsin dragging me. The bite of steel at my throat, and then my mixed heritage.

You are innocent of any crime against your a'Shara, the Sada, or A'tal. Would it help if Pell knew you're half A'talan?

I shake my head no.

Kemu rises and addresses Pell. "As Venari and mindhealer, I attest your daughter betrayed neither you nor A'tal. A'Shara, I beseech you. Set aside this outcasting."

We all know better. Whatever my motives, I've crossed an inexcusable line.

Pell laughs, a bitter sound. "A Venari-to-be who lied to my face? The outcasting stands. Ask Gayleen what she'd do should your loyalty waver."

We turn as Charra yells for people to move. She and Atar support Mora between them. At their side, Selene sees me and comes running. She leaps, paws to my shoulders, and licks my face.

Sorrow chokes me as I whisper her down. For once, she obeys, then parks her rump on my boot, laugh-panting up at me.

Tears pour down Mora's face as she reaches for me. "My beloved child, somehow you must make a life off the grasslands." She pauses and rubs her breastbone as if it pains her.

"Grandmother, I beg you, calm yourself."

She takes my hand, and kisses my birthmark, the bane of my existence. "Ask the Mother of All for guidance. She brought you to us, yet now, destiny takes you away."

Charra and Atar slide their forearms under hers, bracing the old woman. My sister spares me a moment's agonized glance. What Sahain asked of her, Charra has accomplished. I, however, will never see their son, nor fulfill my sworn duty. Equally chilling, I've lied to Atar. He's losing me, right now.

Kemu's concern is ours. He whispers to Mora, her decades heartrendingly clear in her lined face and trembling body.

None of which eases my father's unyielding expression. "Daharshan, by choice, you have aligned yourself with A'tal's enemy."

Even as he casts me out, hate's bitter poison darkens his voice.

"Hear me, believe me, Sha'jin. I never want to see your face again."

Sha'jin: Daharshan for a stranger, a word used all too often as an A'talan obscenity.

Had the a'Shara foresight, he would have crushed my infant skull the morning he found me. This thought brings caustic, silent laughter. Had Pell killed me, he would have died with my sire's arrow in his heart. Were this a tale told around a gathering fire, the irony would have the listeners shaking their heads for such a paradox.

I pray my sire and brother escape because the one lie I've told has cost me everything.

Lycan arrives with Windsong. He's tied a bedroll and saddlebags to her saddle skirts. Does Pell let me take her because she'd remind him of me? If so, this is hate at its most absolute.

As my weapons master bulls through the crowd, Venari dive to get out of Aryren's way. To hell with outcasting. Having made a mockery of what it means to be Venari, she wants me dead.

Death is better than this. I stand my ground as she addresses Pell. He considers a moment, then nods.

As Aryren draws her blade in an arc across the setting sun, I tell Kham "Ameen," then sink to my knees, awaiting the stroke that will part my head from my shoulders.

Mora cries out, her voice fear shrill. "NO, NO, NO!"

For a moment, I give up dying and look to the wise woman.

Face in a rictus, Mora clenches her chest. Kemu speaks to her, and at her nod, blocks her pain.

As if the burden on my soul wasn't dark enough, I've broken the heart of the woman who sought to guide me off my path to self-destruction.

Kemu lifts Mora in his arms, his gaze fixed on Aryren. "Hurt Thea, and I will see you dead."

Aryren coughs laughter. "Get over yourself, a'Rowan. You're not the only one with a dog in this fight."

There's no hate in Aryren's eyes as she draws my practice sword, then slams her blade home in my sheath. "I won't have you dying, trying to defend yourself with this piece of trash. Send my sword back whenever you get where you're going."

She heaves a sigh, then turns away, my practice sword slung over her shoulder. "What an incredible waste of talent."

With Mora's life hanging in the balance, Kemu cannot linger.

Be safe, be strong. I'll find you in Azalaïs.

Selene fills the void of their departure, but even as I hold her, I seek someone to take her.

Atar answers my plea. He blesses me with a kiss, then draws Selene into his arms.

As she licks his tear-wet face, I reach back, then slice through the mass of my braid at the base of my neck. It falls to the ground, long as my forearm, and bound by leather strips. Had I ascended, I would have given it to Pell. Cutting it now is simply an empty act of defiance.

I stalk to Kham and toss my quiver on the ground. Jam one end of my bow into the earth, grab the top, then drive my boot into the grip. Bowstring binding the shattered pieces, I take Windsong's lead from Lycan.

He sweeps me into his embrace, and kisses me, murmuring he loves me.

Distant from my life and its many wounds, I feel only loss.

I back out of his arms, then swing up onto Khamsin, and rein my horses to the nearest gathering fire. The crowd parts, familiar with the damage Daharshan warhorses can do.

The fire is Nana's, the woman who wouldn't affirm my innocence. Eyes huge, she backs away as I ask Kham to rear.

Despite the youth of our relationship, he knows my request as a call to battle. He rises on his hind legs, and screams a challenge.

I fling my broken bow into the flames, thus disavowing a lifetime of striving to become Venari. Rather than a symbol of moving from child to adult, this is a mockery of ascension, signifying the end of a life filled with derision, and now despair. Not Sada, not Venari, not A'talan, not Daharshan.

I face Pell, who's flanked by my little brothers and Atar. Lycan stands with Sojur, their eyes awash in darkness, both helpless to turn this tide.

I make reverence to my father, who looks straight through me.

This is the burden I will bear the rest of my days. The father I'll never be free of loving, casting me out.

As I leave with the horses Khalil gave me, Pell's gift, Selene is the only one begging me to stay.

ACT TWO

OUTCAST

EIGHTEEN

THE WASTELANDS

W ith only stars to see by, I pray the markers we've passed are those I sought, and we're off the grasslands, thus out of danger.

A messenger with a string of remounts might reach Azalaïs' wastelands in five days' time. We've made the trip in three: literally running for our lives.

Waves of exhaustion gray my vision. I sway as Windsong settles to her hindquarters, then forehand. I'm not the only one who needs rest.

Having already fallen so far in life, all that's left now is to roll off the saddle, and onto the ground.

I stare up into the heavens. Panic fades. Desolation fills its void. My brother is dead, and the man who raised us called me Sha'jin, then cast me out.

I weep into my throbbing, festering hands, and beg sleep to take me.

And when it does, I go willingly into the darkness.

Nineteen

SEA CHANGE

Lightheaded with hunger, I brace against the wind streaming up and over the chalk cliffs of Azalaïs. Atar fretted at how lean I was when Leander split my lip. My brother should see me now. Three weeks an outcast and I'm down to skin and bone.

Below, the coastline embraces a churning sea. To the east, the city of Azalaïs hugs a deepwater port that hosts trade from all over the world. Beyond that, extends the largest, most luxuriant stead in A'tal: Solara, more land than the city and racetrack put together.

If I weren't an outcast, we'd be at the racetrack now. Those Venari arriving early for fall racing might take justice into their own hands should they learn Pell cast me out.

As for Kemu, he sent neither help nor a message of hope when I most had need. It rankles, the reminder of trust offered, then broken. Beyond that, I lack the means to feed and house the most valuable horses in A'tal. Yet, if I'm to find work, their tack can't be sold. In short, I'm damned if I do and damned if I don't. Thus, I stay put and slowly starve to death.

We could descend to shore, then head west on the hard-packed beach. There's work for horse handlers in the ports between here and Daharsha. Come dark moon, we could swim past the border, provided we could evade the notice of sharp-eyed Khadir Venari.

Khalil's bow, Aryren's sword, and Khamsin's vigilance would get us to the crown jewel of Daharsha, the port city of Anaïs. There, people aren't as intent upon the letter of Daharshan religious law, their outlook sweetened by trade with distant lands. Cover my birthmark with dirt and I might evade notice. Just one problem. Women don't train horses in Daharsha and I can't grow a mustache.

What little I know of my homeland ends there, which leaves only imagination, and none of it good. I've lost two families, two fathers, and two would-be lovers. With my faith shaken and heart shattered, it's time to accept I'm on my own.

Khamsin leaves off grazing the wiry grass, the wasteland's chalky soil barely sustains, and joins me. His soot-black nostrils flare as he takes in the sea's scent.

The love between my Daharshans: like a fairytale. With summer at its peak and Windsong unbred, Kham's ardent wooing sped her into heat. The days he covered her, I carved notches into a kanga twig. If settled, twelve moons from now, her first purebred foal will be born. On that same twig, I scored a star for the day I left childhood behind. Seventeen years old, without rights, family, or a foreseeable future.

Windsong joins us, disgusted by what she must view as lackluster grazing. As they greet each other, I loop my arms over her back.

Below us, their crests frothing gold in the setting sun, waves roll to shore.

"So, what do you think, 'Song? Do we go east or west?"

She tosses her head as if considering the question, in truth delighted by my scratching her withers. Often as I've brought her to Azalaïs, never like this, riding hell-bent. While the horses found forage and water, I slept like a corpse. I'd wake, choke down food, then ride again. Upon reaching the wastelands, I claimed a share of Azize's kills while my burns healed. Once able to master Khalil's bow with its stronger pull, it didn't take long before I sickened from eating only meat.

Eyes shielded, I watch Azize come in for a landing, some ground dweller dangling from her talons. Were it more appealing, I might consider claiming her kill. My stomach says don't bother. With a belly in knots, starving hurts less than eating.

Tail ruddering, the little hawk lands. She sinks her talons to their brassy toes, and rips a chunk of dead rodent free. She tosses the bloody bit into the air, setting it to rights for a craw-bulging swallow.

I look away.

It's time, more than time. Either I find food that stays down or starve to death. Do so, and my horses' fate will lie in another's hands, which cannot be.

My history in Azalaïs, a Venari's cropped hair, and Aryen's sword on my back will keep the watch from demanding proof of my marks. Yet as a foreigner, a belt knife is all the steel I'm allowed. Whoever said, better the devil you know must have suffered through a similar thorny choice.

No matter. Azalaïs it is.

While saddling Khamsin, I wince for how I smell. Most innkeepers would put my horses in a room and me in the stable. Not that I have the silver to pay for either.

I swing up and whistle for Azize.

The little hawk arrives with a sharp-shinned flutter. She settles on the saddle swell, and preens. While passing her silver-gray pinions through her beak, she finds a bit of meat and flicks it onto my cheek.

I hiss at her, the same sound she uses when peeved, then brush the meat off. She ignores me while continuing her grooming. I've made no headway with this creature whatsoever. She shares nothing willingly, be it food or companionship. Her obsidian eyes tell me to keep my distance, and I do.

With Windsong at our side, I rein Khamsin toward one of the many steep roads that will take us to sea level. While doing so, we pass some poor bastard dancing from a tree of bones, their carrion-stripped remains clattering in the wind. Yet another grisly reminder of the arbitrary nature of Covenant justice, and why I don't want anyone questioning Aryen's sword.

Sojur detests the Venari tradition of descending these hills at breakneck speed, which is why I've never indulged. Till the horses' hooves cease sliding in the soft chalk and we reach level ground, my heart stays in my throat.

First up: the racetrack, site of my life's greatest achievement. Carved into the towering chalk cliffs framing the track awaits seating for the thousands who will attend the races. Beyond lies the stables, gathering halls, and craft shops supporting hundreds of horses and their riders.

Last year I won the Champion of Champions title on a Windsong granddaughter. The Sada partied till dawn, drumming, drinking, and dancing, celebrating a sixteen-year-old rider winning on a junior horse. The same rider now slinking back into town,

Next up is the port where the air smells of fish, damp canvas, and tarred wood. In the gathering dusk, the horses' hooves echo while crossing a bridge over one of the Dark Tide's many tributaries.

We enter the city's outskirts, and I turn north.

Here, nothing's done by half measure. The top training yards and their attendant inns face the ocean. All fencing built of sturdy planks, the paddocks within, meticulously groomed. Even at the height of summer, these stone stables remain cool.

All this luxury is one of many reasons racing in Azalaïs is a beloved pursuit of the rich and titled. Every fall, Sojur argues that the Sada should house at one of these inns. That, this is where those who can afford to buy our horses stay. And every fall, Pell tells his Master of Horse to do just that, yet he will be at The Sun, owned by Enya, the woman he loves.

Hearing voices behind me, I twist in the saddle.

A dozen grooms stand on the road and wave. "Welcome back, a'Sada!"

Guts in an uproar, I raise my arm in acknowledgment. They know me from the color of my skin, and Windsong's trademark silver-white mane and tail. It's a fair guess I'm now Venari, thus able to go where I please.

Nothing could be further from the truth.

I conceal my lack of marks, left hand low and tight to my hollow belly. I don't relax till night overtakes day, and we reach the market where shopkeepers and craftspeople ply their trades. At this hour, shutters cover windows, and bars block doors. No one's around to question my right to the sword across my back.

The space between street lamps grows as we near the part of the city where brick replaces stone. Go deep enough into the bowels of Azalaïs, and true poverty appears. Paint fading, glass broken, repairs never begun. This darker side of this city is an invitation for trouble, which is why Covenant guards patrol this area.

A pair of them now ride this way, their helms crested with crimson horsehair and drawn swords across their brecca. Show these thugs disrespect and they'll drag you to jail, arms damn near yanked out of their sockets. Duck down a side street, and they'd be on me in a heartbeat. I whistle Windsong up close, then halt Khamsin as they block our passage.

The senior guard's voice comes out gruff as shifting gravel. "A'Sada?"

I make reverence, left hand buried in my midsection and heart skipping a beat.

"Bit late to be out and about, eh?"

I shrug, then tip my head toward the sword hilt behind my left shoulder.

"Where you off to?"

My guts wrench. I've not questioned the reception that may await me. "The Sun."

He laughs. "Excellent choice. Tell Enya we'll be there later."

I nod and keep my legs on Kham as they pass. The elder to my right, his partner to the left. Sensing Khamsin's threat, the younger guard's horse shies. "A thousand pardons, guardsman."

He grunts, too busy containing his skittish mount to acknowledge the apology.

I wait till their hoofbeats fade, then dry my sweaty palms on my filthy leggings. Have yet to achieve calm as we round the corner I've anticipated.

Come dawn, the Sun's east-facing windows will blaze with the light that gave the inn its name. Now, stable boys scurry, assisting recent arrivals in the courtyard. Amidst this bustle, Enya greets clients, asking after families, steads, and businesses.

My first time in Azalaïs, I witnessed the wonder of Pell flying off his warhorse even as Enya raced to his open arms. Five years old, and still I understood my father loved this woman. That those he laid within camp were mere diversions.

The courtyard empties as grooms escort horses into the stables, and their riders enter the inn. Seeking to name who waits in the shadows, Enya shades her eyes against the lantern light, body framed in waist-length, honey-colored hair.

With Windsong at our side, I ease Kham's reins.

He marches into the courtyard, and Enya's expression shifts from puzzlement to horror. She knows. Pell's written her, which is why she stands statue still and equally welcoming.

When I was little, this woman shared the marvels of her inn with me, a place where death and war did not complicate life. She'd raise me up to pick pears or apples, and help me find kittens in the haymow. Come bedtime, she told me marvelous stories. Little did I know: every act of kindness and tolerance was for Pell.

It's of no consequence that the tantalizing aroma of baking bread has me swooning with hunger. Yet another beloved person has rejected me, and for that reason, I turn Khamsin, with no idea where to go next.

Enya breaks free of her frozen stance and rushes our way. "Thea, don't go."

I murmur, 'Ameen,' as she halts at Kham's shoulder and takes me in, her sky-blue eyes huge. "Lady above, how could he tell me to turn you away? My sweet, sweet girl, you're home."

Overwhelmed as I am by her willingness to risk Pell's temper, when she reaches for my hand, it's not there. It's over my mouth, holding in my pain.

Understanding this, she opens her arms.

I fly off the saddle, only to pull back. "Enya, I'm beyond rank."

She gets a whiff and waves the air. "Oh, Heavens, you are. First a bath, then a hug."

Hand beneath Windsong's jaw, she leads us into the stables. "So, tell me, my beauty, who is this amazing man at your side?"

Doing everything she can to lighten the mood and pretend nothing is wrong.

We both know better. From this moment on, I'll live from one breath to another, the same as I have ever since my father called me Sha'jin.

TWENTY

MY LORD

Kemu's mantle over fresh-cut hay makes our bed. Often, as we've been one, every time feels like the first, yet aches with the anguish of the last. This man is a compulsion I cannot resist, a need begging to be sated. He brushes the hair off my neck, then breathes me in. Sensation blazes through me. Enthralled, I hook my leg over his and capture his lips. A horse kicks. Wood cracks. My eyes fly open.

I'm not in Kemu's arms. I am alone, on the haymow over my horses' stall at the Sun.

Kham screams, enraged.

My heart hammers as I somersault off the mow. My bare feet smack onto the aisle's stone pavers. I hiss at the sting.

"Ameen, Kham!" This shouted as I rush past the man gaping at Kham as he rips hunks of wood out of the stall door.

You can't race in Azalaïs without knowing something about Lord Aaron, the richest, most influential noble in A'tal. The grooms who saw me ride into town last night spread the news:

last year's Champion of Champions is back, and this time with a Daharshan stallion!

"Please, my Lord, give him some space!"

Even as I make this request, Kham's roar vows this bastard's blood will flow.

Aaron reaches for me. "This isn't possible. She's dead!"

In his frenzy, Kham rears, front hooves battering the stall front.

I am bare-footed and barely dressed, face caught in the hands of a man who could buy this entire nation even as my sire's stallion tears down the wall between us.

Aaron's only half right. We're both dead. Him now and me once the watch arrives.

No, no way will I leave my horses in the lurch.

"My Lord, release me or he'll savage you."

Aaron's a horseman. He knows I speak true, yet hesitates. As he tips my face upward, the heady aroma of dark spices eddies from his hands. "Your eyes, Mother in Heaven. Sapphires cannot compare."

Khamsin redoubles his assault.

At last, Aaron releases me, then takes a reluctant step back. While doing so, he steadies the sword hanging from a remarkably lean waist for a noble of his age and status.

I give my head a toss, and shed some of the straw picked up from rolling off the mow.

Attention, the very thing I hoped to avoid from the watch and now, from A'tal's foremost aristocrat, whatever his delusions. A man who wouldn't give a second thought to squashing a pissant like me.

I fake calm while finger-combing more straw out of my hair. "Let's give this another try. Who is dead?" A soft tone doesn't disguise the tremor in my voice.

"Sabita a'Falili, the woman who gave birth to you." As he gestures to the straw scattered over the pavers, a restrained smile etches no creases in his clean-shaven face.

"All the years I've watched you race, yet never saw the resemblance. Your mother's hair was sun-streaked year-round. When I saw gold in your hair, my heart screamed, *Sabita!*"

I school my face to the composure lacking inside. This man has grasped a truth that's evaded all others, including me, till days ago. Equally chilling, he plays a game beyond my grasp.

"Surely, you get I'm Daharshan."

All my life, believing I couldn't lie. Honesty has proven a broken jar I've yet to mend.

His laughter mocks any such possibility. "If your blood is pure, I'm poor." Taking care not to touch me, he traces the arch of my cheekbones. "Sabita's bone structure." Taps his lower lip. "Fuller than the upper." Chin. "Stubborn."

Hand-to-heart, he makes reverence. "Thea, welcome back to Azalaïs. Please forgive my lack of manners. Chalk it off to the shock of seeing my beloved in your features."

While answering his reverence, I reach for Aryren's sword, only to remember it's locked in Enya's treasury. I turn the gesture into a bow.

"Lord Aaron, it is an honor."

The substitute for an ingrained Venari habit doesn't escape notice. With boyish charm for a man in his forties, he smiles while extending his hand. All of which Kham supervises, alert for anything not to my liking.

It's no secret Pell raised me to the height of grassland custom, and for which I clasp Aaron's forearm. While doing so, I acknowledge the irony of paying homage to a father who rejected me, thereby creating a wound that will never heal.

Aaron's eyes go wide at the sight of my ruined birthmark. "You've been in a healer's care?"

I ease my hand free. "I'm lucky this turned out well as it did."

His brows rise toward a close-cropped hairline. "Lucky? Last year's Champion of Champions and Pell's pride? Thea, I'm no soothsayer, able to read the past in your palm."

I sigh, my heart-wrenching at 'Pell's pride.'

"While on patrol, I met my sire, who recognized my birthmark, and gave me his warhorse."

"This superb stallion who protects you with such valor?"

"Yes."

"Then what?"

Then, my life ended. I fight to keep the anguish off my face.

"Pell judged my loyalties divided and cast me out."

Aaron scoffs. "Plainly, there is a great deal more to this story." This said while flicking away a strand of straw caught in the half-moon fringe of my bangs. Enya set them to rights last night. Expression bland, his gaze follows the gleam of gold downward, only to recoil.

I step back, and shove the rose-colored cami Enya lent me deeper into my leggings. While I better cover myself, his gaze remains elsewhere.

Theocratic law rules A'tal, yet the true power lies in the first one hundred families. Among these tag ends of the monarchy, Aaron is the wealthiest, most powerful of all. Considering my utter lack of status, his next words prove him equally gracious.

"Thea, please forgive me. Try as she might, Sabita could not cure my ingrained reserve. That she laughed, rather than sent me packing, was one of the many things I adored about your mother. So, what are your plans arriving ahead of the Sada?"

My plans are to run, first chance I get. If Aaron whispered into a friendly judge's ear, then sweetened his request with gold, he would own my horses. Swimming to Daharsha would have been a cleaner death.

His smile grows with my silence. "Or did your a'Shara send you away with all the silver you've earned from your wins and horses sold?"

Aaron knows I'm a pauper and house here only because Enya didn't request payment. It's not the poverty or second-hand clothing which shames me. It's being stripped of everything I earned through hard work and bruising effort. In Aaron's privileged world, none of this holds sway. Here, I am nothing and have no right to protect what is mine.

Metal buckets clatter as Valan, one of the Sun's younger grooms, enters the stables. The sight of the first Lord of A'tal turns Valan's eyes plate-round. Make the wrong assumption and he may leave me in the lurch. He's young enough at fourteen to do just that.

I take the buckets into which he's mixed a cautious handful of grain into a generous serving of mash. "Thank you."

There's a breathless quality to my voice I could do without.

Smile shy, he opens the door so I can slip inside their stall. "Long as they were on scarce grazing, best to bring them back slow."

Khamsin sets to the moment I hook his bucket on the wall. The noise brings Windsong in from their paddock. Her bucket I brace on my thigh while savoring the nutlike aroma of steamed bran. My heartbeat slows. My hands steady.

Considering the stink eye Kham continues to give Aaron, he keeps his distance. "Once they finish their grain, do me the honor of breaking your fast with me? I've been told the food here is exceptional."

The honor? This man is as smooth as he is dangerous.

Windsong lifts her head, her beauty reminding me of who she is, who Kham is, who we all are: Daharshans in a nation that detests us. With this thought, resolve arises. Let this country hate me as a pureblood, rather than a half breed.

Aaron waits patiently, doubtless marveling at his beloved giving birth to a simpleton.

I need to knock this man off his high horse. Tell him what he wants to hear, then get the hells gone.

"Perhaps in the gardens, with a view of my horses in their paddock?"

Valan coughs, seeking to disguise a blurt of laughter. Young as he is, he knows having the advantage can prove fragile. "My Lord, I'll see to everything."

He bows, then departs at a run.

Eyes chilly, Aaron watches Valan go.

Me, I'm in a cold sweat. My lie didn't fool my father. What makes me think I can pull the wool over this aristocrat's eyes? Inept as I am at fabricating lies, somehow, someway, I must get through a meal with this man, then the moment he's gone, disappear.

I bid farewell to any hope of putting some meat on our bones. My horses and their half-Daharshan rider will soon be running fast and far as we can.

TWENTY-ONE
EVERYTHING AND NOTHING

You'd think Lord Aaron at ease if you didn't know who and what he was. A noble at an inn, he must regard as marginal, following rumors of a purebred Daharshan stallion. Imagine his delight at discovering their owner may be Sabita's mixed-blood daughter. I truly live under an unhallowed star.

I'm in the stable's shadows, hands atop my sire's bow. Having a weapon and a plan is of no help. This man scares me. Like Pell, he gets what he wants. Be it the height of wisdom or depth of stupidity, I hope to remind him I am not helpless, even without my marks.

An extravagance of the pink-hearted roses Enya raises to such success doesn't impede his view of the paddocks. As I come his way, he rises, paying homage to my being female. Yet more oddness. On the grasslands, we honor courage, not gender.

In Azalais, people call pigeons winged rats. They befoul everything: walkways, courtyards, and water troughs. Enya will view what I am about to do as a service.

I nock an arrow and track the flock circling above the stables. In search of a mate, a gray male rolls. In a seamless motion, I draw and release. The skewered cock plunges to earth.

Valan sees the strike while turning out my horses and raises a fist in victory before heading for the dead pigeon.

I wave my thanks before looking back to Aaron. Who has his attention: me, or my horses?

The question proves idiotic. My warning has fallen as flat as the pigeon Valan has pitched onto the trash wagon.

Arron's mesmerized by my Daharshans, by the poetry of their conformation and the authority of their movement. He's here to feast upon Windsong's lyrical beauty and Khamsin's majesty. Not to share a meal with the failure whose mother he once knew.

A breeze rustles the pear tree shading the table he's at. Sunlight streaks his dark chestnut hair. Born to A'tal's premier bloodline, this man holds sway over more lives than any a'Shara, and for that, I make reverence.

He answers in kind, then pulls out a chair with a nobleman's flourish.

Nerves snapping at having him behind me, I hook the bow and quiver over the chair, then sit.

He gestures to Khalil's bow. "Daharshan, yes?"

I nod, wishing I could enjoy the feast Hilen, the Sun's cook has orchestrated: fruit, cheese, hard-boiled eggs, bread, and delicate pastries.

Aaron gestures to the pitchers, their sides water-beaded. "Sweet or tart?"

I point to the garnet, my favorite mix of pears, strawberries, and cherries.

He fills the goblets with the same grace of service expected of a Venari, then hands me one, and raises the other. "To the woman who gave you birth, Sabita a'Falili."

This is the Sun's finest crystal. As the rims touch, they ring out a warning. 'Thea, pay attention!'

It's excellent, albeit useless advice. I am painfully out of my depth, and he knows it.

The ritual of Thanksgift belongs to the grasslands, yet when I spill a few drops onto the grass, Aaron does the same, supporting his story about Sabita. I take a sip: yet another mistake. He reads my enthusiasm with ease.

"A rare treat?"

I look to him through my bangs, unsure of how to back this man down. "Lord Aaron, have you ever done without?"

His gaze goes distant. "Yes, on the grasslands, with your mother. Sabita taught me the Venari way."

My mother loved this man, yet fell for her captor? Could my inconstant heart be hers?

The morning would be lovely if my stomach weren't churning. I break a round of bread, then seek a tentative gratitude for being alive. Knowing Aaron could have sired me is of no help whatsoever. I would not trade a noble for Pell, or the Haj who gave me life and my horses.

When I offer Aaron bread, he takes the smaller half, once more affirming his understanding of the Venari principle, others before self.

The bread, slathered with butter and honey, helps ease the knots in my belly.

Aaron eats with fork and knife. Using the latter, he gestures to my burns. "So, what happened?"

"One of the Sada found me wanting."

"Did you get justice?"

I nod.

"And?"

"I took nothing."

He pauses, knife blade midway through a peach, its scent warring for ascendance over the roses.

"Did this play a part in Pell casting you out?"

"No." This answered as a rider trots into the courtyard and Khamsin bellows a challenge.

Aaron watches with obvious admiration. "Windsong is legend. The stallion's name is?"

"Khamsin."

"Ah, the West Wind. Is your mare in foal to him?"

He's toppling my so-called secrets without effort.

"Most likely."

His eyebrows rise. "They deserve better than a paddock or the wastelands, Thea."

Eyes shielded against the sunlight filtering through the leaves, I study his expression. My silence doesn't deter him.

"Correct me if I'm mistaken. You have nothing, yet everything, to wit, the only purebred Daharshan breeding horses in A'tal. Come to Solara. Breed your magnificent stallion to my mares. I will happily pay your price."

This I didn't expect. Aaron has a reputation for getting what he wants, by whatever means necessary. Yet with me, he has chosen the indirect route. "May I ask a question?"

He nods.

"What happened to this woman you loved?"

"She went into Daharsha on patrol and never returned. I rode with the Falili Venari for moons, yet we never found a trace of her."

I raise an eyebrow, yet say nothing.

Had Sabita been less obsessed with the rush of a Venari's life, I might have been born into A'tal's first family.

My mother and I: both of us, victims of our mutual fixation.

My continuing silence convinces him he has not offered enough. "Sabita: beautiful sunshine. Solara: of the sun. I built Solara for your mother, then waited three years, hoping she'd return with a marvelous story. I didn't marry till my father's health failed."

He holds up his left hand. On his ring finger, two plain silver bands rest one atop the other. "Sabita and I were to be handfasted. I had a jeweler expand her band so I could wear both."

He rolls his thumb over the bands, a gesture that seems more habit than playacting. "Your mother taught me to live a simpler life, to cut to the essence of all things."

He looks into the distance, then speaks with the lilt and sibilance of the mid-south, of the Falili. "Aaron, don't backhand your competition into submission. Use the sword, my love. It's never misunderstood."

He smiles fondly. "Being Sabita's choice, both stunned and honored me, for when your mother decided, she acted without hesitation."

As does her daughter, but without her mother's acumen.

"If you loved Sabita, why handfast another?"

This earns me a somber look. "To place a child in my dying father's arms. A day later. I lost both wife and father."

We rise as Enya approaches, her smile bespeaking ease around men of power. How could it be otherwise with Pell in her life?

"Lord Aaron, I hope everything is to your satisfaction."

In the main, Aaron has treated me like a Venari. By contrast, Enya receives the full blast of his courtly manners.

He bows, then breathes a kiss over her hand. "Completely. My compliments."

What an artist of tone this man is, praising the Sun in three words, albeit words of consequence.

"Are you here to see Thea's horses?"

"I am. Permit me to repay your courtesy. Tomorrow, please accompany Thea to Solara. I'll send a carriage."

She looks to me, thrilled by the invitation.

Come to terms with Aaron, and it could save me from a life of poverty, even as I learn more about my mother and avoid Pell.

I meet Aaron's amused gaze. He knows he's won, that only a fool would refuse such an opportunity.

None of which silences the voice of reason screaming in my head.

Wrong! Bad choice! Run, you fool! Run!

If Aaron doesn't get what he wants, with his wealth and influence, no one would question if they found my body in some dark alley.

He holds out his forearm. "Tomorrow afternoon?"

Dread heavy in my belly. I clasp his arm. "Tomorrow afternoon."

TWENTY-TWO

SOLARA

Hands clasped behind my back, a Venari habit I'm not likely to lose, helps contain my astonishment.

An open carriage painted in Solara's race colors, black with gold accents, blocks the Sun's front gate. Glorious as this presentation is, the four bit-jangling, black mares who make up the hitch are the greater treasure.

A bear of a coachman keeps their dancing hooves in place. From beneath a broad-brimmed hat, he notes the admiration I lavish on his team. As he does so, a postilion rider assists Enya into the carriage.

When she whispers to him, he grins, then addresses the driver. "Kane, let Thea ride topside?"

A half-smile twitches the driver's impressive mustache as he dips his clean-shaven chin toward the coachman's stairs.

At the top, I pause. A hound lies sprawled on the seat beside him.

The coachman gives her a gentle nudge. "Down, girl."

She does without rancor, and once I'm seated, lays her slick head on my knee. As I pet her, longing for Selene rises.

Rather than swing astride the lead mare, the postilion rider joins Enya. "Kane, I'll keep the lady company. Drive on!"

He sits across from Enya, who now arranges the folds of her rose-colored gown. Were Pell to see this upstart flirting with the woman he loves, it would not end well.

Kane flicks his whip, and the team surges into their harness, haunches round with muscle. They take the first curve without slowing, the wheel mares collect as the headers stride long. We reach the sett-paved straightaway, where the carriage's iron-rimmed wheels rumble with authority. He clucks, urging the team into a high-kneed trot. Horses, patent leather harness, and polished brass: all aglitter. Little as I know of driving, I understand Kane's enjoying himself.

Merchants arranging wares, waggoners making deliveries, and food vendors grilling meat, all take in the glory bearing us from the common, and into the extraordinary.

The mares, moving in unison, continue to draw attention as we pass the racing inns along the city's seaside outskirts. Only when fields fill the horizon does Kane ease the lines, and the foursome charges down the road.

I revel in the speed: the mares' manes flying, and the leather lines fluttering in Kane's deft hands. When moving camp on the grasslands, plodding oxen haul our carts.

A sharp turn lies ahead. The lead mare slows, which forces the outer pair to lengthen their stride. Boot hooked under the toe bar, I lean in with Kane as we thunder around the curve. Despite the speed, all four wheels remain on the road.

The road straightens, and yet again, the mares move as one.

The delighted grin I offer Kane earns me a mustache-raising smile.

"If you wish, take up the lines."

"Master, I can't drive a four-in-hand."

The honorific broadens his smile. "Girl, I know who you are. You'll do fine."

I close my hands around the lines and mimic his grip.

The leather sings with messages, born of each mare's sensitive mouth. The lead mare frets to go faster even as her partner steadies her. Like Windsong, the wheel mares are pure alpha. There is a sacred trust here, same as riding.

Lacking eloquence, the best I can offer is a simple "Thank you," as Kane takes up the reins again.

"You're welcome." This spoken with the tone of a man who's been seen and acknowledged.

The road straightens, giving me my first glimpse of Solara.

My imagination has fallen far short of reality. This is a horse paradise. Long, lush pastures encourage running, which a pack of yearlings do now while keeping pace with the team. Then, tiring of trotting, they tear off at a gallop.

In every pasture, mature trees shade shedrow barns. On the stead's highest promontory, a sprawling mansion overlooks both city and sea: the home built for my mother.

Kane chuffs at my slack jaw. "Not to your taste?"

"More like not in my wildest dreams."

"Aye, there's that."

We near a massive double gate of black iron and bright brass. Lord Aaron's coat of arms, two horses rearing, face each other across the entry, above which scroll-work arches. At its peak, a polished brass sun gleams, bright as the orb in the sky.

Lances in hand, two black-uniformed guards walk the gates open, their faces shadowed by hats broad as Kane's. The mares sweep through the turn, then charge down the lane for an expanse of stables ahead.

It is one thing to know wealth equals power, and another to see it. As we near our destination, the unease I felt in Aaron's presence returns with a vengeance. On the grasslands, we value honor and courage. Here, they worship silver and gold.

The Lord of Solara and a contingent of grooms await at the main stables. Kane steers the mares into the last curve, their black hooves flashing in the midday sun. With a long, soft "Whoa," he brings the team to a halt.

The postilion rider jumps to earth, then lowers the steps for Enya. As I rise, a man in his early twenties exits the stables. It's Aaron's son, Seth, whose birth ended his mother's life. Flawless face clean-shaven, and tawny hair knotted behind his neck, he does nothing to hide his pique at being summoned to greet a two-horse wonder and an innkeeper.

None of which surprises me. In four years of racing in Azalaïs, Seth has never come near winning the Champion of Champions title. Returning his aloof stare comes without effort.

Kane coughs into his gloved fist. It sounds remarkably like laughter.

Rather than use the coachman's steps, I leap and land bent-kneed. A skill learned on the off-chance some renegade might heave my ass out of the saddle.

Forefinger-to-hat brim, Kane acknowledges his employer, then steps the mares off. The postilion rider runs alongside before swinging onto the lead mare's back.

As the carriage disappears behind the stables, with an expansive gesture, Aaron sweeps his arms wide. "Enya, Thea, welcome to Solara."

Seth regards me, hands-on-hips, and wrists strapped like a bull dancer or fighter. Had I the silver, I'd wager this man has never fought. And should he risk his life for the thrill of dancing the bulls, he's an idiot. On the grasslands, the bulls I rode as a child were selected for their hardiness and mild temperaments. Here, they breed killers.

Aaron's eyebrows rise at the dogfight brewing. "Enya, we thought you might enjoy touring our gardens while Thea and I rode out to see my mares."

Seth gets his sire's not-so-subtle alteration in plans. With precise formality, he offers Enya his arm. Perhaps the flowers will make up for her companion.

Liveried grooms lead two saddled, younger mares from the stables.

Aaron smiles with justified pride. "Four-year-olds, bred to our current senior stallion, Obsidian. Half-sisters to the three-year-olds I would cross with Khamsin."

This man needs no lesson in making his case. Riding these long-legged mares either will or won't convince me. Say yes, and I can fade into Solara's woodwork till racing is over and Pell returns to the grasslands.

We ride toward the sea, a distant slice of lustrous blue. Aaron asks, and his mare answers with a fluid canter. Not only does this man breed extraordinary horses, he's a competent rider. We could get along.

I test my mare's temperament by keeping her at a trot. She tosses her head, yet obeys. When I ask for a canter, her break is gigantic, catching her sister within strides.

The turf is perfect. The day is perfect or would be if I were with Sojur. He would love the exhilaration of charging over this carpet of green, with the salt-laden wind in his hair.

Aaron points to a band of mares coming our way, curious like all horses. "The young ladies I propose for Khamsin's court."

From my vantage point, I can see why Kham intrigues Aaron. "You seek a higher neck set and stronger hindquarters?"

"Exactly." His gaze goes distant to a year from now and half-Daharshan foals gamboling at these mares' sides. "There are twenty in this band. What say you to two thousand tallens?"

What I say isn't much. Actually, it's nothing. That much silver? Ten times what Kemu paid for Phillea, obscene as that amount was. Two thousand tallens could buy me a stead and mares for Khamsin. I could make a quiet, comfortable life for myself.

Aaron's brow furrows. "Please tell me if I've insulted you."

I shake off the dream of having a home. "They are maidens. Not all will settle."

"If only one did, I would count myself well-rewarded. Or agree to only breed my mares and I will double the price."

Four thousand tallens! Beyond a fortune.

Before I can wrap my head around his offer, a horse screams, a cry of such pain and panic, it would shatter any rider's heart. As one, we gallop toward its source, a tree-sheltered stable.

Reaching its courtyard, I skid my mare to a halt. Once her reins are tied to a rail, I race into the stable's dim interior.

Some bastard's thrown a lead rope over the top of a stall, then hauled a red filly's muzzle higher than her ears. She hangs, front hooves grazing the straw, her hindquarters oozing blood from a whipping. Tied short as she is, only one wild eye shows. Unable to ease the pressure on her neck, she groans and rears, seeking to climb free of her predicament.

Knife clamped between my teeth, I swarm up the stall front. Toss one leg over the shuddering top rail, then saw through the rope knotted there. Throughout, I keep an eye out for the frantic hooves seeking to scrabble over the wall.

As the rope parts and the filly crashes to the straw, Aaron arrives, his face a portrait of outrage.

"This time, he's gone too far." Soft as he speaks these words, it takes nothing from their intensity.

Eyes glassy, the trembling filly staggers to her feet.

I ease down into her stall. "Sa, sa, little one."

I offer my hand and let her take my scent. If to help her, she must understand I'm not the sadist who strung her up, whipped her, then left her to suffer.

My gentle voice and hands calm her enough she doesn't draw away, which lets me cradle her head to my chest.

I look to Aaron. "If I had the supplies, I think she'd let me care for her wounds."

He nods while backing away. Moments later, I hear him depart at a gallop.

I ease the filly's halter open, then heave it over the wall. It lands on the stone pavers with a clash of brass buckles.

Time passes, heavy and hurtful. Every moment testifies to the savagery of the so-called person who did this, yet hasn't returned to end the torture. I pray they don't till I dress her wounds. She'd panic all over again, and I'd not get a hand on her.

A galloping horse approaches the stable, then booted feet thud down the aisle. Kane appears at the door, edges it open, and slides a bucket inside.

I cup water to the filly's muzzle. She drinks, her lips brushing my palm. Pail leveraged onto my thigh, I scoop another handful. This time, she follows my hand down to the bucket. A sip becomes a drink to the bottom.

Kane whispers. "There's a soporific for pain in the water."

"Anything for the lash marks and the skin behind her ears?"

He passes me an open jar.

The filly flinches despite the care with which I coat the gaping wounds. By the time I'm finished, I want to hunt down the fiend who did this, then return the favor.

Boot heels ring. A man roars. "Who cut that red bitch down? If she rears again, I'll scourge her to the bone!"

Eyes white all around, the cinnamon filly throws herself into the corner farthest from the speaker. Till this is over, she'll have to endure as best she's able.

I exit the stall, then clean my hands on the towel Kane offers.

The man with the big voice and bigger opinion of himself arrives. Blue eyes dismissive, Seth brushes past me and steps into Kane. They are almost the same daunting height and breadth.

"Get out. How I train and discipline Solara's racing stock is none of your business."

This man has shattered every value I hold dear, and for which I launch into the air, then drive my knees into Seth's kidneys.

With a garbled scream, he slams face-first to the aisle.

There's a moment's glimpse of Kane's shocked expression while I yank Seth's whip out of his hand. I send the lash hissing forward, then put my all into the strike, and haul back, clawing a bloody furrow into his skin.

He howls while rolling away from me.

I follow him, then praying not to break the bones in my hand, bring the whip's ironwood handle down on his nose.

Blood gushes, and he groans.

Neither keeps me from dropping the lash over his bull of a neck, tie it into a sliding knot, then dragging his mass to the opposite side of the aisle. There, I toss the heavy whip handle over an open stall door, leap and grab it, hauling him to his feet, then off the floor.

He scrabbles at the noose, eyes bulging, spittle on his lips, face turning the color of dusk.

Only then do I let go.

Seth crashes back to the aisle, and still this idiot reaches for me.

I raise the whip handle over his head. "Be done."

He subsides, but not in silence. "You bitch, you abomination, you Daharshan filth!"

I've grown up with every permutation of such obscenities, thus lean in. "Where I come from, they'd drag a perversion like you to death. If I ever hear of you abusing another horse, I will hunt you down, and kill you myself. However long it takes to die on a tree of bones, I will celebrate, knowing you are no more. Should you be so arrogant as to believe I won't come after you, ask anyone what it means to have a nomadi on their tail."

Using the curse which has dogged all my days brings bitter satisfaction.

I straighten, only to discover witnesses to my vow: Lord Aaron and a companion, both bearing down upon us.

The companion grabs a towel, which he tosses to Seth, and keeps coming, his hands in fists.

Either I move or this muscle-bound bastard will break my jaw.

He leaps, grabbing for me as I fly up the nearest stall front, balancing on its top rail.

Aaron seizes the back of his shirt and pulls him down. "Hemming, don't shame yourself by defending my son's atrocity."

The Shadrean, his dark brown eyes wide with shock, wheels on Aaron. "That stray bitch battered your heir."

A dismissive hand gesture accompanies Aaron's bitter laughter. "My heir, the man who abuses horses, and presumes upon the blood in his veins?"

He rounds on his son, now wobbling to his feet, then rakes him with an expression I know all too well. It's the same look Pell wore while casting me out.

"I *will* have answers why a filly I bred, and you believed would be your three-year-old entry, cowers with her hindquarters bloody."

He addresses the pair with cold deliberation and narrowed eyes. "Solara is mine. Who comes, who goes, all such decisions are mine. Unlike the pair of you, that so-called 'stray' was last year's Champion of Champions. If she needs 'dealing with,' I will do it."

I land light-footed, then lock gazes with the man who will 'deal' with me. I am furlongs beyond disgust, and so far beyond fury, there's no reasoning with the words that arise.

"All the stories I've heard of Solara being A'tal's brightest star, yet your son isn't fit to work in a slaughterhouse. Do what you will. Haul me into court. Even as a condemned Daharshan, I can deed my horses to another. You will never lay a hand on them."

I turn and stalk down the aisle, prepared to walk back to Azalaïs, provided the watch doesn't get me first.

Aaron speaks in an emotionless tone. "Thea, a moment, please."

This is it. Me on a tree of bones for righting a wrong. I pivot. "What?"

He places the bloody halter across my hands. "Her name is Cinna."

Now that I'm not saving her, I see the engraved nameplate.

"I would heal the trust broken between us. Shall we say I gave you Cinna, what, an hour ago?"

I look from the bloody evidence of the damage done to the man who did it.

Seth's gaze promises if he ever finds me alone, he will kill me. Yet his father has handed me a pass on jail. As Cinna's owner, even as a foreigner, I had every right to pummel Seth.

I meet his glare and vow if we ever meet in a dark alley, only one of us would walk away. And should Aaron give me Cinna, I will get her out of here before Seth kills her, then ride the horse he whipped. Maybe even race her. Provided I can solve a host of other problems: food, shelter, and not running afoul of the man who raised me.

TWENTY-THREE

THIRD RATE

E nya pays the city Kane drives us through little mind, likely envisioning my bleak future.

I'm little better. Cinna's halter lies across my knees, the leather now clean and brass polished. If Aaron keeps his word, in a few days, I'll have another mouth to feed.

Valan awaits us at the Sun's gate. He hops onto the running board, then hands Enya a ribbon-bound, wax-sealed Venari missive. "This just arrived."

With a long, soft, "Whoa," Kane halts his mare in the inn's courtyard.

As I come to earth, Enya reads, her consternation growing. She reaches the end and crushes the letter. "This is a travesty! You acted with honor in protecting your sire and brother. Same as you did today, in saving that filly."

"Did Pell explain how he discovered I was here?"

She accepts the hand I offer, then steps down. "Some Covener bespoke a Sada healer, who told Pell. He says either I turn you out, or we're finished. Thea, how am I to make peace with him? Fighting is all he knows."

There's an unhinged element in my soft laughter. "Obedience is the only language he understands. Once he learns I'm gone, he'll mellow."

She wraps me in a fierce embrace. "I prayed we'd have more time. Where will you go?"

Kane clears his throat. "More to the point, what will you do?"

Horses, hunting, and fighting are all I know. With Solara no longer an option, Khalil's bow is all that's left. "I'll hunt and sell game."

Kane arches a bushy, unimpressed brow. "Last year's Champions of Champions? I think not. A friend of mine runs a training yard. No lords, no ladies, just ordinary folk who want sane and biddable mounts. Convince him you can work with others, and he'll hire you in a heartbeat."

The thought of Seth tracking me down, then taking his sweet time putting me out of my misery arises. "What would this man say about my being Daharshan?"

"Trust me, it won't be a problem. Rafi's a horseman. He'll understand the advantage in having a Champion of Champions riding for his yard."

If Kane and this man are friends, they may share similar values.

"I'd like to meet him."

Enya rests her hand on Kane's knee. "A tankard of ale while Thea gets her horses?"

He ticks forefinger to hat brim. "I'd be much obliged."

With a sad smile, she heads for the inn, her hair and gown a vision in pink against its gold stucco walls.

As Kane watches her go, his expression regrets she's given her heart to another. Still, unlike the postilion rider, Kane has the good sense not to mess with Pell's woman.

I leave him to his musings to round up my threesome and meager belongings.

With Windsong at our side, and Azize on Kham's saddle swell, I ride out of the stable.

Kane gives my Daharshans the respectful study of a true horseman. "Godsdamn, they are gorgeous. Had you killed Seth, Aaron would have paid the blood price to keep you off a tree of bones. Is the mare in foal to the stallion?"

"I think so."

"All the more reason she gets proper care."

He shakes his head when I rise in the stirrups and seek Enya. "Don't bother. She left a message with me. If Rafi's yard doesn't suit, you're to return, and she'll sort something out."

He sighs. "What a waste."

I rein alongside his cart as he steers for the gate. "How so?"

"A woman that beautiful, alone for most of the year? And for what? Nothing more than a pole-up-his-arse Venari. You ask me, that's just plain wrong."

We pass through the gate, then turn south.

My conflict with his assessment about Pell must show, because, again, his brows rise. "Tell me I'm wrong. After what he did, you still care for that asshole?"

The ale or Enya has loosened his tongue. Tears threaten, and I duck my head.

"Son of a bitch, you do. Never in all my days could I credit such a wonder. The man doesn't know what he threw away."

When I look to Kane, my wordless grief pierces his indignation.

"Sorry. Me and my big mouth."

Best I change the topic. "Do you think Lord Aaron will give me Cinna?"

"He damn well better. Seth hoped she'd be his qualifier in this year's Champion of Champions race. You saw how well that worked out. Man's a first-rate bull dancer, but put him on a temperamental horse and he pisses himself."

None of which addresses the anxiety gnawing at me. "Kane, how much danger am I in?"

"Plenty, which is why I hope you and Rafi get along. Did you see Black run in his qualifier last year?"

"Black?"

"Sorry, that's what we call Obsidian at Solara."

"No, I was caring for a horse with a pulled tendon."

Horse people live for gossip, and Kane is no exception.

"Shadrean entries are rare, especially rider-owned, but when Aaron saw Obsidian go, he had to have him. Hemming made becoming Solara's head rider a condition of the sale. Turns out the man can ride, but like Seth, is no great shakes as a trainer. The public won't see Black again till Hemming gets him under control."

Puzzling as all this is, it's not what's bothering me. "Why does Aaron tolerate brutality?"

"He doesn't, hence the scene you just witnessed. Nor does Hemming have any say over what Seth does. Even so, I doubt there's a limit to what Hemming will do where silver is involved. Thus, he and Seth get along, especially when it comes to 'pay to play.'"

My brows furrow, for which Kane winces. "Pay me no mind. That sort of shit's alien to the culture you grew up in. Bottom line. The two of them cat around in low places."

"Are you talking about sex for silver?"

"Damn, girl, are you always this blunt?"

"As you say, I grew up on the grasslands."

"Where you absolutely absorbed Venari principles. Back to what brought this mess about. Cinna reared and dumped Seth during this morning's breeze. Mind you, you heard none of this from me, but he got back on and that's the last we saw of Cinna till later."

He laughs, and it's not a pretty sound. "What I would give to be a fly in Aaron's office about now. Seth screwing up Aaron's deal with you will have repercussions. And should he rein his son in, all of Solara will celebrate."

We enter the guts of Azalaïs, then reach a street so narrow Kane drives ahead. While the area's familiar, not so the yard he turns into.

The coachman comes to earth and greets a man more my height. "Rafi, my old friend, it's been too long!"

They slap each other's backs like brothers.

As I take in the yard, Azize chitters on my saddle swell.

There's stabling between the outer walls and a circular track, around which seven riders work horses in round pens. Other than living quarters above the stables, it's much like the layout Sojur uses for the Sada horse.

A rider leads Kane's mare toward a shade tree, which has Rafi turning my way.

"So, Kane, who have you . . ." he breaks off, and gapes at me, looking more the cutthroat than horse trainer. "Thea a'Sada?"

Kane's choice to bring me here makes sense. A black leather patch covers Rafi's right eye, and his Falili Venari marks have been struck out.

I rotate my left thumb and display my lack of marks. "It's just Thea."

Upon seeing my burn marks, he takes a step closer. "Just 'Thea,' my arse."

I hush Kham when he snorts a warning.

Rafi looks back to Kane. "You bring a Venari-to-be and two purebred Daharshans here, of all places?"

"Rafi, she needs work."

"A rider of her quality? Is the watch on her tail?"

I answer for myself. "Not yet."

Kane drapes his arm over his friend's shoulders. "She chanced upon some of Seth's less-than-stellar training methods, then broke his nose and strung him up."

Any pretense of working horses ends. The riders rein their mounts as close to the conversation as their round pens allow.

Rafi barks laughter. "This little girl got the drop on that jackass?"

"Then told Aaron she'd never bring her horses to a place that permitted mistreatment. To keep her off a tree of bones, Aaron gave her the filly Seth abused."

"You want me to feed her and three horses?"

It's posturing. The grins on his riders' faces tell me as much.

Kane gives the smaller man's shoulder a squeeze. "Rafi, don't play the simpleton. A Champion of Champions, riding for you? Taught by one of the greatest living horsemen? Bringing the only purebred Daharshans in A'tal to your yard? Surely you see the benefits."

Rafi snorts. "Not to mention a crapton of complications."

He runs a hand over his clean-shaven jaw, then looks to me. "If you came, how long would you stay? Till racing is over?"

No dust on this man. He knows I need to lie low. "Yes."

"Then what?"

Though it's none of his business, I replay the dream I destroyed with Seth's nose. "Then, I'll find a breeding stead with grazing for my horses, and work their young stock for our keep."

Rafi grunts. "Happen to have an open pen in need of a rider. We provide morning and midday meals and housing above your horses' stalls. How many can you ride a day?"

"Finishing or starting?"

"Bit of both."

"Eight."

"That's all?"

"If you want it done right."

He grins. "Right works for me. Tallen a day."

It's my turn for laughter. "While you flog your customers for what, say ten tallens a day per horse?"

"Feeding you and your string won't come cheap."

"But you do."

Our audience guffaws. "Make that stingy sonofabitch pay what you're worth!"

Rafi pretends to yield to opinion. "Fine, ten tallens a day."

That paltry amount won't restart my life. I swing my reining hand for the gate.

Rafi's lips thin. "Final offer, twenty."

I duck Azize's snapping beak while dismounting, then point to the empty stabling behind an open pen. "There?"

He nods, then whistles to someone in the gathering area.

An older man responds with an irritable gesture, then finishes what he'd been writing. "What?"

"Get word to those on our waiting list with racing stock. First come, first served. And Idry, tell them who's riding for us . . .," he fixes me with a steely, one-eyed gaze, ". . . at great expense."

The scribe chuffs. "Relax. Her work list will be full by day's end."

Rafi flaps his hands at our audience. "All right, you laggards, show's over. Back to work. Kane, get yourself something to drink while we settle her horses."

He leads the way between the empty pen and its neighbor, whose rider greets me with a grin. "Welcome!"

Somehow, I find an answering smile. Thanks to Kane, we have a roof over our heads.

While I unsaddle my horses, Rafi swarms up a ladder, then drops forage in the feeder below. He descends, checks the water level in the stall's trough, then leans on the top rail. "Any extra clothing?"

Even here, ragged mourning black won't cut it.

"Not really."

"I'll tell you where to look. Move your bones, girl. Paying you what I am, I need a drink to steady my nerves."

Bow and quiver on a peg, I unhood Azize and loft her into the air.

Rafi follows the little hawk's upward spiral. "She's welcome to every pigeon we've got. Bastards crap on everything."

Seeking to hurry me along, he reaches for my shoulder.

Kham slams his hoof down and snorts a warning.

"I warrant there's one hell of a story behind that horse."

I contain the wince this produces. "There is. What's yours?"

"Fraternizing with the enemy. I put myself between the head of my company and his target, which is how I lost my eye. The bastard was fast."

This close, I can see the diagonal scar starting on his cheekbone and ending in his eyebrow. "They didn't drag you?"

"My second swore he'd sit for Inlooking and prove I was in the right. I told him not to bother. What our so-called honorable captain wanted to do was sick. They were only little girls, maybe thirteen or fourteen, rounding up sheep that had strayed across the border. I took my discharge and got the hells off the grasslands. I'd had a gutload of that 'we're better than the people we kill' Venari bullshit."

In short, this is the reason Kane wasn't worried about my 'nationality.' I've never met anyone like Rafi, someone who sees good in my sire's people, and for that reason, I hold out my forearm.

"My thanks for the job and your honesty."

He answers my grip with chilling strength. "Trust me, you'll earn every tallen. As for honesty, best that river flows both ways. Azalaïs seethes with your story. How Sahain died. How you reacted. You ask me, your a'Shara should have taken that into account . . ."

I stop him before he continues. "I threw away my warning horn to protect my sire and brother, then lied to my a'Shara, and got what I deserved. Are you sure you want a traitor working for you?"

No sooner are the words out than I realize I am at peace with what Pell did.

Rafi takes his time in answering. "Since we're telling truth, here's mine. Shielding family doesn't make someone a traitor, any more than war permits rape of little girls."

It takes me a moment to grasp his words come from the heart, and how much we have in common.

"I want to introduce you to Khamsin so he'll know you are someone he can trust."

A massive grin lights up Rafi's face. "After Kane leaves. Speaking of which, dawdle any longer, and he'll drink all our wine."

We fall in step, two failed Venari, perhaps friends?

TWENTY-FOUR
A JOB WELL DONE

I find heat in my training colt's tendons and swear under my breath. The reason stands at his three-year-old's sweat-soaked shoulder. I've ridden Dree's horse for a week, yet we only met today.

I glance at the teamster over my shoulder. "Dree, how long has Silver been under saddle?"

He counts, thick fingers rising and falling. "Eight, no, maybe nine rides?"

I refrain from blurting, 'Are you crazed?' I've been riding his youngster at speed.

He flusters, reading my dismay. "I meant to tell Idry how green Silver was, but the thrill of you riding him knocked it clean out of my head."

The next hard rain may split Dree's worn boots, but it didn't keep him from putting his horse into training. I don't need telling Silver is his Khamsin.

I force a smile while coming to my feet. "He'll be fine. He could have done this, goofing off in a pasture. I'll poultice his legs, and once the swelling's eased, swim him in the ocean."

Rafi sited his yard well. The best part of the day is breezing my training horses along the shore.

Dree takes my hands, his knuckles work-swollen. "Can I come by the same time tomorrow to help you change the poultices?"

"I look forward to it."

He offers me another apologetic smile, and heads for his team, off to deliver grain to another yard. He's one of eight owners I ride for. All bring something different to the mix, yet all treat me with welcome respect.

Once Silver's untacked and loose in my round pen, I head for the gathering pavilion.

As I enter, Idry's head down, writing. "What do you need?" The scribe only looks like he's not paying attention.

"Clay poultice for four legs and a set of standing wraps."

A girl, maybe thirteen or fourteen, standing beside a wall of supplies, selects a pouch and tosses it to me.

I sniff the contents. "What's in here besides clay?"

"Coltsfoot, mullein, and wormwood. Reduces swelling and eases pain." She extends her hand. "Hi, I'm Ainee. I gather herbs for Rafi and a few other yards."

Like most people here, she reads my awkwardness with this mainland custom when I take her hand. Dark, unruly curls tumble over her shirt, threadbare as my own. Whatever his opponent's age, Rafi has no qualms about driving a hard bargain.

"I need enough for five days and four legs."

"You'll have it." She points to a supply rack. "Wraps and bandages there."

She takes a jar off the shelves and hands it to me. "Use this on those burn scars. It will help. A Champion of Champions, here! Now I know why Rafi's been in such a great mood."

As I gather the needed supplies for Silver, Ainee rests her hand on Idry's shoulder. "Tomorrow?"

"No, today, as promised." He points to a bundle at the entry.

"Idry, you're the best!" She kisses the crown of his close-cropped hair, more silver than brown, then bundle in her arms, leaves skipping and shouting goodbyes.

Idry hooks a thumb at the table where we eat. "That came for you this morning."

On top of a parcel sits a rectangular, official missive. I break the seal, read what's within, then toss the document on Idry's desk. "My work papers."

He inserts the page into a folio with my name. "So, how does it feel being declared a foreigner in the land you grew up in?"

I swallow the profanity churning inside. "The country I was ready to die for? Telling me I'm nothing, less than nothing? May the Covenant and its laws rot in the deepest of the seven hells. As of this moment, I have fewer rights than any A'talan beggar."

Idry's brows rise. "I'd feel better if I knew you understood just what that piece of paper means."

"Oh, I know what it means. Step a finger-joint out of line and my Daharshan ass lands in jail—or worse."

My outburst only serves to increase Idry's disquiet.

"Thea, new as you are here, your work thrills our clients. I beg of you, keep that Venari temper in check. Trust me, I know how much this asks of you, but for everyone's sake, please try."

With a curt nod, I acknowledge the justified warning before turning my attention to the package. There's an envelope tucked under its twine.

It's clothing, from Enya. Though out of sight, I'm not out of mind.

"Idry, does anyone grow desert roses in Azalaïs?"

At his nod, I turn the card over. Without my having to ask, Idry offers his pen so I may thank Enya for the gift. "You'll take the cost from my tally?"

He reads what I've written and smiles. "I will."

By the time I'm finished with Silver, it's midday.

Mealtimes at Rafi's are raucous affairs, with much laughter, teasing, and grousing over client expectations. As I enter the pavilion, Rafi gestures to sit in the chair next to him.

As I do so, he slides a mug of ale my way. "To a job well done."

"How so?"

He clinks rims with mine. "I met Dree on my way back to the yard. He told me how you handled him, not explaining how green Silver was. It meant a lot. He's not the only one praising your work. Once racing's over, we are discussing your future. Breeding farm, my arse. Hard as this is to accept, your a'Shara did you a favor. You're no archer. You're a rider."

I laugh. "Sojur said the same, hours before Pell cast me out."

Rafi arches a 'did it take?' brow.

We fall silent as women chattering in Daharshan arrive with our midday meal. As of today, I've joined their ranks as a non-citizen.

They bear tureens wrapped in towels, bread hot off baking stones, and the finest fruits of the season. The food here is why Rafi may not get pushback about my staying on. After establishing the yard, he sought Azalaïs' tiny Daharshan community. Upon learning why he was no longer Venari, they welcomed the chance to cook for the yard in a city that regards our kind as undesirable.

The eldest trails her fingers along the bottom of my cropped hair. "Jadeen kala, al-Rafi?"

Rafi translates. "Boy's hair." He points to his marks. "Nam, Venari-to-be."

She looks at me askance. "Nam khadeen?"

He laughs and shakes his head. "Nam, Champion of Champions."

Unconvinced, she arches a brow, yet on her next trip past, lowers a domed brass platter before me. An ibex etched into its gleaming surface courses, beneath which lies a mound of buttered saffron rice and raisins. I fill Rafi's plate till he signals enough, heap my own, then slide the platter down the table.

Next to arrive is flatbread for scooping up rice, herb-crusted lamb, and white goat cheese. Between Hilen's cooking at the Sun and this exotic largesse, I've regained the appetite lost on the wastelands. Knowing the meal will end with kaf and flakey pastry oozing honey and nuts, I pace myself.

Someone pounding on the outer gates has us looking their way.

Rafi's brows crease in irritation. "Everyone knows we're closed at midday. Tell whoever it is to get lost."

Blows continue to rain upon the double doors even as one of the younger men strolls toward the racket. He shoots the bolt and the gate blasts inward, forcing him to scramble out of its way.

A bay warhorse marches into the yard even as his rider reverses the sword hilt with which he attacked the gate. Kemu sheathes his blade, dismounts, then long-strides my way.

His confidence, nay arrogance after a moon-long silence, enrages me.

Rafi begins rising. "Who the hells is this?"

My hand on his shoulder urges him to remain seated. "Kemu a'Rowan. I'll deal with him."

Deal with him *and* tell him where he can go.

We meet midway, and he reaches for me, like a little boy for a toy.

I slap his hands away, then plant my feet and straight-arm him in the chest. "Too little, too late, a'Rowan. A moon ago you told me, be safe, be strong, that you'd find me in Azalaïs."

Rafi's on his feet, ready to wade in at any sign I need help.

All of which Kemu sees and reads wrong. "You found someone else?"

His incredulity insults both Rafi and me. "You thought I'd wait for you?"

I am learning how to lie.

Kemu notes Rafi's struck-out marks and reaches for his blade.

That's not happening, not if I have anything to say about it.

I grab his bearded chin, breaking his fixation on Rafi. "You knew how much pain I was in, but what did you do? Nothing! Didn't send a mindhealer. Didn't write a letter to explain what detained you or tell me if my sire and brother escaped. Why bother showing up now?"

As if questioning whether any of this is worth the effort, he passes his hand over his forehead. "When the ulans reached your post, it was too dark to track your family. They are safe."

I send a prayer of thanks heavenward. Some good came from my sacrifice.

As he takes in my worn clothing and cropped hair, his face tightens. "While you rode for your life, I kept Mora alive even as the head of her croft rode hell-bent to the Sada. All of Lord Karlis' skill, and still it was touch and go. She was so frail, we kept her in a healing sleep most of the time. While awake, she begged me to go after you, and I promised I would, the moment she was better.

"Thea, it took all of my skill and Karlis to save Mora. Was I wrong, counting on your grit to see you safe in Azalaïs?"

A fist to the face would hurt less.

Yes, he's still the man of my dreams. Just as beautiful, just as potent. With his beard trimmed in the Daharshan manner and his sun-darkened skin, he looks like a Kian. So much so, the women send him warm, appreciative gazes.

Me? Not so much. While I can accept Mora owes him her life, how much time would it have taken to write a letter? Or bespeak another Covener, and ask them to find and help me? Very little, and I'll be damned if he's claiming otherwise.

"A'Rowan, if your idea of caring is counting on someone else's grit, it explains why you ride alone. Who'd want you as their second?"

My vindictive tone makes his gray eyes go wide.

"The moment I transferred Mora to my Master at Land's End, I left for Azalaïs. Not only that, I damn near foundered Gamar getting here."

I cough laughter. "And that's supposed to make up for a moon of silence?"

Comprehension dawns—for him—for me. I wouldn't be this angry had I not counted on him.

His gaze softens, and now that he's not glaring at me, the grime on his face and road dust on his haaka registers. None of which makes up for what he didn't do, and he knows it, just refuses to admit as much before our avid witnesses.

He steps into me and speaks for my hearing alone. "Don't do this. Don't end us before we've begun. I was wrong. I should have sent a message. Woman, I have chased after you the better part of our lives, and still, you confound me. Teach me what it will take to please you."

Some of the iron comes out of my spine. Still, there's enough anger left to drive my forefinger into his chest, right over his heart. "Surely you can read what I want!"

"You'll give me that privilege?"

Despite saying yes in my mind, I cock an eyebrow.

He brushes his thumb over my palm, deflecting my anger. "Do these scars constrict?"

"They did while I struggled to feed myself with my sire's bow."

His brows crease in puzzlement.

My peeve returns, this time with myself. "I dithered on the wastelands for three weeks, unsure where to go, or who to turn to."

His skin blanches. "I thought you'd go to Enya, and she would do what I could not."

Unable to meet his gaze, I look away. "After last year, I couldn't face Azalaïs as a failure."

He gusts a sigh. "Pell's rage doesn't make you a failure. Plainly, we have much to discuss once we have some privacy."

Sensing an opening, Rafi joins us. "The food is getting cold."

I get a grip on my manners. "Rafi, this is Kemu a'Rowan. Kemu, this is Rafi a'Falili, for whom I work."

Rafi extends his forearm, his struck-out marks compelling Kemu to pick courtesy or departure.

Kemu grips Rafi's arm. "A'Falili."

Rafi closes his hand around Kemu's forearm with equal force. In doing so, the pair acknowledge the adage, once a Venari, always a Venari.

"A'Rowan, join us. From the look of things, you could use a meal. Thea, show him where he can wash up."

There's a wry bent to Rafi's one-sided grin as he returns to the table.

I heave an annoyed breath—for Rafi steering my ship—for Kemu leading Gamar to a water trough beside which a rider has delivered a double armload of forage.

They're going to do this, subject me to their teasing and scrutiny. Still, what am I to make of someone who says we've shared lifetimes, but couldn't spare a moment to send word or succor?

This leaves me asking, who should he have helped? A woman who did everything in her power to raise me, or a girl who couldn't get over her pride and seek Enya help?

Truth be told, I don't much like my answer.

TWENTY-FIVE

AN ITCH

Sunset has come and gone, yet the day's heat lingers.

I behold the stars, chair tipped onto its back legs and boots up on a round pen rail.

When we were little, Pell would walk our band of three out into the summer grasslands. We'd lie on our backs as he told us tales about how the constellations earned their names. Even then, Sahain was the tallest. I'd rest my head on his shoulder with Atar on the other. Whoever fell asleep first, Pell would carry back to camp—the same man who consigned me to fate's dung heap.

Longing for all I've lost casts a pall over the evening and I sigh while finger-combing my drying hair. Thick as a horse's tail, it has grown out enough to brush my shoulders. Cutting it proved a meaningless act of defiance.

I'm considering heading out for supper when Rafi comes up alongside me. I drop the chair's front legs back to earth. "Thought I was the only one here."

He rests his forearms over the pen's top rail, his body outlined by stars. "For how long?"

When I give him a puzzled look, he laughs.

"After today's performance, you didn't think the Rowan would return?"

"Oh."

"Oh, indeed. May I offer some advice?"

"On?"

"Love, when to say yes. When not to."

"Please do."

He tips his head back and takes in the heavens. "You might think a man with one eye wouldn't appeal to the fairer sex, but you'd be wrong. I spend my nights alone only by choice, but trust me, I don't equate scratching an itch with being in love. Do yourself a favor. Set the same standards."

I give him a sour look. "You're solving a problem that does not exist."

"Hah! A superb trainer and rider, who next year will own three pureblood Daharshan horses? To whom Aaron extended an olive branch in the form of a racehorse? Who, in any sensible person's estimation, is beautiful? Men will do whatever it takes to please you, which includes setting aside their own agendas."

He shakes his head at the jaundiced, doubting look I give him. "For once in your life, Thea, go slow. If you leave, please close the gates."

A half-smile on his lips, he strolls from the yard.

Lantern light halos my last glimpse of Rafi as he turns a corner. In search of a meal, drinking partner, or lover?

Meanwhile, I sit alone and unsettled by his insight.

I'm giving thought to catching up with him when the sound of a horse walking approaches the yard. Our owners know we're closed. This leaves . . .?

Kemu halts in the gate opening, a living statue framed by streetlights. No haaka, only a sword belt slung over his shirt. Gamar lacks a saddle, yet a bedroll and saddlebags drape the big bay's shoulders.

He says nothing, yet a great deal while holding out his arm to me.

Take it and I'm pretty certain how this night will end.

I walk the gate shut, slide the bar into place, and swing up behind Kemu.

TWENTY-SIX

SONG OF THE SEA

The roar of the surf intensifies as we descend to the sea. When Gamar's hooves slide in the soft chalk, I tighten my grip on Kemu's waist.

We reach the last bit and Gamar leaps, landing in a fountain of sand. He prances, proud to have brought us to shore safely.

Kemu slaps the bay's muscular neck. "You big clown."

This horse's playful spirit reminds me of Kitan, which nicks my deepest wound. Any day now, the Sada will arrive and the complications of my life will triple.

Kemu rolls the gear off Gamar's shoulders onto the beach. "Wait here. I want to show him where there's fresh water he can drink."

I slide off and watch as they head for where seagrasses grow along the ghost-white cliffs. When the tide comes in, the way we came will be the only access to this cove.

Here, everything tastes of salt, of beginnings and endings.

I turn to the sea where waves rush to shore, their crests pulsing in the same advance and retreat as the grasslands. As a child, Pell would let me play in the ocean's shallows till, blue with cold, he'd pull me out despite my protests.

These memories, at this moment, couldn't be any farther afield. I shuck my boots and socks, then wade into the shallows.

A sliver of light pierces the riot of clouds overhead, signaling moonrise. I clasp my elbows, swaying in the ocean's ebb and flow. Was it wise, accepting Kemu's invitation? I remind myself, he's A'talan, he's Venari. A woman's 'no' will mean just that. This reassurance doesn't ease my trepidation when he splashes up behind me.

He wraps his arms around my waist, resting his cheek against mine. "It's beautiful, yes?"

I murmur affirmation as our bodies move in time with the sea.

His deep voice melds into the sibilance of the sea. "Today, your anger ate a hole into my gut, that and the inability to express how much it meant, seeing you again. Would it help if I told you my belief in your ability to care for yourself arose from the past lives we've shared?"

He's made this claim too many times. "It would not."

The fluidity with which he mirrors my motion ceases. One breath becomes several before he rests his fingers on my temples.

"Stop me if you don't want to see this."

The beauty of the ocean fades, replaced by a world I don't recognize. A boy and girl, maybe twelve or thirteen, race hand-in-hand through a field of ripe grain, then tumble into the golden bounty and kiss. This fades, to be replaced by a man and woman torn from each other's arms as darkness blots out the sun. Next, a potter pauses at his wheel, clay-coated fingers clenching, then ruining an elegant spinning carafe as a blue-eyed youth kisses his shoulder and reaches between the man's spread legs.

I pull free of his touch. "That was me? I was a boy, in love with a man?"

He laughs. "Not just any man—me. In that life, we almost burned at the stake for loving our own sex."

"I . . . ." break off and sag against his chest. The boy's hair, so like my own, his eyes the same blue. A'talans embrace the principle of every person expressing elements of both sexes, yet the vision of me as a boy astounds with the authority of truth.

Kemu brushes salt spray off my face. "Our prayer to be born again amidst those we love urges everyone to live a worthy life."

He frames my face between his hands. "This isn't the time for faith or philosophy. Light of my all my lives, trust your heart. Trust your instincts."

He tips my face upward and kisses me, softly, slowly, deeply.

All this man has to do is touch me, and I am ready to fight or melt in his arms. Tonight, I melt, fingers tangled in his thick hair while returning his kiss.

He groans, then slides his hands into my leggings, fingers splaying over the small of my back. Heedless of the edge of his teeth, I return his kiss. My senses reel as he lifts me in his arms till we're face-to-face.

I wind my legs around his waist, kissing everything within reach. His breath catches as I press my need against his, affirming my willingness. He splashes back to shore, lowers me to my feet, and yanks off his shirt.

Bathed in the lambent light of the ocean and stars, this man's majesty staggers. Even so, he waits till I make my consent clear.

I do so, sliding my hands down his stair-stepped belly, and revel in the beauty and strength there. Hesitate only upon reaching his leggings.

I want this, body and soul. So much so, I find myself trusting his visions of our past lives, and cannot wait to join again. Breath shallow, I peel off my leggings and small clothes, then shirt and cami.

So much for the girl who thought she'd rather stand naked before the Sada than wear an abaya. My ribs heave and heart flutters as, for the time, I offer myself to love.

Before panic has me snatching up my clothing and fleeing, Kemu gathers me into his arms. Fear becomes hunger as he cradles my bare skin to his.

Gratitude wells for his persistence in the face of my pretense of disinterest. This makes him the right man to take me where I want to go now.

Anticipation sizzles. We're both riders. Where we contrast becomes heat—undeniable heat.

He endures long as he's able, then rolls down his leggings and kicks them away.

With the moon yet to rise, the white cliffs behind him outline his body. He straightens, standing tall and proud.

Artless as I am, there's pride in having brought this transformation about.

As he sweeps us together, and scatters kisses along my neck and collarbones, his laughter comes from deep down inside him. I gasp when his beard brushes my breasts. A part of me I've made little of, a reminder of the woman who gave me birth, then gave me up.

Shock and startle give way to a tenderness that swells into need. Belly clenched to backbone, I press my hips into his, and beg for union.

With this affirmation, he lowers me to the beach in this our lover's melee, where both win.

Possessive as a courting stallion, he closes his teeth on the nape of my neck. My head falls back, from maiden mare to mare in heat. As my body welcomes him, he traces kisses along my shoulders, then cups my breasts. I gasp, and then sigh. Everything taught by my sword master—never let a man get too close—ignored.

"Too close, my love?"

I close my teeth on the curve of his ear, putting an end to the teasing and attention to my every thought.

He takes me with him as he rolls onto his back. "Often, as I've dreamt of this moment, I never foresaw the jewel you'd be in such a setting."

Driven part by want, part by fear, I straddle him. I kiss my way up his midline as he cradles my bottom, my back arched as a cat. Sensation coils through me. As it settles heavy and hungry between my legs, I give my hair a wanton toss. This is play, something I never did as a child. Always too busy getting where I thought I was going.

My hands glide down his knotted stomach muscle till reaching the place where laughter ends and imminence looms. I shift from side-to-side, bringing myself closer to him.

"Thea, if you want me to. . ."

Finger to his lips, I hush him, then part myself.

Am I ready? Oh, Mother in Heaven, please let it be now.

This is worlds apart from on my own and desperate for sleep. All the mares I've bred, yet what happens between men and women remains a mystery to me.

I lower myself. My mind jumbles, part need, part terror. Kemu clasps my hips and holds me above him. I am Azize, sailing on the wind that will make me a woman.

Face buried against his neck, I ease down, yet stop within moments of starting, breath hissing past my teeth. No one told me this would hurt, and I'd been too shy to ask when Mora blocked my courses. The immediacy of him has me poised between panic and an irrational fear of suffocation.

Kemu groans, arching upward. I slide onto him and a guttural cry tears free.

Thea, let me block the pain. I can make this wonderful.

I nod. Without his help, I may lack the courage.

His mind-touch races across my skin, filling my body with warmth, welcome as fire in winter. My clenched muscles ease as he kisses me, then moves his hips, inviting me to do the same.

This time, when I gasp, it isn't from pain so much as fear of the unknown. With a prayer for courage, I push aside sand, then grasp the small of his back. While his steady breathing reflects a Venari's discipline, mine's a racehorse's as I swing down.

He groans. I stifle a scream of revelation. He moves. I moan.

Trust me. It will be fine.

He pulls back, then sinks into me fully. As he does so, I find my voice. As a lifetime spent following a horse's movement takes over, a shuddering cry ends in his name.

Where is the girl who spent her life in reticence and doubt? This stranger's skin glides over her lover's, urging him to take us wherever we are bound.

I am all in, words gone, worlds gone as he becomes the whole of my universe. My soul cries out, telling him, telling myself, telling the Mother Moon rising above: *Yes, oh, yes!*

The ferocity, unexpected. The instinctual animal nature, welcome. Muscles boil. Sinew dances on bone as my world surges, then collapses in a medley of light. Back arched, I drive to the finish and whimper upon reaching the stepping-off place.

I throw myself into the void, and cry out as he fills me with the potential of radiant life, and his voice joins mine.

Incoherent with the splendor of union, I exalt.

I am a woman!

I wind my arms around his neck and kiss him even. He rolls me onto my back and murmurs my name. With Heaven this close, I am ready to ride again.

My legs around his waist have the desired effect. He groans and rises again. In every sense, this man is now my mate. As he seats himself inside me, our hearts thunder in a wild, matched rhythm while we race for the precipice beyond which freedom waits.

His sweat-covered body shudders as he once more offers me the possibility of life.

I hold him and love him, our spirits coursing as we meld into the other. At long last, I am home, where he ends, and I begin unclear. This is the reason we fight to live, so that we may achieve this union, this ecstasy, this completion.

With my face nestled in the crook of his neck, his husky voice is as much sensation as sound. "Thea, look."

He lifts my hand to the backdrop of the surging sea where light dances across our limbs. The ruin of my birthmark glows, not with starlight, but with a Luna's shimmer.

"My love, this magic isn't mine. It's yours, that, or the Mother's blessing."

His lips cover mine.

I promise myself to ask more about this, only later.

TWENTY-SEVEN

RIDE LIKE A POET

I 've seen women entangled in love's spell, yet never believed I'd join their sisterhood.

Today, I rode like a poet. Every shift in the saddle, a lyrical stanza in celebration of love. My hands on the reins, gentle as if they were spider silk.

All of my training horses have rejoiced with me, including my latest conquest, Silver. I think 'canter,' and he lofts into a depart.

Outside my round pen, Dree, and Rafi beam. Beside them, an older Covener in a deep bronze tunic nods approval as I halt the colt beside them.

Dree can't stop smiling. "Did he feel as good as he looked?"

I nod while dismounting, then reach for the girth.

The Covener holds up her hand. "If you wouldn't mind, I'd like to try Silver."

Rafi extends his arm in a gracious invitation. "Be our guest, Lady Edan."

A croft head, here?

Even as I ask myself this, she slides between the rails, then greets the colt, who wuffles her hair, cut shorter than most men's. With practiced ease, she swings up and puts him through his paces. Unruffled by the change in riders, Silver does everything asked of him.

I whisper to Rafi. "Mind if I go for water?"

Gaze intent on Edan, he nods permission.

Idry isn't in the pavilion. Odd enough any day, but startling considering the crimson-robed member of the Mother's Order who sits at one of the tables. The silver in her waist-length hair suggests she could be in her late forties or fifties.

As I fill a beaker with water, she closes her book.

"As suspected, you impressed Edan enough to try the colt. So, Thea, how do you find life in Azalaïs?"

"Odd."

"As do I. Were it not for the races, I'd be at Land's End, doing something more edifying than reading. Still, love is wonderful, isn't it?"

Refilled beaker halfway to my lips, I gape at her. Does she guess, or know, what happened last night?

She smiles at my amaze. "The first time I saw Edan, I thought the sun had risen in the west. Nothing made sense, yet everything did. Was it the same for you?"

I shake my head. Despite her light touch, I sense deep currents run below this woman's placid surface. "Lady, how is it you know what few others do?"

"With Edan insisting on our attending the fall races, I've watched you for many years. Mind you, never like today, in total harmony with your horse. Have you known your beloved long?"

I force my answer. "Since childhood."

"Ahh, and how will that play out, a Venari and an outcast?"

I'm still slack-jawed when Rafi enters, then tosses me a pouch I catch one-handed.

"Edan just bought Silver, but is keeping him in training with you."

He shakes his head at my blank expression. "Five of the gold coins in that pouch are yours. As Silver's trainer, you get your share of the commission. Buy better clothes."

I glance at my shirt. Though clean, it's seen better days.

He scrawls a note for Idry, then weighs it down with the pouch. "Idry will give you a note of credit, which is safer than carrying gold. Stay put. Dree needs to sign Silver's papers and wants to thank you."

Smile well-content, he heads for the colt's new owner, who now speaks with Dree.

Just like that, all my money problems, solved.

The Mother's Own smiles at my bemusement, then pats the bench beside her. "Sit. I'm Kylin."

I do, but across from her. Having worked horses since dawn, I am in dire need of a bath.

At ease with a rider's life, my not accepting her invitation creates no ripples. "May I see your Luna?"

I contain my aversion to her kind, then slide my hand across the table.

She brushes a fingertip over the burn scars sullying my birthmark. "Tragic, the damage a small-minded girl did to a gift from the Mother of All. Have you kept its Covenant and harmed none?"

"I have, other than the self-damage done, lying to protect my sire and brother."

"As Mora suspected. The Sada miss her greatly."

"Is she well, Lady?"

"Yes, and speaks of you often."

My sigh is bittersweet. "Had I heeded her counsel, rather than this . . .," I gesture to our surroundings, ". . . I'd be a journeywoman healer and citizen now."

"True, and your plight causes Mora no end of anxiety. So much so, she seeks to craft a path that will let you become an A'talan citizen."

As I absorb this astounding news, Kemu rides into the yard. In a heartbeat, I'm on my feet, and fighting the urge to race to him.

Kylin waves me on. "Go. The Mother will never stand in the way of true love."

The world disappears as we kiss, and my tension falls away. It takes Gamar bathing our faces in hot horse breath to break us apart.

Kemu pushes the big bay away. "Sorry about that. He insists on being part of everything I do."

"Yet, last night . . ."

Kemu grins. "I didn't feed him, so he'd graze. He needs water. Come with us?"

Arm-in-arm, we head for one of the yard's many oak-shaded troughs.

Gamar drinks deep, then raises his head, eyes bright while taking in all the activity, which includes Edan and Rafi speaking softly while coming our way.

Rafi shakes his head. "Nor do I look forward to when it all goes to hell, and it will. An outcast and Gayleen a'Rowan's rising star? It'll never work."

Kemu's eyes narrow with no small fury as he thrusts Gamar's reins into my hand. "Please, stay here."

He meets the pair midway and makes reverence to Edan, who smiles and keeps walking. Rafi, he steps into. "A moment, please."

The two Venari stand toe-to-toe, their arms thankfully crossed. Rafi's expression is that of a closed door.

Edan pays them no mind and rests her hand on my shoulder. "I cannot wait to work with you."

It would be an understatement to say she doesn't have my full attention. "Ahh, why?"

"Ask Sojur a'Sada a question, and you get a polite answer that seems astute, but upon reflection, proves empty as a hollow gourd. Through you, I hope to gain insight into your teacher's methods."

"That's the reason you bought Silver?"

"Yes, that and unlike the horses you and I love, Silver's biddable. Should he remain a gentleman, I'll turn him out with a select band of mares next spring. He could be the perfect sire for the sort of mounts we need for Coveners who aren't raised riding."

What she says about Silver seems possible, yet I question whether Sojur wants his methods shared. Even as I consider voicing my reservations, Kemu comes our way, his stride that of a man who's had his say.

Rafi follows with a pissed expression that paints scorn across Kemu's sword-crossed back.

Just what I need: the two most important men in my life, at odds with each other.

As Rafi escorts Edan into the pavilion, Kemu turns his back on them, then breathes a kiss over my temple. "I love you, and hope to share your life. Know that Gayleen is my problem, not yours, whatever anyone else says."

Have I made a world-class mistake, condemning myself to Enya's lot, yearning for a man who can only be with me on rare occasions?

No, not possible.

I rise on tiptoes and kiss him.

Let them speculate. Let them gossip and predict. Little as I know of this man, I know I love him, and pray for the day I can say so to his face.

TWENTY-EIGHT

SWAGGER AS IF ASCENDED

A zize plummets, her golden talons outstretched. Moments later, an unsuspecting shorebird's life ends in a flurry of speckled feathers.

Woe betides any vermin that dares cadge grain at Rafi's. Khalil's cranky little hawk has turned into the yard's darling. So much so, there's a running bet on her daily tally.

When offered a long rein, my training horse blows, stride relaxed despite the spindrift bobbling along the beach. When we first arrived, the shifting clumps of sea foam justified spectacular leaps and feints. Now, with the silly out of her system, I delight in the sea's glory as we trot along the shore.

Three riders crest the rise between us and Azalaïs.

I swear, and not under my breath. It's Seth and Hemming, accompanied by a man of truly immense proportions. Absorbed in their conversation, none look my way.

The damage I did to Aaron's son is nothing short of astounding. His bruised eyes look as if outlined in kohl. The swelling on the bridge of his nose has yet to subside.

Busy talking, they don't see Azize on the beach ahead of them.

My sire's brat bird has no intention of abandoning her meal. She continues to eat till they are almost upon her. At the last possible moment, she rises, wings a blur while blasting through their horses' legs, and screaming abuse.

It's a toss-up if any will stay in the saddle.

I stifle laughter even while seeking an escape route.

Moments later, Azize slams into my wrist bracer. She chitters at me as if I were the one who almost trampled her.

As she grouses, I start up the nearest dune, with no idea of what's on the other side.

Hemming gets his mount under control, then points my way.

Seth sees it's me, his battered face twisting into a snarl. Sword drawn, he comes at a gallop, even as Hemming and the fat man yell at him to stop.

My mare bounds up the ridge. Upon reaching the soft sand near the top, she sinks to her knees. I sling Azize into the air, and wince as her pinions crack me across the face.

Seth reaches the dune, and comes out of his saddle, unlike my mare, able to traverse the treacherous sand at a run.

There's nothing for it. I dive off my saddle, but one of my boots catches in the stirrup. As I seek to free it, Seth's blade slices into the saddle's seat, lodging in the tree below. His face that of a madman, Seth yanks back so hard, he topples my mare onto her side. A boot to her ribs frees the sword. He vaults over the frantic mare and stabs where I was only moments before.

I lurch up the hill, hardly able to walk, much less run in the shifting sand.

"Bitch, you're dead!"

Seth's taller and stronger than I am. Every stride carries him farther and faster. I snatch at the sea grasses making their meager living here, and seek to drag myself onto higher, sounder ground. It's all too easily imagined, my lifeblood soaking into this sand, then come high tide, my body washing out to sea.

Steel slices a handbreadth away from my left foot. I shriek, hurtling the opposite direction, only to lose my footing, and sprawl face-first in the sand.

Seth's knees slam into my back, and he roars with laughter as I scream. Grabbing a fistful of my hair, he yanks my head back, then slams my face into the sand. "This is for Cinna."

He punches the back of my head, further rattling my already dazed brains. "And this is for my nose, and making me look the fool before my father."

Again, he pounds my face into the sand.

"And this is for watching your narrow ass pull ahead of me and my racehorses, time, after time, after time."

The sun paints a shadow of Seth on the sand as he draws back his sword arm. Soul consigned to the Mother of All, I wrap my arms around my head.

Something hot and sticky splatters onto my skin. The pressure on my back eases, and I roll onto my side.

Rafi has a belt knife to Seth's throat, from which blood trickles. "Drop the sword or I will happily end your worthless life."

Seth does as ordered, for which Rafi fists his hair, then drags him screaming off me. "Thea, get our horses up on the top of that ridge."

I do so, walking backward, unwilling to miss a moment of such delicious justice.

As the mares clear the two opponents, Rafi grabs Seth's ear like an errant child's. "Asshole, that's my rider you almost killed, and my godsdamned saddle you ruined. You want this sword back, get your unappreciated ass to Gardan's and pay for its replacement. I'll give you till tomorrow. Don't, and I'll sell this blade to the highest bidder, then pay Gardan, and give Thea what's left."

The gemstones in the hilt would buy three, maybe four steads.

"You can't . . ."

Seth's protest ends with a grunt of pain when Rafi slams the sword hilt upside his head. "I can and will. Whether I do is up to you."

He shoves Seth's face into the sand, then keeps him there with a knee between his shoulders. "Stay away from my riders and yard. Stay away from our horses or, as Heaven is my witness, I will end your miserable life."

He clouts the back of Seth's skull with his fist, then swarms up the rise and onto his ruined saddle. "Let's get the hells out of here."

I glance over my shoulder before the ocean disappears from view.

Hemming has an arm around Seth's shoulders. Their enormous companion remains a'horse. His canny expression suggests he believes an opportunity may arise from this debacle.

Rafi grunts in disgust. "Can't wait till Seth figures out just how far beyond the pale I went. Are you alright?"

I wobble my hand. "So-so. Who's the fat man?"

"Vitrine, an esteemed purveyor of perversions and whore-monger to the corrupt rich. Don't let him anywhere near you. He could charm the skin off a snake. So, how did this mess come to be?"

"That threesome almost ran Azize down. Before I could get gone, my mare sank into the sand."

"Let me guess, those assholes were too busy talking to look where they were going."

"Basically."

Now that it's over and we're headed back into town, the shaking starts. My skin goes clammy and stomach contracts so hard, there's barely time to lean sideways before it empties.

Rafi grabs my arm, keeping me upright as I suck air into my lungs. While doing so, Azize returns to her perch on my saddle swell, and gives me the stink eye.

"You rotten, godsdamned bird. You'll be the death of me."

She faces forward, patently ignoring me.

Rafi dry-laughs. "Good thing you didn't ascend. You don't have the stones for battle."

I hold out a still-trembling hand. "You think?"

"I do, and will say this again. Your a'Shara did you a favor, casting you out. Can you get back to the yard by yourself? I want to drop this saddle off at Gardan's so he can start its replacement."

I nod, offended with my weakness.

"Good. Done riding for the day?"

"Yes."

"Put my horse away, and I'll do the same for yours when I return."

He tries for a smile, but it comes out more of a grimace. "How about we become each other's seconds? After humiliating Aaron's asshole son, Heaven knows I'll need someone watching my back."

"A second who trembles and pukes after a fight?"

"You'll get a grip on it."

I cough a laugh. "I'll do my best, such as it is."

"Your best will be more than enough."

I watch till Rafi's out of sight before heading in the opposite direction. He can't take Sahain's place, but his offer comes when most needed.

Upon reaching the yard, I'm still off balance, so much so that when riders call out, asking how Azize did, the best I can do is raise three fingers.

With the little hawk in her mews and Rafi's training horse groomed, then stabled, I head for the gathering area.

Idry's head down, immersed in the paperwork that consumes most of his day.

"Idry, have you seen Ainee? Silver needs another day's worth of poultice."

He shakes his head, then leans back in his chair, and shouts with unexpected volume. "Does anyone know where Ainee is?"

No one has an answer till all have spoken. The last to see her was Idry, two days ago.

He looks back to me. "This isn't like her. Do you know the herbwoman, Nahla?"

I nod. She and Mora are friends.

"Ask her if she's seen Ainee. Before you go, this just arrived from Solara."

Wax over black and gold ribbons seal the stiff envelope. A family could eat for a week on the cost.

I crack the seal, read, then hand the page to Idry.

As he reads, he misses my lack of enthusiasm. "I'll be damned. Aaron's making good on his word. After what Seth did to her, will this filly run?"

I shrug, fearing after today, Cinna may not live long enough to leave Solara.

Idry pulls a tallen from the pouch on his writing table and tosses it to me. "Seeing as I'm sending you on a yard errand, perhaps something will catch your fancy."

I smile my thanks, then make my way to the marketplace.

Each racing season, Pell would bring us here, not that we had need of anything. We had each other. We had our father. I was the odd one out, laughing at Sahain's lame jokes, eager for what the day would bring. The reminder of us swaggering as if the toughest thing in boot leather re-opens a wound I doubt will ever heal.

The sun-warmed, sweet-tart scent of apricots wafts my way. I follow it to the source, where a card in a basket declares the price as six coppers. After losing so much food, I give the vendor Idry's tallen.

"How many do you want?"

I cup my hands.

Eyes wide at my burn scars, he fills a bag, then hands it to me.

I take a bite, and moan as honeyed sun-ripened fruit floods my mouth.

"Like them, eh?"

With a full mouth, the best I can manage is a nod amidst pocketing the coppers he returns.

"Girl, a word to the wise. From here on out, count your change."

Reticent of outsiders, I've avoided these sorts of exchanges. I can only hope my shy smile makes up for a silent departure.

Inept as I am while dealing with strangers, Kane saved us all from starvation by taking us to Rafi's.

As I approach the herb woman's kiosk, Nahla sees me coming.

She purses her wrinkled lips. "What do you want, a'Sada?"

She sees my lack of marks, thus nicks a vein intentionally. I smile as if that weren't so, and hold out the bag of apricots.

"Idry sent me to ask if you've seen Ainee."

She takes two apricots, pops one into her mouth, and chews. "Idry, eh? Tell that cheap boss of yours if he wants someone reliable to come see me."

If Ainee's found another patron, Rafi may have to court, then deal with Nahla. I incline my head and make reverence. "I'll give him your message."

"You do that." She spits out the pit, then points to a narrow alleyway. "When Ainee shows up, that's where she arrives."

A customer approaches. Like an a'Shara, Nahla waves dismissal at me. If forced to buy from her, Rafi's in for a serious drubbing.

Crossing the square is a game of duck and weave. People yell greetings while others hawk wares, then bargain hard. I aim for the tall, mud-brick building that casts shadows over my destination. Their chill raises gooseflesh when I enter the alley.

The deeper I go, the worse it gets. Rotten food, broken barrels, unraveled baskets, then the body of a starved dog. No matter Ainee's threadbare clothing, her attitude never suggested such depths of despair.

Sleeve across my nose, I pick up the pace, peering into nooks and crannies. While giving thought to turning back, I spot a body lying in a thin ray of sunshine, curls tangled over her face, legs tucked like a foal.

"Ainee?" I kneel and rest a hand on her shoulder. It's cold as snow.

When she doesn't wake, I work my arms under her, brace, and rise. No Venari ascends if they can't carry an injured companion to safety.

As I leave the stinking labyrinth of discards behind, people see what's in my arms and part.

I bellow Nahla's name, who sees my burden and sweeps her goods into a basket. Together, we ease Ainee onto the table's planks.

Her breathing's fast and shallow, her skin paper white.

Nahla runs her hands along Ainee's torso, then frowns upon reaching her belly. "Thea, by the melon vendor. Quick, get Hilen."

I bull past anyone who doesn't move out of my way.

Ever imposing, amidst her kitchen staff, Hilen conveys sufficient authority to lead an ulan, for which I make reverence.

"Nahla's asking for you."

The Sun's head cook thrusts her purse into a companion's hands. "Not a copper more, understood? The rest of you, with me."

We follow Hilen's crowd-dispersing wake.

Nahla has Ainee wrapped in a mantle. She begins talking before we reach them. "Hilen, this child needs a surgeon. Will Enya let us use the Sun's mederi?"

Hilen gestures to her four sturdiest kitchen boys. "You, you, you and you, grab a corner of the table top and go." Picks an older boy next. "Find a healer." Turns to a taller girl. "Stay with Nahla's things and explain why she's gone. The rest of you, divvy up my shopping. Tell any vendor, overcharge, and I'll be back tomorrow to take double the difference out of their hides. Off with you, now!"

Her crew makes a start of sorting out who's doing what.

As I turn to go, Nahla snags my wrist.

"Mora's always bragging about your stitching skills. If a Covenant surgeon can't reach the Sun in time, I'll need your help."

I put years into becoming Venari, all for naught.

"What can I carry?"

Nahla cackles while gesturing to a pair of laden bags. "You walked Ainee out. Surely you can hoist these."

I draw the straps over my shoulders, tighten my belly muscles, and straighten.

Nahla's eyebrows arch in approval. Moments later, she's plowing through the crowd, counting on me to keep pace with her.

I do.

TWENTY-NINE
THE PRICE OF A HORSE

A wall of windows illuminates Ainee's naked body in the Sun's mederi. I've never been one for flesh, but this child looks starved. With her consciousness blocked by a mindhealer, she can't explain how this came to be.

One of the two Covenant surgeons examining Ainee straightens. "Nahla, good thing you sent for us. This child's intestines have ruptured."

The herb woman's lips thin in subdued gratification. "I would have preferred being mistaken, Lord Karlis."

What were the chances? The boy Hilen sent for a healer returned with the head of Mora's croft, likely here early for the fall races.

Lord Karlis looks my way. "Wash up. Mora says you're an asset during surgery. We may need an extra set of hands. Maret, let's begin."

I strip down to cami and leggings. Scrub my arms and hands while Nahla binds my hair, then holds open a smock for me.

They've made the first incision by the time I join them.

Maret gestures to the clamps holding back Ainee's skin. "You've done this before?"

I nod.

"I'll show you where I want each clamp placed." As she speaks, muscles part beneath Lord Karlis' blade. Maret wipes away the blood, then points to where she wants the skin clamped.

Down they go, layer by layer, with Maret keeping the field clear for Lord Karlis. He doesn't pause till reaching a film of milky tissue, beneath which intestine coils like snakes. "Breathe shallow. This will reek."

The stench of rotten meat billows into the room: bad as a body nine days dead. Even after a lifetime of cleaning game, I'm repulsed.

Karlis angles into the cavity, clamps a bloated tag of gut, then cuts through it.

Maret floods the area with cleansing tincture, then sops up the resulting mess of blackened blood and pus. The process is nasty as it is necessary. "Thea, do as I am."

Not wanting to harm Ainee's insides, I keep my touch bridle-light. We flood, sop, and toss wads of sodden wool into nearby basins, till Lord Karlis holds up a restraining hand.

With a clean tool, he seeks, but finds no corruption. "We can close."

They stitch the cut edges back together, their focus complete, movements precise. When the repair holds without bleeding, they share a smile. Next up comes reassembling the milky tissue, then layers of muscle. Familiarity lets them work without words, that or they bespeak each other.

When skin is all that's left, Lord Karlis hands me a threaded needle and pair of scissors. "Show me the skill Mora brags about."

If she seeks to create a path to citizenship for me, it could be through apprenticeship with this man. If so, now is the time to impress. I march a line of stitches, needle in, then out, knot made, and snipped while closing the incision. This is effortless compared to sprawled over a hobbled horse, ducking teeth and hooves.

Maret dabs a cleansing tincture over my finished line of stitches, then holds the back of her hand to Ainee's cheek. "Her fever's down."

Karlis affirms Maret's assessment. "Nahla, the infusion, please."

She hands him a cup. "Any changes you want, I can formulate."

He smiles. "As always, our thanks for your expertise."

Twenty years his senior and still, Nahla blushes. "For you, Lord Karlis, always my best."

As the surgeons ease the liquid down Ainee's throat, I gather the soiled tools for cleaning. While doing so, a knock at the outer door precedes a smiling Enya. "For those who can tarry, refreshments await in the gardens."

Nahla makes a beeline for Enya.

Lord Karlis acknowledges the invitation, then replaces his blood-spattered smock with a tunic and surcoat. "Maret, you'll set a schedule for the mindhealers?"

"I will, and should you prefer staying with the patient, I can represent our croft at tonight's Council of Covenants."

"Please do."

She turns my way. "Now that I've seen you in action, I know why Mora hopes you will apprentice with us."

I answer with an uncertain smile, wondering if Lord Karlis feels the same. As a Covenant healer, Pell couldn't keep me off the grasslands. Kemu and I could be together.

The healers trade the mederi for its balcony overlooking the gardens, their conversation too soft to overhear.

Once dressed, I return to Ainee's side. Even through a sheet, her ribs resemble a scavenger-picked carcass. She shouldn't be this thin. Rafi's cheap, but he pays.

My order of go for what's left of the day: tell Rafi what's happened, where Ainee is, then find her family.

I exit onto the balcony where Lord Karlis stands alone, his hands on the half-wall, surveying Enya's gardens with their riot of roses.

Typical of Coveners, his hair's close-cropped and face clean-shaven. It's within this man's ability to solve the many complications Kemu and I face. Still, a comparison to Pell comes all too easily.

When I join him at the balcony railing, he offers me a distant smile. "This is my first visit to the Sun. No wonder your father brings the Sada here."

He faces me, his expression unreadable. "Tell me, did you give any thought to the consequences of accepting your sire's stallion?"

In a heartbeat, I'm back on the grasslands. Mora presses her hands to her heart as my unavoidable choice ruins everything.

"All Mora's children and grandchildren, a credit to her upbringing, yet you slipped through her fingers like the red sands of your birth."

Mouth swimming with salt, I beg my stomach, please, not twice in one day and not before this man. Moments later, I'm on my knees, spewing apricots.

As I collapse in the shadows of the half-wall, he goes for water, which he holds to my lips.

"Mind you, only a sip. Will there be more?"

I shake my head, albeit cautiously.

"Mora says this happens when you're under pressure. I'll tell Nahla how to make the tincture Mora used."

I wish Mora were here now, rather than bespeaking him.

He crouches, pushes aside my bangs, then places his palm on my forehead. "I began my studies as a mindhealer, only to discover the mechanics of the body fascinated me more than the oddities of the mind. Ainee lives here."

A vision forms in my head of a wreck of a barn, its doors akimbo in a weedy field.

He removes his hand. "You'll find her family there. It's due east, perhaps a half hour's walk."

I swallow hard, ill at ease. "Is that permitted? Taking an image from one person's mind, then showing it to another?"

"It is, so long as I keep the Covenant, weighing whether my actions help or harm. In my estimation, why a child is a walking skeleton begs an answer."

He looks to my burn scars. "Regrettable, the timing. Mora's heart and Pell casting you out. Had you remained in her care, those burns would have turned out better."

He lifts me to my feet, then makes certain of my balance before letting go. "For some inexplicable reason, Mora misses you. Visit her when racing is over. See the wonders of Land's End."

He reads my lack of trust with ease. "Refresh my memory. What is Pell's favorite adage?"

The casual cruelty with which he reminds me of all I've lost comes as a welcome reminder. I draw myself erect.

"Stand strong. Never show weakness."

He starts down the stairs, his voice growing softer as the distance between us increases. "Heed your father, Thea."

Which one? The man who made me, then gave me up, or the man who raised me?

No matter. No way will I ask anything of this covener.

THIRTY

BEGGAR AT A FEAST

Ainee lives in a barn, its roof swayed as an old horse's back?

I look to the boy at Kham's side. "You last saw people here . . .?"

"A few days ago."

In the surgeon's vision, this place didn't look so desolate. The windows lack shutters. Broken beams pierce ancient thatching.

"What did this used to be?"

"A dairy. Sorry, I must leave. My da' will pitch a fit if I'm not home in time for chores."

I raise a hand in distracted thanks.

Before leaving the Sun, a kitchen worker gave me the saddlebags now on my pommel: food packed by Hilen, paid for by Lord Karlis. His generosity did nothing to alter my opinion of the surgeon. Thanks to his 'directions,' it took me hours to find this place. With Kane bringing Cinna tonight,

I must return to the yard. Return tomorrow if I can't find anyone?

Crickets thrum, birds chirp in dusty-leaved trees, an erratic breeze tosses the weeds while Kham snaps at flies biting his flanks. And still, there's no sign of anyone besides us in this broken-down stead.

On the grasslands, we had no poor. We had lazy. We had shiftless, but with Pell at the helm, not for long. He made their lives such misery that all gained a willingness to work. Were the problem luck, lost stock, or illnesses, everyone pitched in. As I suspect Ainee has, to her detriment.

Her family could be wary of a 'Daharshan' rider on a Daharshan warhorse. To make my intent clear, I pull a loaf of bread from the saddlebags. Having lost two meals already, and missing another, the fresh-baked aroma has my belly grumbling.

The barn teeters between happenstance and despair. Dangling off its hinges, a ramshackle door frames a patch of light, into which a little boy steps. He's perhaps nine or ten years old. Eyes huge in a face defined by hunger, he stands poised to flee.

I lower the bread till within easy reach. Despite that, he hesitates, a wild animal weighing the risk. My immobility tips the scales. I whisper, "Ameen, Kham," as he pelts our way.

The boy snatches the bread, then disappears back into the barn's gloomy interior. His fear has my heart skipping a beat.

Crickets *cheep, cheep, cheep* as I display a second loaf.

Just when I think he's gone for good, he reappears. At his side, a smaller child gnaws on the bread. Both look like starved chicks, ready to flee from any threat. Good thing I didn't bring Azize.

A third boy joins them, maybe thirteen, or fourteen, with a scowl on his face and sturdy staff in hand. Just as thin, just as ragged as the others. He signals the little ones to stay put, then swaggers our way.

"Is that for them?" He points to the bread in my hand.

I nod.

The bones in his face remind me of a fox, eyes angled, and skin tight to the bone. "Why are you here?"

"Ainee."

His hands fist. "Is she alright?"

"When she didn't show up at Rafi's, Idry sent me looking for her."

I steady Kham as the boy takes an aggressive step closer. "Did you find her?"

"Yes, in an alley, barely alive. Covenant healers had to open her belly to fix what was wrong."

He grips the staff, knuckles stark. "Will she heal?"

"Land's End's best surgeon said she'll be fine."

The breath he's been holding escapes. "Sometimes she stays with friends in Azalaïs. I didn't start worrying till this morning."

He gestures for the other children. They come at a run as I dismount.

Kham nudges the giggling bread-snatcher, who strokes his neck with grimy hands.

I mouth to the eldest: *Boy or girl?*

"Girl, Mina." He points to the littlest. "Eisa." Himself. "Mahir."

Mina's entranced with Khamsin. I get it. At her age, horses took precedence over everything, including food.

I sink to the ground, passing out bread, fruit, and cheese.

Were this trio my brothers and self, about now squabbling would break out. Arguments over who got the karakal's share. All of us oblivious to the privileges we took for granted.

Mina has her arm around Kham's front leg while eating with the other. Mahir feeds Eisa before he takes anything for himself. Me? I'm the beggar at their feast of love.

I gesture to Mina's hair. "So, no one would know she's a girl?"

Mahir grins. "Yes, not that it worked with you."

This comment has me wondering if he's older than his build suggests. "So, no parents, aunts, or uncles?"

He shakes his head no.

"How long have you been on your own?"

"Three years." Plainly, this isn't a topic he wants prodded.

"Why not ask the Covenant for help?"

His face goes tight with rage. "The same bastards who had our parents marched away in chains? Who seized our racing stock and stead to pay their debts?"

My eyes go wide. "Where are they now?"

"Indentured, who knows where. We walked days before finding this place, Eisa, just a year old, in my arms. Ainee and Mina carrying what little the Covenant left us."

So much for the Covenant's vaunted dedication to the Mother and Father of All. What was done to this family fits my definition of barbaric.

Mahir falls silent as they seek to fill stomachs unable to hold everything Hilen sent. Eisa is the first to finish. He scoots closer, then points to my birthmark.

"Mama's Blessing?"

"Yes, the Mother of All."

He crawls into my lap, and finding a welcome there, nestles. It's clear his siblings have put all they could spare into their littlest. Equally clear is my awkwardness around children. I missed something important by not spending more time with my younger crèche brothers.

"When everyone's done eating, I can take you to see Ainee."

Mahir looks to the sky. "Will we get back before dark?"

"Doubtful. You can bunk with me at Rafi's tonight."

At his nod of agreement, I hand him Eisa, then rise. "Mina, can you ride?"

She answers by grabbing the saddle horn and swinging up. When she scoots back, Mahir lifts Eisa onto her lap. While Mahir retrieves his staff, I fasten Hilen's saddlebags behind the children.

Mahir falls in alongside me as we head for Azalaïs.

Between a full belly and the sway of Kham's walk, Eisa's soon asleep in his sister's arms. For a chance to ride a horse like Kham, Mina would keep her eyes open with twigs. Mahir, I can't read. Despite the load he's carried for so long, he keeps his burdens close.

The Venari precept, others before self, urges me to help this broken family.

However little I have to offer, I will.

THIRTY-ONE

ROCK-SOLID NO

E nya insisted on baths and clean clothing before allowing
Ainee's siblings into the Sun's airy mederi. Throughout,
their eyes remained huge: for their sleeping sister and after that,
for the meal Hilen provided in the gardens.

Their awe only grew upon reaching the yard, while meeting
those riders yet to leave for supper. Fit, easy-going men who
may remind them of their indentured father, even as I may
remind them of their mother, odd as that thought is.

As Rafi descends the stairs of his apartment above the
pavilion, I gesture for the children to turn. "And this is Rafi
a'Falili, this yard's owner and head rider."

Mahir bows. "Sir, we are forever in your debt."

His manners suggest there's more to the children's story
than privation.

Rafi takes them in, especially how Mina clings to Khamsin.
"Where will they spend the night?"

"With your permission, in my loft."

"That'll be fine so long as you're here to watch over them."

I groan for what this renders impossible.

From behind Mahir's legs, Eisa peers up at the one-eyed man.

Rafi pretends not to see him. "When will Ainee be back on her feet?"

"There wasn't a chance to ask, but I suspect it won't be soon."

I can easily imagine his thoughts. For now, Nahla is his only option. At the sound of hoofbeats, I turn, expecting Kane. I smile, delighted at the puzzling sight of Kemu on a bedroll-festooned Gamar.

No sooner than he comes to earth, and I'm in his arms, kissing him. The day's been interminable, apart.

He laughs, framing my face between his broad hands. "You missed me?"

"How could I not?"

We share another breath-stealing kiss, only to break it off when the riders' catcalls begin.

"What's with all the bedding?"

He grins. "What's with the crèche you just acquired?"

"It's nothing so formal. I'm just trying to . . ."

He holds up a hand, silencing me. "Mora bespoke me about Ainee's siblings. Was I right about them staying here tonight?"

When I nod, he passes me a bedroll, and takes the rest himself. Children in tow, we climb my stairs.

Little as I have, there's plenty of room. While laying out the beds, Rafi's whistle draws me to the loft's half-wall. Cinna trots alongside the one-horse cart as Kane steers through the gates.

"Kemu, stay with the children while I see to my new horse?"

He nods, at ease with the request. I leave him to it, my boot heels clattering down the stairs.

Kane tosses me Cinna's lead, then gestures to the polished trunks in the back of the cart. "With his Lordship's compliments: Cinna's saddle, bridle, blankets, and grooming tools."

Rafi grabs one trunk and Kane the other, then head for my stalls.

In the setting sun, Cinna's copper hindquarters glisten with ointment.

"Hey, mare, remember me?"

Forelock flying, she flips her head, then rests it on my shoulder.

Her sweetness makes the potential for disaster even greater. When Aaron gets word of what Rafi did today, he may reclaim Cinna. The thought of her near Seth now fills me with dread.

I lead Cinna into the empty stall beside my Daharshans, who whicker a greeting. I'm glad Cinna isn't in heat. Windsong has proven possessive about 'her' stallion.

Cinna grabs a mouthful of hay, then, eyes bright, takes in her new surroundings. As she does so, Rafi and Kane join us.

The coachman leans his elbows on the top rail of her stall. "Good thing she could travel today. Aaron told me what happened this morning."

Naturally, that's when Kemu joins us. "Something happened?"

Rafi answers before I can. "While breezing one of our training horses, Thea crossed Seth's path."

Kemu looks to me. "What happened, and are you all right?"

"A few days, and I'll be fine. No worries. Rafi put Seth on notice."

"What the hells will 'putting him on notice' do?"

I draw him down till we're eye-to-eye. "After which, Rafi beat the crap out of him."

"A'Rowan." The authority in Rafi's voice has Kemu turning his way.

"No sane person does what Seth did today. You have my word that, unless on Kham, Thea isn't riding anywhere without one of us at her side."

Kane clears his throat. "I brought food and wine. How about we move into the pavilion and I tell you what's changed since Thea's visit to Solara."

I look to Kemu. "Are the children all right?"

"They were well on their way to sleep when I left."

Kane's brows crunch together. "What children?"

Again, Rafi beats me off the line. "Long story short, our herb girl went missing. Thea found her deathly ill, got her to a healer, then found her starving siblings and brought them here. I'll feed and water Kane's team if the rest of you take the food and wine to the pavilion."

The coachman passes us two large baskets, then hefts a case of wine.

As we enter the pavilion, Kane bellows. "Idry, join us!"

While we unpack the food, Kane opens wine.

Overhead, the scribe's apartment door opens. Idry clears the landing, then smiles for the bounty Kane has brought. "Is the filly settled in?"

Kane hands him wine. "Like she was born here, thank the stars."

Rafi joins us, and Kane raises his glass. "Let's drink to last year's Champion of Champions, now this year's champion of innocents."

Despite my embarrassment, I give thanks for friends who ease my ever-present melancholy over the family and home I've lost.

Sensing my mood, Kemu pats the bench, inviting me to sit beside him.

As I do so, Kane continues, his words and tone carefully crafted.

"A condition of employment at Solara is what happens there, stays there. I can tell you this much. Were Cinna Aaron's only racehorse, she'd still be Thea's."

He looks to me. "Her transfer's filed at the track, and in the courts. You'll have her papers soon."

Kemu takes my hand. "Kane, how much danger does Seth pose to Thea and to the yard?"

"If the story of Rafi humiliating him spreads, all bets are off."

Hand to aching forehead, I meet Kane's concerned gaze. "In short, I can't race Cinna?"

"Doing so would expose you to immense danger. That said, Aaron would rejoice if she ran."

I groan, for which Kemu whispers into my ear. "Straddle the bench. I'll ease the hurt."

He blocks my aches, then massages the knots between my shoulders.

Unaware of how much I'd been guarding against the damage Seth did, I melt into Kemu's touch.

Rafi narrows his eye at Kemu. "A'Rowan, do we need to be privy to this?"

Kemu doesn't look Rafi's way while running the heel of his hand up my spine. "A'Falili, did you ride eight horses today, then almost lose your life? Carry a child out of Azalaïs' alleys, assist in her surgery, then retrieve her siblings and see to their well-being?"

Rafi grunts, conceding Kemu's motivations might arise from more than intimacy.

I sag against Kemu's chest.

He kisses my cheek. "Any better?"

"Much."

Kane makes the rounds and refills our wine. Only Idry declines, as always, tending toward the austere.

Once all are served, Kemu raises his cup. "Mora, the Mother's Voice who played a large part in Thea's upbringing, just bespoke me with wonderful news. Lord Karlis, head of her croft, has agreed to accept Thea as an advanced apprentice. Thanks to all Mora taught her as a child, her education will take a fraction of the normal time."

My jaw drops.

Immersed in the future he foresees, Kemu doesn't read my qualms. "Think of it, come Years' End, I'll be a Master Mindhealer. We'll see each other often. Once you're a journeywoman healer, the grasslands will be yours again. Who knows, a few years from now and we could start a family. As much as Pell loves children, he may forgive you."

The skepticism on Rafi's face reflects my own. It gives me the strength to go with my gut.

"Healing isn't my path."

Stunned silence greets this statement, for which I add an explanation. "The day Pell cast me out, Sojur said I was a rider, not an archer. And when I got here, Rafi said the same, then added Pell did me a favor in casting me out. Then, there's what happened today."

No matter how ugly, I speak the truth.

"I did not defend myself against Seth. I consigned my soul to Heaven, then went down, and stayed down. War is not my calling, any more than healing. And after what the Covenants' courts did to the children and their parents, I want no part in a system that makes injustice possible. Please excuse me. I need rest."

As I come to my feet, Kemu catches my wrist.

"What aren't you saying?"

In the wake of my silence, he draws my hand to his chest. "Gayleen made this time together possible, yet the moment racing is over, I can't return to Azalaïs till next year. If we are to have a future, Lord Karlis is our only hope."

I go board stiff. "You want to do this before everyone?"

His gaze hoods. "What difference does it make? By tomorrow, the entire city will know."

His being right doesn't make what I have to say any easier.

"Mora did her best to make me a healer, but the idea of suffering through Lord Karlis' judgment turns my stomach. Not only did he blame me for Mora's heart, he gave no credence to the sacrifice I made by setting my sire and brother's lives ahead of my own."

I take a deep breath. "As for our future together, Rafi gave me sound advice. He said any man who wanted to be with me would do whatever it took, including setting aside his own agenda."

I reclaim my hand, then back away. "Whether we have a future is up to you."

As I make reverence, Idry rises. "I'll come with you. I want to check on the children."

A pierced lantern's soft lighting illuminates my loft. Eisa lays curled in his big brother's arms, both of them sound asleep. Mina is on my bed with her face buried in my pillow.

Expression pleased by the peaceful scene, Idry gestures to the landing. "Let's talk."

We sit side-by-side on the top riser.

"He loves you, body and soul."

I heave a sigh, then swallow my pride. "As I love him, not that he's likely to alter his life path."

There's a pause before Idry speaks again. "Would that be anything like you?"

I groan, conceding his point.

"Both of you, praying for a miracle, yet unable to bring one about. Saddest of all, love that deep rarely comes around."

"You make it sound as if I'm the one ruining everything."

He raises a brow. "You've chosen the children over a man who loves you."

I rear back. "Rafi said the only way they could stay here is if I kept an eye on them."

"And you believed him?"

He chuckles. "He's right. You are gullible."

When I rise, he catches my wrist.

"Let me tell you a story. Rafi and I met while he was scouting for a place to site his yard. He had a dream. I had the means and the business experience. Thus, I went from a man who worked alone to riding with an ex-Venari. Together, we made a team, as could you and Kemu. For once, set aside your stiff-necked pride. Admit how much better life would be with a man like that at your side. If I don't miss my guess, he's on his way out now."

What Idry says is true. I can make out Kemu on Gamar, looking this way.

I give Idry's hand a squeeze, then fly down the stairs.

As I do so, Kemu reins my way.

I leap into his arms. We kiss as he turns out of the yard.

As for the future, tomorrow is another day.

THIRTY-TWO
DESTINY

With the children still sleeping and the day's work yet to begin, I have time to clean Khamsin's saddle. The connection with my sire turns the work into a dream of what might have been yet will never be.

Once the leather gleams, I tackle the silverwork, then buff it to a glow. I'm almost finished when hoofbeats approach the yard. A rider knocks on the gate. I draw the bolt, hoping it's Kemu.

Instead, it's Kylin, riding a sweat-streaked mare. This morning the lady wears the black robes of a Mother's Voice, their hems embroidered with golden ivy. Like Mora, Kylin is one of the few, and for that, I make reverence. "Lady, I didn't realize you spoke for the Mother."

She comes off her horse and grasps my shoulders. "Name of Heaven, why refuse Lord Karlis' offer?"

"I don't want to be a healer, any more than I did as a child."

"You'd be a citizen! Protected by Covenant law and able to move freely! Abandon this foolish dream of becoming Venari. Don't, and you condemn yourself to a foreigner's life."

A Mother's Voice, thrusts her fist into my soul? I back out of her grip.

"Even as a healer, Pell wouldn't tolerate my presence."

"Yet toy with returning to the forefront of racing? Do so, and you confront Pell with the disservice he did to Sojur. The consequences could be dire."

I laugh, a bitter sound. "Damă, Pell a'Sada would admit no such thing. I am dead to the a'Shara for all eternity."

She rubs her forehead as if it pains her. "Remember, my asking if you'd harmed none, and kept the Covenant your birthmark symbolizes?"

I nod.

"Ours is a flawed country. For all the good, there is ample bad. While matters have improved without the monarchy, inequities still exist, as you well know. Why else do Venari die protecting our way of life, while the rest of this country goes unscathed? When children starve, where is the morality in the first one hundred families' wealth? Or how can the Covenant see itself as a good steward when its laws take parents from children for debt?"

I sigh exasperation. "What does any of this have to do with my failing a 'foolish' dream of becoming Venari?"

She gestures to my birthmark. "Is that happenstance?"

"No, it's irony. A motherless child, marked by the Mother of All?"

She steps into me, forcing me to yield or brace. I choose the latter.

She snatches my wrist, thrusting my ruined birthmark into dawn's light. "This 'irony' is the sign of a peacemaker, a healer, an Ah'rēnē whose soul the Mother of All has anointed. Fulfill its destiny, and you will lead your two countries out of war."

I wait for the punchline. It doesn't come. "No way am I an Ah'rēnē."

"In short, you won't accept Lord Karlis's offer?"

"Correct."

"And in its place, you'll let the seven hells take the hindmost over earning a citizen's privileges?"

"If that's what it takes to avoid the Covenant, yes."

"What if this block-headed stance destroys your relationship with Kemu?"

Now I really wonder what's being said behind my back. "Why? Because I can't travel the grasslands?"

As if unable to grasp my lack of comprehension, she sighs. "How strong do you think Kemu is? What must he do to prove his love? Give up everything to be with you?"

While her questions bite, their answers are none of her godsdamned business.

In the wake of my grit-jaw silence, she shakes her head. "I swear you're like talking to a brick. I try saving you from yourself, yet you'll have none of it. Now, thanks to your stubbornness, all too soon, I'll get to pick up the pieces."

She remounts, then reins her mare alongside me. "Till that day arrives, do all of us a favor. Stay alive. Die and this messy, imperfect society will disappear, dust beneath the hooves of your sire's Kian. This entire country, enslaved. Our faith driven underground while the balance of power between your two countries shifts. All because you wouldn't hear reason."

She glares down at me as if her harsh expression will break my will.

When it doesn't, she spins her mare and exits the yard.

I give up on making any sense of what she said, then prepare for my first ride of the day.

Ah'rēnē, my aching ass!

THIRTY-THREE

APRICOTS & A KITTEN

I'm teacup over teakettle, filing one of my training horse's hooves when Mahir's boots step into my field of vision.

"Thea, I can't find Mina."

I straighten and wipe sweat from my brow. "When did you last see her?"

"Idry sent her on an errand an hour ago."

Idry wouldn't send Mina anywhere dangerous, yet the thought of her wandering in this city tightens my belly.

"What is it with your sisters and going missing?"

It doesn't bring the desired smile.

I try again. "Where did Idry send her?"

"To the market, for apricots."

I hand him the filly's lead. "Stable her. I'll find Mina."

When I reach the market, the apricot vendor sees me coming and holds up a bag bulging with fruit. "The girls said something about a kitten and coming right back."

Every time we visit Ainee, Mina won't leave till she finds the Sun's current litter.

"I'll get the apricots after I find them. Which way did they go?"

He hooks a thumb toward the alley behind him.

The deeper I go, the more unsavory the surroundings become. Equally unsettling: the trade in these narrow streets has nothing to do with children and kittens.

Hip-cocked and smile smarmy, a wispy man hails me from a doorway. "For a blue-eyed beauty, only a tallen."

I hold my hand level with my bottom ribs. "I'm looking for a little girl about this tall. She has curly brown hair and is with another girl of the same age."

His kohl-lined eyes widen. "Pretty young for the trade."

"She is my groom." My tone conveys what I think of his assumption.

"No need to be snippy. They went by not long ago."

I take off at a lope. Rough laughter and rougher language add speed to my gait.

The alley opens into a courtyard cluttered with castoffs: baskets more hole than withy and barrels unfit for service. Mina's friend holds a pale orange kitten, the two girls hemmed in by six looming toughs, their backs to a wall.

If I were on Khamsin, this would be over in moments. "Mina, quick, return to the yard."

At her gasp of relief, the men turn my way, their grins predatory. Their moment of inattention gives the girls a much-needed opening. Kitten yowling, they dart past the gauntlet, then disappear the way I came.

The six brutes spread out and flank me, favoring ripe fruit over green.

Certain of how this will play out, I drive my hip into the nearest barrel, its bands rust-laced. The iron cracks on the cobbles, sending clanking metal and oak staves sprawling. As the pack closes in, I snatch two of the staves from the wreckage.

Their leader, his hair greasy and skin pitted, sneers. "Them little hunks of wood supposed to scare us?"

I don't answer, too busy tracking one of his henchmen now edging up behind me. The moment he's within range, I spin.

The first stave catches the thug upside the ear, and the second drops him to the cobbles. Completing the turn, I face the leader again.

"You might reconsider. I left the grasslands only days shy of becoming Venari."

Another of his feral dogs plucks up his courage, coming at me with the inevitability of a falling tree.

I leap, driving my boot heel into his chest. Break one rib, possibly two.

With a groan, he grips his ribs, then staggers after his companions, who now even the odds by racing for the exit.

Their leader draws a forearm-long knife, sharpened to the point of fragility. He flicks it my way, but I stand my ground. Surely, this idiot gets the risk he's taking

Like most bullies, he counts on intimidation, feinting a slash at me, yet doesn't make use of my need to rebalance.

Disgusted, I shake my head. "Cease this nonsense. Tell your lackeys you beat the crap out of me. They'll be none the wiser."

This has him lunging, his blade point aimed at my heart.

I drive one stave onto the knife tip, then whip a turn. Shatter the cheap steel on the brick wall behind me, then complete the rotation with both staves held out at shoulder height. Bone cracks. Blood spurts. Teeth shatter as the man topples face-first onto the cobbles.

I wait, my heart pounding. When he doesn't move, shove a boot under his ribs, lift, then let go. He lands limp as the garbage he is. Staves tossed aside, I head for the market. With any luck, I'll reach the yard before Mina raises the alarm. One thing is certain: from here on out, she's going nowhere without me or Mahir.

The apricot seller sees me coming and holds out the bag of fruit. "The girls tore past so fast, I couldn't stop them."

"No worries. They're headed for Rafi's."

"Please, thank Idry for his trade."

"I will." I wave farewell, then apricots over one shoulder, dart through the crowded marketplace.

Upon reaching the yard, Mina's in the gathering pavilion, shrieking at Rafi.

"Mina, where are your manners?"

She whirls, pelts to me, and throws her arms around my legs. "I've never been so scared."

I stroke her curls. "What about the fright you gave me?"

Mina's new friend cradles the cause of all this uproar, now sound asleep despite the hysterics. "What's the kitten's name?"

"Can we keep her? Tria's mom said no."

"That's up to Rafi, to whom you owe an abject apology." All this, a bit of theater from my childhood: adults dishing a lesson over a meal of crow.

Rafi seconds my displeasure by adding the full weight of censure to his scowl.

At complete odds with moments before, Mina uses her little voice. "Please, Rafi?"

"Please, what? Stuff wool in my ears the next time you scream 'Fire!' After you didn't do as Idry asked, I should say no."

Granted, he's laying it on thick. Still, it's warranted if we're to impress on her there are places in Azalaïs not suitable for people her age.

Horses entering the yard have us all turning.

The same captain who questioned me the night I arrived, leads a full contingent of the watch. His lancers have their spears horizontal, prepared to skewer anyone who doesn't get out of their way.

The yard's riders grab the wide-eyed children and pull them to safety.

As the captain halts his horse a length away, Rafi closes ranks with me. As he does so, the watch parts, letting six riders through: Seth's riding companion Vitrine, and the five thugs who abandoned their leader in the courtyard.

Fat cheeks quivering with indignation, Vitrine points at me. "That's her! She broke my servant's jaw, and then killed him with his own knife! Seize her! These five upstanding citizens saw it all!"

Upstanding citizens, my arse. More likely pimps in Vitrine's pay.

"Care to explain how I murdered someone with a shattered blade?"

His answering smile is that of grease oozing from a roast.

Realization dawns. No knife lays shattered in that courtyard. The blade buried in the dead man belongs to one of these thugs. Bizarre as this thought is, laughter bubbles out of me.

Rafi grips my shoulder. "What the hells is wrong with you?"

The knife sheathed in my boot won't stop a spear, arrow, or sword, but only a stride away lays a solid wood breadboard on a gathering table.

The captain tosses Rafi a sealed order even as a member of his watch dismounts, clanking manacles in hand.

As he reaches for my wrist, I grab the breadboard and swing. For a moment, it looks like he'll stay upright.

As the captain drives his horse into the pavilion, a lance sails past my head. Bowls shatter. Iron-shod hooves mash spiced food into apricots. All this seen in general, with my gaze fixed on the sword point now poised over the notch between my collarbones.

"Ah, at long last, I have your attention."

I call him a name used only on the grassland. My tone, however, that's universal.

I back away, but he rides forward, his laughter low and ugly. "Keep moving, you murdering bitch. I'll happily run you through."

His blade lodges over my heart, for which I still.

"Someone shackle this murdering bitch."

If I were willing to die with the children watching, I'd try taking out the man now, closing manacles around my wrists. Vengeance won't fix what's wrong with this situation. Not with Idry on his knees, his arms around a wailing Mina and Eisa. Not with Rafi restraining Mahir, who curses with a horse person's creativity.

I bellow to be heard over the noise. "I killed no one!"

This brings relative quiet. "Mahir, tell Rafi what the Covenant did to your parents. Idry, please witness my testament. I give all my horses to Rafi a'Falili."

All this accompanied with the sound of Khamsin tearing his stall down, board-by-board.

"AMEEN, KHAM!"

Thankfully, he subsides.

A member of the watch passes a raita between the chains linking my hands. As he does so, I look to Rafi.

"If you sell my horses, please, only to Sojur a'Sada. Better yet, stand Khamsin to stud so you may help the children."

Rafi yells for a saddled horse.

The watchman tosses the raita to the captain, who loops it around his saddle horn, then backs out of the wreckage he created. From beneath his steel helm, he smirks at me. "For your sake, I hope you're fast on your feet."

These words, spoken while spurring his horse into a canter.

No human born can keep pace with a horse.

I am no exception.

THIRTY-FOUR

WORSE YET TO COME

I lay sprawled on a prison cell floor. Everything hurts. My skin is either bloody or raw, and muscles are bruised to the bone. Yet the worst is yet to come.

Damp rot oozes from the walls. Vermin squeak and skitter in the shadows. Amidst all this fetor, the sour stench of my fear reigns supreme. Gone is the maniac who rode her horses above and beyond our abilities. The fighter who, when sparring, went for blood. The Venari-to-be who leapt the Horns of the Bull.

Get up. Show at least a shred of pride.

It won't help. Vitrine's testimony sufficed. Any moment now, they will haul me from this noisome hole and 'elevate' me on a tree of bones.

No Inlooking was offered, nor do I possess the build worthy of ending my days cutting stone in a Covenant quarry. Thus, I am dead. A'talan courts 'remove' murderers from society. And after the sadistic joy the captain took dragging me, it's only a matter of how long I will last, perhaps a day, maybe two.

I pray Rafi keeps Khamsin, and that together, they will earn enough silver to free the children's parents. If so, I will have done some good with my wasted life.

As for me, I'll be a raven-pecked skeleton, bleached bones dancing on sinew, reunited with my beloved brother. Two children of violence, dying the same way we lived.

The memory of Sahain's gentle smile while bidding farewell to life makes for a stark contrast to these vile surroundings. Rather than pray for his strength, I pray for his courage. I wish for a way to fade into nothingness rather than endure the pain now marching my way.

A key grates. The cell door crashes into the wall behind it. Hard-muscled hands reach beneath my arms, then drag me groaning into a dim passageway. My jailors exhibit the same care as the captain did while hauling me over Azalaïs' filthy cobbles. Neither one hesitates when I stumble or gasp as flagstones peel yet more skin off my body.

Up, up they drag me, into a night shot with stars and sharp with sea air.

A dead tree appears backlit by lanterns, against which two ladders rest.

The white chalk ramparts surrounding this courtyard tell me we're behind the High Court of Azalaïs, visible throughout the city. The boneyard in which I'll die makes for a stark reminder of the extreme cost of breaking A'talan law.

At the base of a leafless tree, they halt, then remove the shackles which grind rust into my bloodstream. These they replace with rough ropes, which they sling over their shoulders, then start up the ladders.

I scream as my feet leave the earth. Something gives way in my left shoulder and the pain triples.

Like dogs fighting over a bone, they wrench me between them, climbing ever higher, jerking my body from side to side.

There's no way I'm doing this with dignity. I will scream my throat raw, begging for steel's kiss. Not that these bastards will give me any such gift. I'll die by degrees, day after stunned night. Muscles tearing, joints separating till I can't draw a sip of air.

Finally, blessedly, the ascent ends. They tie the ropes between two branches and suspend my body between them. I hang, not in ecstasy, but in agony. These wings cannot fly.

They descend, shove my booted feet into where the branches join, then leave me to my misery.

My muscles quake as I straighten my knees, seeking to ease the strain on my shoulders.

I can't. My hands are already too numb to grasp the rope, yet the pain has only begun.

This will take days, during which the heinous and morbid will gather to watch, as last year's Champion of Champions dies by degrees on a tree of bones.

THIRTY-FIVE

THE TORRENT

Lips dry as dust, I beg the Mother of All to take my soul, and free me of the torment in which I drown.

The pain staggers. It's said, given silver, executioners will break the condemned's legs, and speed death. I had none, thus hang limp, staggering from one labored breath to the next.

Hours pass. I slip in, then out of consciousness, yet wish for the latter. Upon hearing galloping hooves, I struggle to raise my head, praying Kemu has a bow with which to give me grace.

A rider shrouded in black tops the plateau.

My beleaguered heart leaps, then plunges. It's not Kemu. It's Seth, his presence confirming just whose lies contrived my doom.

He reaches the tree and reins back with such force, the stallion paws at the cobbles. Sparks rise from his iron-shod hooves. Enlightened rider that Seth is, he saws at the bit till it drips blood.

I force dust-dry words past my drought-constricted throat. "You, unspeakable bastard."

His laughter malevolent, Seth regards my contorted misery. "True to form, Daharshan. Vile even in the extremity of death."

Had I the means, I'd spit in his face.

He reads my wordless wish and reins the stud closer. "Take a good look, bitch. This horse is one of the many reasons you are on that tree. Had you come to Solara, my idiot father would have had you training, then riding for him. Having lost Cinna to the likes of you, no way was I standing aside while you raced Obsidian." The same stallion now battling for his head.

Seth blocks the attempt with vicious hands and spurs. Before the imminent explosion occurs, he eases the reins, aware he too may live on borrowed time.

"So, tell me, did you find Vitrine's performance convincing? I hope so after what it cost to deliver you to this well-deserved fate. Vitrine, his thugs, and mob of informers: every one of them panting to claim my reward."

He sighs, hand-to-heart. "Sadly, I must depart. Linger till your last agonized breath, and I implicate myself. Please, tell the seven hells I sent you."

He spins the stallion, then spurs him into a gallop. The black horse and his black-hearted rider disappear into the darkness. Were it not for the acrid stench of steel horseshoes on stone, I might have thought this visitation an aberration of extremity. Instead, know I'm dying for a horse I hadn't seen till moments ago. All of which would be laughable, were I capable of such a feat.

In this moment of comparative lucidity, my right leg spasms, jettisoning my boot off the branch. Pain cudgels into me. I scream, teetering on blacking out. Do so and the mercy for which I plead will be mine.

No, I'm stronger than this. Surely, I can endure till Kemu arrives. My last words should be, 'I love you.' Then I'll embrace the grace he'll grant me.

I bend my arms, howling anguish as the rope bites deeper into my wrists. The pain grays my vision as I pull my body up till able to wrestle my boot back onto its perch.

When my quaking legs finally give way, my chest will arc and rip my arms from their sockets. They say it's a slow, excruciating death, able to breathe in, but not out. As the stars pass through their stations, the claim proves true.

When the sun rises, those ghouls fascinated by suffering will arrive, hurling insults, garbage, and mockery. The same people I would have laid down my life to protect from my sire's Kian.

All my dreams of becoming Venari, and still I refused the perverted allure of witnessing death. When the ulans stormed the ways, dragging Daharshan warriors to their deaths, I found other tasks. The thought of my color of skin shredded to the bone repulsed me.

In short, I lived a delusion, believing I could kill those who gave me life. That accuracy as an archer somehow made death more humane in that it came swiftly.

In short, drivel. Dead is dead.

My legs cramp, boots skidding off the fork. I scream as all my weight smacks into my shoulders. Praying not to faint, the tendons in my arms creak while I regain my footing.

No one is strong enough for this. No one, and in my weakness, I yield, seeking the one person who should be here.

Kemu, if only in the name of mercy, end this!

The woman who eschewed magic, tries mindspeaking?

There's no response.

What did I expect? Whatever Kylin's delusions, I don't have magic. Why fight the inevitable? Let it happen, now, before the crowds arrive and the circus begins, jeering the Daharshan, pelting her with rotten food.

I unlock my knees. The wood beneath my boots, polished smooth by countless others who perished this way, jettisons my body into the air.

Muscles rip.

Ligaments strain.

My body sags from howling shoulders, and head falls forward. So much for days of dying. This ends now.

It's a prediction that proves all too true.

My breathing turns sporadic. Idle thoughts eddy through my dimming awareness. If only I were in Pell's arms. If only he could whisper, 'Let go,' as he did for Sahain.

Something brushes past my face. I open my caked eyes.

Lunas, thousands upon thousands of them, ride a soughing wind, encircling me. Amidst my marvel comes a revelation. I've misread my birthmark. It isn't a sign of the Mother of All's dubious favor. It's an invitation to return home.

As my heart falters, the Lunas' moon-silver wings brush past me, blessing me with their iridescence. Everything their wings touch glows. As I revel in the euphoria of suffocation, my cracked lips twist into a rictus of a smile.

"Thea, hold on!"

A heavy mass smacks into the tree trunk. Footfalls hammer up a ladder. Someone's hand grasps my forehead, and the hurt everywhere fades.

A second ladder joins the first as another person crashes up its rungs. My vision clears. I recognize Kemu as he climbs above me.

"Kane, are you ready?"

"Do it!" The coachman bellows from below.

Kemu saws through the ropes on my left wrist.

My arm drops like dead meat, body skewing. I slam into Kane, who supports me as Kemu slices through the bond on my right wrist. I crumble into Kane's powerful arms and the world tilts as he descends.

As I'm lain to earth, many hands support me. I stare up into dove-pale skies, marveling at every breath I take.

When Rafi holds water to my lips, I drink too fast and cough before speaking. "Did you see the Lunas?"

He strokes sweat-soaked hair off my eyes. "Yes, we saw them. Your face glows with their iridescence."

Rafi makes way for Lord Karlis, who kneels at my side.

Expression dispassionate and movements precise, the surgeon manipulates my arms back into their sockets. Gruesome as the sound and sensation are, thanks to Kemu's mindblock, I don't pass out.

A contingent of the watch, led by the captain who dragged me, comes our way.

I look to Lord Karlis. "Promise me something."

The surgeon's brows lift. "What?"

"In mercy's name, slit my throat before those bastards 'elevate' me again."

He grimaces. "There'll be no need. Lord Aaron convinced the court to Inlook you. The head of Kemu's croft is here to do just that."

Long black robes stark against the dawn sky, a master mindhealer kneels beside me. "Thea, my name is Mikha'el. Do I have your permission to Inlook your memories?"

I nod, bemused when the others back away.

Mikha'el offers me a reassuring smile, then places his hand on my forehead. "If an Inlooking is ordered as a legal testament, only a master may touch the accused. Have no fear. I will only access memories of the event that condemned you."

I close my eyes as what has become the familiar feather-light touch of magic enters my thoughts. Despite dismissing the possibility Mikha'el will answer the question at the forefront of my mind, I still ask it.

All those hours on the tree, why didn't Kemu bespeak me, and say help was coming?

Turns out I'm right. There's no response.

ACT THREE

MY WAY

THIRTY-SIX
COME AWAY

Weak as I am, Kemu braces one forearm, Rafi the other. The yard's riders make way, their expressions haggard for last year's Champion of Champions, but this year's near-corpse.

Too weak for the burden of their pity, I keep my gaze on Windsong, now arching her neck over the stall she and Khamsin share. I reach her and bury my face in her silver-white mane.

"Sister of all my days and woes, I never thought to see you again."

Khamsin joins us, and breathes me in as if reassuring himself this bedraggled creature is indeed Khalil's daughter.

I rest my forehead against his. "Honest, it's me."

Still unsure, he snorts.

Hand-over-hand along the top rail of their stall, I make my way to Cinna. "Hey, girl."

She nuzzles my cheek, and I blink back tears. Defending this sweet mare almost killed me.

"Somehow, someway, Cinna, we'll show them."

Rafi reclaims my elbow. "Damn straight you will, just not today. Come away. Your horses are fine. We would say the same of you."

While passing the other riders, they murmur, "Born again."

I try making little of it. "Just think. Another hour and Rafi would have been three horses the richer."

It doesn't earn me a single smile.

Losing patience with my shambling progress, Kemu scoops me up. "Another hour and we would have joined you on that tree for murdering Seth."

I subside, head on his shoulder.

Rafi leads the way up the stairs to his apartment over the gathering pavilion. Never having been here before, the crows-eye view of the place I now call home brings a strange peace.

Kemu lowers me onto a chair. "I'll get you clean clothing."

I nod as he leaves, distracted by paintings of illustrious horses hanging between shelves of leather-bound books. "Rafi, you're a scholar?"

"Of horses and riding."

He hands me a cup of water, positions a chair across from mine and sits, the pitcher on his knee. "Let's get this over with. What the hells were you thinking? You damn near got yourself killed."

Almost word-for-word what Pell said when this whole downhill plunge began.

Though I rub my forehead, the pain is in my heart. "Rafi, please, don't . . ."

"Don't what, speak the truth? That doesn't fly between us. While Kemu sought help from his master, I rode to Solara. Kane got me to Aaron. Still, it was damn near dawn before the court assembled a tribunal. The moment the judges arrived, Aaron told them in an enlightened nation, a lack of citizenship wasn't a presumption of guilt."

"But when he called for your accusers to be brought forward, we discovered all had fled, including Vitrine. At that point, Aaron demanded they affirm your innocence by offering Inlooking. Still, any more delay, and all our efforts would have been for naught."

A truth of which I am painfully aware. "Did Lord Mikha'el see Seth wish me a good death?"

Rafi's laughter comes out horehound-bitter. "Yes, not that the court will call Aaron's asshole heir to account, especially for a non-citizen. Thus, we can add injustice to the horror that will haunt the rest of our days."

I rest my hand on his knee. "No second could have done more."

As he refills my cup, the strain on his stubbled face eases. "Where are the children?"

"Idry took them to Enya, and she got them through the night."

As if I haven't caused enough trouble.

Boots clomp up the stairs. Two of our riders enter bearing steaming bathwater. Kemu follows with clean clothing.

As the others take their leave, Rafi waits at the door. "Kemu, if you need anything, just ask. Thea, my room is yours, long as you need. Rest. Our clients will insist on seeing you tonight, even if only for a while."

Once we're alone, Kemu removes the boots Pell tooled for me, and in the doing, sees their worn soles. "You'll be days out of the saddle. Shall I take these to a cobbler?"

For once, someone grasps what I prize, but doesn't question my values. Throat thick with emotion, I nod. As he helps me undress, I pray for an explanation for his silence during all those brutal hours on the tree. When no answer comes, tears do.

"Are you in pain?"

Mute with hurt, I shake my head.

"Thea, tell me, whatever it is."

I swallow and find my voice. "Why didn't you bespeak me?"

"I couldn't. Your battle to live blocked my every attempt. My choice was to help convince the court to Inlook you, or give you grace. I couldn't kill you, thus fought for your life."

A sharp in-breath treads hard upon the heels of this admission. I bury my face in my hands. Had we traded places, I would have done the same.

"My love, you had every right to ask. I've failed you before. For the time being, can we leave it at that? I want to get this blood and filth off you."

There's pain in his eyes, as there is in mine. Yet within this hurt lies affirmation. He didn't abandon me, and for that, I manage a faint smile.

Once he's washed away the worst of the dirt and stench, he lowers me into the steaming bath. He strips down and joins me, then scrubs away the last of last night.

I'm half-asleep by the time he pours fresh water over my blessedly clean, albeit bruised, body. He brushes aside my damp hair and kisses my neck.

The reminder of life's preciousness has me returning his kiss. "Kemu, prove this isn't some afterlife dream. Hold me. Tell me everything will be all right."

He answers by carrying me to the bed, then enfolding me in his arms.

This man is a joy I didn't think would be mine again. Amidst crisp, sun-dried linens, I celebrate the gift given.

Voice gentle as soft rain, he whispers. "Rest, my beloved. I'll be with you throughout. Any nightmare that dares raise its head, I'll chase away."

I yield to sleep's embrace, but know it could have been eternal.

When awareness returns, it comes on a scream.

I'm on my stomach, arms above my head. The bed lurches as they once more rip from their sockets.

A woman's gentle hands ease me onto my back.

"Thea, be at peace. You're safe, at Rafi's."

Once able to focus on Kylin's crimson robes, I manage a breath that doesn't end in shrieking. The setting sun haloes her body as she brushes hair away from my eyes. I've slept the day through.

"I know you'll ask, so here's the answer to your question. Last night would not have happened were a Mother's Voice allowed to interfere with free will."

I clutch the sheets to my naked body. "You foresaw me on a tree of bones, yet did nothing?"

"Our vows forbid altering destiny."

It takes me more than a moment to recover from this shock. "How dare you claim to harm none? You stood apart while an innocent died!"

"No, I did not. I affirmed everything said in court. Nor may a Mother's Voice question the Goddess' methods of annealing a soul."

About now, the urge to hit her is nigh on irresistible. Teeth grit, I fight my way up to sitting. "Lady, I am not a sword. I am a living being."

"Whom the Mother has instructed me to guide."

Aghast, I gape at her. "You expect me to believe that?"

"I do, nor am I the only one watching over you. Mora has done the same all your life. Speaking of Mora, would you speak to her like this?"

I groan. I don't need her reminding me about my manners atop my many other problems. "Where is Kemu?"

"Gayleen arrived in Azalaïs and summoned him. He asked me to watch over you."

"In short, the Sada aren't far behind?"

"Correct. This mess could not be more monumental."

She withdraws a linen packet spun gossamer fine from her pocket. "These are showing up all over Azalaïs: pinned on shirts, hooked on bridles, and painted on banners. I thought it might bring you some comfort, knowing what the miracle of your survival means to this city. You are the first condemned foreigner to be proven innocent."

She spills a pendant of enameled silver onto her palm. It is a Luna, her outstretched wings touching a crescent moon. This is no trinket. It's a Covenant work of art. Even so, I know a peace offering when I see one.

"Damă, I couldn't . . ."

"I insist." She lowers the chain over my head. "Rafi's Daharshan ladies have brought you a gift as well." She gestures to a garment draped over a nearby chair. "Will you wear it tonight? They've gone to great lengths, preparing a feast in celebration."

The riding coat is the same color my sire and brother wore, a blue darker than my eyes. Tiny buttons and gold braid adorn its edges. The gift's extravagance far outweighs my relationship to its givers.

Kylin brushes the hair off the back of my neck. Moments later, a mindhealer's spider touch races across my skin.

I send her a questioning look as the ache in my body departs.

"Mindhealing was my first calling. Service to the Mother came later. Shall I help you dress? Your friends and clients await."

I feel all of four years old as she helps me into undergarments, shirt, and leggings, then eases my arms into the coat's sleeves. My boots I manage on my own, same as I do my progress down Rafi's stairs.

The children wait on the landing. Nahla's with Ainee and Rafi has Eisa. Mahir has his hands on Mina's shoulders. Ranked behind them are the yard's clients, suppliers, and many Daharshans, most who are strangers.

Rafi offers me reverence, and the group follows his lead.

Overwhelmed, I answer in kind. When Kylin gestures for the crowd to make way, they willingly do so, suggesting that my fragility has been explained and forbearance has been urged.

Mahir releases Mina so she may do for me what I did for Sojur: lend a shoulder. Her expression suggests she blames herself for my travail. Though untrue, I hope yesterday's events taught her choices have consequences.

Kylin stands guard throughout the well-wishing and hopes for my swift return to riding. I do my best to respond in a manner that won't draw pity.

When there's a break, the Daharshan ladies bring their artful delicacies to the tables. The air fills with inviting aromas.

I rise so they may see their gift, then mimic the reverence they pay me: hands crossed over the base of my throat. It delights them, as they do me by speaking in my sire's language, however limited my understanding.

The children scatter to play.

Kylin's posture softens as Edan comes our way, with Rafi at her side. He shrugs when I ask if he's heard from Kemu.

The sight of my bruised face has Edan shaking her head as she sinks into a chair across from mine. "More I get to complain about at the Council of Covenants. That captain beat the crap out of you."

I brush a finger over where a shackle cut through my eyebrow. "Some of which I had coming."

"Bullshit. Those assholes take the law into their own hands much too often."

She pauses. "Speaking of the devil . . ."

The man who dragged me across Azalaïs' cobbles now limps our way, one eye swollen shut, and nose broken. He halts at the far end of the table, then tosses Rafi a leather pouch. "Payment for the damage done yesterday." Not waiting for a response, he hobbles away.

Rafi topples the contents onto the table, then flicks through a pile of silver coins. "There's got to be a hundred tallens here. Any idea about who beat the crap out of him?"

Edan laughs. "Obviously, Kemu a'Rowan. While discussing silver, if Thea were to ride with us to Land's End, how much income would the yard lose a day? Fifty tallens, or more?"

Rafi furrows his brows. "As it is, our clients scrape to pay our price. Were they intimate with the details of our business, they wouldn't hesitate to barter."

"Fair enough. What if Land's End puts fifty tallens in your coffers for each day she's not here?"

Rafi nods, cautious. "It would help."

"Just give me a number and I'll cover it." She looks to me. "What say you? Once racing is over, load the children into a cart and ride with us? I know you don't want to be a healer, but think of the joy seeing you would give Mora. Beyond that, my students would get to see some real Daharshans."

Not aware she's talking about my horses, not me.

Kylin gestures to where Nahla holds forth on some arcane bit of herbal lore for a mesmerized Ainee. "Think of it, the girl's the perfect age to apprentice, and Mora would love teaching her."

"Nahla might think otherwise."

"Actually, it's Nahla's idea."

Rafi grimaces. If Ainee goes to the Covenant, Nahla gets his account.

Edan raps a knuckle on the table, reclaiming my attention. "Would you be up to watching me ride Silver tomorrow?"

I welcome the thought of normal back in my life and smile my yes.

The sight of Eisa thumping Kane's broad chest, urging his 'horsey' to go faster, brings me to my feet.

The coachman deposits the wriggling boy on Rafi's lap, then wraps me in a careful embrace. "Our miracle."

I return his hug. "There'd be no miracle without you and Lord Aaron. Is he here?"

"Sadly no, and sends his apologies. The search for your accusers took precedence."

"Please thank him, and tell him I am forever in his debt as I am in yours."

He smiles, then steps back, studying the blue riding coat. "So, this is you in your native dress. Can you imagine the dropped jaws if you raced Cinna in this?"

I laugh. "Yes, but not with approval."

"After what you've been through, why would you care? The city's already abuzz. So what if they have more to gossip about?"

Considering who tried killing me, the answer to my next question is vital. "It's not the city that concerns me. It's Lord Aaron. Does he want me racing Cinna?"

Kane beams. "Name of Heaven, yes, race her! It would mean the world to him if one of his horses had a shot at winning."

His expression sobers. "Sadly, with His Lordship in the city, I must return to Solara. Be well, Thea. Be blessed."

As Kane departs, Mahir collects Eisa. "Time for bed."

I nudge Mina. "You too."

Edan rises, as does Kylin. "See you midmorning?"

I nod and make reverence as they leave. Strange, now the First Lord of the Land and the head of a Covenant croft are my patrons.

The yard empties. Our guests know tomorrow's a workday.

As people leave on foot, horseback, and in carts, I check on my horses, a welcome, albeit slow task. Kemu is right. It will be days before I'm back in the saddle.

With the children asleep, I sit on my landing, telling myself nothing is amiss, yet don't believe a word. What's so pressing that Gayleen detained Kemu tonight of all nights?

The sound of someone entering the yard brings me to my feet. It's Kemu. I am down the stairs far swifter than my ascent.

He dismounts and comes my way as I do his, hungry for his arms around me, arms he does not open. Equally shocking, he's clean-shaven and rather than a haaka, wears a journeyman mindhealer's black tunic.

Hand to throat, I halt an arm's length away. "What's wrong?"

"So much, I don't know where to begin." Blessedly, he closes the space between us, then rests his forehead on mine.

I sink into him, but there's no kiss, only silence as we share breath.

When he speaks, sorrow deadens his tone. "Did that captain of the watch show up?"

"Yes, and paid Rafi for the damage done. Edan says you were the one who thrashed him."

He nods as if it were inconsequential.

I rest my hand on his clean-shaven jaw. "What brought this about?"

"I asked to speak to the Council of Covenants. What that captain did, and what that tribunal almost didn't do, needed addressing. I told them, any person accused of a crime should be offered Inlooking. It did not go over well. There's more. The head of my ulan announced he's retiring at year's end. My father named him as his replacement. He's asked me to be his."

I shove my trembling hands beneath my arms while screaming inside, No, no, no! Once capable of speech, my tone could announce the end of the world.

"Your family will be very proud."

"What of you?"

Me? I want to turn back time and not love this man.

"Will you accept?"

"We both knew this was a possibility."

"A possibility you seem inclined to make a reality."

The muscles in his jaw tighten. "How can I not take up my father's legacy?"

"Apparently, you can."

His eyes narrow with no small amount of anger. "Do you know what I went through last night? I feared you'd give up, same as when Seth attacked you on the beach, and you did."

I stare at him, incredulous. "What of it? I'm not Venari. My failure didn't endanger others."

"You think so little of me, and my love?"

Fury scorches the tears now gathering in the corners of my eyes. "Who knew? A mindhealer who can't perceive the pain he causes. If you lead your ulan, we're done. I will not live Enya's life."

The following silence bristles with thorns. When he speaks, those thorns become swords.

"Accept Karlis' offer, and our problems disappear."

That he would ask this of me, stuns. "I am a rider, not a healer."

This, he lets lie, no amendment, absolution, or solution, his expression stricken as if I lay on my bier.

In the breach of his silence, my heart breaks.

I step back, hands pressed to my churning insides. "And to think, I would have given you my last breath."

Hard as these words hit, they change nothing, fix nothing, which he proves as much.

"Thea, this is real, not some dream. Mora and I opened a path for you to become an A'talan citizen. If you can't see fit to serve A'tal, I pray you find the partner you so richly deserve. Should you change your mind about Karlis, ask Kylin to bespeak me."

I stand there, arms leaden as he swings up onto Gamar, then reins away.

Rafi's reservations about Kemu have proven prophetic.

As he disappears from my life, I know only one thing.

I will never love again.

THIRTY-SEVEN

HEART BROKE OR NOT

With every shutter Rafi throws open, I burrow deeper into his bed covers.

He sits beside me and swats my rump. "Be done with this. Three days of mourning a man is more than enough. It's high time you rejoin the living."

I groan and roll onto my back.

His lips narrow with irritation as I rub the sleep from my eyes. "I swear I've seen livelier corpses."

It's a tad too close to the mark. To prove him wrong, I snag an apple off a tray on the bedside table and take a bite.

That I'm eating eases his irritation somewhat.

"You won't want to hear what I have to say, but too damn bad. First, you're a professional, and should be in the saddle, heart-broke or not. Second, Khamsin lacks his papers of lineage, thus can't race, but Cinna can."

I regard him through bangs lank from lack of washing. "What's your point?"

"She isn't good. She's great. While you wallowed in grief, we turned her out on the track. The horse Aaron gave you may well be this year's three-year-old filly champion."

I wedge my elbows into the mattress and leverage my back against the headboard. "Gave me? That mare damn near cost me my life."

"Quit milking it. The healers say they've met no one better suited to recover from such an ordeal—provided you get moving. Obviously, they don't know what it takes to be Venari."

His backhanded compliment doesn't address a multitude of issues he hasn't touched upon.

"Hardiness won't pay Cinna's entry fees or keep Seth off me. Beyond that, if I race, only Heaven knows what Pell may do. While casting me out, he called me Sha'jin, then said he never wanted to see me again."

Rafi snorts. "He may not want to see you, but an a'Shara's honor won't let him hurt you. I'm not saying he'll make it easy, but you can handle tough. As for Seth, I'd welcome an excuse to beat the crap out of him again. In so far as the expenses, we have a solution."

"What, me in debt for the rest of my life?"

"No, you have a slew of backers, namely Kane and everyone else here. Whatever you win, you keep half. We get a percentage equal to our contribution. You get to show the world you're still on top of your game, and while doing so, prove Pell threw away Sojur's legacy."

He pauses, a restrained smile on his lips. "Beyond that, you'd see Kemu again."

"The man who wished me well in finding the partner I so richly deserved? Trust me, I have no interest in seeing him again. Besides, whatever happened to the pair of you hating each other?"

"Between saving your life, and Kemu breezing his horses along the stretch of shore we use, we've gotten to know each other."

"You speak to him?" My tone's incredulous.

"Every day, and you're mistaken if you think this separation is easy on him. It may not show on the outside, but inside, he's kicking himself for the stance he took."

The question is off my lips before I can stop myself. "Has he asked after me?"

Rafi sighs in exasperation. "What do you think?"

"And?"

"I told him the truth, not that it helped his state of mind."

I send him a peeved look. "That's supposed to get me back in the saddle?"

"Damn straight. This wallowing solves nothing."

He stands. "I'll send bathwater and clean clothes. One other thing—you're back in your loft tonight. Unlike you, I didn't grow up in a crèche. I've had my fill of puppies piling me while trying to sleep."

I raise a hand in acknowledgment as he departs, then haul the food tray over my lap.

There is honor in riding well, just as there is in living well. And then, there is love, the most precious gem of all.

Be that as it may, I will not subject myself to Lord Karlis' acid tongue, even to heal the ache in my heart which is Kemu a'Rowan.

THIRTY-EIGHT

SEE ME

It's been five days since the 'miracle' of my survival, and still, people dog my path. Some hoping to partake of the blessing bestowed. Others, seeking insight into whether I'm still a contender. And then there are the morbidly curious. Thus, like Mina, I go nowhere alone.

Company helps keep melancholy at bay. Bad enough, I dream of Kemu. Alone, and the song of the sea would reopen the all-too-fresh wound of his absence. The day I returned to training, he ceased breezing his horses along this stretch of shore.

Rafi's on Silver, swimming through a churning sea. Mina and I are on the beach. Helping me leg Cinna up for racing has brought Windsong into near-peak condition for a mare in foal.

When I signal the little girl for another sprint, Mina and my beloved break well. I give them a head start.

As I release Cinna, Rafi shouts my name, then points toward Azalaïs.

A man on a gray and a woman on a blood bay come our way. It's my father and Charra, walking at ease, the long journey almost over.

Sojur sits Amir, watching them ride away, but does not follow.

I scream, my voice fear-shrill. "Mina, up on the bank, NOW!"

Charra hears me and looks my way.

Pell tracks his daughter's moment of inattention, and jaw set, puts D'jhat into a canter.

All the aching, empty places which are my father bleed afresh.

Sha'jin, listen and believe. I never want to see your face again.

Arms out in supplication, I slide off Cinna, then sink to my knees.

Sojur has Amir at a gallop, not that he'll get here in time. The a'Shara will accomplish what Seth didn't on a tree of bones.

If this is my death, I am not running.

I make reverence even as my father prepares to kill me.

Charra's voice rises above the crash of the sea. "Father, don't!"

I tell myself, take the blow. Be tempered steel. Break, don't bend, and end this misery now.

Pell's unreadable gaze does not acknowledge what he is about to do: kill a daughter who still loves him. So much so, she embraces death just to be near him again.

The wet sand throbs beneath my knees at D'jhat's approach. At long last, this horse will realize a life dream: ridding the world of the Daharshan he hates most.

Three voices beg the a'Shara for mercy: Rafi's, Charra's, and Mina's.

I take my last breath, praying this bastard horse's first blow will be to my head.

A blast of wind rocks me as sand peppers my skin.

D'jhat thunders past me, a breath away from where I kneel. In my heart, I beg Pell to turn back and forgive me. None of which happens.

While Rafi roars out of the sea, Charra gallops my way.

Mina's the first to reach me.

She flies off the saddle, then throws her arms around my neck. "Don't leave me!"

She's crying, out-and-out sobbing, but this isn't the time for comfort or explanations. I pry her hands free, then come to my feet.

"Mina, see to the mares."

My brusque tone brings silence, then compliance.

Rafi gives me a *'what the hells'* look as he halts before us.

There's no time to explain, not with Charra reining in at my side. She catches my hand, then presses my palm to the slight swelling of her belly.

"Sister, what of your promise to Sahain? If dead, you can't help me raise this child. I beg of you, don't challenge Pell again. He won't even speak your name."

She takes in the fading bruise on my cheek and now healing slice through my eyebrow. "Somehow, I come up with a better argument to plead your cause."

Withdrawing an engraved silver locket from her pocket, she folds my fingers around it. "Atar sent this. Foul as Pell's temper has been, I don't dare tarry. Where can I find you?"

I point to where Rafi sits Silver. "I work and house at Rafi a'Falili's yard."

His smile enchanted, he makes reverence. "Charra au'Sada, welcome back to Azalaïs."

She answers with a pained smile, emerald eyes immense at his struck-out marks. "Thank you for helping my sister."

Though physically impossible, Rafi seems to grow a hand taller.

She looks back to me. "Please, take better care of yourself. Sadly, I must go. Sojur will explain what's happened since your outcasting."

Her smile wistful, she canters after her father.

Charra's skill in the saddle used to irk me, confirming as it did Pell siring my greatest misery. No more. Now, scars I never believed would need stretching must make room for a sister and nephew.

My reverie ends when Sojur reins Amir to a shuddering halt before me. "Name of Heaven, Thea! You, better than most, know Pell never changes his mind. Push him any further and he will kill you!"

I make reverence. "Master, where are they going?"

"Enya sent Pell a letter that questioned him casting you out. It put him in such a rage that we've been fighting ever since. He and Charra are staying at the Black Swan. The rest of us will be at the Sun as usual."

I look over my shoulder to where my sister and father's forms grow smaller.

"Godsdamnit, Thea, don't even consider it!"

The Swan, Azalaïs' premier inn for the wealthy and titled, yet now, Pell's punishment for Enya's so-called betrayal.

A mad bubble of laughter arises inside as I turn back to Sojur. "All the years you've urged him to house on the fancy side of town, and now he agrees?"

Sojur nods, his gaze on Mina. "Who is this child you trust with Windsong?"

Her gaze darts between Sojur's bearing and his mangled hands, then fixates on the sword across his back.

"Her parents lost both their freedom and stead to the Covenant. She's one of four siblings I seek to help."

I clear my throat, reclaiming Mina's attention. "This is Sojur a'Sada, Master of the Sada horse, the man who taught me all I know about horses and riding."

Mina's been around me long enough to know the only proper response is silence or reverence. She offers both.

Sojur's gaze shifts to Cinna and the still-healing lash marks on her hindquarters. "And the red mare is . . .?"

"Cinna, a gift from Lord Aaron."

"Racing bred?"

"Top and bottom."

Rafi clears his throat, reminding me I'm one introduction short.

Before I can do so, Sojur speaks in a tone conveying a marked lack of enthusiasm for a Venari drummed out of the ranks.

"Rafi a'Falili."

The snub doesn't keep Rafi from making formal reverence. "Sojur a'Sada, it is an honor."

My teacher's gaze hardens. "What is your association with Thea?"

"She rides at my training yard."

"How fortunate for you."

The bite of sarcasm in Sojur's tone is something I've known and dreaded my whole life.

He looks back to me. "I want you at my side when I tell Enya where Pell is. Your presence may ease the blow."

Such kindness emulates Sojur's training methods in that he seeks gentleness rather than domination.

Rafi nods permission. "Send word and I'll come for you."

Sojur shakes his head. "No need. I'll bring her to your yard."

I swing up behind my teacher, aware a discussion about how he's treated Rafi must wait till we're alone.

Amir explodes into a canter, fit and full of it after five days of travel. The horse I bred and hoped to race, now bearing ill tidings to Enya.

THIRTY-NINE

NEVER CALLED TO QUESTION

Face between her forearms, Enya sobs at one of the Sun's garden tables. A letter written in Pell's hand lies before her.

When Sojur rests his maimed hand on her shoulder, her head flies up. "My dearest friend, I didn't hear you arrive." Tears still flowing, she looks to me. "All the years I've loved your father, not once has he been so cold, so ruthless. My defense of you convinced him I, too, have betrayed his trust. He's forsworn me as well."

Sojur and I share an anguished glance. Never having seen the a'Shara fresh off a battlefield, his blade running crimson with Daharshan blood, Enya doesn't know just how brutal he can be.

My teacher clears his throat. "I, for one, don't give a damn about Pell's wounded pride. He's wrong, just refuses to admit it. We've gone from fighting to not speaking."

The Sada a'Shara, never wrong, never called to question. Though free of his rule, his disdain casts a long shadow.

Enya gestures to a passing server, then points to Sojur. The man nods in acknowledgment of her silent request.

She looks back to us. "Thea's choice didn't make Pell cruel. That, he managed on his own. Sojur, how long before the Sada finish at the track? Two, maybe three hours?"

He nods, then accepts the stirrup cup brought by the server. This, he raises to Enya, then makes Thanksgift, and drinks.

Calling upon the calm with which she runs the Sun, Enya dries her eyes. "Pell's mistaken if he thinks we'll roll in ashes and mourn his absence. Thea, I want you here tonight. Come early and bathe in my rooms. I have something for you to wear. Tell Rafi if he doesn't accompany you, I'll be crushed. He deserves our heartfelt thanks for all his help during your ordeal."

Sojur gives me an odd look, then looks to Enya. "If Pell learns you've thrown a welcome party in his absence, the Swan may not survive his temper."

Her lips purse. "If so, so much the better."

She rises. "Please, excuse me. I have much to do." She heads for the inn. While passing meat roasting on a spit, Pell's letter gets tossed into the flames.

Sojur snorts. "Not quite the seasoning you'd expect in fine cooking."

I sit across from him at the table. "Enya has loved Pell longer than I've lived. Yet, like me, she too has had her love sacrificed on the altar of male pride and ambition."

He slants me a questioning look. "Plainly, a great deal has happened since last we saw each other." While sliding the ale across the table, he takes in my hair, now shorter at the sides, and longer in the back. "Enya's doing?"

I nod before making Thanksgift. "The night I arrived."

"Looks like a bobbed horse's tail. Will you let it grow out?"

I shrug. He's not addressing that I made a Venari's choice, cutting my hair as if ascended.

"Insofar as riding for Rafi a'Falili, why not a more reputable yard?"

I drink, heart divided between my two fathers and lands. "Ten days ago, I was accused of killing a man, and 'elevated' on a tree of bones. Rafi, Lord Aaron, and two Coveners convinced the court to Inlook, thereby absolving me. Thus, thanks to Rafi, I am alive, with a roof over my head and food for my horses. While it's true that he lost his commission for attacking the head of his company, the reason he did so confirms his honor."

"Which would be?"

I return the ale. "Preventing the rape of little Daharshan girls."

Sojur lowers the mug without drinking. "Not the story I heard."

I meet his doubting gaze. "Pell cast me out for putting my sire and brother's lives ahead of my own. Rafi lost his commission for exemplifying that same precept, others before self. So, while a more 'reputable' yard might have been possible, a more honorable man was not."

Sojur drapes his ruined hands over the chair's arms. "Indeed. Has the student outstripped her teacher?"

"Master, there's nothing I could teach you."

He arches a brow as if unconvinced, and sorrow punches into me.

I will never equal the man who made me the rider I am, particularly now, lacking his instruction.

Seeking to ease my many losses, I retrieve Atar's locket. Within is a portrait of Sahain and a lock of his hair. The thick in my throat goes down like day-old porridge.

Sojur slides the ale my way. "Drink."

Before doing as told, I pass the chain over my head, settling the locket beside Kylin's Luna.

Sojur waits till I regain my composure. "So, tell me about the red filly, and about the man who sacrificed your love on an altar of prideful ambition. Tell me about the tree."

In a few words, he's redefined our relationship, releasing me from the role of student, while opening a door to mentoring. And in the doing, he has shouldered the role Pell rejected.

Knowing this as a rare opportunity, I force a smile, savoring these precious moments against the drought the rest of my life will surely be.

FORTY

AN INEXCUSABLE LINE

Blue eyes haunted, and hair freshly trimmed, the girl in Enya's mirror contemplates the locket and pendant laying side-by-side over the notch in her throat.

Three men should be here. Sahain, who can't. Kemu and Pell, who won't. If my father changes his mind, the vision of my blood splattered across Enya's sleeping room comes all too easily. Gorge rising, I draw the bath sheet closer.

Laughter and conversation drift through the doors open to Enya's balcony. Glowering clouds and the occasional rumble of thunder be damned. Tonight's party has begun.

Enya returns from her sitting room, a ribbon-bound bundle in her arms. "The plan was for you to wear this at the Champion of Champions' Ball. If you go, you can't wear Sada emerald, but you and Sojur back together, that's worth celebrating."

As she frees the ribbons, a gown the color of spring grass gushes across her bed covers. The dried rose petals between its folds scatter, filling the air with their sweet perfume.

I swallow a persimmon-sized lump, and raise my arms so Enya can draw the fabric, fluid as water, over my body. My first dress, its back open to the waist, its edges a riot of leafy cutwork. With my body's warmth, the roses' perfume grows.

"Did Atar design this?"

She nods, then gestures for me to stand.

I watch in the mirror as she ties the cords that will keep the dress's cap sleeves in place. "Enya, the time it took to embroider this . . ."

She straightens a seam as if doing so will distract me from the tears glittering in her eyes. "Time, I had in abundance with your father on the grasslands."

Mother in Heaven, haven't we shed enough tears for Pell a'Sada?

I don't speak till she's able to meet my gaze. "He won't be able to endure being apart from you."

"With the Swan treating him like royalty, highly unlikely."

"Give him more credit. He won't last the night."

"Hah! If so, I hope it's sheeting rain."

There's an edge to her voice that's at odds with her nature. For that reason, I try again.

"Whatever the weather, I cannot be here. In this dress, I couldn't run fast enough, far enough."

"If Pell shows up, he will contain his temper or leave. Sit facing me."

I shut my eyes as, with a feather-light touch, she draws kohl lines above and below my lashes. "Thea, look."

I turn to the mirror.

A stranger looks back at me, her Daharshan eyes huge with sorrow.

Enya draws my necklaces out from under the gown and puts a period to Pell's assertion. Thea of the Sada is no more. The girl who would be Venari, renounced by father and lover, now vanquished by an exquisite gown.

"Join us when you're ready." A sad smile and she departs.

I look to the carved roses framing the mirror, among which grasshens fly. Designed by Atar, and commissioned by Pell, the day this gift arrived, we didn't see Pell or Enya till the following morning. Even at that age, I knew what they shared was irreplaceable. Yet now, they are apart.

As for me, I left the grasslands as a girl on the cusp of womanhood. A border I crossed in Kemu's arms for a love now lost to me. Ten days and still no sign of him, yet he and Rafi speak often. When I ask after Kemu, Rafi only shrugs.

Regret will only cost me time with Sojur. I rise and head for Enya's balcony, the emerald fabric swirling around my legs.

In the gardens below, night birds serenade a rising wind. A multitude of lanterns hung in the fruit trees cast a golden glow over the Sada riders. Men and women I've raced with the past four years. While it's doubtful a welcome awaits me, I descend the stairs.

A rider halts a red horse in the courtyard, a silver-white dog at their side. Throughout racing, Sojur insists his riders maintain spit-and-polish formality. Golden hair gleaming against an emerald tunic, Lycan gives Hanan to a groom.

I come down the steps two at a time as Selene bounds my way, then crouch and catch her, my laughter joyous as she covers my face with frantic kisses.

One of Lycan's friends comes at a run. He puts as much excitement into his voice as she does into gamboling at my side.

"Selene, let's eat!"

We're all back at the Sun. Everything is right in her world. Tail wagging, she follows the Venari-to-be as I rise into Lycan's brilliant smile and breadth of chest.

Despite my discord, I find words. "Thank you for bringing Selene."

The way gossip seethes through Azalaïs, it's likely he knows about Kemu. If so, it doesn't keep him from taking my hand in his.

"When Selene realized you were gone for good, she refused to eat and howled constantly. With Atar's blessing, I took her into my tent. Still, it was weeks before she'd hunt for me."

In the awkward silence that follows, he traces the fading scar through my eyebrow. "You survive what no other has. Are the rumors true? Did the lies of Lord Aaron's son condemn you?"

"Such is the suspicion." My reluctance to go into the details astounds me.

We're drawing attention, so much so, he leads the way under a pear tree's arched branches. There, we sit on a bench, knee-to-knee, and my hand still in his. He's the first to break the silence.

"When I asked permission to leave early, the a'Shara said either I trained with Sojur and raced Hanan or not ascend. Tell me, did Kemu play a part in your absolution?"

This he lets lie, no additions or subtractions.

Insides churning, I look away. "He did."

Fingertips under my chin, he urges me to meet his gaze. "Despite wishing it were otherwise, I knew Kemu had the advantage. A blooded Venari, able to travel as he pleased, that and an accomplished racer and successful horse breeder? Low fruit for the woman I love."

"Lycan, I . . ."

He silences me, his fingertip to my lips. "Venari honor the day and worship the night. You have been my hope since the first time you smiled at me. All I ask is that you let me prove I have your back and can go the distance."

I'm appalled at how much his constancy means, yet know it will go nowhere if Kemu and I can resolve our issues.

In the wake of my silence, he smiles ruefully. "Thea, I know Kemu ended your relationship."

Blood rushes to my face. Nothing's private in this damn city, nothing.

"It's no cause for embarrassment. It's just life, in all its many imperfections and possibilities." He gestures to the courtyard. "Someone else wants to see you."

I throw myself into Atar's waiting arms. He blesses my hair with a kiss, then takes my hands, and spins me in a bittersweet tribute to the brother whose death shattered everything.

The reminder is too sharp, too fresh. With a half-sob, I plant my feet, then wrap my arms around my last beloved brother.

He kisses my cheek, then steps back and takes me in. "Do you like it?"

I sweep my hand over the silky fabric. "My first dress? I love it almost as much as I love its designer."

He grins. "Enya and I hatched this plan a year ago. Once certain you were done growing, I sent her the patterns."

Our voices bring Selene. When she tries to jump on me, Lycan points to the ground. "Selene, sit."

She does, then laugh-pants up at me, her long tail sweeping the grass. Marveling, I pet her. "You trained her?"

Lycan smiles with justified pride for something I couldn't do.

We fall silent at the sight of Enya reviewing her staff's offerings for the Sada's first night at the Sun. She pauses at the main table's centerpiece: the pink-hearted roses she raises to such success. Before them rests a silver stirrup cup which should be in Pell's hand.

I look to my companions. "Give me a moment?"

Selene bumps my hand with her long nose as we walk. "Enya?"

She turns.

I gesture to the stirrup cup. "Perhaps, Sojur?"

She considers a moment, then fills the cup with ale, and hands it to me. "It will mean more coming from you."

Sojur's surrounded by his top riders. Their gazes hood at the sight of the outcast with Enya.

She pays them no mind. "Sojur a'Sada, the Sun gives thanks for you and your riders."

He salutes her with the cup, makes Thanksgift, then drinks, his expression bespeaking of our common wound. The man who should be here to take this welcome from his lover's hands.

Enya turns to the massed Sada, arms held wide as she speaks with a serenity born of making strangers friends, and friends into family. "You are all welcome. Eat, drink, enjoy."

The riders offer her hand-to-heart reverence, then dissolve the moment's solemnity with a ringing shout.

With a gentle smile, she leads the way to the tables. Yet another tradition, Enya welcoming each rider personally.

As the crowd departs, Sojur gestures to the empty place beside him on the bench.

A gust of wind shakes a nearby apple tree, which rains pippins as I sit.

Sojur tilts his head, watching them fall, the silver in his hair gleaming in the lantern light. "The first time you saw apples 'fall from Heaven', we couldn't convince you they weren't a gift from the Mother of All."

While passing me the stirrup cup, he smiles at the memory.

Legs curled to the side, I sip, pretending everything is as it should be, that any moment now Pell will arrive and greet us with a smile.

Sojur, rarely physical other than while correcting my position when riding, brushes an errant lock of hair behind my ear. "Lycan's still enchanted. What of you?"

I keep my answer soft. "I have a heart to heal."

He nods acknowledgment of Kemu quitting me. "When Pell gave Lycan his ultimatum, the boy clawed his way into the first rank of my riders. While I have hopes for how he'll do racing, I have none for him remaining with the tribe. Furthermore, if Amir wins, I'm resigning my commission. My plan is to establish a racing stable and stud farm here in Azalaïs, then, hopefully, hire two ex-Sada riders."

I'm grateful I don't have a mouthful of ale. "Whatever brought this on?"

"When I told Pell you were the only one who could do justice by Amir, he ordered me to find another rider. I've tried, yet failed, thus I will be in the irons for Amir's run for the Championship."

"Sojur, no!"

He takes the cup from my nerveless fingers, then drinks deep. "I'm open to suggestions."

I keep to myself what we both know. Namely, racing is for the young, for those who lack qualms about insane risks, and have all their fingers and feet.

Lycan's been waiting for a break in our conversation, for which he makes reverence, then gestures to the bench across from us. Receiving Sojur's permission, he sits.

Our teacher smiles for the younger man's enchantment. "An amazing rider and . . ."

Lycan leans forward, taking my hand in his. ". . . and blindingly beautiful."

Even as I welcome the sight of Rafi coming our way, I dodge the compliments with a question. "How was Hanan at the track?"

"Loud. He announced his presence to every mare within earshot."

Sojur chuckles. "As to be expected of a young stud in a strange place."

I can't tear my gaze off the crimson Falili haaka Rafi wears. A gold letter 'C' is embroidered over his heart, above which five stars arch. The man I work for is a Champion of Champions, but never said a word.

He inclines his head to Sojur. "Master."

My teacher meets Rafi's one-eyed gaze. "A'Falili."

"May I join you?"

When Sojur gestures consent, Rafi sits beside Lycan, brow arched at the young man holding my hand. "Watching Thea train is a daily privilege. Your protégé drew Lady Edan to our yard, and she proved instrumental in saving Thea's life."

As if comforting me, Lycan strokes my ruined birthmark.

Before I can reclaim my hand, the sound of a karakal preparing to kill has all of us seeking its source.

Kemu stands an arm's length away, his expression feral with rage. "Get your hands off her."

Lycan bolts upright, inadvertently splaying me across Sojur's lap.

Into the midst of this tangle, Kemu tosses an antique folio onto the bench, then launches at Lycan.

The two men come together with the force of two bulls determined to destroy the other. As each seeks the advantage, their muscles strain while their boots grate for purchase.

Sojur's hand on the center of my back keeps me out of the melee.

Kemu slams Lycan to earth, yanks Lycan's back over his thigh, then bears down, forearm jammed across the younger man's throat. Lycan's back arches in an excruciating, sacrificial curve.

Sojur's tone turns icy. "A'Rowan, kill this Venari-to-be, and not only will you pay reparation, his family will be your responsibility for the rest of your days."

Lycan's face darkens. He can't get his right arm past Kemu's shoulder, not with his left arm pinned to earth by Kemu's knee.

I eel out of Sojur's grip and bolt to my feet, seeking Rafi, frantic for his help. Failing to find him, I haul on Kemu's arm, getting nowhere.

"Thea, move!"

It's Rafi, double-handing a bucket of sloshing water our way.

I move, and he arcs the contents over the fighters' heads. "Kemu, either let him go, or I'll crack your skull wide open."

The only change is Lycan's growing desperation.

I grab Kemu's chin and make him look at me. "Kill Lycan, and I'll never speak to you again."

There's a faint easing in Kemu's corded arms as he considers my threat. The release, when it comes, is as sudden as it is unexpected.

Rafi pulls me out of the way as Lycan stands and coughs like a blown horse.

Before the fight can erupt again, Sojur shoulders the two men apart. "Lycan, I want you alive and racing. Return to the track. I'll see to your interests."

"Master." His voice ragged, Lycan makes reverence to our teacher, then looks to me. "For your love, no price would be too great."

Kemu goes rigid, his fury now a barely contained storm. Only when the younger man disappears into the stable does he scoop up the folio, then extend it to Sojur. "I knew you sought this treatise."

Expression rife with disapproval, Sojur reads the title, then accepts the book.

"With your permission, I would speak with Thea in private."

"A'Rowan, while I thank you for the gift, you have crossed an inexcusable line. You may speak with her, so long as you stay in my sight."

Without a by-your-leave, Kemu grabs my wrist and takes off. It's follow or be dragged. No one handles me like this. No one.

Skirts swirling, I pass him in a few long strides, then spin and slam my unhindered fist into his chest. "Let me go."

"You want to discuss this in front of everyone?"

"I'm not some bitch to be hauled around on the end of a leash!"

"Even though you act like one?"

Before my hand can connect with his face, he steps into me, pinning my wrists to my sides. "We're not doing this to each other again. Choose or this ends now. I won't compete with any would-be Venari or one-eyed horse trainers."

Choose? You said we were done.

It takes a moment to register. I've bespoken him. Not only that, he heard every word. His expression tells me so.

"Thea, answer me."

I'm so angry I can't see straight. "A thousand pardons. I thought you said we couldn't make a life together."

"So long as you pursued a life of racing rather than healing."

"What I do is no longer your concern."

I writhe against his grip, and his gaze consumes my body. Then, as if waking from a dream, he groans, and pulls me close, putting an end to my struggled.

"Please, forgive me. I can't sleep, eat, or stop thinking about you. I found Sojur's book and thought we could discuss horse breeding, only to arrive and find you in the arms of a boy."

When he eases his hold, I'm able to rear back and see his expression. The hurt there curdles my smile. "Trust me, Lycan's no boy, and would leave the Sada for me."

"That blond lout? Any man with half a brain would curry the favor of a Daharshan beauty and her two purebred horses."

"Just what does that say about you?"

"That I can't be bought."

My laughter rings bell-clear. "Unless the prize is a title, say Master Mindhealer, or future Rowan a'Shara?"

He visibly wrests his emotions under control. "We'll see how you handle life with a man overshadowed by your talents. As for Rafi a'Falili, Brava! From the patronage of the first Lord in the land to a third-rate drummed out of the ranks."

I gape at him. "Why, you gutless coward. You seduce an innocent, yet have the gall to belittle those who come to my aid? Lycan is a friend who, in my absence, eased Selene's sorrow."

I'm crying, tears of rage, tears of desolation, all the while praying he'll heal the wounds we've sliced into each other.

Instead, he steps back, then arms crossed, regards me in stony silence, for which I lash out.

"A'Rowan, your conceit far exceeds your worth."

His eyebrows rise. "And this is you, *not* doing to me what Pell's done to Enya?"

Gooseflesh shudders down my near-naked back. While I strain to keep my horses and self fed, his future shines bright. How is it a man with freedom, rights, and citizenship can accuse me of 'punishing' him?

No way will I give in to him.

I turn and stalk away, screaming inside with every step I take.

Don't do this. You love him.

Love him almost as much as I hate him.

FORTY-ONE

MY WAR ENDS

In the Sun's crowded gathering room, rain sheeting off the roof blurs the gardens beyond. As I enter, the better part of Sojur's riders fix me with unyielding gazes. Those few who offer stilted words of greeting do not detain me for long.

Amidst this press, Rafi sits with a table of Venari. They hang off his every word and well they should. If he hasn't coached me out of deference to Sojur, he must if I'm racing Cinna.

He spots me and gestures between us, indicating a desire to speak, then points to a window alcove apart from the tables.

I nod and make my way there.

As Rafi comes my way, many offer him good-natured greetings. By the time he arrives, he's grinning. "I forgot how much I enjoy being around racers."

He sits beside me, brows creased at my grim expression. "Are you alright?"

I wobble my hand. "So-so. Even in this dress, I don't cut it with this crowd."

"What you wear won't make a difference. They know you have what it takes to shove them to the rear of the pack."

I laugh, a bitter sound. "While on the topic of racing, any plans for coaching me?"

He hooks a thumb at his award array. "Are you peeved about my not mentioning this?"

I nod.

"Don't be. Your plate's been full. The last damn thing you needed was me messing with what Sojur had carved into stone. Mind you, I'll have plenty to say at the track, but only in private. No way will I tarnish your reputation. That's gold in our coffers."

I heave a sigh. "Speaking of coffers, Silver's my first ride tomorrow, and Edan will be there."

"We'll get you home in time. Want to talk about what happened earlier?"

"Not particularly."

He narrows his eye at me. "For once, indulge me. Kemu's mother may not have taught him manners, but Gayleen sure as hells did. That woman won't take shit off any Venari. But you, in that dress, with Lycan holding your hand, no way Kemu would let that pass."

I rear back. "You're blaming me?"

"Imagine how you'd feel, seeing Kemu with his arm around another woman's waist."

A flash fire of anger consumes any reasonable response I might cobble together, for which Rafi snorts.

"Smarts, doesn't it? Kemu didn't quit you. He set conditions you spurned."

I shift onto a hip, then trail my fingertip along the windowsill. "He said what Pell's done to Enya, I've done to him."

"I can see the similarity. What will you do about it?"

"Do? All my life, I've done whatever it took to prove my worth, yet have created one disaster after another."

"Does that include last year's Championship?"

"No, but in the long run, how did it help?"

"It brought us together."

I manage a faint smile. "For which I am eternally grateful."

"Good to know. Do me a favor, no more fights tonight."

"Damn it, Rafi, I didn't start . . ."

Him, blessing my forehead with a kiss, silences me.

"You may not have started it, but damn well ended it. Best you figure out what you want before Kemu calls it quits. Can't remember the last time I saw a man that angry. Come get me when you're ready to leave."

The Sada make way as Rafi returns to his companions.

Rather than test their tolerance, I take a circuitous path to where Atar sits in his favorite nook, two steps above the main floor.

He sees me coming, pushes aside his drawing board, then scoots over, making room for me on the bench. Arm-in-arm, we take in the oddness of the Sada without their a'Shara.

Soul weary, I rest my head on his shoulder.

He slides his fingers through mine. "Tiring work, breaking men's hearts?"

I straighten. No way is my no-luck in-love brother taking me to task about my behavior. "Just what are you suggesting?"

Rather than answer, he opens his portfolio, then turns the drawings within. There's Selene greeting me, then Sojur tucking a lock of hair behind my ear. One of Lycan holding my hand, then his back arched in an agonizing curve over Kemu's thigh. Last in the array is the grace cut. Kemu's tortured expression as he watches me stalk away, my bare back rigid with indignation.

Rafi is right. I may not have started the fight, but damn well ended it.

I offer my brother a wan smile. "File these away under some of my less-than-spectacular moments?"

He tries holding back his laughter, and fails. "More like scenes I won't weave into any tapestries. Do you want these drawings?"

"Is this your way of telling me that actions have consequences?"

To my chagrin, he nods.

"Bring them to Rafi's tomorrow morning?"

"How about midafternoon? My ass is flat after five days in the saddle."

No sooner are these words out, than he slaps his hand to his forehead. "Pay me no mind. I'm an idiot."

"Just be glad you've never had to ride for your life. Be there before noon and you'll have an amazing meal, cooked by some truly beautiful Daharshan women."

Mood somber, he nods.

"How has life been without Sahain?"

"Wretched. The only good is Charra, and I can share our misery."

He touches a fingertip to Sahain's locket, where it rests beside Kylin's Luna. "This was her idea. Me, I just struggle from one day to the next."

"As do I." I kiss his cheek, then rise. "Tomorrow?"

Incapable of words, he nods.

After the crowded gathering room, I welcome the cool of the outer stairs. Strong winds have driven the storm back to sea. Once I've changed, we can leave.

I lift my hems while climbing the stairs to Enya's balcony. As I do so, overhanging trees scatter raindrops onto my bare back. Before I reach my destination, angry voices ring out in the courtyard below. It's Enya and my father.

Bent double to avoid being seen, I fly up the remaining steps, then retreat into the shadows of Enya's balcony where terror frosts my skin.

The a'Shara's tone strives for reasonable. Enya isn't having any of it. Her sharp words gain in volume, then end in a slap. Puddles splash as she races across the courtyard, then up the stairs and into her bedroom. Her door slams shut.

While peering over the half-wall, I stay in the shadows.

Below, my father stares up at Enya's balcony. D'jhat is at his side. Without warning, the a'Shara drops the reins, signaling the stallion to stay put, then pounds up the stairs.

As the door to her bedroom opens, I cower in the dark.

Enya shouts, calling him stone-hearted, cold, and calloused.

His deep-voiced answer is too soft to hear.

Silence follows yet more silence. Then, one by one, the lights in Enya's room go out. The balcony door opens, through which my father's tall form strides to the half-wall. He draws his arm back, then arcs a bundle through the air, which lands with a splash below.

The door shuts. The curtains close. That bundle? My boots and riding gear left in Enya's room. The a'Shara has just told me to get out and stay out.

Trembling hands on the rain-chilled stucco, I wait while cool breezes raise gooseflesh on my skin. Only once certain they are in each other's arms, do I creep down the stairs.

At my approach, D'jhat snorts.

My hatred for this horse shames me. Only someone with shoulders as broad as Pell's means anything to D'jhat. Me, he treats like the enemy I am.

When I reach for the reins, his teeth snap shut a whisper away. I snarl, "Quit," then slam my knuckles into his jowl when he doesn't.

Three times this stubborn bastard tries taking a chunk out of me as, at arm's length, I lead him into the stable.

My next chance to duck teeth comes while snubbing him to a wall. He glares at me through his unruly forelock, then flips his head, trying to slack the rope.

I find an empty stall in which a full water bucket and stocked hayrick await, then return to D'jhat and drop his girth. His back hoof barely misses my arm.

For once, I don't knee him in the guts. So long as he doesn't connect, my war with this horse is over. I ease the saddle onto the aisle, then lead him into the stall. I keep my fist around the cheekpieces, ready to use the bits as a weapon if he comes after me again.

Thankfully, food takes precedence.

The saddle and bridle go on the rack outside his stall. Pell's bow and quiver go on a nearby hook. All tasks I would have performed with joy if I were still his daughter.

On the groom's chalkboard, I write: *Enya, thank you. T.*

My father is with the woman he loves and for that, I am glad. Yet, amidst collecting my sodden clothing and boots from the courtyard cobbles, I marvel leaving the Sun doesn't hurt more.

Then again, as Pell says, I've been known to lie.

FORTY-TWO

THE HELLS WITH GRACE

In my round pend, Edan sits on Silver. "He did what?"

"Pitched my boots and riding clothes into a puddle. The a'Shara has unerring aim."

"Yet you stabled that nightmare he rides?"

"How can I not honor the man who raised me?"

She sighs while dismounting. "You want my take? He doesn't deserve you or Enya."

Kylin nods agreement from where she basks in a sunbeam, steaming teacup between her hands.

I run my hand along Silver's chest. "Edan, he's cool enough to be stabled. If you'd like kaf, I won't be long."

By the time the colt is untacked and groomed, the rest of the yard has begun its day. Men shouting, pails clattering, and horses whinnying.

As I rejoin them, Edan passes me kaf. "You seem at peace with your father winning last night's round."

After spending most of what was left of last night tossing and turning, I take a welcome sip of kaf. "Not so much at peace as realistic about the futility of resistance."

Rafi clatters down the stairs of his apartment. "Futility, my arse."

Before I can steer the conversation in a better direction, a member of the watch rides through the front gates, spots us, then reins our way. As he salutes the Coveners, the yard's noise level plummets.

"Thea, formerly of the Sada?"

I come to my feet. "Yes?"

He tosses me a beribboned, wax-sealed envelope, then turns and trots from the yard.

I stare at the missive in my hand. Nothing from these assholes is ever good.

Kylin holds up a hand before I can crack the seal. "May we explain our reasoning?"

Sensing what's coming has an element of pain, I widen my stance.

Edan rises, then closes the space between us. "After meeting the children, we searched for the court order that indentured their parents. Finding none, we opened an investigation into how such an injustice came to be. As you know all too well, A'talan law can be manipulated for gain."

She taps the envelope. "Within is a writ to surrender the children to Enya. They will remain wards of the state till their parents' fate can be determined. We advocated for leaving them here, but the court deemed it best to place them in a more homelike environment."

Expression anxiety-ridden, Kylin joins us. "Thea, can you accept this with the same grace you exhibit in most things?

Trust that your life path has only begun, and now is not your time to mother?"

Rather than respond, I crack the seal. While it takes only moments to read, it will take a lifetime to grasp. I am to surrender the children by day's end and thereafter, have no further contact. As a foreigner, my involvement in their lives has been deemed unseemly.

I look to the women. Edan, at ease with life's harsh realities and Kylin, apprehensive about my response. Neither perceives they've perpetuated the parents' fate upon their offspring, for which I sling the writ onto the table.

"The hells with grace. You're getting honesty. Your ilk has no concept of a life without rights. That explains how 'justice' can be bought here, and why children starve. Should the Venari who do this country's dying ever fail, this whole cobbled-together mess will crash down upon all our heads. Please excuse me. I have a child's heart to break."

I stalk to where Mina waits, Windsong and Cinna's reins in her small hands, then sink to a knee before her. "Mina, the Court has ordered a search for your parents. Till they are found, you and your siblings will live with Enya and Ainee. We'll take you to the Sun tonight."

For a moment, she stands stricken with shock. When able to speak, her voice quavers. "Leave you? Leave Windsong?"

At my nod, she throws her arms around my neck, sobbing so hard she can scarce breathe. I rub her heaving back, my gaze on the creators of her sorrow as the mares nudge her, seeking to comfort the little girl.

Edan's eyes are granite. Little wonder, with Kylin weeping in her arms.

It's their problem, not mine.

I lift Mina onto Windsong, then come up behind her.

Rafi doesn't need asking. He swings onto Cinna, and side-by-side, we ride out of the yard.

If I have one fewer training horses tomorrow, so much the better.

FORTY-THREE

DENIED TEARS

On the street we walk, fog born of last night's rain, billows knee-high. My arm around Mina's shoulders doesn't stem her tears. A subdued Eisa rides astride Rafi's shoulders. Beside him, Mahir trudges alongside Idry. The hope their parents will be found has proven no solace against leaving the yard.

We round the last corner and halt.

Between the Sun's entry, two wraiths sit dark horses: Pell on D'jhat, and Sojur on Amir. D'jhat frets the inn's welcoming lantern light, an unholy fire in his eyes.

Pell eases the gray's reins. The stud's iron-shod hooves bell as he marches our way. Danger that this horse presents, his rider personifies every inequity opposing me.

Sojur follows at a walk, as if unwilling to take part in the injustice his second commits.

How did my choice curdle Pell's heart? Always a hard man, he was just until I committed 'treason.' This quandary merits consideration, provided I can keep my head and neck together.

He halts before us, then spins the stud about-face.

It's a battle maneuver taught all warhorses.

Mina shrieks as D'jhat's forelegs fly past her. I don't flinch, having expected this. Still, the little girl's terror opens a window into my childhood, asking why I never questioned this man's will defining my life.

Pell side-steps D'jhat, closing the space between us. Were the a'Shara not in control of his bastard horse, I'd be minus half my face.

He smiles while holding out his arm to Mina, offering her a ride on a horse I'd rather eat.

Rather than accept, she cowers and clings to me.

You'd have to know my father to read his ire: the hooded gaze, the tight lips. No one refuses the a'Shara without consequences, and for which, my heart sinks.

If Mina sets her will against Pell, he will make her life a misery by excluding her from the favor he'll shower on her sister and brothers. Envisioning this storm of calamity for Mina comes all too easily.

D'jhat huffs fiery breath into my face, breaking my fixation with the future. If that weren't a sufficient challenge, Enya, and Selene arrive at the inn's entryway. Seeing me, my dog comes at a gallop.

I crouch and brace.

Selene slams into me, wriggling like a puppy. My heart breaking, I hug her, then turn her to face Mina.

"This is my hunting hound, Selene. Now that I can't watch over you, she will."

Shyly, Mina strokes Selene's silky coat. Within moments, my dog is in her arms.

This is the end. If I see them again, it will be at a distance.

Denied tears well in my eyes as Mahir shakes my hand with adult formality.

Everyone's joy, Eisa, wails as Rafi sets him down. He doesn't quiet till in Enya's arms. It's of small consolation, but Enya will love and mother these children in ways I cannot.

Throughout, Pell's gaze remains opaque. It's D'jhat who reveals his rider's impatience by stamping his hooves.

Heart stuttering, I lift Mina onto Sojur's lap.

He shakes his head, confounded by how we've achieved such devastation.

I make reverence to my teacher, then to my father, who does not acknowledge me as I turn and walk away.

My tears don't fall till I'm shrouded in fog, disappearing like the nomadi Pell believes me to be.

FORTY-FOUR

MY WAY

From the yards' entry, Rafi beckons to me. "Come see this."

After last night's excess of ale, I'd prefer the midday meal now arriving. "Can it wait?"

"Just come."

I heave a vexed breath, then join him.

A sheathed sword, bow case, quiver, and saddlebags lie against the yard's outer wall. Among the arrows fletched in my signature blue, a single crimson ascension arrow laments all my lost chances.

Familiar with the lengths Pell will go to leave no enemy standing, I slide the bow from its case. The ends of the layered Silkwood stave have been carved into horse heads, their mouths open for the string's nock. The bow's length, its depth of recurve: all specific to my height and build. Ascended, I would have wielded this work of art to deadly effect.

I trade the bow for the sword. Marks incised into its collar confirms the blade as Covenant forged. Drawn, the hammer blows stippling its curved edge, affirms the core as malleable, but spine unyielding. I stack my hands one atop the other, then swing.

The blade hisses through air, and would whisper through flesh. In my tawny hands, this symbol of honor, duty, and valor breaks A'talan law. Despite aching to claim this blade as mine, I slam it home in its sheath.

Rafi watches without comment as I crouch and open the saddlebags.

In the first is the haaka I wore the night of Sahain's ascension. The second contains a pair of new sakier boots, their shafts partially tooled. Bow, sword, boots, and haaka: all treasures Pell ordered dumped in our less-than-stellar neighborhood.

Rafi gestures to the blade. "May I?"

I proffer the pommel.

He frees the sword, sending it singing through the air. Comprehending the masterpiece he wields, words fail him as he returns the blade to its sheath.

I sling one saddlebag over my shoulder, quiver and bow on the other. "He's taunting me, daring me to break the law."

"Sounds about right."

"It won't work. These so called 'gifts' are going back now."

Rafi slings the sword across his back, then shoulders the remaining saddlebag.

When we arrive, the Sun's courtyard resounds with laughter and music. Most Sada prefer Hilen's cooking over the racetrack's mid-day meal. Those who see us cease what they're doing, aware my presence could end in disaster.

The thought of knocking at Enya's door makes my gorge rise. Instead, I rein Khamsin below her balcony, then shout loud enough to be heard. "Pell a'Sada, your outcast would speak with you."

At this time of day, I know he's here. Here, and heard me, just chosen to ignore me.

When I dismount, and hand Rafi Khamsin's reins, he catches my wrist. "Be smart about this."

"I will, if he permits."

I cross to the drum circle, among which is Garin, head of Pell's elite guard. He's always been decent to me.

"Garan, may I borrow your drum?"

He grimaces. "Thea, you must leave. Pell's here."

"I'll leave once he speaks with me." The tremor in my hands is such, Garin passes me his tabor.

I heat the drum head by one of the cook fires over which Hilen's people will soon hang kettles of magnificent soup. My palm swirled over the taut skin, has it hissing like a snake. Struck, it bells high and true.

On the courtyard pavers beneath Enya's balcony, I sit cross-legged, tabor wedged between my thigh and waist, take a deep breath, then consign my soul to Heaven.

Ferocity and speed recreate the sound every Venari dreads: a Daharshan war chant that promises blood will flow and lives end.

As the drum's piercing howl reverberates off the stucco walls, the shrill rhythm shreds the garden's peace. The Sada regard me as if I've taken leave of my senses, which I have in summoning my father to this particular battle.

Atar, frantic, comes darting through the crowd. "Thea, cease!"

Those Venari unaware that it's me, free their blades, their expressions strained at the unexpected Daharshan threat.

A door crashes into a wall above me. Moments later, Pell appears at the balcony, his sword drawn. Taking no longer to grasp what I'm doing than it did for me to plan, he comes down the stairs two at a time.

Atar puts himself in front of me, even as Enya screams from above. "Pell, no!"

The a'Shara slams Atar out of his way. Blade held to the side and expression stone-cold, he addresses me. "I see you, Sha'jin. Say your piece, then be done."

I strain for reason. "Outcasting wasn't enough? You had to heap yet more shame upon me, discarding my ascension gifts for all to see?"

"I needed no reminder of your squandered life."

"Squandered? How? By loving you? By honoring everything you represent?"

His laughter, bitter as kaf, forces me to admit a denied truth. All this man ever wanted was my obedience and homage, not my love.

Blade edge glittering, he leans in. "I cast out a traitor, only to have her prey upon Enya's tender-heartedness, nearly destroying our love. And to think, I was only days from making my enemy's child into an A'talan weapon."

My sanity shatters. I launch at him, fury with a single purpose: to hurt him as much as he's hurt me. He slams his sword hilt into my shoulder and sends me flying. Stars burst in my vision as the back of my head smack against the stone pavers. And still, I rise.

It takes his boot on my breastbone to keep me down. "You will not make me the weapon of your self-destruction. Are you done, or is there more?"

Rafi comes at a run, my ascension sword drawn.

I hold up a hand, begging him not to interfere.

He slows, then halts when Pell remains still.

In the breathless silence which follows, the only sound is the soft plop of blood dripping from my scalp onto the paving stones. My bad blood, hell-bent upon destroying us both. I blink away the haze of anger, and at long last realize this warrior could never love what he's dedicated his life to destroying.

Enya remains poised on the stairs, hands over her mouth. Pell spares her a moment's glance, then speaks in a voice meant to carry.

"Sha'jin, three times I've given you a pass. The morning I found you, the evening I cast you out, and now, for seeking a Venari's grace. If you want death, take your own life. I will not kill a child I raised and once loved."

Once loved. When a dream dies, does it cry?

When able to speak, my every word stands poised on a knife edge of pain.

"I am dust beneath the a'Shara's boots, and will burden him no more."

There's a flash of doubt in his dark eyes as he judges my sincerity. Surely, after seventeen years, he knows I'll keep my word.

His boot comes off my breastbone, and a good thing. With my stomach in knots, I twist onto my side, spewing blood-flecked vomit over the paving stones.

Somewhere in the crowd, Mina screams my name.

Head throbbing, I make it to my knees, throughout wishing I could turn back time and make different choices, and earn different results.

Pell narrows his eyes in disgust. "What was I thinking, trying to teach honor to a nomadi?"

My already-broken heart shatters. Never has he cursed me, calling me the hated other. Yet, even as I have broken faith with him, so has he with me. None of which matters anymore. My war is over. I have lost. It's time for surrender.

"You believed birds swam and fish flew. You believed I loved you."

Yes, I am lying to him, pretending my love has died, and to myself, insisting I no longer care. Yet with this candor, my former reason for living, earning his approval, fades.

As they clear the crowd, Sojur grips the back of Mina's shirt. The sight of me kneeling before my father has Mina wrenching free and racing our way.

She slams her small fists into Pell's unyielding belly. "I hate you! I wish you were dead!"

She whirls and clings to me with all the strength in her wiry body, and keens as if I'm dead.

I rest my cheek against hers. "Shh, Mina, you mustn't disrespect a man that stands between you and people like myself."

Plainly, I can't stop goading him.

"He hurt you!"

I dry her tears with my sleeve. "What I did was stupid. I'll be fine."

This is for Sojur, who now holds out his hand to Mina. "Child, come away."

I kiss her forehead, then urge her toward my teacher. While doing so, Sojur and I share a dark knowing. By seeking to force Pell's hand, I almost squandered his teaching.

However unsteady, I rise. The babble of voices fades as time folds in upon itself and the man I called father meets my gaze. In that moment, the past turns to dust, then drifts away.

Ribs aching, I straighten best I'm able. "A'Shara, the day you cast me out, you didn't give me time to share something only few know. I'm not Daharshan. I'm half A'talan."

There's a collective in-breath from our watchers.

I savor my next words like ripe fruit, yet know they will go down sour. "What little time I spent with my father convinced me the crazy in my blood came from my Venari mother."

Pell's eyes go wide as I call the Haj who gave me life, father. From the start, his obdurate adherence to A'talan superiority raised a barrier between us. What must he feel, discovering the child he repudiated isn't flawed in the manner he thought?

Sorrow deadens my tone. "You taught me your values, but cut me free when I proved the quality of your instruction. We have both won, yet lost. Would that it were otherwise."

Pell's gaze remains opaque. Mine's bereft.

This is the image I will carry the rest of my days. The man who saved and raised me, now righteous in his anger even as his second comforts another little girl who has lost far too much in her brief life.

I whistle for Khamsin and Rafi does the same for Silver. We lower my ascension gifts to the pavers with the respect they warrant.

I have done one thing right. Cut myself free of the misguided worship that defined my life and made me believe my blood would tell.

I swing up on Khamsin, then make reverence to Sojur and Mina, now joined by her siblings. Receive reverence back for the foreigner who found them, fed them, then brought them to safety.

Only then do I look to the man I have worshiped all my life, yet to whom I do not make reverence.

Though bruised and bleeding, his hold on me is forever broken.

I am free. To make my own way, whatever that proves to be.

ACT FOUR

FOR EVERY RIGHT A WRONG

FORTY-FIVE

QUITTING ME

I endure without whimpering as Idry dribbles water over the wound in my scalp.

At the sight of blood darkening the basin over which I lean, Rafi brings his fist down on the table. "Godsdamnit, did you have to goad Pell?"

I ignore him while drying the back of my neck. "Idry, how bad is it?"

"Enough that it needs stitches. I'll send for Nahla."

A nearby rider nods, then takes off at a run.

Rafi raps his knuckles on the table, retrieving my attention. "Can't you think under pressure? No, godsdamn it! You race. You knew exactly what you were doing."

This said as Idry places a goblet of cider before me.

I narrow my eyes at Rafi. "Whatever gave you that impression?"

This time he brings his fist down with such force, the goblet topples, then shatters on the paving stones.

Idry sighs. "I'll get a broom."

"No, damn it! You need to weigh in on this."

"Rafi, it's her life."

"Bullshit! We're talking about the best rider in A'tal. Meanwhile, the bastard who raised her . . ."

Idry grips Rafi's shoulder with such force he falls silent.

The scribe looks at me. "Thea, what do you want?"

"To keep breathing, odd as that sounds after the stunt I just pulled."

Rafi grunts. "About time. What else?"

Before an answer presents itself, my vision grays.

Rafi lunges across the table and grabs me under the arms. "Easy there, I've got you."

Idry replaces the basin with a folded towel. "Rest your head here till the dizziness passes."

I close my eyes, but can't silence the voice in my head.

I've ruined everything. My relationship with Kemu, a chance at citizenship, and now, any possible reconciliation with Pell. In doing my best to hurt the man who raised me, I exhibited neither honor nor restraint. Yet again, I've ended a fight, this time to irrevocable results.

Rafi sits beside me and rests his hand over mine.

I tilt my head his way. "You should have left me on that tree. I am the worst of both my countries."

He tightens a whipcord firm hold on shoulder. "Bullshit. Think of all the times Pell could have ended you, yet didn't. He knows he's wrong. That's why he didn't lash out, no matter how much you had it coming."

I groan while sitting up. "Rafi, what's wrong with me?"

"Girl, if I had the answer, I'd tattoo it on your arm. Is what you threw into Pell's face about being half-A'talan true?"

I nod, unsure whether letting this particular cat out of the bag was wise. "Yet, like my horses, have no proof of nationality."

We fall silent as the rider who went for Nahla returns. He has a healer's wound basket over one forearm while she holds the other, nattering on at his side.

Rafi rises, making room for her. "You took your sweet time."

Paying him no mind, she places a clean towel before me. "Your head, here."

I do so, injured side up.

She probes the wound. "You'll hold still if I numb this?"

"If you don't mind some screaming, I will."

"Scream away so long as you don't move."

Whatever she uses to coat the wound stings, then numbs somewhat. A clamp closes on my skin. A needle punches through my scalp. Gut skitters and drags. By the time she's drawn the first two edges together, I have a death grip on the table's edge. "How many more will it take?"

"Four, no, maybe five stitches. Sure, you don't want a mindhealer?"

"Positive." Justifying my actions to someone like Kemu is the last thing I need now.

By the time Nahla pats my shoulder and tells me she's done, I'm regretting my decision heartily.

She places a cup of pale liquid before me. "Take your time sitting up, then drink this."

Same as Mora's concoctions, honey can't disguise the underlying vileness. Rafi reads my expression and brings water, which I sip while looking to the heavens. "Storm's back."

In more ways than one. Two riders enter the yard. As Lady Edan and Kylin dismount, Rafi makes reverence.

While considering seeking sanctuary in Rafi's rooms, Nahla's hand on my shoulder keeps me seated. "Any dizziness or double vision, send for me."

"I will, and thank you, damă."

She smiles, then crooks a finger at the rider who walked her supplies here. "You get to carry my things back, then return with my bill."

Rafi stiffens, only to reconsider. He lays a hand over his heart as the herbwoman departs. It earns him a sardonic smile.

The Coveners join us in the pavilion, for which Edan arches a brow at Nahla's handiwork. "The Sada a'Shara: never boring, and never predictable."

My flat expression has the desired effect. Gaze hard, she sits across from me. "Are you quitting me?"

Kylin joins her lover, lending weight to Edan's question.

For once, I am not alone in a fight. Rafi's behind me, his hands on my shoulders. "Edan, you don't need Thea training for you."

Her gaze stays on me. "Need and want are two different things."

I put Rafi's unspoken accusation into words. "The Covenants' courts deemed me unworthy. You should do the same."

The change from horsewoman to covener takes all of a heartbeat. "You ingrate, without us, you would have died on that tree."

"True, but minus your 'help,' the children would still be here."

Then again, no one would be searching for their parents.

Edan rises, only to have Kylin pull her back down. "Both of you, quit. Thea, we were wrong in not telling you, and for believing there'd be some leeway in the court's ruling. Still, this is better for you and the children."

"Better how? The Covenant didn't give a damn while they starved to death in that wreck of a barn, yet somehow, deemed my influence inappropriate."

After the events of the past hour, the irony isn't lost on any of us.

In the wake of my mute dissent, Rafi speaks. "Everyone here had a hand in caring for those children, and other than Thea, we're all citizens. Why take them from a woman they adore?"

Edan sighs. "Chalk it up to the disparity between our lives and yours. While an apology changes nothing, please accept it."

If I respond, it will only be to lash out, which Kylin knows. She gives Edan's hand a squeeze, then lets the silence grow, lending weight to what she's about to say.

"Whatever you decide, let me add yet more for consideration. You've survived abandonment, outcasting, and execution. Such miracles are signs of Creation's favor. And then, there's this." She gestures to my ruined birthmark.

"Everything about your life is miraculous. What you are capable of astounds, including your ability to mindspeak without instruction. Mora and I agree it's only a matter of time before your gift reveals itself. Please, don't distance yourself from the Covenant. The day will come when you'll need our help, especially mine."

Expression flat, I regard her. Calling my life a miracle comes under my definition of delusion. As for my 'gift,' I have none other than riding. Even so, I need to keep my mouth shut. If Rafi wants me riding Silver, I will just not happily.

Sensing this, Edan rises and assists Kylin to her feet. "Please, Thea, ride for me. It's been a continuing revelation into Sojur's process. We'll return tomorrow, hopefully still as clients."

I stand, make grudging reverence, then diminish its significance by heading for my stalls.

Rafi calls after me. "Where are you going?"

I keep walking. "Does it matter? I'm taking Khamsin."

Only once Edan and Kylin have departed, do I turn back to him. "Rafi, whatever Nahla charges, take it from my tally?"

He gives me a crooked grin. "You thought I wouldn't?"

A moment later, his gaze sobers. "Send word if you're not returning."

I wave acknowledgement, then once more, head for my father's warhorse.

FORTY-SIX

A SIGN

High above a roiling sea, my battle-inured stallion takes in the scent of the returning storm.

The weather during racing, one day it's sweet as summer's kiss, the next, autumn's harsh backhand. Thunder fists lofty, soot-black clouds. A heartbeat later, a flash of lightning razors the sky. No better than the day I leapt the Horns of the Bull, I flinch. Chin-tucked-to-shoulder, I steady my breath as afterimages fade from my vision.

Somewhere west of us comes the clatter of a tree of bones. I, too, could make macabre music. The Daharshan who fought to rise above her station in life and did, literally. Those unfortunates executed here were non-entities unworthy of pelting with garbage. They elevated me where all could see.

The reminder brings laughter morbid as my thoughts.

No doubt about it. There is something wrong with me.

I hold my arms out to the sea and envision my love for Pell sifting through my fingers. How am I to cease loving the father who bundled me into furs, then rode out into the winter grasslands with me in the crook of his arm? The same man who carved wooden horses for me to play with while he and his ulan commanders strategized. Who made my first bow, who tooled images of my beloved animals into my boots, including those I wear tonight.

The same man who hates me now.

Khamsin snorts as if reminding me that kingdoms have been built by less likely persons, none of which had him or Windsong. He's right. The blood flowing through my veins, though mixed, is rich in battle's fierce heritage.

Such whimsy brings disparaging laughter. Battle's rich heritage is exactly what got me into this mess.

Below, the storm whips the sea into a fury.

If Aaron wants me racing Cinna, I can't cower at Rafi's till the tribes go home. Win and it's easily imagined, my Venari mother and Haj father celebrating their daughter's audacity.

I look beyond the web of lights that define Azalaïs to where Solara stands. A near-infinite expanse of land in a city where most have none. Yet who permits this imbalance if not the same Covenant whose laws 'elevated' me on a tree of bones, then deemed me unfit to assist A'talan children.

Injustice, thy name is A'tal.

Thunder rumbles. Moments later, a bolt of lightning lances into the shore below us. I'm still gulping my heart out of my throat when Kham spins, then bolts. A roar pursues us as the ledge we were on plummets into the sea. Even as this disaster completes itself, further inland, a downpour of lightning daggers to earth.

I'm still shaking and wiping chalk dust from my eyes when, in the distance, flames appear. Starting small, then growing, likely one of the racetrack stables struck by lightning. Any rider seeing this will rush to help any horses trapped within.

I rein Khamsin east, and seek a path down this hill.

When the going's too steep, Kham braces his front hooves while his hinds skid. Only upon reaching level ground do I ask for speed, which Kham has in abundance.

Urged on by horses screaming in the burning stable, he closes the distance between us and a growing mass of light.

I find an empty pen away from the conflagration, then turn Kham loose inside it. Secure the gate with a knot that signifies hands-off. Any idiot ignoring this warning will be met with teeth and hooves.

Hald over my hair and lower face, I hook my rump on the edge of a water trough, then sink beneath its surface. Come up gasping with the cold, then grab a lead rope, and enter the burning stable.

The heat sears my skin as billowing smoke forces me onto hands and knees. Elsewhere in this inferno, others cough, and curse, begging horses to remain sane.

This must be a taste of the seven hells, every breath a gulp of live coals. All that keeps me going are the consequences if I don't.

The heat redoubles, forcing me onto my belly while, fear-crazed, the horse I've fixed upon screams.

Brains near boiling, I reach my target, and pray this horse has sufficient sense to comprehend I'm here to help. Stand and my skin will fry. Thus, I hug the wall, groping for the latch, then find it, and shove upward.

The stall's occupant slams the door open, then scrabbles to make the turn into the main aisle. Swift as a karakal, I swing up onto the panicked animal's back.

As we burst through a wall of flame, those outside hurl buckets of water over us. After the heat, the shock all but stops my heart. I gasp, inhale water, and go into a paroxysm of coughing.

As my mount rears and plunges, a riata sails around their neck. I time my dismount, then slide off, rolling out of harm's way.

What starts as laughter becomes a racking cough. I ride it out on my back, and welcome the rain. I've survived baptism by fire, returning to a place where I have every right to be.

It's like this, staring up into the cloud-shrouded Heavens that I find resolve. I will race Cinna, prove Seth's a brute, and Pell threw away Sojur's legacy.

As for this city and its people, this 'Daharshan' will no longer cower in the shadow of their hate.

FORTY-SEVEN
SIT YOUR ASS DOWN

I'm just one of many soot-covered riders in the gathering hall nearest the burnt-out stable. Bangs a damp veil over my eyes, I sit apart, hoping to avoid notice. Once done eating, I'll return to Khamsin.

As I sop up the last of my soup, polished boots step over the bench across from mine.

A grizzle-bearded Venari in Falili crimson sits, then pushes a mug of ale my way. "Salût."

Astonished at the courtesy, I clink rims with him, then make Thanksgift, and drink.

As he studies me, the sun-scored lines around his eyes deepen. "They say you crawled into that fire on your hands and knees, then rode my filly out, bareback and bridleless. You're not Falili or Venari. Why come to our aid?"

Does he bait me because I'm an outcast? If so, better I answer rather than cause a scene.

"Horses were dying."

"Same as Aaron's filly, or those orphans? You charging in to save the day?"

Anger puts some steel into my spine, repairing my elbows-on-table hunch. "Who are you to take me to task?"

In the wake of his silence, I rise, empty soup bowl in hand.

"Sit your ass back down, granddaughter."

Rather than gape at him, I gesture to the ale. "How much of that have you had?"

He guffaws. "After what you told Pell at the Sun, you didn't think your mother's sire wouldn't take a closer look? I swear you're just like Sabita, wilder than a spring hare and equally willful. Plainly, the apple didn't fall far from the tree."

"Your name, sir?"

As if questioning my ignorance, he cocks his head to the side. "Leonas a'Falili."

This venerated doyen of racing fathered Sabita? I sink back onto the bench, then wince when he brushes his forefinger over my cheekbone.

"Have that seen to. You ride for Rafi, yes?"

I nod.

"A fair number of us didn't buy into his dishonorable discharge. Tell Rafi his second's racing this year, and wants to see him. What about you? Will you run Aaron's filly?"

"Such is my hope."

"He's offered stabling for the Falili horses displaced by the fire. Join us. We'll see to it Pell leaves you alone."

Mug, now empty, he rises, but does not leave.

His patience morphs into amusement as I stare at him, overwhelmed.

"Manners, Granddaughter."

I bolt to my feet, offering an embarrassed reverence.

There's a tinge of regret on his face while he rests his hand on my shoulder. "If only we knew what happened to your mother."

The invitation to claim kinship, however exhilarating, daunts, yet words never before possible leave my lips. "Grandfather, be well."

A smile lights up his face. "The same for you, granddaughter."

He leaves, gait hitching like many of his age, the byproduct of a wound or renegade horse. With the life we live, sooner or later, it happens to everyone.

Bemused, I watch till he's out of sight.

While in Azalaïs, especially at the racetrack, Pell, and Sojur kept me on a tight rein. They feared someone might take exception to the color of my skin and eyes. Yet once an outcast, I never thought to seek a face resembling my own.

An influx of grooms in Solara's black and gold enters the hall, bearing all manner of horse equipment. Aaron and the Falili a'Shara arrive next. Having known these people from his search for Sabita, Aaron has come to their aid.

The a'Shara whistles to his racers, who gather around, accepting the supplies. As they do so, the Lord of Solara surveys the crowd, then spots me. He gestures from his chest to mine, indicating a desire to speak.

I meet him midway.

"My congratulations, Thea. I hear you just saved another filly. Speaking of which, should Cinna need anything, just ask."

As he speaks, one of his people hurries our way, a missive in hand.

Hand-to-heart, I incline my head. "My Lord, I must return to Khamsin."

He gestures permission. "Be well, Thea."

At the exit, I pause.

Unread letter in hand, Aaron stares after me and raises the envelope in farewell.

I answer in kind, sensing he'd prefer coming with me rather than deal with his life's many complications.

In my absence, someone added hay to Khamsin's rick and watered him. The golden stallion ignores both while pacing and calling.

Arms over the top rail, I wait for him to engage.

On the first pass, he brushes my forearm. The next, he halts, then arches his neck over my shoulder. I turn to discover what's caught his attention.

With the stud pen behind me, I have nowhere to go when Kemu strides from the dark. Without a by-your-leave, he splays his fingers over the back of my neck, putting an end to the physical hurt, just not the heartache.

He remains silent for so long that I want to scream: Just tell me I'm a maniac and begone!

Finally, blessedly, he draws back, and studies my face in the light of the remaining flames. "The past few hours, I've been a beat behind you, first at the Sun, then at Rafi's. When the fire began, I broke off, then missed you in the gathering hall. Can you forgive your mother?"

My breath catches. "You know about Leonas?"

"Your grandfather told me everything."

I lower my gaze, unwilling to share the heartache of a mother who didn't assure her daughter's citizenship.

Fingertips beneath my chin, he urges me to look up. "How is it Pell has brought you to your senses, while everything I've said or done has failed? You would be dead if the a'Shara didn't love you. And yet, you couldn't resist sticking the knife in, just like you did to me."

"And just how did I 'stick a knife into you?'"

"By replacing me, rather than seeking a solution."

"If you mean Lycan, he's just a friend."

"Who, given any encouragement, would bed you in a blink."

Exasperation slams into longing, only to bounce off anger. "Kemu, what in the seven hells do you want?"

"A way out of this mess. What about yourself?"

What would I give to heal the wounds between us? The truth? Everything.

In a moment for which I had no expectation, he reads my willingness, and gathers me into his arms. His kiss is of such tenderness that my breath catches, but all too soon, he breaks it off.

"Can we take things slow, then see how it goes? Race Cinna, and you'll have a mountain to climb."

My nod denies what I really want.

"Shall I ride with you to the yard?"

"No need. Kham will get me home safe."

"I'll find you here in the morning and renew the mindblock."

Thoughts in a jumble, I slip through the pen rails, then swing up into Kham's saddle.

Kemu frees the knot on the gate, but ill at ease with leaving matters so unresolved. Halfway through, I halt Khamsin.

Kemu rests his hand on my knee.

For once, rather than shy away from his strength, I thread my fingers through his. "Kemu, can we find our way back to each other?"

If we both try, yes, absolutely. Sleep well, my beloved.
I will, if you're in my dreams.

He smiles, then kisses the back of my hand.
I'll be there.
And he is.

FORTY-EIGHT
ORPHANED

After yesterday's events, I would regard half-awake and somewhat capable as an accomplishment. Cinna offers me no such option. It's early morning, we're at the racetrack, and she's acting the total idiot. Any new sight, and her head is in the air as she spooks, spectacularly.

Word has flown. Last year's Champion of Champions will race a stead-bred horse, and not under the aegis of the filly's breeder or her former tribe. Brows raised for her behavior, Rafi, and my grandfather are among those watching.

For them, I manage a wry smile. Venari will rate Cinna's behavior as deplorable. Not so the people of Azalaïs. Any rider who can stick with what I do comes under their heading of genius. Besides, I want Azalaïs talking about Seth's brutality. About his inability to ride Cinna, and whether there's any truth to the rumors, he sent me to a tree of bones.

The order of go-in-training runs comes down to who wants to run against your horse. I steer Cinna into the holding pen and wait. Word has flown. Shun her, don't breeze your horse against hers.

Losing patience, Rafi stabs his forefinger at the track. "Take her around by herself. Give these assholes something to worry about."

As the last group of riders crosses the finish line, I canter Cinna onto the backstretch, then circle her. Upon spotting Lord Aaron in Solara's box, I wave even as his filly rises on her hinds and paws at the air.

Aaron gives me an enthusiastic thumbs-up. A row higher, Seth and Hemming sit, arms crossed and glowering.

For them, I thrust my fist skyward and dig my spurless heels into Cinna's flanks.

She catapults all four hooves off the ground and lands at a full gallop. In battle, this maneuver would mow down the fiercest of enemies.

As she blasts down the perfect footing, I keep my gaze straight ahead. Many must wish Sojur's best student wasn't in the red filly's irons, foremost among which is her ex-rider.

We cross the finish line full out, yet when asked, Cinna rates herself, coming down from gallop to canter, then trot. Delighted that the nonsense is out of her system, I croon praise, and angle her for the sidelines where Rafi and Leonas wait.

As I do so, hundreds of people manifest a sudden need to look at anything besides the bright red filly and her ex-Sada rider.

Rafi laughs as I halt beside my grandfather. "Just be glad the Falili don't have a three-year-old filly entry. Thea, your grandfather will walk you back to our stalls. There's someone I want to see." He grasps Leonas' forearm, then strides toward a tall Falili coming this way.

Leonas' smile approves as the pair throw their arms around each other. "That's Rafi's second, Aza. It means a lot, you getting Rafi back on the track."

I drop to earth, the loosen Cinna's girth. "Actually, it's the other way around. Rafi's the reason I'm racing."

Leonas pats Cinna's neck, and my filly, still full of herself, flips her head. "Girl, you are some horse. Let's get you out of here before Seth arrives and starts sharing his self-serving opinions."

As we head for the back barns, Leonas threads his arm through mine. "Good thing you didn't take me up on the offer to stable with us. We can't get rid of Seth or his shadow."

"His shadow being Hemming?"

My grandfather nods. "Don't know what to make of the man. Word is we won't see Obsidian run unless Hemming pulls off a miracle. What a shame. The horse was brilliant last year."

We've almost reached our destination when Leonas halts, then spins us in a half circle.

A short distance away, Pell sits D'jhat. As always, a sword rides across the a'Shara's back.

This is the moment I've dreaded: pushing a river that won't leave its bed.

My grandfather says nothing, yet a great deal when he drapes his arm over my shoulders.

Pell inclines his head. "Leonas."

Amusement eddies in my grandfather's tone. "A'Shara. No need to introduce my granddaughter."

Pell's brows raise enough to acknowledge the claim, yet convey doubt.

Leonas blesses my temple with a kiss. "Join me for dinner in the main gathering hall tonight?"

Inherent in his invitation is faith I'll be alive to do so.

I nod, gaze on the man who raised me.

Allegiance made clear, Leonas takes his leave. Should Pell get physical, the Falili veteran just put him on notice.

With my grandfather gone, my status as an outcast proves a blight keeping others away.

Into the resulting silence, Pell eases a question. "Why save Leonas' filly? To validate your lie about being half-A'talan?"

My laughter comes out horehound-bitter. "Leonas sought me out. I didn't know my mother was his daughter."

Reading Pell's temper, D'jhat surges.

Cinna yanks back far as her reins will allow. Last damn thing I need is this filly running amuck. "Either get your bastard horse off us, or I'll take a fist to his nose."

There, I've said it. I hate his horse. As expected, Pell does nothing. Instead, he forces me to grab D'jhat's bridle, then heave him off us.

My father's gaze evidences fleeting admiration for flouting his will. All too soon, it hardens into a demand for docility I have no intention of offering.

"A'Shara, you taught me to honor my father, yet sent Venari to kill the man who made me. Mercifully, someone told me he still lives."

The blow hits. His lips tighten.

None of which silences me.

"Despite lacking citizenship, as last year's Champion of Champions, I have every right to race. Do what you will. I won't lie down. I won't go quietly."

There's no challenge in my tone. Just a simple statement of purpose. Yet this could be when he frees his blade and puts the mass of his shoulders behind it. If so, little wonder. I've thrown my blood father into his face, again, and in the doing, proven I'd rather die than cower in the shadows.

Hand-to-heart, I make a curt reverence, then let Cinna drag me away from D'jhat. As we head for our stalls, my neck prickles, half-expecting my head parted from my shoulders.

Instead, Pell a'Sada, the scourge of Daharsha, displays restraint in the face of extreme provocation. Same as he did at the Sun.

Out of respect for Leonas? Or could a shred of fondness remain for the dark-skinned child who loves him still?

FORTY-NINE

DEMENTED

The wine of ripening apples intoxicates as I make my way to the racetrack's gathering halls. By now, the home I will never see again is a waist-high sea of shimmering gold, set against Daharsha's red sands. Here, the seasons turn slower. Only a few fallen leaves crunch beneath my boots.

Heads swivel. Conversations start or stop as I seek Leonas in the hall. Yet who deigns to speak to me if not Gayleen a'Rowan, boots up on a second chair while sipping kaf.

"I'll be damned. Just look what the karakal dragged in."

I've witnessed Gayleen's acrid temper often enough, just not as her target. Her Venari, dozens deep, pay their a'Shara the tribute of silence. Having taken her stance, they have the good sense not to challenge it. Nor will I. Her legendary sword hangs from the back of her chair. Give Gayleen trouble, and she'll end me.

"So, Thea, what's next? Start a war? Destroy Azalaïs? Oh, never mind. Let's just keep this simple. Why the hells are you here?"

This woman doesn't give a damn if I respond to her needling, likely hopes I will. I offer her reverence, with no expectation of acknowledgment. "Same as you, a'Shara. I'm here to eat, in my case, with my grandfather."

Her eyes go wide at the claim. She tosses back the last of her kaf, then holds the cup above her shoulder.

One of her Venari takes it and strides away.

I arch a brow. "Not looking to sleep tonight?"

Her eyes narrow at my audacity.

Gayleen has opted for informality tonight. Rather than battle braids, she's bound her hair at the nape of her neck. While it makes her look approachable, it's an illusion, done for her beloved, now nursing their latest child in a group of mothers.

She snaps her fingers, retrieving my attention. "Is it true that you told Pell, 'I won't lie down? I won't go quietly?'"

"It is."

"Are you demented? Your father is, hands down, the best among us. If Daharsha declared war, Pell would command all five tribes. Should he take exception to a Covenant decision, this nation would demand he had the final say. Surely you get this?"

The question is rhetorical. I don't respond.

She passes a breath over her clumped fingertips. "Just like that, every A'talan would answer to Pell a'Sada, because he is fair, and because Venari respect him. And then there's you.

"Remember the night I said I'd take you into my ulans, naked as the day you were born? Venari-to-be come and go. Some make it, some don't. But you, you had it all: grit, will, talent, determination. And what did you do? Challenge Pell, not once, but three times. I won't piss him off simply because you lack self-control. Can you grasp what I'm saying?"

I've had a gut-load of powerful people seeking to intimidate me. Though aware I'm about to go too far, it doesn't stop me.

"No, a'Shara, I can't. Please spell it out for me."

As if seeking restraint, Gayleen takes a deep breath. "Simply, the Rowan need Kemu, a mindhealer who wields a sword better than most in my ranks. A man whose courage, honor, and dedication inspires, so much so, his company voted him to be their captain come year's end. Mind you, provided his fixation on an errant lover doesn't distract him to ruin."

She rises, then thuds her forefinger against my breastbone. "Either Kemu gets his head back on straight or he'll wreck entire career. That's why you'll never earn the name Thea a'Rowan."

Comprehension dawns. "He asked you to overturn my outcasting?"

"Exactly. I gave the idea consideration till you attacked Pell at the Sun."

Just like that, everything turns upside down.

"While feeling sorry for yourself, here's yet more misery. Pell and Sojur are ready to call it quits as each other's seconds. After watching you ride that red filly today, your teacher demanded Pell make an exception, then let you race Amir. Naturally, Pell refused. Thus, what your father sought to prevent will happen. Sojur, minus five fingers and a foot, will ride against Aaron's stallion, Obsidian, the most out-of-control creature I have ever seen on four hooves."

Tongue to the roof of her mouth, she clicks a slow, unimpressed rhythm. "Well done, Thea. Well done, indeed."

Her Venari returns with a steaming cup of kaf.

Gayleen waves it away. "Leave it. This knothead needs the kick in the ass more than I do." One more pointed glare for me and she leaves, her retinue trailing behind.

My presence has cleared a goodly swath in a hall that's elbow-to-elbow people. What did I expect? I am an anathema.

I sink onto Gayleen's chair, then take a tentative sip of kaf. She's right. I need this, this and a real kick in the ass. Under no circumstances should Sojur race. The danger is just too great.

Kemu knows I can't kill my own kind, not after meeting my sire and brother. Why ask Gayleen for an exception?

Sojur enters the hall with a group of Sada riders. Mina is at his side, her gaze bounding between those asking him questions and his answers. Despite breaking the Court's injunction against contact with the children before hundreds of witnesses, I must convince Sojur not to race.

Mina tugs on Sojur's wrist, then points to me. With a weary smile, he nods permission.

The little girl darts through the crowd.

I rise and catch her in my arms. Bless her hair with a kiss, then step aside so Sojur may use Gayleen's chair. While we wait, I finger-comb her curly hair off her face. "Are the others with Enya?"

Head tipped back, and expression dazzled, she nods.

"Is Sojur teaching you?"

She bobs her head, eyes awash with hero worship. "He's . . ."

". . . Amazing?"

She beams agreement, then joins me in making reverence as Sojur arrives, and sits with obvious relief. A good twenty years older than most here, his missing foot makes these pre-race days brutal.

The lines in his face deepen as he takes in my worn brecca and battered boots. "Just think, had I sent you to a different guard post, you'd be in Sada emerald today."

This can't go anywhere good for either of us.

"Master, who can grasp Heaven's purpose?"

Mood dark, he nods. "Yet, miracle of miracles, you're racing."

"As I hear you are."

He tilts his head back and regards me with a weighing expression. In the past, whenever I argued with him, he'd give me "the look," and wait till I came to my senses. Since calling him on his treatment of Rafi, he's given my concerns measured consideration.

"Master, I beg of you, pick another rider for Amir. No one knows if Hemming will race Lord Aaron's Obsidian, but everyone says he can't control the stallion."

A tinge of bitterness taints Sojur's half-smile. "While I appreciate your concern, the only ones who can do justice by Amir are us. His bid for the Champion of Champions is now vital. I've penned my resignation for once racing is over."

I rub my forehead, weighing how far I can go. Sojur cannot risk his life. Nor is he more crazy than sane, which riding at speed in a crowded field demands. With all that's at risk, I say what I feel.

"Don't, Sojur, not for any reason. Horses are the heart of every ulan, and you are the soul of the Sada. Don't abandon those who need you."

His gaze shifts to something behind me. When his posture stiffens, I turn.

Riders dive to get out of Pell's way. He knows there's a fox in the hen-house and intends to be rid of me.

Mina presses her back into my legs, her posture stiff and defensive as my own.

The a'Shara ignores us, his gaze on Sojur. "Ride with me to the Sun?"

Sojur shakes his head. "I'm not done here yet."

Had I any doubt, the lack of warmth in Sojur's tone and his remaining seated underlines just how at odds they are.

Pell rests his hand on his friend's shoulder, inviting further explanation.

I grew up on stories of Pell's agony, of how, hounded by guilt and desperation, he refused sleep and food. A moment's inattention and the enemy seized his second. Two weeks later, Sojur rode back into camp, more dead than alive and forever changed. From that day forward, Pell visited the seven hells upon any Daharshan who crossed his path.

Now another 'Daharshan' stands between them, for which there is only one solution, however much I wish it otherwise.

"Mina, please watch for Leonas a'Falili and explain why I had to leave."

The nothingness in Pell's gaze is worse than hate. Having created the fracture in their relationship, I pray not to make it worse.

"A'Shara, I beg of you, craft the means to protect the greatest horseman alive. If not for your friendship and the Sada, then for the world."

I bless Mina with a kiss, make reverence to them all, then turn and walk away.

While doing so, I pray somehow, some way, my father will make it right.

FIFTY

AN UNCANNY
SIMILARITY

A man sits in a two-horse cart near Cinna's stable. The nearer I come, the greater my certainty. "Kane?"

He swivels on the driver's seat. "Thea! I was about to seek you at the pavilions. Lord Aaron requests your presence at Solara."

I stifle a sigh. "Do you know why?"

"He said you'd ask and to say he'll explain everything. Two of the yard's riders will stay with Cinna. Have you eaten yet?"

"Sadly, no." I settle in the cart beside him.

"A meal waits at Solara. So, how was our filly today?"

He clucks, and the matched pair step into a brisk trot.

Plainly, there won't be any details forthcoming. I content myself with the day's tales about the horse we saved, yet fall silent as the gates of Solara close behind us. While passing the main stables, I search for life yet find none. Equally puzzling, Kane doesn't offer an explanation.

Being Solara, it takes time to get where we're going. Tall grasses toss and rattle between us and our destination: a rectangular pavilion overlooking the sea.

Kane halts the team, then points to a path winding through the seagrasses. "That will take you to Aaron. Good luck."

Puzzled, I clasp the hand he offers, then watch him out of sight.

Surrounded by the rush of the sea, I make my way through the maze of towering white plumes and rustling fronds.

The grass thins, then ends, revealing the pavilion. Its barren simplicity emulates the chalk cliff upon which it stands. The long south side is open to the sea. Aaron sits beneath its portico, his brooding gaze on a life-sized painting.

A Falili Venari sits a'horse, reins in one hand, the other on her brecca. Her posture in the saddle bears an uncanny resemblance to mine. I don't need telling this woman gave me birth.

I halt and clear my throat. "Lord Aaron?"

His spurs sing as he rises. "Ah, Thea, thank you for coming."

He gestures me closer so I may better regard the mother who hoped I'd live a 'spiritual life.'

Harsh realism portrays Sabita's clarity of gaze. Behind her left shoulder, Covenant steel juts. Her haughty expression suggests her choice to deny Leonas his Mother-marked granddaughter arose from pride.

I clamp down on the fury this guess brings.

"When was this painted?"

"Shortly before she disappeared." His gaze moves between the portrait and me. "Sabita must smile, seeing us together."

It's obvious he still worships the woman Khalil made his Haj'ene. Me? Not so much.

A wine service and covered platters rest on a linen-covered table facing the portrait.

"Please sit. Which would you prefer: red wine or white?"

The red's blood-rich minerals dance on the salty air. "Red, please."

Unlike our first meal together, intuition offers me no counsel as we chime wine glasses, then make Thanksgift.

Held to the light, rubies dance in the wine. I take a sip, and as the vintage fills my mouth, a murmur of appreciation comes easily. "Sojur would love this."

"I'll have a case sent to him. May I serve?"

I nod, bemused at an aristocrat treating me like a member of his class. Aaron's egalitarian nature may have been a quality my mother found attractive.

The plate he fills would be greeted with favor on the grasslands. "Did Kane tell you of my search for those who perpetrated your false accusation?"

"He did."

He sets the filled plate before me. "Please eat. Leave anything not to your taste. After today's events, I have no appetite."

Sensing there will be no rushing him, I eat in the mainland's manner: knife in one hand, fork in the other. Aaron drinks with equal deliberation.

Only after refilling our glasses does he speak. "Today at court, I received confirmation your accusers have fled to Shadreal, and are beyond A'talan justice."

I trade the fork and knife for wine.

"The proof of yet another conjecture awaited my return home. Namely, half my stables empty with an equal depletion of my grooms, with Hemming nowhere to be found. Seth's horses, tack, clothing, and furnishings, all gone, most likely to his mother's estates, endowed to him at birth. Had Kane not been here, my son would have taken Obsidian as well. A horse for which I paid a fortune, and have entered this year's Champion of Champions race. Mind you, done in hopes Hemming would get the horse under control."

A horrible question arises. Could Seth have done something dastardly as contriving the conflagration at the track? Idiot! He damn near killed you. What's keeping him from thinning his competition?

I yank myself back into the now. "Obsidian's not ready to race?"

Aaron's lips tighten. "Not by your standards. Still, I paid his fees and prayed for a miracle."

The suggested betrayal cuts deep.

Uncertain how my words will be received, I speak softly.

"That night on the tree, Seth arrived on Obsidian. He told me to die well, and that it cost him a great deal to deliver me to my fate."

Aaron regards me with a grim expression. "After my wife's death, I didn't have the heart to deny my son anything. As he grew older, his cruelty surfaced. I set limits, for which he'd promise to do better and did, in that he hid his aberrations. Can you forgive me for drawing you to his attention?"

I swallow. My first apology, and it's from the first Lord of the land. "There's nothing to forgive. Seth's choices are his alone."

Aaron fortifies himself with yet more wine. "Thus, we arrive at why you are here. Word is my son has leased the best unclaimed stable at the track, and that Hemming is now his head rider and trainer. I have a great need for someone of your caliber. Name your price and conditions. Whatever, whoever you want, it's yours."

He looks to Sabita's portrait. "I met your mother during racing, the ten most exhilarating days of my life. When she returned to the grasslands, I lasted a week before following her. Thus, I, better than most, appreciate the quality of blood flowing through your veins.

"Before Sabita's death, she was well on her way to commanding a Falili ulan, and had her eyes on the ultimate prize: a'Shara. And then, she was gone."

I can't let him continue, not in good conscience. Whether for good or ill, however this plays out, it won't take long.

"Lord Aaron, the morning we met?"

"Yes, what of it?"

I gesture to the painting. "When my sire gave me Khamsin, an older brother rode at the Haj's side. This brother spoke near perfect A'talan."

I steel myself. "The woman you love lives."

Aaron looks from the hard-eyed Venari to me, the hurt on his face palpable. "You couldn't tell me this sooner?"

"When we first met, I didn't know or trust you. Nor did my being half-A'talan become common knowledge till my set-to with Pell. You and one other know the truth about my mother."

"That person being Leonas?"

"No, he's next. He knows I'm Sabita's daughter, just not that she lives."

As he considers the implications, Aaron's brows rise at my status as a Haj's daughter. Yet, when he speaks, sorrow burdens his tone. "Why trust me with something so precious and personal?"

On this, I have no reservations.

"How can I not? I owe you my life."

He smiles at the tribute paid. "We share so much. Will you take up Solara's reins and ride for me?"

"Ride for you, yes, yet I lack the experience of a Master of Horse. Rafi a'Falili and his scribe, Idry, would be the better choice."

"Are they a condition of your employment?"

Bad enough, answering to this man for what I can or cannot do in the saddle. "Yes, they are."

"Kane would second your request, and after what I saw of Idry and Rafi at court, I'm inclined to agree."

"It would give Solara the best of all worlds. As for myself, I ask only one thing."

"Which would be?"

"That you heed my counsel, however outrageous you may find it."

A ghost of a smile touches his lips. "I will, provided an explanation accompanies said outrageous counsel. Is that satisfactory?"

"It is."

He stands and offers his forearm. "What will Sojur say about his most gifted student running against him, perhaps beating him on Obsidian? The horse is just that talented."

With a tentative smile, I clasp his forearm. "He will say, 'May the best horse win.'"

Aaron beams. "Thea, welcome to Solara. Do me and your mother proud."

I smile while making reverence.

This man, I will serve. The woman who left me in the lurch? May our paths never cross.

FIFTY-ONE

SHOW ME

No doubt about it, summer's wriggling her backside at fall.

We canter along the shore, our breath white as hoarfrost on the chill air. Scavenging seabirds rise on sharp wings, shrieking their disapproval as we pass. Grooms at seaside racing inns pause, their speculative gazes taking in last year's Champion of Champions riding at Lord Aaron's side.

The morning fog thickens.

Aarron's people light our way into Solara's racetrack complex, where, in the main stable, Kham greets me with a stallion's deep whicker. Windsong and Cinna whinny greetings, all safe and opulently housed.

The noise brings Rafi and five of the yard's riders, like me, dressed in Solara's black and gold. When I slant Rafi a questioning look, he mouths, 'Later.'

Aaron gestures for his still loyal grooms to gather around. As he speaks, these men evidence tension, their arms crossed and gazes hooded. With two ex-grassland riders at the helm, a change of guard may mean jobs lost.

I've lived their lives, pushing hard, praying sleep would heal any damage done, and enduring when it didn't. Prove my value to Aaron, and I'll have the luxury of not battering my body during racing.

Kaf arrives, then Aaron, who asks about the day's order of go and which horses we want first.

I sip and consider. I must prove myself equal to the challenge. "Obsidian?"

Arron smiles, pleased by my willingness to take 'the bull by the horns.' "Come with me. He's in a different stable."

As we walk through the still-dense gloom, the sound of horses starting their day emphasizes my altered life. Were I still Sada, I too would be feeding and grooming, wondering which rides Sojur would assign me. There'd be no need to prove myself capable of riding a stallion this entire city calls brilliant, yet uncontrollable.

Before we reach the last of Solara's stables, a groom detains Aaron for a question. He motions us to go on ahead.

We share a puzzled look for the empty, albeit impeccable one-horse stable.

While we wait, Rafi strikes a pose, sweeping his hand across his polished, knee-high black boots. "No expense spared: made to measure overnight. Talk about rising above and beyond." All this accompanied by a waggling eyebrow.

"Listen, you peacock, I prefer everyday riding clothes."

"In which you'd be believable as Solara's head trainer and rider?"

I glare at him, for which he makes a placating gesture. "I get the pressure you're under. That said, why not accept the role of Master of Horse?"

"Are you kidding? Doing a decent job in the saddle will take all I have. Last damn thing I need is the burden of Aaron's people and herds."

Rafi sighs. "Far too often, I forget how young you are. Truce?"

I manage a half smile. "So, how did my horses and half your riders get here?"

"Aaron met with us last night. He offered lavish payment in advance for anyone willing to help. We sorted out who wanted to race, then put it to a vote. Those not racing will keep the yard going. Those clients who stay on will get free board till we're all back to work."

My eyes widen. "Does that include Lady Edan?"

"Not only did she accept, she sent her congratulations and hopes if the opportunity arose, we'd invite her and Kylin as our guests."

I groan. "That woman won't give up."

He laughs. "Neither will Kylin."

Before I can respond, a stallion's scream tells me my day's about to begin. Good thing my stomach is mostly empty. It's hard to impress, bent double, puking. "If I were you, I wouldn't get too comfortable. This whole arrangement could come apart in a heartbeat."

Rafi grins. "Not likely with you in the irons."

Four grooms appear, struggling to lead my ride. Obsidian's body billows steam. He screams while straining against a war bridle, its narrow cords wound behind his ears, then through his mouth, from which blood drips.

Rafi and I grew up riding spirited horses, just not horses crazed by incompetent or brutal handling. We share our mutual distaste for the violence being done to an animal now under our care.

I shout to be heard over Black. "What configuration of bit?"

Forearms bulging, a groom blocks the stallion's bid to take a chunk out of his arm. "Twisted wire."

As expected, and for which I draw my belt knife, then get a hand on Black's scalding shoulder. As I work my fingers up to his poll, his eyes show white all around.

Once there, I discover the cords have sliced through the delicate skin behind his ears. "Someone, pad a halter's crown, then add a set of reins."

A groom departs at a run, and returns equally swiftly.

Getting the halter on Black takes speed, me quick as a striking snake while pulling it over the war bridle. He heaves us skyward, his blood-engorged nostrils flaring as he comes down trembling, expecting yet more abuse.

In that fragile moment, I slice through the bridle and the bit falls from his mouth. I pull the severed bridle pieces out from under the halter, then toss the reins over his neck, and vault onto his bare back.

Nothing happens. He quakes, awaiting further brutality.

I chirrup. Black goes vertical, and lands like lightning. The steam billowing off his body engulfs me.

Knowing he's not done, not by a long shot, I ask again.

He lets loose with another buck, high as the first, this one fishtailing at its peak.

I'm not built like a bull, like Seth. Without a saddle, this horse may well unseat me. It wouldn't be the first time, just the worst.

Hide twitching, he returns to earth.

I stroke his neck and croon. "Black, my beauty, surely you'd rather run than buck."

At my soothing tone, he swivels his ears, listening to my voice.

I hold my hand to the curve of his jaw, then whisper, "Show me, horse."

He takes a board-tense step as I close my lower legs on his ribs, for which I ask no one in particular. "Which way to the track?"

A dozen arms point.

I squeeze again. This time, Black jumps forward. Not upward.

The grooms run ahead, their lanterns marking a path through the fog out of which a practice track appears.

Black goes up onto his hinds and screams. For him, this is a place of pain. It takes everything Sojur taught me to get him on the track. Twice he tries to spin and bolt.

Rather than punish, I keep asking for forward, then accept the stiff, defensive canter he offers.

Gradually, his gait loosens, and gives me a glimpse of what this horse can do at speed. Even so, a single veer or buck, and he'd slam me to the turf or hurl me against the rails. No matter. This horse needs me to be with him now, rather than worrying about myself.

As if reading my thoughts, he extends his stride.

Even as his breathing fountains over me, his speed rips tears from my eyes. Doubtless, he's puzzled by what I'm not doing: yanking, spurring, or kicking.

Lord Aaron and Rafi's faces blur as we pass.

The stories about this horse have not done him justice. Black's extreme height and ferocity has him charging down the straightaway as if crushing enemies beneath his hooves.

Muscles molten against mine, he exalts in his speed as the first rays of dawn pierce the fog, and ignite the coat for which he was named.

Fearing he could run till his heart bursts, I burr a low, calming sound.

His ears swivel as he shifts from gallop to canter, then to a walk, stride long and loose as he clears his airway.

When grooms start our way, I hold up a restraining hand. "If someone will show me where everything is, I will care for him myself."

A brief discussion ends with one groom remaining.

Reins still over his neck, I slide off and stroke his shoulder. "Horse, it's just you and me from here on."

He walks at ease as I lead him to Rafi and Aaron, who doesn't approach the horse he owns.

"Can you race him?"

"I'll ride him back to Solara tonight, then see if he'll let me make the decisions."

Rafi nods approval of my plan. "Earn this horse's trust, and he may well win you your second Champion of Champions' title."

Aaron smiles, delighted with our consensus. "Once you've bathed him, join us in the main stable."

I acknowledge his request, then follow the groom.

As we move through the brightening dawn, Black moves closer till the slip of his shoulder brushes mine.

This is when I vow, whatever I can do for this horse, I will.

FIFTY-TWO

MASTER OF HORSE

Rafi and I indulge in an entrenched Venari habit, resting whenever and wherever we can. Today, it's at the track in Solara's private viewing box, our boots up on the rail below us.

Though approaching midday, the field is still crowded. Every savvy rider takes advantage of running on the track we'll race on. We've been doing the same ever since I rode Black this morning.

To my left, Aaron passes me the next horse's records. "Yuni, a three-year-old colt. This summer, a first and two seconds, then a couple of starts we'd just as soon forget."

He's making little of the less-than-stellar runs where this colt came in dead last. "His dam is the mare I rode this morning."

He taps the sire's name on Yuni's papers. "After his death last summer, I bought Obsidian."

I hand Rafi Yuni's pages. The ex-Venari has proven at ease with the role of Solara's Master of Horse. Not only that, he looks the part he's playing. So much so, I question his oft-declared distaste for the upper classes.

At his right, Idry takes in everything with a quiet dignity that befits Solara. Heaven only knows what Azalaïs makes of me.

Yuni and his rider are next up at the starting line. For the practice runs, riders break in twos and threes, with no interference from track officials. The congestion doesn't faze Yuni, a lively black bay. While awaiting their turn, another rider blasts across the finish line.

It's Kemu, on Celio, his four-year-old stallion.

In a heartbeat, Rafi and I are on our feet, shading our eyes as the pair eases down to a canter.

Aaron rises as well. "Will they be a problem?"

Rafi voices my thoughts. "That horse will be everyone's problem."

Aaron sends me a piercing look. "Better than Black?"

I'm still framing an answer when Rafi directs my attention back to the track. I look, then, do a double-take. Kemu's brought Celio around. A victor's spray of red roses with blue ribbons now rides in the crook of Kemu's arm.

Rafi guffaws. "Brace yourself. He's about to embarrass you in front of everyone."

Another rider in Rowan sapphire catches Celio's reins when Kemu vaults from the saddle into the viewing stands. Gaze fixed on me, he does not engage with those razzing him with their lewd suggestions.

My stomach knots. This is his idea of taking it slow?

He reaches Solara's guards, for which Aaron gestures permission for his entry.

Smile contained, Kemu goes to a knee before me and proffers the roses. "My lady, please accept this token of my devotion."

I hesitate, unsure about what's called for in such theater.

Rafi elbows me in the ribs. "Take them. Now's the time, and he's plainly made this the place."

At my stiff, discomforted nod, Kemu returns to his feet, and lays the long-stemmed roses in my arms.

They are beyond perfection: gem-bright dew on scarlet petals: leaves glossy, every thorn removed. Thanks to Enya, I know such masterpieces may please the eye, yet lack the soul-melting savor of a rose's sweetness. Not so these with their intoxicating perfume of honeyed spice.

Hand along my jaw, Kemu leans in and kisses me. Not some here-and-gone kiss. More of a statement meant to be witnessed by any rivals.

I'm breathless by the time he breaks it off, breathless and speechless at the avowal he's made.

Smile one-sided, he reads my wide-eyed shock. "I meant what I said about Gayleen being my problem. Hence the public declaration."

Aaron holds out his forearm in welcome. "A'Rowan, good to see you again. Your stallion, however, worries me."

Kemu laughs, at ease with the awkward situation he's created. "As he does many people."

I know Aaron well enough to read the tension this statement produces. Still, he smiles.

"Please, join us at Solara tonight. Arrive around sunset. We'll dine in our stable offices, where you can tell me more about Celio."

"I'll be there and thank you for the invitation." Kemu makes reverence to Aaron, then turns to me.

"You are ever in my thoughts." Yet another blinding smile, then swift as his arrival, he clatters down the stairs.

I'm still staring after him when Rafi taps my shoulder, then gestures to the starting line. "Yuni's ready to go."

I breathe in the roses' fragrance, heady as what's just happened, then force my attention on the track.

While Yuni runs well, the same can't be said of his rider: whip flashing and spurs relentless.

I add Sojur's notation for lackluster to this rider's name. "Aaron, please call them back. I want to try this colt."

He crooks a forefinger to a Solara groom below, his signal for 'Bring them in.' It's the first time he's used it today.

I remove my riding coat. Yuni is young and I may need the freedom to move. "Is Yuni's rider one of Seth's or Hemming's hires?"

Aaron nods. "One of the few they didn't take with them."

"Can I fire him?"

"If you deem it prudent, yes."

Not only is this rider incompetent, if in Seth's camp, he's a spy. I go down the steps two at a time, then loft over the rail onto the track.

Yuni's rider is more than ready for a fight. "Why call us back? We were doing fine."

"Not in my estimation, you weren't. Get off."

His face goes brick red. For a moment, I think he'll refuse. Instead, he kicks out of the irons, then leaps to the ground.

While I shorten the offside leather, this clod doesn't have the manners to ask what change I want on the mounting side. Instead, he forces me to walk around him and change it myself.

I make peace with the bit in Yuni's mouth and swing up. Now is as good a time as any. "Something you want to say?"

He spits and mumbles a rank description of my character. The gist of which is I'm better suited for work in the alleys where I found Mina. Not only is he a shitty rider, he's fathoms off the mark.

"You're fired. When I return, don't be in Solara's stables."

I request a canter, and Yuni responds enthusiastically. So much so, he forces his former rider to lurch out of our way.

A stream of invectives peppers our backs.

I don't respond, having grown up with more creative descriptions of my worth.

Another three-year-old joins those waiting their turn: Hanan, who now exhibiting a warhorse's steady confidence. His rider is another story. The same man who said no price was too high for my love glares at me. Either Lycan saw Kemu's extravagant gesture or someone told him about it.

I rein Yuni head-to-tail with Hanan, for which Lycan's shock battles with outrage.

"After everything Sojur did for you, you'll race against the horse you bred and gave him?"

In short, the Sada are at a boil, believing I intend Sojur harm. Aware my behavior must befit Aaron's standards, I school my tone to mild. "If someone else became Solara's trainer, would that help Sojur?"

Lycan's anger becomes confusion. "What are you suggesting?"

"What I am about to say is for Sojur's hearing only, and Lord Aaron wants this to remain a secret. Obsidian will run only if I have him under control."

His expression swings between doubt and relief.

Odd how life plays out. Without my help, Lycan would not own Hanan.

Aza, Rafi's second, whistles approval as he comes up alongside me. "Just look at you, in Solara's colors, and on a Solara horse! Want to run against my colt?"

Aza's grin suggests Rafi's shared details about my love life.

He looks to Lycan. "Hey, Sada, join us. We'll make this a real race."

Grudgingly, Lycan joins us at the line, where we count to three, then release.

Yuni approaches racing as if it's nothing to get excited about. If I'm to validate Aaron's confidence in this colt's bloodlines, the colt's attitude needs changing. I bring my lower legs down hard on his sides.

Startled, Yuni squirts forward, pulling up even with Hanan. The red horse goes faster. I draw my legs off a second time.

It's all the threat needed. Yuni accepts, with me, a lackadaisical attitude won't cut it and extends his stride. The fence posts blur as we fly down the straightaway, then lean into the last turn.

Aaron, Rafi, and Idry are on their feet, yelling for yet more speed.

Yuni complies. We cross the finish in a storm of hoofbeats, nose-to-nose with Hanan and Aza's colt.

I rise in the irons and pat Yuni's neck. As he rates himself from gallop to canter, I tell him he's wonderful.

Aza gives me a thumbs-up before peeling off to where Leonas stands beaming at me.

I answer by kissing my knuckles, then thumping fist-to-shoulder. The salute turns my grandfather's smile into a grin.

Expression impenetrable, almost Daharshan, Lycan heads for where Sojur waits.

The reverence I offer my teacher receives no response. If Lycan delivers my message, I hope things will go better next time.

As we come off the track, our head groom hands me my coat. "Midday meal will be in Aaron's office. By the way, well done unloading that jackass. Will you ride Yuni back to the stable?"

I nod. "Anything else of that nature, please give us a heads-up?"

He ticks finger-to-forehead. "Gladly."

I smile, then offer him reverence.

The formality pleases him, so much so, he smiles back as I rein away. If this man sides with us, it may ease some of our challenges.

I jog Yuni past riders, grooms, farriers, and enthusiasts, in short, the noisy sundry of racing. Oddsmakers yell, asking if I'll race Yuni in his qualifier. I answer with a smile and shrug. They know better than to ask such questions.

Solara's main stable entry allows riders to enter without dismounting. I do so to find a groom awaits us. Together, we strip Yuni's tack, then sponge and scrape him down. While the groom wraps the colt's legs, I study Yuni's conformation.

The groom talks as he works. "This boy's a good 'un. Didn't understand why Seth passed him over."

"Just be thankful he did."

He laughs. "Aye, there's that. I'll get a cooler on him, then walk him out."

"Is his tack stored in the main get-ready area?"

"It is. You'll find his name above his rack."

Feather-light racing saddle over one arm, bridle on the other, I make my way into the get-ready. This orderly haven of oiled leather meets Sojur's exacting standards.

With Yuni's saddle on its rack, I turn my attention to switching out his bit. Tomorrow, I'll be able to rate Yuni without hurting his mouth. I like this colt, so much so, I'm considering racing him, thus need to know how much horse I can save for the finish.

While coiling the reins, then fastening them into the bridle's throat latch, I hear someone come up behind me. Thinking it's the groom, I don't turn.

Gloved hands close around my throat.

Yuni's bridle crashes to the stone floor as Seth speaks, his voice an eddy of winter's cold. "Race Obsidian, and I *will* see you dead."

Desperate for air, I reach over my shoulders and claw at his face. Short as my nails are, blood greases their progress through his skin.

A moment later, I'm face down on the floor, dazed from a blow to the head. I groan, and wrench onto my back, ready to kick.

Seth is nowhere to be seen. The only proof he was ever here is my bruised throat and the eddy of scent, depraved as its wearer.

Still woozy, I pull myself upright on a saddle stand.

No one witnessed this event. Raise the alarm now, and it will only complicate what's left of this day.

I pray I'm equal to the stakes for which I play, and yet again, heartily regret the steel not riding my back.

FIFTY-THREE

FOR EVERY RIGHT, A WRONG

G ravel crunches beneath my boots as I walk to Solara's stable complex. Tonight's meal will be formal, thus I wear a form-fitting coat and skintight leggings no sane person would swing over a horse.

My disquiet overshadows anticipation even as color fades from the western sky. While I have every expectation of Kemu joining us, his 'let's take things slow' gnaws at me. In twelve days, racing will be over. Time in which we must heal the trust broken between us and seek solutions to our many problems. Fail, and he'll return to the grasslands while I remain here. Having witnessed Enya's life of yearning, I won't live like that.

This day's brutality may have brought on my unease, not that tomorrow will be any better. We'll put to test the twenty horses we select tonight, racing flat-out on the private track where I rode Black. Solara's grooms will keep the curious at bay as Rafi and I discover which of Aaron's horses are the true contenders.

The welcome aroma of warm food guides me to the main offices. There, I pause in the entryway.

Four men sit at the table: Aaron, urbane and confident, Idry, gracious in his asceticism, and, as ever, Rafi with a sardonic half-smile on his lips. It's Kemu, possessed of the look of eagles that topples my hard-earned calm.

He senses me and rises to come my way, yet halts a few steps distant. "What's wrong?"

My attempt at a smile fails. "Are you inside my head?"

He shakes his.

"Best I sit before answering."

Brows creased, he offers me his arm.

Rafi draws out a chair. As I sit, Idry fills a glass with wine, then places it before me.

Kemu takes the chair to my right as Aaron raises his glass.

"Join me in saluting the three brightest stars in Azalaïs' constellation of Champions of Champions: Thea of Solara, Kemu a'Rowan, and Rafi a'Falili."

We make Thanksgift, then drink, in my case, only a sip. While racing, less is more, especially after two blows to the head. I cradle the goblet in my hands before speaking.

"Today, while racking Yuni's saddle, someone I believed was his groom came up behind me. I was mistaken."

However onerous my news, Aaron's puzzled expression drives me to continue. "Your son throttled me, then threatened to kill me if I raced Obsidian. I scratched his face, for which he clouted me. I went down hard. By the time I could get up, he was gone."

Kemu's stillness bespeaks a prelude to the violence so inherent in Venari. It's Idry who raises a hand, silencing the tirade Rafi's about to spew before looking to Aaron.

"How do we deal with this?"

I slide my fingers between Kemu's. There's a pause as he regains control, then closes my hand between his. As one, we look to Aaron, who now stares into a future only he can see.

When he speaks, resolve fuels his words. "One of us must be with Thea at all times. We'll double our guards, both here and at the track. Tomorrow, if my son won't receive me, I will send an affidavit vowing to haul him into court for any further harassment."

Idry looks to me. "Are you good with this?"

I nod, despite praying it's enough.

Kemu, squeezing my hand, reclaims my attention. "How hard did he hit you?"

"Enough I saw stars."

His jaw stark with clenched muscles, he addresses Aaron. "While it's a given that Thea's hardheaded, she needs rest after two blows to the head in as many days."

He looks back to me. "Have you picked the rides you want?"

When I nod, Rafi hands me a pen and paper. "Make a list. We'll sort out which of Solara's horses might challenge them."

As I write, Kemu comes to his feet. "I'll accompany Thea to her lodgings, then stand guard over her tonight. Can someone bring us food?"

Aaron nods. "Thea's staff will provide anything you want. Break your fast with us here tomorrow? We've yet to discuss your Celio."

As I slide my list to Rafi, Kemu pulls out my chair.

"Let's go."

I'd protest the coddling were the prospect of getting out of these clothes less appealing.

When night is our sole companion, I ask the first of the many questions troubling me. "Whatever provoked today's display?"

"Did it anger you?"

"No, it made me question your intent."

"My intent was simple. To tell Gayleen and the world just what you mean to me."

"Your a'Shara is already pissed at me. Beyond that, why does the world need to know?"

The only break in the long silence which follows is a horse's occasional call. By the time he answers, I'm ready to send him packing.

"Because if we fail in this life, I'm holding myself accountable."

It's my turn for silence, silence, and panic. "You think that's possible?"

"We're bucking serious odds: Seth, your outcasting, and my commission."

Anger takes panic's place. "If you aren't leaving the ranks, infuriating Gayleen doesn't make sense."

"True. While we're asking without answering questions, why accept the job as Solara's trainer?"

"I owe Aaron my life and he needs help. Beyond that, I'll be able to assure Sojur isn't at risk should Obsidian race."

He gestures to the vastness of our surroundings. "This ornate lifestyle wasn't your goal?"

I tip my head at the three-story building we're approaching. "Hardly, just look at this place. All this for a woman who called a tent home?"

I halt as he does, then faces me. "Beyond putting Gayleen on notice, my intent today was to warn off other interested men. Now, I can tell my family and ulan about the change in my plans, resign my commission, round up my horses, and return to you."

He waits patiently as I grapple with his startling accommodation to my life's many constraints. Yet, words fail me, not for this moment of which I had no expectation so much as the abrupt shift in his attitude.

What would I give for us to be together? The truth is, anything.

This he reads with ease, elation bubbling in his husky tone. "Think of it. Aaron's a realist. Convince Sojur to become his Master of Horse, then hire me. With the three of us riding for Solara, under Sojur's direction, we'd be damn near invincible."

"Come Year's End, we could ride to Land's End. You could spend time with Mora while I took my tests of Mastery. We won't be Venari, but their values are ours. We can still make a contribution."

His plan, so much more than I dared hope, has me up on my boot toes, kissing him. When we finally step apart, we're both smiling.

Curious about my early return, my 'staff' appears within moments of our arrival. I explain without going into detail, then rest my hand on Kemu's wrist. "Give me a few moments to change. We can eat on the roof with a view of Azalaïs and the ocean."

He nods approval of my suggestion.

As I start up the stairs, he's introducing himself to the bemused staff.

Once free of my boots, I look for clothing in which I can breathe. Among my meager belongings, the deep blue of the

Daharshan ladies' gift beckons to me. I exchange the skintight leggings for loose, find slippers, then head for the roof.

Aaron's people have outdone themselves. On a linen-cover table, silver and china shimmer in firefly-soft lighting. Domed platters keep food warm, while a variety of wines await in crystal decanters. Ordinary people don't live like this. I certainly haven't, till now. Yet of those who brought this fantasy to be, there's no sign.

I exit the shadows.

Kemu's transformation from Venari alert to danger to a man in a woman's presence is instantaneous, as it is gratifying.

For once, words fail him, his gaze traveling from top to bottom, then back again. "That night after the tree, the origin of your coat didn't register. How could I have been so blind?"

I rest my hand along his clean-shaven jaw. "Of greater import, why can't you see the color of my skin and eyes?" Forthright, as these words are, I do not regret them.

He draws me close, then shares breath with me. "My love, I see Daharsha in you, yet your beauty both within and out, silences the expected Venari response."

He rests his hands over the delta between my shoulders and neck. "May I?"

At my nod, he eases the tightness there.

I yield to his touch, only to gasp when his teeth close on the nape of my neck. Endure long as I'm able before drawing his lips to mine.

It's been twelve interminable nights since he quit me. Fourteen since we were one and life was this sweet, this precious. He slides his hands beneath the fabric covering my breasts, and the stars overhead fade.

What comes after comes like lightning. Our clothing falls with the inevitably of autumn leaves. Our hands find what they seek. Kemu sweeps the seat cushions to the floor and then lowers me onto them. He joins me, warm skin to warm skin. Desire rules both of us as he straddles me, and kisses his way down my throat, then lower.

No one told me need would rule in the arms of the right man. I arch my hips. Our union is swift, as it is all-consuming. Driven by our uncertain future, what we wish for must be now. We love with abandon, and seek to hunger no more.

However great Kemu's art in love, I dare not give my ecstasy a voice. Believing Seth had murdered his rival, half of Solara would crash up these stairs. The reality is far more wonderful.

We drift, bodies sated and limbs tangled, rapture sweet as honey in our veins.

Night birds and crickets serenade us as the lanterns gutter inside their pierced metal shields.

As I waver between sleep and wakefulness, my gaze drifts over the sharp-edged shadows cast by the risen moon. Shadows, out of which, death approaches on swift and silent feet, steel glinting in the invader's fist.

I scramble to my feet, screaming Kemu's name.

He comes off the floor as the invader lunges. A blade slashes through the moonlight, scoring a bloody line across Kemu's chest.

I hurl our clothing aside, seeking Kemu's sword as another assailant comes over the parapet. Unable to find the blade, I hurl a lantern at the newcomer, who bats it aside. While crashing to the floor, the lantern splatters burning oil over the cushions, which catch fire.

The man prowls my way, his leering visage painted orange in the flames. There's a blur in the corner of my vision as Kemu roars, then turns with astonishing speed.

A burst of light blinds me. My eyes strain to adjust.

A gristly sound of tearing flesh ends in a gurgle. A body smacks into me. I flail, stumbling over the man who cut Kemu. Lifeblood gushes from a mortal wound in his throat.

The second assailant lunges at me, which is when a karakal leaps from the shadows. One swipe of its massive paws and the man's face opens to the bone. With a ghastly crunch, the beast sinks its scimitar teeth into the man's body, then hurls it aside. It leaves me naked and weaponless as the supreme hunter of the grasslands stalks my way.

I scream Kemu's name. He doesn't answer.

It can't end like this, not now, not when we're one again. The ground is three stories below. Jump and I'll die. Nor will screaming help. I'd be dead before anyone got here.

I scrabble at the parapet, seeking to free a brick. All that gives is skin, and I turn to face my death. Throughout, beg this to be one of my nightmares, yet know it isn't, not with the musk of big cat in the air. All that's left is a faint hope the karakal will feed on the carnage done, giving me time to escape.

No such luck. The karakel stalks my way, dense muscles jouncing. I whimper as the cat coils up onto its hind legs, long tail whipping, eyes awash with green fire. Claws that reach for me, becoming fingers even as fur shifts into summer-tanned skin.

What cannot be stands before me. Kemu, naked in the moonlight, his hands low and open. Not predator, not karakal. All that keeps me upright is the brick half-wall behind me.

"Thea, say something."

I gasp. "You're a . . .," I can't get the word out.

"Please, let me explain."

"Explain? There aren't enough words in the world!" Fists failing, I come at him.

He snatches my body into his, for which I sink my teeth in his shoulder, then spit blood. "You lied to me!"

"How, by not telling you? I knew this would be a free-for-all, but not whether you could handle the truth."

I'm so hurt, tears spill. "I gave you everything: body, heart, and soul. No secrets, while you kept the darkest secret of all. A threat used to scare children into behaving. Do you know how many times I've screamed myself awake, believing a karakal had me in their jaws? No, wait, you know, because you know everything about me!"

I shove against his chest, hard as I can. "Let . . . me . . . go."

His hold tightens. "This is why I didn't tell you. You can't just take the good. There will be bad, and you know it."

"Do I, truly? How bad can it be? Something worse than a shapeshifting, mind-reading mage? Speaking of which, get out of my head and stay out!"

He clenches his jaw. "No."

This man has made a mockery of what it took to overcome my aversion to his magic, all so I could love him. The only thing that keeps me from saddling a horse and seeking Lycan is the very real fear of crossing paths with Pell.

I want to hit this man, and hurt him like he's hurt me. "Venari, mindhealer, liar, and thief, yet the Sada call me nomadi."

Let me go.

This bespoken, aware he's heard my every thought.

He rests his forehead on mine.

I was eleven the first time I shifted. Mikha'el was with the Rowan and sensed my wild magic. Once I was human again, he found me and explained what had happened, why, and how.

He's gone leagues beyond too far. Not questioning the possible outcome, I jerk my knee upward.

Only instinct saves him. My knee glances off the outer meat on his thigh as he twists, then whirls me about-face, pinning my back to his chest with a male's infuriating strength.

With both of us breathing hard, he whispers into my ear. "If you have any hopes of my siring a child for you, a blow there, not wise."

If I could reach his face, I'd rip it off. "And why would I want your child? As a reminder of you in another woman's arms? I think not."

"Thea, I've loved you for centuries. Since we've been one, it's been only you."

"The same man who wished me well in finding another partner?"

He sighs while giving me enough freedom to face him. "I am indeed that fool."

"The same fool who believed I'd buy a cock-and-bull story about a thorn bush cutting your shoulder? Speaking of which, whatever possessed you to track me as a karakal?" This asked, while not quite believing I'm having this particular conversation with this naked male.

A faint smile finds a home on his lips. "Whatever makes you think that was me?"

I inhale so fast, my breasts brush the blood on his chest.

As I pull back, he tightens his hold. "Yes, that was me. I knew you'd pitch a fit if I just showed up. Was I right?"

I ignore the question. "Were you the least bit embarrassed when Sahain told his tale of playing a similar stupid prank on me?" This asked as a grudging acknowledgment arises. Sahain's story gave Kemu ample reason not to reveal his secret.

"Pursuing 'prey,' elusive as you? No, not after learning of your nightmares. Had I explained when provoked, I shapeshift, you would have shown me to the door. Speaking of which, can we agree my magic is the only reason we're alive?"

I heave a sigh. "Yes."

My admission adds warmth to his tone. "Seth knew Aaron would act the moment today's attack came to light. Hence this slipshod plan and its wretched execution. Seth won't make the same mistake twice. I want your word, no more going it alone. Promise me, and I'll promise you, no more secrets."

"And if we slip up?"

"We make it right, swiftly and humbly."

"Humbly?"

He joins my laughter. "Perhaps not. So, any suggestions how we explain two bodies savaged by a big cat? The last time this happened, I was on a battlefield."

"Is that why you've never had a second?"

"That, and shapeshifting, is too like Shadrean sorcery, which is why the Father's Order keeps it a secret."

My hands on his chest fist. "There are other mages like you?"

It's his turn to sigh. "Yes, which is why the day I came of age, Mikha'el initiated me into the Order. Its members and Mikha'el taught me to control the change, yet my Venari ethics assure I use it only for good. You are the only person not in the Order who knows my secret."

My whole life, I have resisted magic. Yet what have I done? Fallen for a mage, for which there is only one solution.

I rise on my tiptoes and claim his lips. "Had anyone heard the noise, they'd be here by now. Let's douse the fire, then clean up this mess and ourselves. With the autumn rains, the Dark Tide runs high. We can toss the bodies into the river. By morning, they will wash out to sea. All Seth will know is went wrong when I show up at the track tomorrow."

He pushes my bangs aside, then blesses my forehead with a kiss. "The world does not know what it lost with you not ascending."

Oddly, the reminder doesn't sting, not with this man at my side. I rest my hands on his face, and marvel at skin that was fur not so long ago. "So, how do we convince Seth not to try again?"

"'We' do nothing. You focus on racing. Aaron, Kane, Rafi, Idry and I will do what it takes to keep you safe. With all we must do before the sun rises, can you accept that for now?"

I remind myself, loving someone means trusting them and rise on my toes, then breathe my yes into his lips.

FIFTY-FOUR

SOLARA'S REINS

A utumn's white-gold sun shrouds Solara's get-ready pavilion in shadow. Those of our grooms, able to shake off other duties, join us as we prepare for our first race of the season, me on Yuni.

While pacing the sidelines, I tell myself it's just another race. Something I could do in my sleep, or would have last night were it not for Kemu loving me into sweet oblivion. I force myself to stop, then stretch my arms overhead.

The Sun's two-horse cart halts in a nearby courtyard. Valan is in the driver's seat. Behind him, the children's eyes are enormous, for where they are, and the company they keep.

Pell's elite guard comes forward to assist the a'Shara and Enya. He passes a giggling Eisa to Garin. The little boy reaches for the Venari's oh-so tantalizing sword hilt. This gets him set down, knee high, to Garin's tall boots.

Another Venari proffers his hand to Ainee. She comes to earth, then sets her skirts to rights, every bit the lady.

Nine days have passed since they watched with fear-round eyes as I lay bleeding on the Sun's pavers. Eight since the courts gave them to Enya and the fearsome warrior I once called father. Before running my first race for Aaron, I could have done seeing none of this.

Pell disembarks, then offers Enya his hand. The wound I opened between them now healed. Every glance, every touch, couched in tenderness. Yet in a week, he will be gone.

Valan gathers the reins as Mahir assists Charra to earth. Beside him, Selene scents the air, then, barks and leaps from the carriage.

I crouch as she courses into our get-ready area, then hug and hush her. Little ears, sharp as a ratter puppy, hear me.

"Tee'ah!" Eisa evades Pell's grab as he pelts my way.

More of what I don't need: breaking the court's injunction against contact with the children. Still, as Solara's trainer, I can't hide, thus step into the light, and catch Eisa in my arms. As I breathe in the sweet scent of little boy, Selene gambols at our side.

When Pell strides our way, Rafi takes a crossed-arm stance at my side. A moment later, Aaron steps in front of us, then extends his forearm, which Pell clasps.

"Lord Aaron."

"A'Shara."

I tell Selene to sit, and for once she obeys, then noses a giggling Eisa as I lower him to the ground. Dreading what will come next, I rise. The sight of Windsong's silver-white tassel hanging from Pell's favorite blade all but stops my heart.

Eisa, oblivious to the undercurrents, lifts his arms to Pell, who scoops him up before looking back to Aaron. "Congratulations on the expert hands now guiding Solara's reins."

I catch my jaw before it drops.

Aaron's smile is, as ever, gracious. "Solara wishes the Sada good running."

"The Sada wish Solara the same." Pell inclines his head to Aaron, then returns to Enya as Eisa waves an enthusiastic farewell over his shoulder.

Bewildered by his lack of comment about my breaking the injunction, I send Selene after them. She bumps Pell's leg. He strokes her head, laughing at something Eisa said.

Rafi nudges my shoulder. "What's wrong?"

"He didn't throw it away."

"Throw 'it' what away?"

"That tassel on his sword pommel. I made it from Windsong's tail hair."

Rafi grimaces. "Who the hells knows what goes on in that man's head? Are you alright?"

"I'd better be."

Yuni arrives on dancing hooves and trumpets his youth. Fingers laced, Rafi boosts me onto Yuni's saddle, then walks around us before giving me a thumbs up.

I salute him, then my patron, throughout praying I'll be worthy of his trust.

Aaron smiles as he and Rafi depart for Solara's private viewing box. I wave my thanks to our grooms, who cheer as I trot Yuni to the inspection area.

Lycan and Hanan arrive soon after. The big red colt looks as battle-ready as his rider. Hanan calls a challenge to another colt now putting on a show for his dazzled, clueless owners.

The qualifying runs are rife with Seth's less-than-stellar entries. Hemming is on a colt better suited as a gelding. Not only is the horse coarse-headed, he has a muzzle the color of mouse droppings. The rider I fired is on an equally inelegant mount, both men in Seth's red and black colors.

Yuni bounces throughout his inspection, which earns him a smile from the race official. She tosses me our starting chit, which I snatch it from the air, note our position, then loft it to the line-up scribe.

As Lycan angles Hanan into the lineup, he looks to me, then holds up four fingers for their draw.

Plainly, Sojur must have adjusted the Venari-to-be's attitude. I hold up two fingers in response, then as we take our place in the line, I shout. "Lycan, I'm riding against Hemming and that shithead grinning at me."

Lycan follows the path of my gaze and laughs. "Idiots. Good running, Thea."

"Same to you."

With twelve in the field, we enjoy some space.

While this starter takes an exaggerated length of time before releasing his arrow, the moment it smacks into its target, we're off.

Yuni has gotten better with every ride, and this looks to be no exception. As we streak past the viewing stand, I catch glimpses of Aaron, Rafi, and Idry in our box, then of Pell and Enya with the children, who scream my name. Pell watches them without rancor, seemingly not in the mood to dissuade them of their favorite. Despite wishing I could fathom his reasoning, now is not the time.

Yuni's hooves scourge the track, the snap of his stride in perfect alignment with his lithe build. With the exhilaration of speed comes the voice of reason: whatever made me think I could live without racing?

At my right, Hemming rides as if his whole body were tied into knots. For him, racing is a brutish chore with enemies to defeat, especially me.

We enter the first curve, and Yuni settles into his rhythm. With every bound he takes, I ask with my lower legs, not containing or abandoning him. He swings his hinds through with enthusiasm, pulling up even with the six leaders now fighting for the rail. Among them are his ex-rider and Hemming. Both grin wolfishly as they veer into my path, seeking to foul Yuni's stride.

My first run for Aaron, and I've made a world-class mistake. I knew I'd be riding against unprincipled bastards, but the enigma of Pell's well-wishing drove it clear out of my mind. With neither whip nor quirt, my choice is to endanger my horse's safety or kiss off a win.

"Thea!"

I dart a glance under my arm.

Lycan lifts the braided quirt dangling from his wrist, something Sojur insists his riders carry when racing. "Let me in."

I check Yuni, forcing him to yield to Hanan.

The co-conspirators think they've won, that it's only a matter of which one right up to the moment Lycan drives Hanan between them.

Battle-trained, Hanan does not hesitate in bringing his broad chest and muscle-bound shoulders into play. He bashes into Hemming's horse while Lycan wields his quirt with expert force. Right, left, then right again.

The skin on Hemming's forehead splits, then bleeds. Half-blind, he swerves for the outer rail. Yuni's ex-rider checks his horse so hard, the colt drops from gallop to canter. Even as this happens, Hemming clears his vision, then comes after me again.

That's not happening.

I chirrup to Yuni, who, intent upon retaking the lead he thinks should be his, buckles down.

We've lost lengths, yet a reserve win would make Yuni eligible for the title race. From here on out, it's a matter of whether he can pull ahead before Hemming fouls us again.

Lycan has the lead and intends to hold it. Meanwhile, I'm rump-high in the stirrups, and seeking an opening.

Vowing to never race again without a whip, I chalk this ride off to a stupid beginner's mistake, and the last godsdamned one I intend to make.

Out of the corner of my eye, I spot the faltering stride of a horse ahead of us, and bring my legs down on Yuni's sides.

The opening's paper-thin, but it's enough. Yuni jams his nose between the fading colt and his companion, then slides between them as if greased.

The straightaway sweeps into the final curve.

Lycan extends his lead. I don't resent his taking advantage of the opportunity presented. I'd do the same.

The screaming reaches for a crescendo as the race comes down to second place, and who's fighting me for it if not Hemming. I call upon everything Sojur taught me over four years of racing. Butterfly soft hands and the sort of balance that invites my horse to outstrip Hemming's.

Yuni does just that, sweeping across the finish line right behind Hanan. I'm still praising him when Rafi and Aaron join us outside the presentation area.

Aaron pats the horse he bred. "No surprise, that pair trying what they did."

I leap to the earth. "And would have succeeded without Lycan's help. Aaron, I apologize. I knew better."

Rafi responds before Aaron can. "The blame is mine. It's been years since I raced. I'd forgotten this sort of nonsense happens."

Aaron waves our concerns aside. "Not a problem. Whoever's in the irons for Yuni's Championship run, we'll use his odds to our favor."

Race officials arrive with a blanket of autumn roses bound by blue ribbons. Hanan sniffs them, only to lose interest upon discovering they aren't edible. A tidal wave of applause greets Pell and Sojur when they join the Venari-to-be. Despite a rocky start, he's proven himself. I can only hope they won't hold the help he gave me against him.

While awaiting our turn in the presentation circle, I'm mindful of how different this moment might have been. Had I not met my sire and brother, I'd be at Pell and Sojur's side, an ascended Venari, and likely one with Lycan.

My sorrow persists even when Yuni dances when draped in roses and red ribbons.

The screaming hordes acknowledge Solara's reserve win, which Aaron accepts with quiet dignity.

Having almost ruined Yuni's first chance to shine, I do nothing to attract attention and welcome when we can exit the presentation area.

Rafi hands me Yuni's reins. "I'm needed at the stable for our next race. Walk him back for me, will you?" At my nod, he departs at a run.

A Solara groom detains Aaron, and I move Yuni to a patch of grass so he may graze while we wait.

Someone behind us clears their throat, and I turn.

Yuni roars a challenge to the stallion Hemming rode, whose reins Seth holds. "Bitch, I'm adding Yuni to your tab." This said in a genial tone of voice that has nothing in common with the venom in his eyes.

Aaron, seeing his son, breaks off his conversation and storms our way. "What part of my affidavit don't you understand?"

Seth's sly smile widens. "Congratulating your rider isn't harassment."

My jaw drops at the bald lie.

Aaron fists his son's reins as a warrior replaces the smooth aristocrat. "If this is how you want to play it, I'll amend the affidavit to any contact whatsoever."

Seth's ugly laughter mocks his sire's icy anger. "Truly, Father? All the hours you spend drilling with a sword, yet when challenged, hide behind the law? If only Sabita could see you now."

I grab the arm Aaron draws back. "Don't, my Lord. That's exactly what he wants."

As if affirming my claim, Seth steps his closer, in hopes proximity will goad his father into striking the first blow.

As I struggle to contain Yuni with one hand, I yank on Aaron's arm with the other. "My Lord, come away. You don't want to miss the four-year-old stallions. You don't want to miss Kemu on Celio."

Aaron rips his gaze off Seth and sees the pleading in my eyes. He visibly calms himself before gesturing to a Solara groom. "Take Yuni back to our stables, then tell our people what just happened."

As the groom trots Yuni away, Aaron looks back to me. "Let's go."

Seth calls out to us as we head for the stands. "Run, old man. Hide. It won't make any difference. Whatever it takes, I will win."

Neither of us looks back nor speaks till inside Solara's private box. As I down water, Aaron downs wine, his boots up on the same rail Rafi and I used earlier.

It's some time before he speaks. "Thea, do you think I'm a coward?"

"No, my Lord. Sink to Seth's level, and you cease being a man of honor."

He regards me for a moment. "From Sabita's daughter, that's high praise indeed. We'll see how Seth handles not being my heir."

While my lips part, no sound comes out.

Aaron laughs, then gestures to the track. "Save your amazement for him."

At the rail below, Kemu sits Celio. He smiles, kisses the back of his hand, then sends that kiss my way.

I catch his kiss and press it to my heart.

Win, my love.

He grins while gesturing farewell.

I will.

And he does.

FIFTY-FIVE

INVINCIBLE

Forearms over the top rail of Black's paddock, I study the stallion who will be my Champion of Champions ride in three days' time. Only while moving from one patch of grass to another does he exhibit a stud's watchfulness. Little wonder. I ride him to the track every morning, then come midafternoon, put him through a blistering workout. Yet with every ride, he's given me more try. Equally astonishing, he's proven impossibly brave, though consistently wary. Given who 'trained' him, Black's discipline under pressure has earned both my respect and admiration.

"Thea?"

I turn, smiling, hand over my heart. "Solara welcomes Leonas a'Falili."

My grandfather's gaze shifts between the black high-collared riding coat I wear and the stallion behind me.

"Aaron's people said I'd find you here. Twenty-two years, Aaron has held this commemoration for Sabita. This year's invitation came doubly welcome with her daughter now as Solara's head trainer."

He rests his elbow beside mine on the top rail of Black's paddock. "Some horse, eh?"

"He is that indeed."

"Aaron tells me he's your Champion of Champions ride. What of Cinna? She won her qualifier."

"Black is the reason Aaron hired me."

"Ahh, such is life."

As we contemplate the stallion before us, our mutual silence acknowledges life's many ironies.

I nudge his elbow in its crimson haaka. "Any chance Sojur found another rider for Amir?"

My grandfather gusts in annoyance. "No, nor is he looking. Pell's stubborn, but compared to your teacher, he's amenable. Word is Sojur's riding as if twenty years old and that, even on Obsidian, you'll have your hands full. Is such a thing possible?"

I hesitate only for a moment. "Absolutely."

His eyebrows rise. "Who could credit such a thing?"

I smile fondly. "Anyone who knows Sojur."

Leonas rests his hand on my shoulder. "Selfish as your mother was, I find your loyalty startling."

All week, I've waited for this moment. "Grandfather, I have something to tell you, something I told Aaron the night he hired me. I am not your only half-Daharshan grandchild. The day I met my sire, my older blood brother rode at the Haj's side. His name is Baseem, and he spoke near perfect A'talan. Baseem is our father's heir."

Fearful of his response, I rush the rest of my confession. "Your daughter, Sabita, lives. She is my sire's first wife, his Haj'ene, his one true love."

Rage contorts Leonas' face. "Yet didn't send me her Mother-marked daughter?"

I nod, startled that this is his first thought.

"I was wrong. You're nothing like Sabita. Damn that woman. She gave me no end of grief, raising her without a mother. Does your brother, my grandson, wage war against A'tal?"

"There was no time to ask. Forgive me for not telling you sooner?"

He waves my concerns aside. "A blooded Venari, cleaving onto a Daharshan Haj? How is such a thing possible?"

"A grand passion?"

"Sabita? The woman's heart might as well have been of stone. Aaron, a man of intellect and experience, never saw it. Do you think he'll try finding her?"

"How could he?"

"We're talking Aaron here. When he sets his mind to something, it usually happens. Damn her! Against a Daharshan Haj, Aaron wouldn't stand a chance."

Before he can say more, someone clears their throat behind us.

As we turn, Lycan makes reverence.

Leonas rests his hand on mine. "Granddaughter, I'll tell Aaron you're right behind me." This said with a grin, suggesting he knows just who has been guarding my nights, and furthermore, approves.

With a hearty, well-met slap for Lycan's shoulder, Leonas strolls toward the grooms holding saddled horses for the trip to Sabita's seaside pavilion.

I wait till he's out of earshot. "Lycan, why are you here?"

"Aaron sent me an invitation, in thanks for getting you out of that scrape with Hemming. Is there someplace we can talk?"

I lead the way to an espaliered apple tree where we sit beneath its arbor.

He says nothing till I take the hand he holds out to me. "I told Sojur you'd ride Obsidian, only if you had him under control. That's when he told me how I came to afford Hanan."

I suck a breath between my teeth. "Are you angry?"

"With a woman who made possible a horse I couldn't afford? No, I'm overwhelmed. That same day, Sojur told Pell about Obsidian, which went far to heal the tension between them."

Thereby explaining Pell's compliment for the "expert hands" holding Solara's reins. Not that I evidenced as much after making a mess of Yuni's first race.

Lycan draws a horsehair bracelet from his tunic pocket. "Atar helped me with this."

Hanan's chili-pepper red tail hairs have been plaited into a flat, multi-stranded braid, each end clamped with silver ferrules. A Luna dangles from one side, wings outstretched. From the other hangs the Sada sigil, all sculpted with Atar's subtlety.

Lycan poises the bracelet below my wrist. "May I?"

I stare at the sheval, dumbfounded. After our conversation about Kemu, whatever motivated Atar to create this symbol that promises handfasting?

"Lycan, you ask something of me I can't do."

"Can't or won't?"

"Both."

"You'll never marry?"

How do I convince him we're only friends?

I fold his hands around the bracelet. "Keep this for a love that won't destroy your life."

Gentleness departs, revealing the man he's becoming. "Where is it written that love is safe?"

The truth he speaks astonishes. So much so, I respond in kind. "Kemu and I are one again."

There's a pause before he rises, pockets the sheval, then does something unexpected. He removes the saddle from one of the waiting mares, swings up onto her bareback, then holds his arm out to me. Shades of the day he took Habibi and her supposedly broken ankle back to camp.

However troubling, I accept his invitation and settle crossways on his lap.

Once away from prying eyes, he halts the mare, then slides the sheval into my coat pocket. "Wear this if you ever want me."

Before I can protest, he asks for a canter.

Kemu is right: the moment is all we are given.

Would I have picked a different love, given different circumstances?

No. Not even for a friend.

FIFTY-SIX

SHAPER THAN A SERPENT'S FANG

The din of voices grows as I near the Black Swan's mezzanine. Aaron's guards see me coming and uncross their lances, so I may join the shoulder-to-shoulder crowd.

Riders, owners, and race officials take note as I exit Solara's suite of rooms. Were I them, I'd do the same. Every stride I take reflects light off my polished knee-high boots. On my black silk riding coat, an embroidered Champion of Champions sigil rests over my heart, above which Solara's sun reigns. Over that, a half-circle of eight stars arches, one for each of the four horses I've qualified this year: Yuni, Cinna, a four-year-old gelding, and the open mare. I am a walking testament that Lord Aaron chose well while replacing Hemming.

No one greets me as I seek the Lord of Solara. Most here wish I'd died on that tree. As I move through the crowd, there are glimpses of Pell and Sojur speaking with quiet formality. Not the back-and-forth of lifelong friends, yet with more ease than the night Gayleen tore into me.

Sojur spots me.

Pell tracks his second's moment of inattention, his gaze remaining on me as Sojur speaks to him.

Dare I? Dare I not?

I steady myself on a rag-tag of breath, then hand-over-heart, bow. Even in the name of courtesy, the infinitesimal flick of Pell's brows is more than I dared hope. Nor does he look away till addressed by another Sada.

Sojur gestures for me to stay put as he comes my way. Paying homage to the legend in their midst, the crowd parts for him. Six qualifying stars arch over a Champion of Champions sigil on his haaka. All earned before I was born, before my father's people took him apart a joint at a time.

I make reverence. "Master."

He smiles while regarding my array. "The student has bested her teacher."

"No, never, not if I live till a hundred." Knowing whose colors I wear and what Aaron expects of me, I temper my tone. "They say the wagering over which of us will win has reached a fever pitch."

He nods, his smile growing. "May I ask who you'll be riding?"

He'll know soon enough. "Obsidian."

Sojur takes a considered breath. "Such was my hope, however great the challenges you faced. You could not have paid a greater testament to my teaching than getting that horse under control."

Had we had that sort of relationship, I would not resist the tears that well. In their place, I manage a weak smile. "Whoever wins, you made me the rider I am."

"While your devotion touches me, I want your word. If you have more horse, you will use him."

"Master, I'll be riding to win."

He clasps my forearm with surprising strength for a hand with three fingers. "Good running, Thea, and may the best horse win."

"Master, I wish you the same."

I track his departing gait, as always uneven, one of many reasons I wanted to be in Amir's irons. Yet, I am at ease with the vow just made. With Kemu on Celio and Rafi on Yuni, the outcome is truly in Heaven's hands.

Somewhere nearby, Aaron laughs. Idry is at his side, both men surrounded by sycophants seeking favor.

No wonder Rafi stands aloof. I approach from his right so he'll see me coming. "Has it been a long time since you attended one of these?"

"Ten blissful years. Still like our choices?"

"However much I'd delight in making Seth eat Cinna's dust, yes. Looking forward to racing Yuni?"

"And prove a decommissioned, one-eyed Venari can still ride? Hells, yes."

The race officials gathering at the top of the presentation stairway are our signal to join Aaron and Idry.

Quiet descends over the vast hall as the herald takes his place at the top of the stairs.

First to be announced for the Champions of Champions run: the three-year-old reserve mare, then the winner. Thanks to Solara's grooms, the crowd greets Cinna's name with cynical laughter. Our people saw to it everyone knew just who put the scars on the gifted red filly's hindquarters and why.

Aaron bows, acknowledging Cinna's win. When neither Rafi nor I start down the stairs, the crowd knows Solara has passed on her option to run. With the price I paid for breaking Seth's nose, I content myself with the vindication to come.

Next up, the three-year-old geldings, then the stallions, starting with the reserve winner: Yuni. Idry joins Rafi as they descend the stairs to the ballroom below, both men waving acknowledgment to those eager to see Rafi racing again.

We add our applause to the tumult, then for the winning colt and rider. Blond hair swept back, and head held high, Lycan begins down the staircase. Hanan's winning star now rides above the Sada sigil embroidered on his tunic. Friends shout their support, and rivals, good-natured assessments of his chances.

My own emotions aren't racing-focused. Lycan's long legs and broad shoulders would make him the ideal lancer, which is why I pray he gets out of my life and becomes Venari. Last night damn near broke me. His offer to handfast, then him savoring a taste of life at Solara. All of which was poised upon a knifepoint of immense risk. Call it love, call it obsession, no one and nothing is coming between me and Kemu.

The roll call begins for the four-year-old reserve stallion. Aaron acknowledges Rafi's win with a bow, once more passing on declaring for the race. The winner's announcement follows: Kemu a'Rowan on Celio.

My heart belies my outer calm. Just seeing this man turns me inside out. As he strides for the staircase, his mild gaze meets mine. Often as he's won, the array over his Rowan crest looks as if the stars have fallen from the sky.

Our paths didn't cross after we returned to the track last night. Lycan left for the Sada, and Solara escorted Leonas to the Falili. After which we made the rounds of those racing stables associated with Arron, then finished at our own party. It gave me time to try making sense of my messy emotions.

That tangle returns as Kemu acknowledges the crowd's thundering tribute with his swordsman's hands. The same hands with which he rendered me incapable of thought mere hours ago, in his rooms here at the Swan.

Aaron reads my fixation, and clears his throat, bringing my attention back to the here and now. The noise swells to a low roar, which forces the herald to raise his voice while announcing the open horses.

"As last year's Champion of Champions, Thea of Solara declares first in the open division. She will ride Lord Aaron's stallion, Obsidian, who qualified last year as the five-year-old stallion winner."

Never in Azalaïs' history has a stead horse triumphed over Venari-bred. Thanks to Black's inspired owner and his two ex-tribal riders, that could change now.

Aaron and I descend to supporters clapping and Venari hissing. I tell myself it's of no import that the grapes evading my grasp have proven sour indeed.

The herald, accustomed to speaking over cheers rather than the chill of Venari censure, waits till we've joined Rafi and Idry on the ballroom floor. Only then does he announce the open gelding and his rider.

"Declaring for the Champion of Champions race, Hemming, riding the open gelding champion, Faharr."

The Shadrean wears Seth's racing colors, but it gains him no respect for having quit a beloved member of the Azalaïs racing community.

The crowd greets his descent with chilly silence. Nor do they approve of his employer, next to be announced.

"Declaring for the Champion of Champions race, Seth, riding the reserve champion mare, Layla."

The scratches I carved into Seth's face and his still-healing nose lend a fighter's character to his patrician visage. As he descends, only the gullible he's lured into his racing stable applauds. He smiles as if not damned by faint praise.

The herald, mindful he holds a plum, waits for silence before making the final proclamation. "Declaring for the Champion of Champions race, last year's four-year-old champion stallion, Amir, to be ridden by his owner, Sojur a'Sada."

Tribal ululation, cheering, and clapping up wells. We add our voices to those saluting the Sada Master of Horse, racing handicapped. Pell remains at his side, lest his second's missing foot betray him. Nor does the tumult ease till they reach the ballroom floor where the crowd surrounds them.

As for Solara, we pass through a groundswell of speculation over this year's potential winner. Upon reaching our tables, would-be breeders to Yuni and Obsidian swarm Aaron even as the yard's clients swamp Rafi and Idry. I remain apart from this free-for-all, yet within summoning distance should Aaron want me. While doing so, I spot Kemu and Gayleen ending a conversation.

As Kemu comes my way, whatever put a burr under his saddle pad, dissuades anyone from detaining him. Has Gayleen advanced some sovereign argument against delaying his resignation?

Dark gaze distant, he offers me reverence. "Gayleen says Solara had tribal guests last night: your grandfather and Lycan." His icy tone affirms he's beyond angry.

Not sure what I can tell him without matters ending in bloodshed, I choose caution. "Leonas, as an old friend. Lycan, for pulling my fat out of the fire with Yuni." My laughter's uneasy. "Not like Habibi, but close enough."

The reminder of the day he braided desert roses into my hair softens his expression somewhat. "How long will you stay tonight?"

"Long as Aaron wants."

"Will Solara exercise horses tomorrow?"

"Other than breezing Obsidian, no. The horse doesn't have a stop in him."

"He and Celio might as well be brothers." He forces a smile. "Such a light workload suggests another night at our ocean cove would be possible."

Another night.

Has he changed his mind about resigning? If so, I have traded days of ecstasy for a lifetime of emptiness. The madness that replaced Enya's commonsense with the fragility of love has taken hold of me as well. A love that couldn't turn the tide sweeping Pell into greatness, and now seems intent on doing the same with Kemu.

He steps closer. "Thea, whatever you're contemplating, pay me the courtesy of time, so I can solve the mess your outcasting put us in."

Anger adds fire to my response. "I am 'contemplating' a man who says he loves me, yet questions my integrity."

In response, he withdraws Lycan's sheval from his pocket. "After you left this afternoon, I found this tangled in the bedcovers."

I answer his piercing gaze with defiance. "It's not on my wrist, nor would it be if you weren't in my life. When I told Lycan we were one again, he shoved it into my pocket, then said, if I ever wanted him to wear it."

A genuine smile lights up his face as he takes me into his arms and kisses me.

I tell myself, life is short, and let him encompass the whole of my world. Yet, all too soon, he breaks off the kiss, then breathes in the attar of desert roses along my throat. While doing so, he slides Lycan's sheval into my pocket.

"Return this. False hope is the cruelest cut of all. If Aaron sees fit to let you go, bespeak me."

He bows, then strides away, gait as resolute as his arrival.

Before anyone razzes me about the kiss, I trade the ballroom for one of its many balconies overlooking the sea. Cold as the salt-flavored wind is, I burn, much like the bridges I've destroyed these past weeks.

Below the balcony, a sharp-angled moon paints the waves crashing to shore in silver and shadows. I could have settled on a man who'd stay, yet have given my heart to a man disinclined to promises.

The door behind me opens.

I turn as Kylin glides my way, her black robes unearthly, their hems whispering over the marble floor.

"You get a moment alone, and I spoil it."

She halts at the balcony rail, then studies the turmoil in the waters below. "In truth, mere mortals cannot keep pace with you. From Venari-to-be, to an outcast 'elevated' on a tree of bones, and now, Lord Aaron's trainer and head rider."

She faces me. "Once racing is over, please come to Land's End. Visit with Mora while Edan and I make amends for the children."

Irritation adds hauteur to my tone. "Finding their parents would be sufficient."

She deflects my censure with a smile. "Thea, do you see Solara as your destiny?"

My guts churn with this woman's obtuseness. "Suggesting what, Damă?"

She answers with silence while tracing a fingertip down my coat's raw silk, then halts upon reaching her Luna beside Sahain's keepsake. "Excellent. You still wear it."

Wear it, but reject the association it claims.

I draw her gift over my head. "I can't carry this burden any longer."

She fists her hand, refusing the necklace. "In this, you have no choice. It is your destiny. It is your fate."

I drape the chain over a nearby balustrade finial. There, the enameled Luna flutters as if flying. "If the Mother of All wants me, she knows where to find me. Enjoy the party."

I make curt reverence, then return to the ballroom. Better on display at Aaron's side than brains scrambled with the obscure and cryptic. Even as I tell myself this, everything changes.

Rafi has his back to me. He's watching the son Aaron vowed to take to court, toe-to-toe with his father, both men anger-rigid.

Seth hammers a knuckle against his father's chest. "You will not curtail my freedom. As for that bitch riding for you, your obsession with her mother has crept into insanity."

Aaron shoves Seth off. "How your mother must mourn, having given birth to a snake."

When Seth draws back his fist, Rafi shoves between them, then, with a stiff-armed heave, sends Seth's backside skidding across the polished marble. "What did I tell you about messing with mine?"

Seth regains his feet and backs away. "Touch me again, and a washout like you will end your days on a tree of bone. A'talan courts are merciless for those who commit violence against members of the first hundred families."

Seth believes the crowd he's drawn assures his safety, and rounds on his father. "You dreamed your life away while Sabita spread her legs for a dark-skinned heathen and made your piece-of-shit head rider. Doubtless, Sabita discovered manners and wealth weren't a substitute for manhood, as did I, growing up with neither father nor mother."

Aaron surges, yet halts when Seth spits on the floor between them. Laughing at the ease with which he's backed down his father, Seth looks to where Rafi and I stand. "You two are going down as well. Count on it."

We watch as he heaves through the crowd buzzing with speculation.

Rafi shakes his head. "Pay him no mind. He's all talk."

"No, he's not, nor dare we behave as if he were. Solara's horses are counting on us, as is their owner." I look to Aaron, who's now in a chair and gesturing for wine, then arch a questioning brow at Rafi.

"If he'll talk, it might help."

It takes Aaron a moment before my presence registers.

"Would you like some company?"

He sees the void surrounding him, then laughs without humor. "You, always." Hooking a chair with his boot, he drags it beside his own.

A server delivers a wine carafe, Thanksgift bowl, and two glasses, which he fills with respectful silence before departing.

Aaron hands me a glass, then raises his. "To the outcast who exemplifies Venari principles, and the man that continued his father's bloodline, and sired a viper. May we both escape the curse which haunts us."

I force a smile, yet see no hope of Aaron's wish coming true.

The crystal sings as we touch rims, then bloody the Thanksgift bowl with wine.

While the vintage warms my belly, my soul grieves for Aaron. A father whose son knows only hatred, and a man that lost his one true love to my sire.

Love, sweet as it is, must it always turn into poison?

FIFTY-SEVEN
FLAWED

The surf's roar enlarges upon the ghost-white cliffs behind us. In the wild dark, our cove revels in the briny nature of change, be it beginnings or endings.

Swathed in our mantles, Kemu strokes the arch of my naked hip where we lay side-by-side. "Thea, we need to talk."

"About what?" My words come out muffled with my face nestled against his chest.

"About what you'll do when I return to the grasslands."

I rear back in a near-futile attempt to see his expression. "Aren't you resigning your commission?"

Scoffing laughter mocks my aggrieved tone. "Just answer the question."

I'm moments from tears, and a day's ride apart from the ecstasy just shared. "Are you asking whether I'll wait for you?"

I sense more than see him shake his head. "You read my purpose wrong. I need to know if I'm in for yet more heartbreak."

The sound coming out of me is more snarl than reason. "Would you just say what you mean? Unlike you, I'm not a mind reader."

"I have, in every way I can, yet get nowhere." He takes me with him while sitting up, which forces me to wrap my legs around his waist.

"That's just so much . . ." His retort powers over the insult I'm about to spew.

"Remember the day we gave Sahain to the wind? When I said one moment, I was a fire in your blood, and the next a pale infatuation? Add all the times I've told you I love you and cannot live without you. Does this sound like a man who wants to leave?"

"No more than it explains your expectation of heartbreak."

"Do you have any idea why that would be?"

If he's not resigning, let the hiss of the ocean answer him.

His sigh is leaden. "What did I expect? You think a set of broad shoulders means a man is impervious to hurt."

Before I can lash out, he touches his forehead to mine.

My inner vision fills with images of the potter and his doe-eyed lover. One moment, I'm teasing him, the next flirting with others, and when found in bed with another, am utterly defiant.

"That's your pattern, Thea, all in or out."

Cold as I was moments before, now the heat of guilt blooms. "I'm the one who leaves?"

His nod shoves aside the hurt, but anger surges into its gap.

"If I'm so damn flawed, why seek me out? Are you a glutton for punishment?"

"After lifetimes of agony and ecstasy, I keep praying we'll get it right."

His tone suggests there's more. "What aren't you saying?"

"You do more than leave. You shove your betrayals into my face, punishing me for our failures. That's why I've held back, out of fear of what you'd do once given the upper hand."

He's right. If he resigns, the balance of power between us shifts to my side. Beyond that, there's truth in that I have an appetite for spite, especially when matters between us go sideways. How many times have I written him off despite wanting him? Could my mother's inconstant heart be mine?

The weight is just too great. I come to my knees, vowing never to hurt anyone again, including myself.

His grip on my waist tightens. "Now isn't the time for shame, pride, or blame. Just tell me the truth. Will you wait for me, or am I in for yet more misery?"

My haze of defensiveness clears, and broken as it is, I find my voice. "I don't know what I'll do on my own, yet know what I pray for, and it's you."

"I know you want me. What I'm asking is if you trust me?"

Kemu's Venari principles are bedrock to his nature. If I can't trust that, I can't trust anything.

"The one thing outcasting taught me is to live in the moment."

"So much so, you'll wait for me if I return to the grasslands without resigning my commission?"

All I am capable of is a defeated whimper. Everyone I love leaves or sends me away.

He frames my face between his broad hands, then urges me to meet his gaze. "There must be peace between us. There must be love. Even the brightest day turns into night if you don't trust me."

The shift from strangling pain to anger takes all of a heartbeat. "You know me, yet leave me?" I heave against his chest, get nowhere, then subside, tears of despair running down my face.

He enfolds me in his arms. "I can take your pain and endure your rage, provided you trust me. Keep my commission, and there's a good chance I can convince Gayleen Pell's good opinion is not worth losing a master mindhealer and captain. Which would you prefer, Azalaïs or the grassland?"

"Kemu, I can't go home."

"You undervalue yourself. The past four years, any rider worthy of the name, including Gayleen, has been at the rail when Sojur let you race. She knows he wanted you to be his quatrain. Why not the same role with the Rowan, provided she accepts I will not be parted from you?"

"Gayleen said after challenging Pell twice, she wouldn't have me."

He laughs. "That was then, and this is now. You're Solara's head trainer and rider. How could she resist such a coup?"

I wait for some unattainable condition that doesn't come. "I could go home?"

"And spend every night in my arms."

Wonderful as all this is, it doesn't eclipse the fear now consuming me of being apart from him, on my own, and lonely.

"How do I deal with my past betrayals, and you with your secrets?"

He shares breath with me.

We'll make a heart-vow, that somehow, some way, we'll make this work, and however long we're apart, we'll hold true to each other.

Can I do this? Can I trust in love? Trust a heart that worshiped Pell and longed for Lycan? Despite my many failures, I yearn to say yes, yes to an eternity in Kemu's arms. I close my eyes and bespeak him.

With Heaven as my witness, I vow to wait for you, however long we're apart.

As I will for you. I am yours, for now, and evermore.

Laughter heady as wine, he lifts me into his arms, his kiss an invitation into the deepest waters of his love. As he eases me down, my skin brushes over the hair on his chest. A sensation so exquisite, it swells into an inchoate moan as we become one.

The sea, the moon, the world, and all its worries fade.

FIFTY-EIGHT
WON'T HAVE THIS MAN

S olara's grooms gather around as Rafi and I strap on our
spurs. The one least enamored with us says what the
others won't.

"I thought Venari didn't punish horses."

This said, not grasping the compliment just paid us.

I slide my boot out to the side. "Look at the spur's neck."

The left spur is on my right boot and vice versa on the
left, rowels angled out, not in toward the horse.

Our critic blinks. "Oh."

"Oh, indeed. Anyone who crowds Yuni or Obsidian . . ."
I stab the knife-sharp steel into the grass, ". . . bleeds."

Rafi schools his tone to milder than mine. "Where we
come from, keeping a horse under you is a matter of life or
death, which means we know every trick in the book."

Not that I evidenced as much while qualifying Yuni, now
being led into our get-ready pavilion.

Rafi greets his mount, who trumpets in his boyish, 'I'll be a stallion soon' hoot. "Ready to dazzle, Yuni?"

After four days of racing, our grooms know to bow their heads when we rest our hands on Yuni's shoulders. We pray for every horse to do well, then return sound.

I hold the off stirrup as Rafi swings up, then walk around them, inspecting everything. It's our signal for privacy, which our grooms honor by heading for where they'll watch the race.

Rafi smiles down on me. "Is your head in the game?"

My brows crease. "What are you suggesting?"

"Any sane person envies lovers. That said, since the Champion of Champions' Ball, it's a wonder you haven't walked into any walls. I need to know your focus is on racing."

"It better be, riding against Seth and Hemming."

"Exactly."

I sigh. He has a point. "I'll be fine once I swing a leg over Black."

"See to it you are. So, what about us? Do we pass muster?"

I rest my hand on his knee, not for the first time, wishing he were Sada. Had I grown up with a childhood friend who saw good in my sire's people, my life might have gone a different direction.

"You're good. Now go be great, and no holding back. One of us needs to make Aaron's day."

"Says the woman riding the fastest horse in today's field."

"And least trained."

His grin fades. "You have my word there will be no holding back, long as you promise the same."

I clasp the arm he extends. "You have it. Good running, Rafi."

"Same to you, Thea." He gives me a thumb-up, then walks his colt off on a loose rein, unconcerned when the youngster prances upon seeing the stands full to overflowing. With every seat taken, those without have spread across the hillsides. The noise level has grown by the moment.

Upon entering Black's stable, I find him ripping hay from his manger. We've compromised. Rather than battle him in the crossties, I get him ready in his stall.

I look to his groom. "Has he been this calm all morning?"

The man nods. "When do you want to saddle him?"

"Once I've groomed him."

Black continues to eat as I run my hands along his legs, then brush out his midnight coat. Once he's saddled and bridled, I grasp his jowls and gaze into his eyes. I hope he understands the significance of what we're about to do.

Rather than impatience, he pays me the compliment of resting his forehead on mine.

Aaron owns Black, yet after everything this horse has been through, this moment of trust makes him truly mine. As I ask Heaven to keep him safe, his calm persists, even as we ride out under a pale autumn sky.

Everyone's been waiting to see this horse. Like a wave sweeping to shore, the crowd shouts his name. The tumult has Black flattening his ears, and knees rising above level as he marches us onto the track.

Strange how life plays out. I am in the presence of greatness, yet without Seth, would have played no part in the glory now bearing me toward the center oval.

As we pass the viewing stands, I glance up to Pell's box.

The children jump like spring frogs and shout my name. Enya and Pell sit behind them, the a'Shara's expression expansive as he meets my gaze, then inclines his head.

Time stops. Hand over exultant heart, I bow my head.

Believing the gesture is for them, the crowd cheers.

Black humps up. Fool thing it is with this horse, I laugh despite knowing if he bucks, he'll give the crowd something worth watching.

Sojur's on Amir at the starting line, his right boot bound to the stirrup leather. If anything goes wrong, he has no exit. Their fates are literally tied together.

Even as I gather Black's power between my hands and legs, Kemu brings Celio up to the line. His smile for me blinds. We have only a moment, yet use it well. The reverence we offer each other bespeaks so much more than respect.

Black surges. Weight deep in the irons, I circle him, yet keep the starter in sight.

Twenty have declared for the race, all assigned our starting positions yesterday, which the others now take. Put Black in the lineup, and he may go after another stallion. Instead, I circle him, his canter getting bigger by the moment. Throughout, I keep my attention on Hemming, Seth, and the rider I fired.

The starting official looks near apoplexy, gaze shifting between the lineup and me. Till the racing officials make their wishes rules with consequences, I'll do what's best for my horse.

My heart beats double-time as the starter draws his bow. Guess wrong and we'll be eliminated.

His posture alters. The arrow flies.

I release Black. Even as the arrow pierces the target, he blazes across the starting line. We've made a clean, legal start.

Sojur claims the pole position while the rest of the field sorts itself out. With these numbers, it's a melee.

I crouch over Black's neck, knees bent, arms following the extension and contraction of his stride.

In a race, everything happens fast, yet slow.

I glance left. Find Rafi on Sojur's tail, chasing him for all he's worth, which in my estimation is plenty. Kemu isn't far behind.

The rider I fired comes our way, as if intent on driving us into the outer rail. Succeed, and the result would be ghastly.

This grudge holder comes within an armslength of Black, yet doesn't see my left boot isn't in the iron.

Black bellows a welcome to the mare while rating his speed to hers.

The mare's rider is a follower of fashion, his riding pants of some form-fitting fabric. He drives our two horses together, sealing his fate.

I lash out.

He screams, blood spurting from the line my spur has ripped into his thigh. Though the wound's not life-threatening, he flings himself from the saddle, then crawls off the track.

At my request, Black bids the mare a reluctant farewell, and moves out at full speed.

They say bad things come in threes, and today doesn't look to be an exception. Seth's in the middle of the pack, riding a mare who's obviously not a contender.

It's Hemming who has my complete attention. The sway of his whip tells me that the core's lead-filled. After inspection, he exchanged his legal whip for this instrument of torture.

My mental discourse sinks to the lowest language of the horse pens. If he seeks to harm Amir or Sojur, I will see him dead and rotting, never to know the fires of rebirth. Use his whip on his mount, and I'll lodge a protest.

I drive Black into the pack, slicing a diagonal for the inside rail. I have one target only: Hemming on Faharr, now closing in on Amir.

I'm not the only one who knows what may happen if I don't get there in time. Hundreds scream and beg me to hurry.

We're in the first curve, about to enter the backstretch. What works in our favor is Black's willingness to do what other horses can't. He cuts off runner after runner, coming in sharp and incredibly fast. We pull up even with Hemming, which puts us between Faharr and Amir.

Hemming uncoils his whip.

I hammer Black's ribs with my boots. "GO!"

Black closes in on Amir, just not fast enough to avoid Hemming's whip if he uses it. If the lash hits my lower leg, bone will break. If higher, it will cut through my brecca. Both heal.

Even as these thoughts flash through my mind, Black gives me his all, pulling up even with Amir.

Even as I praise him, I see Hemming's whiplash coiling between Black's hind legs, then fouling his stride. He stumbles, coming down wrong on his left hind. There's a gut-wrenching sound, the same as when I shattered the recurves of my childhood bow.

Black strains to take another stride, but screams as only a horse in pain can as his left rear hits the track. The leg, unable to bear weight, folds.

Faharr slams into Black. Our bodies fly end-over-end. In a tangle of red and black, a hoof sails a hairsbreadth away from my cheek as we crash onto the track.

Ribs crack or break.

Stars burst in my vision.

Breath refuses to draw.

I'm face down, more dead than alive. The ground beneath me trembles as the pack sweeps past. In a moment of comparative silence, a pool of blood gathers under my head, my nostrils recoiling at iron's raw stench. My heartbeat, now as much sensation as sound, joins the hammer of those horses still racing. All but my horse, all but Black, who screams, the sound sharper than steel. I have made my sacrifice his, yet try as I might, cannot move. For all I know, I may have broken my back or neck.

Without warning, my ribs spread like a boot to the guts, and I gasp air. Focus returns as a horse's leg flies past my face.

It's Black's, who fights to stand, yet cannot on a broken hind leg.

I strain to rise, agony billowing. Vision graying, I drag my body over Black's shoulder, doing my best to keep him from threshing. Throughout, I beg Heaven to take this horror from us, despite knowing it can't.

The screaming continues, not from me, but from the crowd, for Obsidian.

Of us all, Faharr is the fortunate one, back on his feet, albeit limping. I don't dare move. Can only hope someone gets here before Black tries rising again. If he does, he'll cast my body over Hemming's, whose eyes are open and empty.

Hemming has killed himself for Seth's gold, and in the doing, doomed the horse he sold.

Heaven won't have this man. After the evil he's done, I pray the deepest pit of the seven hells takes his soul and never lets it go.

FIFTY-NINE

WHOLE AGAIN

Kemu skids Celio to a halt and runs to me.

Black heaves against my shattered body. My vision darkens as I tighten my arms around his neck and beg him to remain calm.

Kemu drops to his knees across from me. He forces the stallion's head to earth, then blocks his pain.

Black subsides. Splayed across his sweat-gleaming body, I surrender to my own hurt.

Kemu rests his hand on the back of my neck, and moments later, pain takes on a less strident hue.

My beloved, you have cracked your ribs and damaged your spleen.

Unworthy of his care, I wrench free of his touch. "I am not Venari, riding into battle, yet what have I done? Sacrificed a horse commended to my care, a horse who trusted me."

Tears falling, I stroke Black's face, and murmur, 'Forgive me.'

With a vagueness born of my injuries, I sense Kemu moving to Black's hindquarters. Despite the wailing crowd, there's no missing the grate of broken bone when he flexes Black's hind leg.

Eyes showing white all around, Black begs me to fix what's wrong.

I can't. No one can.

Kemu crouches across from me. "The tibia is broken between the stifle and hock. For his sake, end it before he tries rising again."

I feather my fingers through the silk of Black's forelock. "Wait for Aaron?"

"Free him, Thea. He can't feel the pain, yet suffers, unable to rise. Give him to the wind."

To find resolve, I must see the damage myself. I turn. Jagged, bloody shards of sheared bone pierce Black's inner thigh.

I know how to take life mercifully, and as Black's rider, this is my responsibility. Yet duty has never weighed so heavily upon my heart.

Kemu offers me his dagger.

Head bowed, I whisper, "Forgive me," in a voice strangled by torment. I stroke Black's face, and pray he goes in peace. Only then do I rest my arm over his eyes.

Be born again, Black, in one of your sons. I'll find you next spring and promise our life together will be splendid.

He neither sees nor feels the blade opening the great arteries in his neck. In a torrent of unrelenting noise, leaden silence envelops us.

Black's nostrils quiver as he takes in the iron scent of blood. I cradle his head, begging his forgiveness as the fire fades from his eyes.

His ribs strain to lift, then settle. His last breath sighs from his body. He is here no more.

Crying so hard I can scarce see, I slice through his bridle. Do the same with the girth, then shove the saddle off his back. This horse will go to Heaven free.

Throughout, I beg Creation to turn back time, give me another chance and choice. Anything besides this heartbreak and horror. I stroke the face of a horse who can no longer complete our bond, pouring all my sorrow into this void.

At first, I dismiss the light emanating from Black's coat. It grows into the brilliance of iridescence, out of which a kaleidoscope of Lunas breaks free.

Hundreds upon hundreds of them, their silver-white wings soaring into the sky. A living symbol of the Mother of All's bittersweet blessing while summoning one of Her children home.

One remains, her wings opening and closing in perfect alignment with the scars over my birthmark. She dusts my skin with her radiance, then follows her companions.

Kemu's grip on my shoulder tightens.

Thea, that magic is this?

The mark I was born with, now restored: a Luna's silver-white wings once more rest atop my amber skin.

Kemu kneels beside me, then takes my hand. He raises his voice in ululation for a warrior lost in battle.

I add my ragged voice to his.

Venari join in our lament, paying tribute to a noble horse, but not the agent of his death. A man who lays unmourned, his body crushed and misshapen.

The Lunas turn south to the sea, south to the warmth of Shadreal as they bear Black's soul home.

I pray he still senses our bond, and come next spring, will be born again in one of his foals so we may share our lives again. The night Sahain died, the morning I almost joined him, and this affirms the covenant we keep with our Creators. In that living just and worthy lives, we will be born again among those we love.

As the Lunas disappear, I look to Hemming's crushed body. He tried, and failed, not valiantly, but in vain glory. And in his wake, has left us to endure what was taken.

A group of Sada riders thunders our way, at their head, Sojur on Amir, both alive and unharmed.

Hands red with Black's blood, I return Kemu's dagger. "Help Sojur?"

The Sada cordon off our tragedy, their naked blades keeping the bold and curious at bay.

Kemu slices through the rawhide binding Sojur's calf to the stirrup leather, then assists his dismount.

My teacher crosses to me, kneels, and embraces me. Often as he's used my shoulder as a staff or shaped my shins to a horse's sides, he's never held me like a father.

I welcome the relief from blood and death, and savor Sojur's scent of horses, dust, and the sweetness of fall pears. "You're safe."

His response comes equally soft. "Thanks to you. Thanks to Obsidian."

The sound of my father's deep voice raises our heads.

He strides our way, his white haaka shimmering in the clear afternoon light. Edan and Kylin are at his side. Were I still his daughter, he'd take me into his arms and make sense of this inexplicable tragedy. Sadly, those days are over.

I'm wrong. Stunningly wrong.

Pell sinks to his knees, then draws me into his arms, unconcerned by the blood. He folds his head over mine, then rocks me as if I were little again, and the pain too great.

"Sa, sa, little one. It's over."

No, not over. This heartbreak will haunt the rest of my days, yet the man I call father holds and comforts me. As he strokes my hair, I find shelter in his powerful arms.

"With impeccable honor, you put another's well-being before your own, saving my dearest friend." Gaze marveling, he blesses my still-glowing birthmark with a kiss.

"Thea, I was wrong. You aren't a traitor. You are the essence of a Venari. Come home, daughter, and heal the wound between us. Serve your father and your country."

Edan silences Kylin when she cries out in dismay.

I look from them to the warmth of my father's gaze, without which I would think this yet more torment. "I cannot be Venari."

Stunned, Pell draws back.

Sojur rests his hand on the a'Shara's shoulder. "My friend, she endured outcasting rather than endanger her sire and brother. Someone capable of such sacrifice should not change. Beyond that, the time has come to train my replacement. Who better than the daughter in your arms, provided you don't ask her to kill those whose blood she shares?"

Pell nods. "My friend, your wisdom exceeds mine."

He looks to me. "Daughter, come home, not to fight, but as Sojur's understudy, his quatrain?"

My dream comes true. Incapable of words, I nod.

Someone gives Pell a waterskin, with which he washes away the blood of a noble horse, and the bad blood between us.

The cordon of Sada opens, letting Lycan and Hanan through. White ribbons festoon the red horse's bridle. They've come in third. Despite his triumph, shame taints my would-be second's expression. Unlike Kemu, he didn't drop out of the race to help me or the dead horse at my side.

Pell rotates his Venari marks toward Lycan. "Fetch malachite." The harshness in the a'Shara's tone suggests he too lacks regard for a man who said he loved me, but did not come to my aid.

Glad for a task, Lycan spins Hanan, then speeds for the stables.

I don't have the strength to comprehend why Kylin sobs as if her heart has broken. I am ascending now, the same as on a battlefield.

Pell takes my hand. "Do you vow to serve your people and nation, knowing only death can break such a bond?"

I'm expected to speak from my heart, and do. "I pledge my life to A'tal and to my a'Shara."

Kemu kneels at my side as Sojur closes his maimed fingers around my left wrist, steadying my trembling hand.

Pell scores three chevrons into the skin between my left thumb and forefinger, starting small and growing larger, one on top of another. Thanks to the mindblock, I feel only the slither of steel through my skin.

Lycan returns with a small pouch, out of which Pell pours the grass-green mineral onto his palm, then holds to the bleeding cuts till they accept no more. He blesses my forehead with a kiss, then lifts me onto my unsteady feet, waiting till I have my balance before letting go.

"Thea a'Sada, speak and be heard. Act and be honored. Ask and you shall receive, for as Venari, you are one with your tribe in all ways."

I make reverence, then speak words I no longer believed would be mine. "My a'Shara."

I look to Sojur. "My master."

The Sada part to give Rafi passage. As this year's Reserve Champion of Champions, white roses festoon Yuni's neck. As he offers me reverence, tears streak my would-be second's face.

I brave a smile I don't feel. Rafi's done for Arron what I could not.

Our patron is next through the gauntlet, tears for his dead horse streaking his face. He extends the Champion's blanket of red roses to Sojur. "No rider deserves this tribute more."

My teacher shakes his head. "No rider ever owed a greater debt than I do to your horse and to his rider. Please, honor Obsidian. He is the true champion."

Weak as I am, I help Aaron drape the blanket of roses over Black's neck, paying homage to a horse who in life commanded fear, yet in death won adulation.

Aaron holds his hand to Black's face. "You were Solara's crown jewel. If only I'd been content to leave you with your mares."

He bends and kisses the broad forehead. "Come back, Black. Live again in your foals."

The Sada let another rider through their cordon, Seth, on his mare, now festooned with the yellow ribbons of fourth place.

He halts beside Hemming's misshapen body, and regards it as if some perverse work of art. "What a hapless fool."

Expression bland, he looks to where we kneel beside Black. "And to think, all we wanted was to improve the odds of Obsidian's victory. The only consolation is the foals Black sired on my mares. In the wake of their sire's death, they will be born priceless."

Lips thin, he shakes his head. "What an ungodly mix: a nightmare and a dreamer who, together, slaughtered the crown jewel of my inheritance."

Aaron rises, rigid with anger. "Other than my complete disdain, you have had all you will from me. As for the foals Obsidian sired upon your mares, I shall have them all. You paid no fees, thus have no contract."

Seth laughs. "We shall see, old man. As for my inheritance, there's a clause in your betrothal with my mother you need to re-visit. The High Court assures me it is ironclad. The moment you're dead, Solara is mine."

As his sire recoils, Seth reins my way.

Flanked by Pell, Kemu, Rafi, and Sojur, I stand my ground.

Seth's smile has all the warmth of a snake's, even as his gaze gloats at my still bleeding marks. "As for your part in this debacle, you will pay blood price. Fail to do so, and as Venari, you are honor bound to do whatever the court orders, including giving me Khamsin."

Pell swears with words Venari favor when things go sideways.

All that keeps me upright is Kemu's arm bracing mine. That I'm swaying on my feet broadens Seth's smile as he departs. The horse dead at our feet means no more to Seth than his father or dead rider.

In his son's absence, Aaron lays hand-to-heart. "Thea, I cannot apologize enough, nor have adequate words of gratitude for all you've done."

His gaze shifts to Rafi. "It is my great hope you and Idry will stay on at Solara."

Before Rafi can respond, the wail of Venari warning horns pierces the racetrack's stone bowl. Each of the five tribes' distinct pattern calling them to battle.

Kemu's gaze shifts from out to in, then back again. "Daharsha attacks the entirety of our border. Our tribes beg for our return."

Pell blesses my forehead with a kiss. "A'Sada, till a healer says otherwise, you will remain in Azalaïs. Heal swiftly, daughter. Your people need you."

A sad smile, then he heads for D'jhat.

Kemu is already on Celio.

I'll find you before the Rowan leave.

As they depart, his stallion's hind hooves spray limestone out behind them.

Pell's on D'jhat, ready to ride. As I strain to come to attention, his gaze remains on me. "Daughter, I pray we see each other again."

I bow my head in formal reverence, as my tone bespeaks the love I bear him. "As do I, Father."

Though it's time he can ill afford, he takes it, yet a moment later, he too is gone.

Amir stands quietly as Sojur prepares to mount.

I cross to them, then square his empty right boot in the iron.

Hand to my cheek, Sojur blesses me. "If only your naysayers could see you now. Be well, Thea. Be blest. By the time you can ride, I will need you, most likely desperately."

It's all the time we have. As he departs, I pray for his continued safety.

All across the racetrack, the same drama repeats, Venari racing for horses and weapons.

My heart constricts. The men I love are leaving for battle. I may never see them alive again.

Kylin, face streaked with tears, and gaze fixed on my left hand, comes my way.

With the price so many have paid for this moment, I put a Venari's harsh demand into my voice. "Mother's Own, did you foresee this?"

She shakes her head in fierce denial.

"Do you know what the Mother wants from me?"

Words fail her, so much so, she resorts to mindspeach.

Thea, you will earn your gift, not learn it. Till then, follow your heart and instincts, just as you do the Mother.

She gets no further, and sobs so hard, Edan leads her away.

Meanwhile, I survey the wreckage of the day.

The horse Lord Aaron entrusted to my care lies dead at my feet. My two nations are at war, and my two fathers will soon be hell-bent upon killing each other.

Amidst all this darkness, death, and destruction, shine two stars: Pell's permission to return home and Kemu's love.

I wrap my arms around my shattered ribs.

Broken as I am, I have been made whole again.

SIXTY

MY NAME

A freshening wind has driven the clouds northwest, and left the western sky a seamless indigo. Beside me, Kane sits on the driver's seat of Solara's four-in-hand carriage, the reins draped between him and his favorite team of black mares. After healers forbade my riding, Lord Aaron assured I would reach this hilltop in time.

Only an hour has passed, yet Venari of all five tribes charge up these chalk hills, heading west to war. Spare horses run alongside their riders. They wear haakas of Falili crimson, Mitanni violet, Khadir saffron, Sada emerald, and Rowan sapphire.

My greatest fear is we've arrived too late, that my a'Shara and Sojur are already gone.

Two riders start up the hill, Sojur in emerald, Pell in silver-white. D'jhat's ash-gray coat and massive build stands out easily against the white chalk.

The winning horse charges up the hill alongside Sojur, undaunted by the race he's just won. This is why my teacher wanted this year to be Amir's bid for the title. A glorious breeding career awaits Windsong's only son.

Even as this thought comes, another refutes it. Next year, Amir will have a half-brother. Deep in my bones, I know my beloved Windsong carries Khamsin's colt, and that he will be magnificent. Heaven willing, I will return to Azalaïs come spring, and seek another colt, a special colt. I'll know Obsidian when I see him in his son's eyes. Aaron and I have agreed upon the price: my breeding Khamsin to a select group of Solara's mares.

Sojur and the a'Shara crest the hill, then wheel east, and salute the anxious people of Azalaïs in the racetrack below. Only then do they join the stream of riders spreading out over the wastelands while heading home.

I stand straighter than my body wishes, left arm across my chest, hand-to-heart. However perplexing Heaven's answers to my prayers have proven, I pray they travel safe.

Their forms grow smaller, then disappear. Before darkness and despair fill my heart, I sense Kemu's approach, then see him on Gamar. Celio runs free at their side.

As much as I want this man, I won't detain him.

We come into each other's arms, seeking to express with touch what words cannot. Fearing we may never see each other again turns our kiss more precious than gold.

My love, a few weeks healing, and Khamsin will take the grasslands by storm, and carry you back into my arms.

He steps back, his gaze memorizing this moment.

"Kemu?"

"Yes, my heart?"

I love you.

I've bespoken him. The best way, the only way, I can say these words.

There's no time, yet he makes it. His smile is transcendent, aware of what expressing my feelings cost me.

As I have loved you over many lifetimes. I will engrave your words upon my heart. Till we are reunited, they will carry me safely into battle.

He runs to Gamar, mounts, takes a last lingering look, then departs.

My world constricts. Once more, I am an unhorsed child left to find my own way home, born beneath an unlucky star, and cursed by fate.

No, not cursed. Loved by a man who is only a thought away. Elevated by the man who raised me.

A sense of strength fills me with the resolve I lacked only moments ago.

I am not alone. I am one with my people.

And my name is Thea a'Sada.

An end, and yet a beginning . . .

Want to know what happens next?

P re-order Luminesce, Book Two of Day Without Dawn with the code below. No charge till the release and it will be in Kindle Unlimited!

Want to see the triptychs I made for the characters in Iridesce?

About the Author

Writing, riding my Morgan horses, meals with friends, time in and on the water, yoga, dancing, gardening and helping other riders with their saddles (as a Society of Master Saddlers Qualified Saddle Fitter) I could not ask for more. And now that you are here, let's get this party started! You can visit me online at:

ACKNOWLEDGEMENTS

So many people, experiences, and welcome influences, first among which, the dream that gave birth to Thea and her world.

To my teachers and mentors who read, crit and taught me, my heartfelt thanks: Ben Logan, author of The Land Remembers, whose concepts tied me into knots that took years to absorb. Cal Moriarty for reading my prologue in the Womentoring Project, then said, "I want the story behind this book as well!" Art Holcomb, Script Doctor to major Hollywood studios, who mentored me on the reality of publishing and storytelling. Mel Williams, a member of the Fantasy Faction online crit group (organized thanks to Janice Hardy's Crit Connection) for her invaluable perspective in grappling with the reality of prejudice.

Next up, the editors who made such a difference for Iridesce, foremost among which is Molly Kalesh, author/alpha reader/editor extraordinaire and artist. Michelle Hazen, and Dario Ciriello, who endured my 'I'm not changing these till I discovered another author using the names/words he wanted changed. Thank you for your patience!

To the fantasy/science fiction authors I've traded beta reads with: Nicholas Wisseman, Mikhaeyla Kopievsky, Sherry Bassette, Caroline Sciriha, Joey Harpel, Melainie Marttila, Taylor Fitzgerald, and J. A. Andrews.

For Grady Earls, graphic artist and movie maker, the insight with which you translated this book into images awes me. My ever-thanks for your vision.

To Carolyn Standlee-Hanson, Winona County Master Falconer, the time we spent with you and your Red Tail Hawk gave me the basis upon which to create Azize.

To the myriad of riders and trainers whose horses I have the privilege of serving as a Society of Master Saddlers Qualified Saddle Fitter, you make life even sweeter.

For those gone too soon from my life, I hope we meet again. Meg Nathan, Karlis, Marie, Tim, and the beloved horses, cats and dogs no longer in my life.

Last of all, to the heart of my life: my husband, our (now) small herd of Morgan Horses, our two born-in-a-barn, we-rule-the-house cats and the myriad of wildlife who share our lives and make our garden and window views such an endless delight—thank you, one and all!

GLOSSARY

- Affonaè: continent shared by A'tal & Daharsha.

- Ainee: herb girl at Rafi's training yard, one of four foundlings.

- Ah'rēnē: person born of ancient enemies, destined to bring unite the two warring nations.

- Amir: Windsong's only colt, winner of the previous years' Champion of Champions race, given to Sojur by Thea.

- Aryren: Sada Master of Weapons.

- A'Shara: one of the five A'talan war leaders.

- A'tal: one of the two nations on the continent of Affonaé.

- A'talan: those born here.

- Atar: Thea's eldest Crèche brother.

- Azalais: largest port city in A'tal & site of annual fall Champion of Champion's race.

- Azize: small hawk born in Daharsha.

- Baseem: Lawaan heir of Khalil.

- Black Swan: the inn preferred by the wealthy of Azalais.

- Charra au'Sada: Pell a'Sada's blood daughter, a member of the Sada Tribal Council.

- Covenant: One of the five institutions of higher learning and lawmaker, led by a member of the Mother's Order, A'tal's spiritual leaders.

- Coveners: members of the Covenant's twelve crofts, each dedicated to a different skill or pursuit of knowledge or magic.

- Croft: twelve to each Covenant, dedicated to a certain craft, art or discipline.

- Dafor: a colt Thea bred

- Daharsha: the desert nation where Thea was born, then abandoned.

- Daharshan: those born in Daharsha.

- Dree: a carter who brings supplies to Rafi's training

yard.

- Eisa: Ainee's youngest brother.

- Enya: owner of the Sun, where the Sada house during Azalais' Champion of Champions race, a longtime lover of Pell a'Sada.

- Falili: one of the five A'talan tribes on the grasslands, just south of the Rowan. Their Venari marks are crimson.

- First One Hundred Families: what's left of A'tal's nobility after the Venari deposed the monarchy.

- Gamar: Kemu a'Rowan's bay warhorse.

- Garin a'Sada: Head of Pell's personal guard.

- Grasslands: the lush lands east of the border, from the northernmost range of the Silverstones, then east to the sea.

- Gayleen a'Rohan: a'Shara of the Rohan Venari.

- Habibi: only child of Leander.

- Haj: a title bestowed upon any Daharshan warrior capable of winning the role of leading his tribe's warriors against A'tal.

- Hemming: head rider & trainer at Solara.

- Hilen: head cook at the Sun.

- Jae: the Sada Headwoman who oversees the tribal council.

- Kane: head coachman of Solara.

- Khadir: a grassland tribe south of the Mitanni. Their Venari marks are saffron. Khadeen: Daharshan for child.

- Khalil: Haj of the Lawaan.

- Khamsin: Golden warhorse bred and rode by Khalil.

- Kian: Daharshan word for warrior or warriors.

- Kylin: a member of the Mother's Order & Edan's beloved.

- Lady Edan: head of the Bronze Croft at Land's End.

- Land's End: northernmost Covenant in A'tal.

- Leander: owner of the largest flock of sheep among the Sada.

- Leonas: Falili Venari & famed racing doyen.

- Lord Karlis: Head of the first one hundred families, the man who built Solara, A'tal's premier breeding farm, and father of Seth.

- Luna Moth: symbol of The Mother of All's peace.

- Lycan: a Venari-to-be like Thea.

- Mahir: eldest brother of Ainee, Mina & Eisa.

- Mina: Ainee's nine year old sister.

- Mitanni: grassland tribe located south of the Falili, by the sea. Their Venari's marks are violet.

- Mora a'Sada: healer and a Mother's Voice, spiritual advisor of the Sada.

- Mother's Voice: she who can channel the will of the Mother of All.

- Nahla: famous herbwoman in Azalais.

- Nana au'Sada: head cook of the Sada.

- Nomadi: vile term to describe the Daharshan Kian who come raiding all too often.

- Patra: Daharshan for father.

- Pell a'Sada: a'Shara of the Sada, who found and fostered Thea.

- Phillea: one of Thea's mares.

- Rafi a'Falili: an ex-Venari who runs a training yard in Azalais.

- Red Sands of Daharsha: the infamous desert which only the desert people can survive.

- Rising Sun: the inn in Azalais, owned by Enya, where the Sada house during racing. Rowan: grasslands tribe south of the Sada. Their Venari marks are sapphire blue.

- Sabita: a Falili Venari Lord Aaron hoped to marry, who disappeared while on patrol in Daharsha.

- Sada: the grasslands tribe closest to the Silverstone Mountains. Their Venari marks are emerald.

- Sahain a'Sada: Thea's beloved crèche brother.

- Selene: Thea's white hunting hound, given to Thea by Pell when she was ten.

- Seth: Lord Aaron's only offspring.

- Silverstone Mountains: northern boundary between A'tal and Daharsha.

- Sojur a'Sada: the Sada Master of Horse and Pell's Second. Captured, then tortured by Kian, he lacks a foot, three fingers on his right hand, and two on the left.

- Stead: private land holdings across A'tal.

- Steadholders: those who hold the land apart, unlike on the grasslands, where it is shared.

- The Guard: the Covenant's watch dogs against law breakers.

- The Mother's Order: Women gifted with magic, prophecy, and healing, sacred leaders of A'tal. Each initiate wears a tattoo of a Luna, sacred to the Mother of All on the back of her left hand.

- Thea: abandoned at birth along the border, a just weaned purebred Daharshan filly at her side. Found, then fostered by Pell a'Sada, for a birthmark on the back of her left hand: a Luna moth, sacred to the Mother of All.

- Valan: a stable boy at the Rising Sun.

- Venari: an A'talan warrior.

- Windsong: a dark chestnut purebred Daharshan filly, with a silver-white mane and tail, left with Thea when she was abandoned.

- Zaria: a female Daharshan name.

SIXTEEN
YEARS
EARLIER

THEA'S ORIGIN STORY

DAHARSHAN DESERT NIGHT

K halil's warhorse snorts, keen to enter the fray below. It's a raucous melee of belling blades and screaming men. He strokes the chestnut's arching neck, his bronze hand the color of the gelding's hide. "At long last, dear friend, these futile battles will end."

For every drop of blood spilt, horse stolen or Venari enslaved, always, always a cost. Families shattered as Lawaan warriors die at the hands of their ancient enemy. Brothers and uncles, compelled by the Heavenly One to take in widows and children. Yet the greatest iniquity of all? To preserve Khalil's new role as Haj, Tahir, his half-brother must die.

On the rocky border between the warring nations of A'tal and Daharsha, the desert's ever-present wind ripples Khalil's indigo riding coat. His gelding's golden mane and tail stream eastward. Were it not for the battle, they'd make excellent targets against the setting sun.

Their shadows lengthen on the shale dividing the ancient enemies. Soon, night will cast its jet-black cloak over the unnatural act Khalil must undertake.

In the battle below, A'talan lancers drive their horses through an equal number of his Kian. Trained to fight in packs, the Venari slay the zealous Daharshans like sheep. Such is the nature of his people: glory onto the individual warrior, no matter the price of pride.

He finds Tahir by his silver-white gelding. The flamboyant mount and gold-encrusted tack speak of the boldness which will prove his brother's undoing.

Khalil detests the slaughter below, yet draws a single arrow from his quiver. On the Daharshan side of the border, his waiting forces cannot see the emerald of the arrow's vanes. Mere days ago, he cut this A'talan shaft out of a dead Kian, then secreted it for this very purpose.

Arrow nocked, he rests the bow's powerful recurves across his thigh. He strokes the silkwood shaft, seeking calm and resolve.

The setting sun turns the desert's undulating dunes to the color of heart-blood. His thoughts drift as he waits for the killing moment.

He and Tahir grew up inseparable, despite good-natured rivalry for their sire's favor. The day their father, Abda, chose Khalil to take his place as Haj of the Lawaan, loathing inflamed Tahir's soul.

That same day, Tahir aligned himself with Šaiṭān, the tribe's new and all too toxic cleric. A Ja'kor who on the outside bore the seeming of sanctity, yet proved a sinner. Šaiṭān led his beloved brother down the path of self-seeking ambition. The unholy pair dismissed the damage they'd do. All the progress

Khalil and his beloved Haj'ene had brought to their tribe, destroyed. All betterment returned to the privileged.

No, not while Khalil still breathes.

He draws his bow, its layered horn creaking. The corners of his chinstrap beard lift in a snarl. "Drink the life of yet another Kian, arrow of my enemy. In the doing, save those who made you by ending the brother who would supplant me."

The screams of the wounded and dying overpower the malediction as he seals his curse. "Die, my once childhood friend and brother. May the seven hells swallow your soul, never to know Heaven's delights."

There's no quaver in his muscled arms while he maintains the pose. Tahir's horse, now a silver wraith in the growing dark, is all the target he needs. He times his exhalation to the arrow's release, then roars as it shimmies into the dark.

"Tahir, beware!"

At the boom of Khalil's familiar voice, Tahir whips his horse around.

The A'talan shaft finds its mark in Tahir's uncuirassed chest. Its triple blades pierce his heart. He topples into a froth of Kian and A'talan Venari battling off horseback and on foot.

Iron to a lodestone, his gaze raises, finding Khalil on the ridge. A single word bubbles on his lips. "Brother?" Then, nothing. Azure eyes empty and face free of pain, his head falls to the trampled A'talan grasslands.

Bile floods Khalil's stomach. He experiences a moment's guilt, regret, then reasoned affirmation. On the desert, only the strong survive. Far better he ends one man's ambitions than losing hundreds in bloody raids upon their ancient enemy. Far better, he ensures their sire's favorite son remains the Lawaan's Haj.

At the sound of a horse coming up behind him, Khalil reins his mount about-face.

"My Haj!" Zadan, his second-in-command, thuds fist to chest. "The Haj'ene asks for you."

Khalil permits himself a sharp inbreath of startle. "She gives birth?"

At Zadan's nod, Khalil swears. "My brother could not have picked a worse time to defy me. Summon my guard."

His second frees a piercing whistle. "All eyes and honor to our Haj, Khalil el'Lawaan!"

As his guard makes the uphill climb, Khalil sounds the call to retreat on a ram's horn. A command he'd rather die than issue were this a battle of his own making. Not this hapless, unsanctioned raid on the Sada.

His men halt in a silent line one hundred strong. The desert wind whispers secrets only those born to it can hear. Tales of demons and devils, of Djinn and Ifrit. Tales Tahir did not heed, thus condemning his soul for all eternity.

Framed against the splendid tapestry of his heritage, Khalil gestures to the battle below. "See the ferocity with which Pell a'Sada's Venari kill those of my Kian Tahir led astray. Witness the profligacy with which my brother risked his life and theirs. Lawaan families will mourn tonight with their beloved men in Heaven. Rue the action you must take, but obey my orders. This alone will let us maintain our strength and prosperity."

A hundred heads, bound from eyes to chin in azure cloth, bow.

"Half of you will remain here under Zadan's command. If the Sada dispose of our dead where you can retrieve them, do so. If not, leave them where they lay. They died for disobeying my mandate. Tell those families who must perform the rites of mourning without a body to inter they must blame Tahir.

"As for those who survive this battle . . ." his gaze shifts to Zadan ". . . either they acknowledge me as Abda's choice as their Haj or die."

Zadan and the one hundred slam fists to shoulders, then respond in one voice. "We obey our Haj, beloved of the Heavenly One, Khalil el'Lawaan!"

That they hold true adds a faint touch of warmth to his grim expression. "See to it you do so. Like my sire, I am done with dissent."

The Daharshan ability to keep their expressions unfathomable does not hide their fear. For that reason, Khalil modulates his tone.

"Think of your families. Think of your children. The sacrifices you make tonight arise out of love for our people and way of life, not from greed for glory. By your acts, you follow the commandments of the Holy Word. You will be a bright star in Heaven's firmament when your day comes. The Heavenly One will not cast you into darkness, demons, and damnation. Would I could say the same of those below."

He checks his horse, now impatient with the delay and lack of action. "Zadan is my eyes and my will. Obey him as you do me, for I must leave as you complete this unwelcome task. My Haj'ene gives birth."

He pauses at the soft murmur of 'May a son bless you,' then inclines his head in thanks. "From your lips to the Heavenly One."

Moments later, he starts down the incline, then out into the desert. The sound of hooves slipping on shale follows him as those Kian Zadan chose as his guards descend.

He turns north. The backside of the Silverstone Mountains looms to his right, outlined by the risen moon. Already, his nostrils thirst for the elixir of water that arose from A'tal's lush summer grasslands.

From spring till winter, A'talan streams rush with the mountain's snow melt. That same water does not flow west into Daharsha. In his homeland, the only green is that of an occasional errant oasis and its date palms.

The land rises as his guard joins him.

The parched air takes on the clarity of stone, of eternity, through which black-winged bats flurry. They bear the spirits of Djinn and Ifrit, damned for all eternity to prey upon the righteous.

Khalil touches the naẓar amulet hanging from his sword pommel. As he does so, he makes the sign of warding against the evil eye.

As they ride, he senses more than sees creatures seeking food, water, or mates. Somewhere in the potent dark, an ibex screams as a karakel, the scourge of the desert finishes its kill. His Kian close in around him. They will not lose the man whose choices made them the most envied tribe in Daharsha.

The sand hisses with the rhythm of their horses' strides. Proud-cut geldings, an ignominy imposed upon all Kian. It's Daharsha's method of denying A'tal access to their breeding horses, the swiftest in the world.

Tahir and Khalil's great-great grandsire, Amir to the then current Sultan, birthed this plan and convinced their sovereign of its wisdom. Every year thereafter, the influence of captured Daharshan bloodstock weakened. No further evidence of the fiery desert horses now lingers in the A'talan cavalry.

Nor did Abda, their current Amir, and his sire, challenge this strategy. Not when A'tal's so-called democracy denied Daharsha access to their ample water.

The band sweeps through the outskirts of the Lawaan encampment. Sheep bleat and camels grumble. It's the horses, their greatest treasure, who whicker greetings to returning companions.

The group slows from canter to trot, then walk. The tribe's tents spread their swooping felt wings over the sand. Small fires glow before tents. There, women bake flatbread on stone griddles while tending brass kettles on iron tripods.

The food's rich scent reminds Khalil how long it's been since last he ate. Once his newest child arrives, he and Sabita can revel in their future and share a meal. They can forget, at least for a while, securing said future required Tahir's death.

The day Khalil made Sabita his Haj'ene, first wife over the others in his hareem, Tahir denounced the act as heresy. In the doing, he won the support of the tribe's Ja'kor.

Emboldened, the priggish cleric railed against an infidel made into more than a Haj's slave. This complication in establishing Khalil's authority brought them to today's breaking point.

He halts before Sabita's tent.

Those Kian appointed to protect her come to attention. Fists-to-shoulders, they salute him, their blue eyes flashing in the lantern light. "Heavenly One's champion!"

With a brusque nod, he acknowledges the respect paid, then swings out of the saddle.

As he enters the tent, a dark silence envelops him. No sound of a woman in labor or a midwife's urging. Has she given birth? Will this child be like their first, Baseem, glorious in his boldness? Undaunted at being half A'talan?

Despite this day's many horrors, the image of two boys with mettle fierce as their sire and dam pleases him. Let the other

Haj shake their heads over Khalil elevating an ex-Venari to his Haj'ene. Not a one of them flourish well as the Lawaan.

Boots silent on the thick carpets, he strides toward the rear of the tent. Aligned to the west, were the sun in the sky, the tapestry walls of Sabita's inner sanctum would glow. It's a sad illusion of the many freedoms denied the women of the Daharshan royalty, be they wife or Haj'ene.

He pauses at the opening to her sleeping room, entranced.

Lost in wonder of the other, his best belovèd cradles their newborn to her white-rose breast. Rather than Sabita's hazel eyes, the child's are azure like his. A glory of black lashes lies against tawny skin. In this child he sees the bones of both nations: his people's high cheekbones and Sabita's thinner upper lip.

"My amorata."

Her fingers cease shuttling through the infant's silky black hair. She meets his gaze. Immersed in her babe, the once always alert ex-Venari had not heard his approach.

Tears shimmer on her lashes as she holds out a graceful, pleading hand. "My life." Words spoken in tones of sorrow.

He sits at her side, drawing mother and child to his chest. "My heart, what brings these tears? Are you in pain?"

She clings to him and shakes her head, muffling her sobs in his robes.

He cups the ivory sculpture of her jaw in his bronze hand. "Tell me. What is amiss?"

Tears fall from her kohl-lined eyes, yet her aristocratic features remain serene. In all things Sabita, subtlety ruled.

She eases her forefinger beneath the child's left hand, then lifts it to the pierced lantern light. "See for yourself."

Despite the plain-spoken words, her tone grieves.

On the back of the infant's left hand lays a birthmark in the shape of a Luna moth, beloved of A'tal's Goddess, the Mother of All. Symbolizing the moon and her cycles, this is the faith Sabita clings to in her heart. This female-centric faith is at the heart of the enmity between the two lands. He's never spoken of his distaste for women making and enforcing their Goddess' decrees, nor has she. It's an unresolved element in their bond.

She reads his stony silence. Her sorrow compounds. "Khalil, my heart, I did not pray for this."

"Are you certain of that?"

She swallows. "As certain as I am of loving you."

Despite this affirmation of what they share, he retreats inward, his gaze locked on the infant's hand. In Daharsha, this mark is abhorrent, nay repugnant, aligned as it is with A'tal's ruling class—the Order of the Mother's Own. Women of such power they can see into the future and control the fates of men. One side, masculine, the other feminine, and rare is their union without inequity.

He adores this woman, yet once capable of speech, his words reek of harshness and misery. "Boy or girl?"

"A girl."

The blow hits hard, only to triple as his daughter reaches for him with her anathema-marked hand. From his many wives, mostly sons. This child should have been Sabita's solace, her confidant, her joy amidst his tribe's hostility. He left Baseem with her a year longer than was fitting for that very reason.

This precious daughter, with whom Sabita could have shared her thoughts, cannot, must not be. His guts twist. Their Ja'kor's vindictive religious mandate will damn this innocent. He will order her tiny body spiked upon a dead palm tree sharpened for that very purpose.

Resolved in his decision, he looks to Sabita. "Did the midwife see this mark?"

Muscles in her face taut, she nods.

Once able to speak, her words come out jagged, stark, and desolate. "She did, then with venom in her tone, said I must suckle the child and tighten my womb. That the Ja'kor would take this 'monstrosity' into the desert and leave her for the jackals. Such an insignificant, cursed bit of flesh was not worthy of impaling."

A serpent's tongue could not wag faster than their midwife's. The moment she gains access to the Lawaan's Ja'kor, he will storm this tent and damn them.

As if reading his thoughts, Sabita rests her hand on his cheek. "My love, what can we do?"

That she asks, rather than insists, urges him into further rebellion. Were his choice not already made, her trust would have taken him there. And yet, he despairs. How will he protect and preserve this child, conceived in love beneath a starry desert sky?

This whole nightmarish situation, brought to be by the Mother of All. Khalil's faith forbids other gods before the Heavenly One as they despoil His chosen people.

His daughter reaches out, grasping at his thumb, already possessed of Baseem's determination. What good will that do her if he does not act?

He draws Sabita's hand to his lips, kissing her Venari marks. His refusal to have them tattooed over? Yet another rock piled on the mountain of complaints lodged against his Haj'ene.

"The Ja'kor won't have her, nor will the jackals."

Sabita stiffens. "My love, your people will judge you, as will your father and the Haj of all the other tribes, and certainly the Sultan. Defy your Ja'kor and the Lawaan will kill you, then every person aligned with you."

"Not if I take our daughter into the desert and 'sacrifice' her."

The irony in his tone keeps her wide-eyed and silent.

"So long as I return without a child, we alone will know she lives in A'tal."

Her expression brightens, then dims. "It won't work. Your Ja'kor will demand a witness to her death. Beyond that, with the color of her skin and eyes, no A'talan will doubt her blood is Daharshan."

He turns the infant's left hand till the blue-toned birthmark rises to the top. "Same as they will see this mark and know what placed it there."

"But what will keep them from killing her first?"

"The birthgift I'll leave at her side—the finest filly born to my herds this spring."

"You would destroy your grandsire's legacy to save our daughter?"

"I would and I will. You convinced me it's a fool's errand to squander Kian's lives in needless raids, for which Tahir died. Without his interference, now I can bring peace to my people. What better way to close this twisted circle than bear false witness while practicing deceit?"

She strokes his beard, her gentle touch filled with a wife and mother's desperation. "Do this, but promise me you will return alive, not as a ghost."

Again, he kisses this woman who tried killing him when he captured her. "Nothing and no one will keep me from you. Take heart, my love. Prepare yourself for the part you must play in this charade."

In this faint moment of lightness, she smiles through her tears.

It's enough. It must be, for it is the only relief they will have this night.

The little one nestles against her mother's breast as her eyes close in sleep.

He kisses his daughter, then his Haj'ene. "This is our only clear path. Once the midwife gains access to the Ja'kor, he will come here. I'll instruct your guards to refuse him entry till my return."

She returns his kiss, her passion for him equal to his for her, yet their kiss tastes of despair and the bitter ashes of loss.

Within the hour, Khalil returns to Sabita's tent riding his finest mare, black as the night itself. Her unweaned filly whirls around them. She treats this nighttime excursion like some grand game. The greater sorrow is that come the dawn, like his daughter, the filly will never see her mother again.

Their gazes in the far distance, Kian line the path to Sabita's tent. Like his sire, their Haj's temper has a quixotic nature, indiscernible till explosion.

The belief Khalil will sacrifice this unhallowed child explains their lack of outrage. His further offer of atonement, the finest filly born to his mares this spring? How could such a gift not appease the Heavenly One?

Khalil imagines their thoughts. 'Tis a bloody price our Haj pays for his presumption, taking our enemy to wife, then naming her his Haj'ene.

Little do they know, nor will they ever. However this plays out, he will do what it takes to save his daughter. That she has a life in A'tal may temper the grief which will haunt her parents. That he emulates his sire in falsely bowing to the Holy Word is of little import. Life first, then honor. As a man, and a Haj, his people come first. This is at the heart of what will assure his father's favor. When the old Sultan dies and his sire ascends Daharshan throne, Khalil will take his father's place as Amir.

Sabita stands outside her tent, gold-streaked hair hooded and lower face veiled. The child of their love lies swaddled and sleeping in her arms.

For a moment, he contemplates adding yet another soul to his tally tonight: the Ja'kor. However satisfying, it would not end well. Nor would retribution fill the soon-to-be empty place which is their daughter. As for the Ja'kor, he will make a reasoned plea for being the sole witness to his daughter's 'death.'

He walks his mare through the mass of Lawaan tribesmen who encircle Sabita's tent.

They part with reluctance, their expressions an odd mix of outrage and sympathy. Under his leadership, they have prospered. Still, will they ignore the curse Heaven has laid upon his line? He prays his so-called sacrifice works.

They crowd him as he halts his mare, then gestures for Sabita.

As she comes his way, her handmaids follow their mistress. She hurls them a harsh look for which they cower, then retreat to the entry.

The tribesmen part with reluctance for this so-called Haj'ene. All hunger for a glimpse of the abomination on the child's hand for which she must die.

The chestnut filly butts her dam's udder, for which the mare squeals displeasure. Presage wells. He will take two daughters from their mothers tonight. This elegant, impetuous brat and a little girl he would have doted upon.

Khalil spots Baseem. His son forces his way through the mass of Kian surrounding the tribesmen. His startling azure eyes glow in a face lighter than Khalil's. Any attempt at restraining him, he evades, a blur of indigo robes swirling around tall boots. The anger his sire has tamped scorches his son's expression. Four years of age and he's already taken on his father's autocratic mien. Nothing and no one interferes with his will.

While Khalil approves of the boy's attitude, now more than ever, it's time to put some polish on his son's manners. At least till he has the size and skill to back up, the command he assumes is his to take.

The tribesmen give way, more out of dislike than respect and little wonder. They view mixed-race children as seconds, off-falls. Useful in the ranks, just not Daharshan.

Baseem nears his sire as an arm shoots out from the crowd. An arm which ends in a hand gripping a blade. His Kian ride into the protesting crowd as Khalil comes out of the saddle. Sword drawn, he reaches his son, then steps back as the Ja'kor presses the knife to Baseem's throat.

"Baseem, do not move." He enunciates each word, his deep voice underlying the gravity of the command.

"I won't, father." Despite the boy's brave mien, there's a quaver in his voice.

Kahlil looks to the Ja'kor. "Šaiṭān." His expression and the use of the Ja'kor's name promises nothing and no one will keep him alive should he harm Baseem.

Righteous in his preeminence, the Ja'kor does not quail under Khalil's impassive gaze. "You shall pay a father's ultimate penance."

The man's lips thin in distaste. "Take this abomination into the desert, then skewer your sacrilege upon a stake. You will remain till she wails her last."

The cleric looks to Sabita. "As for you, heathen, you will humble yourself before the Heavenly One. I am not content your conversion is real, not rote."

He lances a glare at Khalil. "Haj, you have sinned, elevating a slave to wife, then making her your Haj'ene. For this, the perversion in her arms must die. Fail and I will end this branch of your line: baby, boy, and the woman who bore them. As the Heavenly One's messenger, this I vow."

More like the devil who led Tahir to damnation. Rather than speak his thoughts, Khalil bows his head. "As the Ja'kor commands."

The tribesmen murmur approval, but Šaiṭān arches a single brow, as if reading Khalil's thoughts.

"Till you return with your hands and sword bloodied by these sacrifices . . ." he gestures between the chestnut filly and the infant, ". . . I will keep your son and Haj'ene at my side. Do we understand each other?"

Khalil restrains the fury boiling inside him to end this man, then nods.

Šaiṭān searches the crowd. "Where is Tahir?"

This zealot knows of the brothers' division. His question reveals suspicions for which a solution for which must wait. "Dead."

The flatness of his tone and lack of explanation leaves the Ja'kor silent, only for a moment.

"How is such a thing possible?"

As if he hadn't goaded Tahir into defying Kahlil's orders. "The fortunes of war do not include safety. If possible, the Kian I left behind will retrieve Tahir's body."

"Let us pray they do so."

Khalil bows his head, as if in submission. He will end this man's stranglehold over his tribe. "As you command, my Ja'kor."

"Then, best you get to it."

Khalil sheathes his sword, then holds his hand out to his son. "Bid your sister farewell."

Šaiṭān hesitates to remove his blade from Baseem's throat. The tribesman murmur disapproval and the Ja'kor relents.

The boy darts to his father's side.

Khalil kisses his son, then leads him to where Sabita stands.

As is proper, she sinks to a knee before them.

Fear strains Baseem's expression. "Mother, who has cursed my sister?"

Fresh tears gather at Sabita's lashes, but anger roils in her tone. "The country that gave me birth."

"Please, show me."

That he asks rather than insists reflects the values Khalil drills into his son.

She folds back the blanket, exposing his sister's tiny hand and the birthmark upon it. As she does so, Baseem touches the luna, confirming it as flesh, not shadow.

Does his son fight to contain his emotions? It seems possible as he bends to kiss his sister's brow.

Separated by custom, burdened by sorrow, mother and son share a brief look. Then, with Baseem's help, Sabita rises.

Khalil vows to close the distance between mother and son, especially now and for both their sakes.

Heart aching, he holds his arms out to her, knowing what she feels isn't his fixity of purpose. She's too deep into the loss, which soon will be theirs, something neither of them can repair. Nor will another daughter take the place of the babe in her arms. The Goddess she loves and worships has blessed, then cursed her. The same Goddess who may curdle her love if she blames Khalil for what may be an act of Heaven.

Tears falling, she lifts her veil and kisses her daughter, then holds the babe out to Khalil. She makes a mother's ultimate sacrifice before the hundreds here. This attests to one of the many qualities he esteems in this woman.

He gathers his daughter to his chest, then places a kiss of blessing upon Sabita's forehead. "This is for the best."

With what little strength sorrow has left her, she grips his arm. Her voice is a tear-choked whisper. "Promise me, no pain."

He nods, rather than speaks, keeping their exchange private.

Her breath catches, then gives way to wailing.

This is something the Ja'kor and the tribesman approve, a conquered woman sobbing. A pure Daharshan cannot sob while crying, nor do those of mixed blood.

Khalil looks to his son. "Stay with the Haj'ene and comfort her in my absence."

He need not say this, not with the tender way Baseem holds his mother's hand. Yet, with this command, Khalil makes his will official, thus not subject to countermand.

It is the only win they'll have tonight. Killing Tahir, though necessary, was and will remain a lifelong loss.

He mounts his mare, gives his wife and son an expressionless nod, then heads west into the desert to do the Ja'kor's will. All Khalil's ethics, morality, and honesty could not save them from Heaven's intervention.

Behind them, the haughty filly squeals while she tears after her dam.

The child, like all Daharshan infants who survive, remains silent.

Into the desert silence he rides, bearing his daughter and a dreadful burden of knowledge.

Fate's brutal hand has closed around the life he shares with Sabita. A life she changed at the deepest level. If Šaiṭān harms Baseem, can he keep her from killing the man? Though out of practice, she does not lack the skill. Do so, and they will lose everything they've achieved. Same as they've lost their daughter, a little girl he would have delighted in, spoiled, and adored.

If to save her, he must give away a piece of his body, a piece of his soul.

When he returns with his sword bloodied and no children, two-legged or four, Šaiṭān will revel in his cruelty. Let him gloat. They won't know the blood belonged to some desert creature.

None of these assurances grant him a reprieve.

The stars above effuse the sky. Their distance affirms the disparity between the hopes of men and Heaven's whim. Has Sabita's Goddess punished her for desiring a man who is contrary to all A'tal stands for? An even darker thought arises. Does the Heavenly One punish him for Tahir?

When younger, he and his half-brother would raid, stealing A'talan horses, cattle, sheep, or women. The day he and Sabita came so close to killing each other, he foreswore all such pursuits. You cannot take what should be given.

They were a'horse, their bows strained and arrows aimed at each other's hearts, so near neither could miss. Despite the confrontation's intensity, Khalil saw what was before him. Sabita's fierce beauty and the deep reserves from which it arose. What gain with both of them dead? Irrational an act as it was, he eased his bow, making the offer of peace, of Ameen.

That he, a so-called 'savage', would stand down made what followed even sweeter. She smiled, the faintest upturn of her lips as she too eased the strain on her bow.

In that moment, Khalil fell under her spell. He lowered his hald so she might see his face. Then, not knowing the words with which to woo her, he held his hand to his chest. It was all the time they had. As Falili Venari boiled up the incline to the border, Khalil departed.

The second time, he took a greater risk, finding her through the distinctive copper color of her horse. They spoke, a broken conversation more gazes than words.

The third time proved the charm, horrible as it was. A raid on the Falili encampment went sideways. He and Tahir were halfway to the border while driving a flock of stolen sheep, when Venari cut them off. Sabita was among that number, not that they knew each other in the dark. The following fight bloodied them both and ended with an unconscious Sabita slung over his saddle.

He battled to gain her trust. At last, that magical day came and their world became the other. Nor has their passion faded, despite differences greater than their similarities.

The border looms in the dark.

Kahlil halts his mare and listens for sounds of the enemy.

Lawaan fathers school their sons about the mighty range dividing northern Daharsha and A'tal. Hearing nothing on the shale-strewn path above, he sends the mare up the incline.

Her hooves, hardened by a lifetime on rock and sand, clatter over the rocky toes of the Silverstones. The filly bounds alongside her dam, undaunted by the long trip.

Father and daughter, mother, and foal crest the hill. There, Khalil halts, once more listening for riders. The only sound is his mare's grunt when the filly rams her udder.

He asks the mare for a walk and puts an end to the filly's greedy feasting.

The stone walls frame their path and loom overhead. The echo of his horses' hooves tells him whenever they stray.

All's well till it's not.

They are almost free of the foothills when he hears voices speaking in A'talan. After Tahir's disastrous attack, little wonder the Sada forces are on high alert.

He arches the small of his back and halts the mare, then blesses her tolerance when the filly latches on again.

Words reach him in bits and pieces. It's two Venari patrolling this section of border. With his daughter in the crook of his arm, he cannot use a bow. It's a grisly image, his saber ending these Venari's lives, splattering him and his daughter with their blood. Do so and he destroys his plan for her survival.

What he knows of the Sada's new a'Shara suggests the man would link an abandoned Daharshan infant to two 'missing' Venari. His daughter's sacred birthmark would not save her.

A hollow sound of hooves on rock approaches. If they enter this passageway, he'll retreat and pray the sound of their mounts' hooves will cover his own.

Heaven's celestial clock, the stars overhead, reminds him time is short. The consequences of failure have him swallowing a knot in his throat.

He retreats, something he's sworn never to do, backing the mare, his gaze swinging from front to rear. The Venari's voices soften and he halts.

Between them, fog rises in lazy spirals, white as the snow that covers these peaks in winter. The whorls thicken into a veil that arches up the stone walls.

South of the fog, the Venari's exclamations fade. They are riding away.

Khalil eases the naẓar between his palm and pommel, then bows his head in silent prayer.

Heavenly One, for this boon, You have my lifelong devotion. Whatever You ask of me, I will do.

There is no response, no inner exhortation, or praise, only the offered salvation. Awash with gratitude, he slides his curved blade back into its sheath. He cannot raise his daughter. Yet, this divine intervention may give her the life of choice she couldn't have in Daharsha.

Judging the time passed sufficient, he urges the mare into the mist.

For the first time tonight, the filly does not forge ahead, instead clings to her mother's side as they part the veil of fog. They enter a stand of kanga trees, their gray-green leaves rustling in the nightwinds.

He halts, bathed in moonlight and marvel. To his right, undulate the desert's red ochre sands. To his left, the grasslands stretch out into what seems an endless horizon of poison green. On one side, the travails of life. On the other, the Heavenly One's promised afterlife reward.

What must it be like, living in a land crisscrossed by rivers and streams? In Daharsha, he's forced to question every day whether there will be enough food and water for the Lawaan and their herds.

The little one ends his reverie with a small waking burble. If she fusses for her mother . . . no, not after the Heavenly One's miracle. He must not draw calumny upon them. Swathed in black, on a mare of the same color, he will trust they are mere shadows in the pre-dawn.

Khalil makes his way through the kangas, then halts at the spring they surround. To the east, he sees a faint tinge of dawn along the horizon. Despite the need for caution, he cannot dawdle, thus dismounts. As the mare and filly drink, he makes a nest in a hollow beneath one of the kanga trees. There, he lays his daughter upon the opulence of his mantle. Its folds will protect her against the early morning chill.

He lingers and caresses his daughter's cheek even as the pressure to depart builds. With a heavy heart and sigh, he bends and blesses her forehead with a kiss.

"Be well, my daughter. May Heaven bless the mark you bear."

Threading his ironweed raita through the filly's halter, he affixes the rope to a kanga near his daughter. When he leaves on her dam, the filly's cries will bring Venari, who, who will find both foal and child.

With a last sorrow-filled look, he swings into the saddle and heads north. The only salve is, if all goes well, his daughter will grow up in her mother's country.

The filly protests, her whinny piercing and imperious. Her dam, ready to be done with this child, does not answer.

Once again secreted in the foothill's rocky folds, he nocks an arrow, this one fletched in Lawaan blue.

The filly wails for her dam, high and unceasing.

Not so his child. Same as Baseem, Khalil's bloodline has prevailed in the daughter he has named Zaria, who while crying makes no sound.

* * *

The night's been long, frustrating, and futile. While cresting the border, Pell, a'Shara of the Sada, looks to his second. "Sojur, any inkling why they withdrew?"

His friend shakes his close-cropped head. "Not a single godsdamned one."

Pell chuffs laughter. "Me neither. Four years minus the 'pleasure' of Lawaan raiders. Let's just hope they aren't back at it again."

He checks Kitan, his warhorse, and looks north. "Did you hear something?"

Sojur swivels in the saddle, joining Pell's study of a stand of kanga trees.

The sound comes again. "How did a foal get up here without their dam?"

"I don't have a clue. Best we get the little one back to our mare bands."

Wanting nothing more than a meal and a bath, the two Venari walk their mounts toward the wailing chestnut foal.

Sojur whistles, a long low note of amaze. "Mother in Heaven, that isn't one of ours."

He comes off his stallion, and crosses to the foal. "Pell, this filly is Daharshan."

He calms the distressed beauty with his maimed hands, five fingers between them. That and his right foot, taken during two agonizing weeks of Daharshan torture.

Pell dismounts and frees the raita affixing the filly to the kanga. "Why is she here? Kian don't ride breeding horses while raiding."

The sun clears the horizon, bathing the border in brilliant orange-gold. As it does, Pell looks to where the raking light penetrates beneath the kangas. "What in the seven hells?"

He strides to the tree, then plucks something off the ground.

Sojur's breath catches as he turns around. "Boy or girl?"

"I'd say girl."

As the azure-eyed baby reaches for him with her tiny hands, tears glisten on her lashes. A birthmark in the shape of a Luna, symbol of A'tal's Mother of All, lies atop the infant's left hand.

They share their mutual silent wonder.

Sojur is the first to voice the question on both their minds. "Will you let her live?"

"How can I not? She's Mother blessed, and beyond that, abandoned with a birthgift beyond price."

"True, but who will take her in?"

Pell laughs. "No one. I'll raise her in my crèche."

"My friend, you push the river for a newly elevated a'Shara. She will be just one more godsdamned thing the Sada will grouse about."

"Once they grasp what a purebred Daharshan filly will do for our breeding stock, they'll get over it." Infant tucked beneath his dense-bearded chin, Pell remounts.

As Sojur does the same, the filly's hooves dance while keeping her distance from his stallion. "It's not the filly they'll complain about."

Pell nods in weary agreement as they head for the descent, which will take them to the Sada encampment. "True. Still, when Mora sees this child's birthmark, she'll silence any detractors. After which, she'll browbeat a Sada tribeswoman into nursing this infant."

Sojur raises a doubting brow. "If successful, even a Mother's Voice would label such a feat a miracle."

Pell fixes his attention on the incline they're descending. He longs to eat, bathe, and rest. None of which will happen soon with the tawny-skinned infant he cradles. How can he justify raising a child whose color of skin and eyes make her A'tal's enemy?

With a sigh, he glances to the tiny weary head resting on his shoulder.

Differences in faith and culture make this innocent his enemy, of which she knows nothing. Nor did she ask for the lot thrust upon her. Who will gainsay him if she's raised to A'talan values? He can give her a life of choice, rather than the injustice of a woman in Daharsha.

Nothing and no one.

It feels as if the Mother of All has answered his question.

He inclines his head while sharing breath with the babe, then whispers. "Thea, I'll call you Thea."

Exhausted as she must be, there's a tiny smile on the little one's lips, and Pell's heart opens.

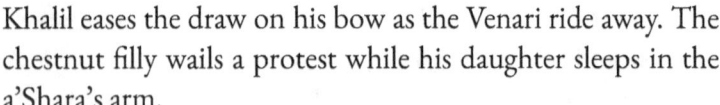

Khalil eases the draw on his bow as the Venari ride away. The chestnut filly wails a protest while his daughter sleeps in the a'Shara's arm.

"Raise her well, enemy mine. May I never face her in battle."

Regret weighs his heart as he reins north. By setting aside his duty to protect and provide, he's opened a wound in his soul which will never heal. Oddly, he believed killing Tahir would be the greatest burden upon his conscience. The guilt of abandoning his daughter has become a jinn riding his shoulders.

He sighs. Nothing happens apart from the Heavenly One's will.

However great the burden Khalil will abide.

Within moments, the Silverstones conceal Khalil. Not so from the vision of those seemingly so distant from life. The Three Sisters: Fate, Portion, and Calling.

Fate, the inescapable. Portion, each soul's lot in life. Calling, their mission. Only time will tell what they've decreed for the child named Thea and Zaria by her two fathers.

Of greater import, will she accept her allotted role?

While the Sisters ponder this improbability, so at odds with the natural order, wings whisper across the border from

Daharsha. A kaleidoscope of Luna moths, their silver-white wings edged in blue-green. They are the only creature to cross this border in peace.

They land among the kangas, and partake of the flowers surrounding the spring. Then, silent as their arrival, they depart, like this tale, their leavetaking both an end and a beginning.

MORGYN
STAR
PRESS

Library of Congress Cataloging-in-Publication Data is on file with the publisher.
Print Book ISBN: 978-1-961283-01-5
Ebook ISBN: 978-1-961283-00-8
Book Cover Design by Grady Earls
1st edition 2023